Solivagant

An Always Alone Novel

Philippa Attwood

Solivagant, by Philippa Attwood
All rights reserved.

Cover Design: Philippa Attwood

Editor: Philippa Attwood

Cover Photo Source: Pexels.com

Follow my social media for updates, sneak peaks, information and all news regarding my books, as well as keepin up to date with me:

Twitter - @authorphilippa
Instagram - @authorphilippaattwood

Table of Contents

Dedication
Author's Note
Prologue
CHAPTER ONE - Robinne
CHAPTER TWO - Robinne
CHAPTER THREE - Robinne
CHAPTER FOUR - Robinne
CHAPTER FIVE - Robinne
CHAPTER SIX - Robinne
CHAPTER SEVEN - Ralph
CHAPTER EIGHT - Robinne
CHAPTER NINE - Robinne
CHAPTER TEN - Ralph
CHAPTER ELEVEN - Robinne
CHAPTER TWELVE - Robinne
CHAPTER THIRTEEN - Ralph
CHAPTER FOURTEEN - Robinne
CHAPTER FIFTEEN - Ralph
CHAPTER SIXTEEN - Robinne
CHAPTER SEVENTEEN - Ralph
CHAPTER EIGHTEEN - Robinne
CHAPTER NINETEEN - Ralph
CHAPTER TWENTY - Robinne
CHAPTER TWENTY-ONE - Robinne
CHAPTER TWENTY-TWO - Ralph
CHAPTER TWENTY-THREE - Robinne
CHAPTER TWENTY-FOUR - Robinne
Epilogue - Robinne
Thank You/Acknowledgements
Song Playlist
About The Author

Dedication
For my 'Christian Grey', you know who you are. I forgive you for deceiving me.
For your deception gave me my wings back.
I'll always treasure you, darling man.
Always.
-

Author's Note:

This is an updated version of Robinne and Ralph's story, complete with revamped scenes, brand new scenes and song playlist for scene moments. I'd previously released 'half' of the intended manuscript back in July of 2018, with full intentions of releasing the latter half when my health was better. Now is that time. I'm pleased to say that my health is better and as a result, I have been able to re-write, add, edit and bring to you all what should've been coming your way in the first place.

This story is very personal and important to me, as I've finally been able to put a lot of me into a fictional character, get deep thoughts, feelings and emotions out there that I've kept inside of me for so long, revealed hidden truths and parts of my life that I've wanted to forget, and so much more. It's all in here, raw and real.

Never have I been more excited and terrified at putting it all out there and exposing wounds I'd closed years ago, but I'm glad that I did and I honestly hope that you all enjoy a read I've worked so hard on for you all.

Love,
Philippa

PROLOGUE
~Robinne~
3 Years ago, September 2015

No other single solitary moment came to mind where she was more terrified this. Not a single one. She was about to do something for the very first time, say something for the very first time, something huge. Well, to her anyway.

Most girls Robinne's age had already said this by now. Weather they meant it or not was another story, it didn't really matter but now, now it was her turn. She'd put it off for almost an entire year, fearing that if she had said it sooner, she would be adding another name to a nonexistent list of friends who'd abandoned her. That however, is a story for another time.

People these days took the word 'love'd all it stands for, for granted these days. Robinne forever hears people tell their boyfriends, girlfriends and other variants of significant others, that they love them. How many she wondered, actually meant it. We've all seen school relationships play out in movies, tv shows and here in the real world, with only a few those real world school relationships actually making it the whole way.

She hadn't been as fortunate as some, she'd never had a secondary/high school relationship. Why was beyond her, as even those who were bullied for being 'fat' or 'ugly' still managed to find someone to love them, except for her. So when the opportunity came up where she'd get to tell someone her feelings, she wanted to be certain that when she did say it, it would *actually* mean something.

Sitting cross-legged in the center of her bed, Robinne held onto her phone as if it were her only lifeline to reality. In a way, it was. Taking a deep breath, she pulled up the conversation she was having with her friend of almost a year, Christian. They'd met on Facebook, not unlike most people these days. A friend of hers had introduced her to him, saying he was looking for new friends. She didn't decline, as she herself was also looking for new friends. Her friend/sister in the States had just secured her first boyfriend, so all her attention had shifted to him, rightly so, so she'd been left without anyone to talk to regularly.

They were introduced through a Facebook group where we were all fans of the Fifty Shades franchise. Having clicked straight away, or at least she thought so, they'd spent the last year getting to one another outside of Facebook, soon messaging one another most days than not.

From the very first day they'd 'met', Robinne *knew* he was the one. Some knew someone was 'the one' from a touch of the hand, when their eyes first meet, or even by the sound of the person's voice. Her way of knowing he was the one was unconventional, yes. It didn't make it any less valid a reason to *know*. The moment he'd sent her the first message, something within her soul clicked with his. Nothing inside of her knew if he felt the same way. In fact, it was extremely unlikely. Nonetheless, she'd kept how she felt from day one, and every day since, locked away not telling a soul. She'd grown so fond of him, admired adored him, that she couldn't see life without him.

She was well aware that it was totally cliché, but she didn't care. Today would be the day she told him how she felt, praying that he wouldn't totally freak out and out and want nothing to do with her.

Please God, let this go well. Please!

Glancing down at her phone, she read his latest reply.

> *Christian: No, there is no one I currently like. What about you? Is there anyone you love?*

Robinne and Christian were talking about their ideal people, what they liked in a person and other such things of the like. By now, Christian knew that she hadn't had a boyfriend yet, but he didn't know *exactly* everything about her situation.

Taking a deep breath once more, she decided to take the plunge. It was now or never.

> *Robinne: Yeah, there might be somebody. But he doesn't know that I like him.*

> *Christian: Who is it? Do I know him?*

> *Robinne: Hmm, yes. You might. You might know him more than you know.*

> *Christian: Who.Is.It!?*

Gulping, she typed her reply that would seal her fate, or cement it.

> *Robinne: It's you.*

Minutes literally ticked by, and not so much as a peep out of Christian. Her worst fears were slowly being confirmed. Everything inside of her was screaming that it was a bad idea from the beginning, yet she still went through with it anyway. Who confesses to a long-distance friend of almost a year through iMessage? Only stupid people obviously, going by how this was going.

It was silly to be worrying about something so small as someone's reaction to something, especially when you don't know what's happening on the other end, but here she was. Worrying. Her hands shook fiercely, something she wasn't used to. Her hands never shook unless her blood sugar dropped. She hated having shaky hands.

Several more minutes passed by with still no word from Christian. Robinne's level of worry kicked up so much that if there was a meter reading it, she would've broken it. What was taking him so long to respond? Surely a guy knew if he did or didn't like a girl (or guy) when they confessed to them? She'd give anything for a reply right now, anything to put herself out of this state of worry.

"I...I've ruined everything." she whispered to herself.

Relaxing the grip on her phone, she let it fall to the bed without a care where it ended up. It was the least of her cares right this moment. She'd risked all, and lost.

You're such a fool Robinne, you're such a stupid...stupid fool.

Not bothering to change into her bed clothes, she flopped down sideways onto the bed, curled up and sobbing her heart out. For the first time in her twenty years, Robinne cried herself to sleep, finding solace only in slumber.

Opening her eyes the next day, albeit regrettably, she was more than surprised to see a message waiting for her when she reached for her phone. It was from Christian.

Christian: Good morning beautiful, I hope you slept well. I've got a busy day today at work. I'll message you when I'm free. Have a nice day!

She stared at her phone not quite believing what she was seeing. Granted she didn't expect to find any message from him at all, not after she dropped the doozy of all bombs on him last night, she never expected such a normal, relaxed answer from him.

Deciding not to press the subject of last night upon him again today, she waited until he was free later on, for her to continue speaking to him.

To her, the value of their friendship was way more important than her bringing up the subject of her feelings for him. On that note, she never brought up the subject again. For the next two and a half years, neither of them mentioned the night of her confession ever again. Their friendship carried on as if nothing had even happened.

It might have meant nothing at all to Christian. He might have forgotten about it, or even had a good laugh at the desperate English girl, but she never did.

Every day for the next two and a half years, she never forgot that night. Did she wish she never had mentioned it at all? Possibly. Would she always love him, even if he never loved her back? Oh yes. If she was to remain his friend for as long as he wanted to keep her, as she didn't have the best luck with friends, she would take it.

Anything was better than nothing.

After all, some of us aren't meant to be loved.

CHAPTER ONE
~ *Robinne* ~
Present Day, July 2018

As an avid reader, there isn't much that Robinne James hasn't seen written hundreds of times, across hundreds of books. It's the same thing again and again, just told a little differently by each author. A boy meets a girl, one or both has a tragic past, it becomes a will they won't they scenario, which is always followed by an explosive coming together, heartbreak or realisation which is usually followed by a happily ever after. Robinne was sick of it. Those stories aren't reality.

They were dribbly fiction.

Unrealistic nonsense.

For once, she wished she could read a story where she didn't have to predict, or know what would happen in the end, right from the outset.

She wasn't a cynic by nature, she did have a soft, mushy, romantic side, but she was primarily a realist. Books which were too far beyond how life truly was, at least for her, were far more in number than stories she could personally relate to.

For example. There was a book that she was reading sometime last week which fit into both the very predictable from the beginning category, as well as the unrealistic nature category. A girl left her hometown broken-hearted by the boy she knew was her true love, she came back years later and of course, ran into the very same guy minutes after arriving back in town. She tried to resist him, he tried to woo her, they spent one night in the throes of passion and badda bing badda boom, they ended up back together by the end of the story.

Predictable. Unrealistic. Repetitive.

If Robinne could count and list the amount of times she'd read books with that plotline or close to, she'd be at least a few hundred pounds richer than she was right now. Perhaps even thousands.

As a freelance editor, and hopeful future author if she could catch a lucky break, she often came across plotlines similar this whilst working, alongside when she read for pleasure when she had the time.

Outside of how strongly she felt about this subject, her life wasn't going as well as she would've liked it have by now. After working only one full time job from when she was nineteen to twenty, having then scored a series of jobs which screwed her over in one way or another, she decided it was more time for a change.

Having taken up freelance editing from when she left school at eighteen, at first as a side job to earn her some money while she looked for a job, she was able to save up money and save it nest egg-style should her circumstances change. When she got that first job of hers, it allowed her to pay the basic bills, while continuing to freelance edit on the side.

Now that she had decided to finally take the plunge to change up her life, she was glad that she had kept up the freelance editing, as what she had managed to save would just about secure her a very minimalist life start-over somewhere else.

Robinne had managed to complete various courses at her local college to earn her editorial and publishing qualifications, equal to what she would've attained at any university. It had been hard and a long time coming, as she was unable to study English literature or publishing at University, due to lack of funds, but she had what she needed and she was proud of herself.

If she had chosen to go to University to get her qualiations in the same subject areas, she would've been looking at a debt of at least £90,000, minus live-in and extra fees. She wasn't prepared to put herself through University to come out with that level of debt against her name, even if people did constantly repeat to her that 'it'll be scrapped when you turn 50', or 'it's only a small payment each month, you won't notice it go from your bank account'. If there was another way to get what she needed to get her where she needed to go, without the debt, that's what she would be more prepared to do.

So, she did.

However, despite what she'd achieved in her tender twenty three years, it wasn't merely enough compared to others her age who'd gone through the conventional educational channels.

Which is what led her to what she was currently doing this very moment.

Packing her last book away into a box predictably labelled 'books', Robinne took one last look around her humble one room apartment which had been her home for the last five years. It was all she could afford at the time others went off to university. She was able to afford the cute little one room bedsit with a full time job at her local bookstore, which went down to part-time when she started her evening/night courses at college.

She wasn't sad to see it go. It had been a good place for her to get a start in life, granted she wasn't lucky to have the privilege of parents and being able to live with them. It was now time for this place to give that chance to someone else, to make this place their home.

All that was left now was to get her ass on the plane. Her stuff would follow her in due course, as she'd been able to arrange moving her stuff with the individual she'd been in talks with where she was now going to be moving to.

As the moving men came and collected her last remaining boxes, she stepped around them and out into the hallway, allowing herself one last look behind her before closing the door as the moving men came out after her.

With the finite 'click' of the door, she happily closed the literal door on this chapter of her life, as a new chapter awaited her across the pond.

Au revoir England, hello America.

* * *

For the first flight in her entire life, second if you count this connecting flight, it hadn't been all that bad as she'd been led to believe. Everyone had been more than keen to throw in their two cents in what she should look out for, what she'd experience and what would be the worst things about flying.

It wasn't like she didn't welcome people's advice or comments, she'd rather not hear the same things over and over that she knew probably wouldn't even apply to her. At least she didn't have to contend with that anymore, now that she had finally landed in Texas, her final stop.

Having collected her carry-on bag from the overhead hold and her two modest-sized suitcases from baggage claim, she stepped out into the late July heat and humidity of Austin, Texas. This was probably one of the few oversights of coming from a mild, gloomy part of England that rarely experienced actual summer weather in the summer season. Derbyshire weather had nothing on Austin.

God, the humidity!

Thankfully the kind driver of the bus, famous to the states as the Greyhound busses, took her cases off her as she approached the bus, allowing her to climb on board and get comfortable on the short so journey to Dripping Springs. Her final destination.

She'd picked Dripping Springs because of its closeness to Austin, Texas' capital. As well as its low population count, its sustainability and for its renowned reputation for its brewery and wine, among other options that she was too tired recall right now. She wasn't a heavy drinker by any means, but the town appealed to her with its eclectic, yet humble portrayal online.

She'd know for sure if she had made the right choice in choosing Dripping Springs, once the bus got there and she'd scoped the place out a little more in her own time.

When the bus had finally filled up with everyone who' planned to be on it, Robinne felt the weariness of long haul travel finally catch up on her.

She'd not managed to sleep on either of her flights, much to her dismay. She'd catnap on this short journey if she was able, then crash into a sleep to last the ages when in her new home Dripping Springs. Or so she hoped.

All thoughts slowly faded into the back of her mind as her eyelids drooped, the bus pulling out of the bay just her eyes closed shut.

Peaceful slumber at last.

* * *

As she was happily slumbering on the bus, she felt herself slowly come out of her lovely dream by something that was...poking at her?

Whatever was poking her should stop. Right now.

She was having the best dream, which these didn't happen often, and it was being ruined by something sharp and pointy poking at her.

"Dear...dearie...sweetheart, we're here." a gentle voice said to her, obviously not wanting to spook her.

Cracking one eye open, she peered up into an aged, but no less beautiful face, of a kind-looking woman. Her tired eyes guessed this woman to be in her mid-sixties.

What did this woman say again?

"Wha…" was all she managed to say, her catnap depriving her of the ability to speak until she was fully awake.

The kind-looking older woman laughed softly, clearly aware Robinne was not used to long-distance travel.

"We're here, dear. Dripping Springs. I take it that's where you're headed?"

"Yes. It is."

"Oh...you're British. How charming!"

Charming? That's a first.

"Thank you. Sorry, I don't mean to be rude…" she hoped she wasn't being rude anyway, she was just trying to form a decent sentence after coming round.

The woman waved her hand, dismissing her apology politely.

"Nothing to be sorry about dear, I can see you're beat. I'm Hannah, it's lovely to meet you. Let's get you off this bus now shall we?" she smiled kindly again, obviously keen to help a person in need.

Another first. Shouldn't it be the young helping the elders? Nevertheless, it was beyond kind of her to help out a sleepy stranger on bus.

"Thank you, that's most kind of you. I'm Robinne, it's nice to meet you too." she said, sleepily rose out of her seat.

The two of them made their way down and off the bus, with Robinne pausing next to it to stretch her tired muscles. All the bags and belongings of the bus passengers were all neatly placed in one spot on the sidewalk, so it was easy to grab her suitcases from the bunch, before heading back towards Hannah.

"Thank you again for waking me up. I thought I'd catnap a while, but I must've gone deeper than I thought."

Hannah gave her that kind smile again.

"Dear you need to stop thanking me, it's no problem. We help one another out around here, strangers included. You seemed pretty harmless enough, so it was no burden to wake you."

Such a sweet woman!

"In that case, I don't suppose you know where I can rent a car? Or perhaps get a taxi to where I need to go?"

Hannah tilted her head ever so slightly, "Where is it you're headed dear?"

Robinne gave her the address, which she'd written and kept in trouser pocket.

"Oh! That's the old Jameson place! I heard someone new was moving in, but I had no idea it was you dear. I heard it's now almost been re-built and ready for the new owner. It should be done tomorrow by my understanding. You'll be needing a room at the B&B on the main street. Just a right turn from here and halfway down."

Not ready? Her contact here assured her it would be.

Well, not much she could do about it. At least there would be a place for her soon, she can manage one night in a B&B. Just. She had just enough money on her to make it work, and she was more than ready to bed down for a while. For the weekend at least.

"Tha--" she almost thanked her again, quickly remembering to stop as per Hannah's polite request. "It's been lovely meeting you Hannah, I appreciate the help. I'll check in there right away."

"You're welcome dear, I hope they treat you good. Nice people who own that place. I'll be on my way now too. Maybe we'll bump into each other again sometime. Take care of yourself now." Hannah gave a last wave before climbing up into a local taxi, which had pulled up just moments before.

Robinne watched the taxi pull away, heading down the road in the opposite direction she had to go. She did wonder if she'd ever see Hannah again, the possibility of it being very high seen as the population of the town was so low, compared to her former home. She looked forward to it.

Hannah had said the B&B was on the first right turn and halfway down. *Right.*

Grabbing the handles of her suitcases, she headed off, holding onto the thought of a rewarding soft bed to rest her weary head.

It wasn't hard to find the B&B, as it was the only facility of its kind on the quaint main street. Once inside, she wasn't disappointed. The place had an obvious small town charm to it, yet it still felt somewhat homely. Yes, she wa to enjoy her short stay here.

"Hello?" she called out quietly when reaching the desk.

Her question was met with silence.

Spotting a bell on the desk, she gave it a few gentle rings.

"Coming! I'm coming!" Another cheery voice called out from somewhere within the ground floor.

Is everyone cheery permanently around here? It's kind of nice.

The source of the voice soon became clear, as rushing down from the stairs was another kindly looking woman no older than her mid-fifties, clearly keen to answer whoever was quite literally ringing her bell.

"Woah, sorry about that! Washing machine would not tolerate its latest load." she said as she came to a stop beside Robinne. "Well hello there, how can I help you today?" she said, brushing a stray lock of hair behind her ear.

Robinne offered her best 'I'm not as tired as I look' smile, before answering her.

"I was told you could offer me a room for the night. I'm moving into a house which isn't ready till tomorrow."

A spark of recognition flashed across the other woman's face.

Uh-oh.

"You're Ms James! Robinne, am I right?"

Spookily right is more like it.

She wasn't fully aware of the outward reaction she'd just shown to this woman, but she was shocked on the inside.

How would she know that I was Robinne?

It had to be this whole 'small town' thing again. She was sure of it.

"That's me. How did you…"

"Small town talk honey, I know the house seller well. I should hope I should anyway, he's my husband after all." she chuckled at her own humour. "I'm Mrs Jenkins. My husband is Joe Jenkins."

Ah, that explains it.

"Nice to meet you. Mr Jenkins has been simply wonderful and so understanding with my circumstances, I'm so grateful for the last minute contract agreement for the home."

"Joe's like that, always has been." she said with a smile in her voice. "Let's see what we can do for you about a room."

Oh yes, a room.

Talking to Mrs Jenkins, even in her tired state, she'd forgotten what she'd come in to ask for.

"That would be great. Something uh…affordable. If that's quite alright."

Looking up, Mrs Jenkins gave an understanding nod.

"Say no more. Joe mentioned your sudden move across the pond, kindly hinting that you were on limited funds. Charming accent by the way."

She was beginning to believe the statement now herself.

"Thank you" she chuckled.

After a few minutes, Mrs Jenkins had found a room for her and had got her signature in the check-in book. "Here's your room key. No charge. Your room is on the top floor, furthest on the right."

Blinking as she accepted the old-fashioned room key, she wasn't sure if she'd hear right.

"I...uh...w-what about the fee?"

Mrs Jenkins shook her head slightly, her cheery smile remaining on her face.

"No fee dear. Since you're going to be renting one of Joe's places, the room's on us for tonight."

This is far too kind. I can't give her nothing. Maybe she'll accept a favour in return or as a thank you?

"Oh Mrs Jenkins, this is too kind of you. Thank you so so much! If there's anything I can do in return for this I'll--" she tried holding it off, but the yawn from hours of tiring travel finally broke free.

Mrs Jenkins moved from her spot around her side of the desk and moved her and her suitcase towards the staircase.

"Nonsense, I won't be accepting a dime off of you. You go on up and head up to bed. You deserve a good bath and bed. Clock out when you're ready to tomorrow morning, I'll have Joe ready to take you over to your new home when you're all rested up. Go on up now dear." she gave her a friendly nudge up the first step.

Who was she to argue? Mrs Jenkins was such a lovely woman on first impressions, and she was hardly powered up enough to refuse her hospitality.

"Thank you. Goodn--" she looked at the clock on the wall. 3PM. "Afternoon."

Mrs Jenkins gave her a finite nod before returning to the back office, closing the door softly behind her.

Well, off to bed at last.

Once inside her room, Room 15, the first thing she did was flop front first onto the bed. The door swung to a soft close behind her, with her suitcases happily situated beside the door.

Ah, heaven.

This quaint room, was not to be sniffed at. Those who demanded luxury wherever they went were clearly out of their minds. Coming from a one-room bedsit to this quaint B&B was an unexpected, yet pleasant experience.

After allowing herself to relax on her front for a short while, she knew Mrs Jenkins was right. What she needed was a bath and bed.

After her bath a little while later, she emerged back into the bedroom. Forcing her tired limbs to move further into the room, she settled down into the modest bed for a good and well deserved sleep.

Ah, thank you Hannah.

Thank you Mrs Jenkins.

CHAPTER TWO
~ Ralph ~

It was thankfully the end of a long, hard, back-breaking day for Ralph. Working on the old Jameson place was something he'd volunteered to help with when his Pa had first mentioned it to him, but he wasn't a builder or carpenter by trade, so working on something like restoring an old house for months on end was finally taking its toll on his body.

Normally, Ralph would be seen working on his family's ranch, doing what all good people of small towns do on their ranches. He'd worked on the ranch since he could remember. Having being born and raised there, he naturally started 'helping' around the ranch as soon as he was able to walk. From carrying a small amount of feed to the chickens they'd once had, to learning how to herd the cattle on horseback, he'd spent most of his life helping to keep the ranch going. Minus the time he'd gone off to college to get his degree. He'd come straight back home after he'd attained that.

On the side, he'd manged to obtain a local licence to be able to qualify to do the odd carpentry/building job. Like this one, for example. Since it wasn't his main plateau of work, he usually offered to help those who truly needed the time and work put into something, who usually couldn't afford a high end company to come in and do the work. His brothers had quickly fallen suit behind him when he'd decided to do this, leading them usually being hired as a team to help out should the occasion arise.

Having worked on fixing up the old Jameson place for three months with his brothers and getting it ready for the new occupant, he was more than happy to stand back and admire the completed build, having put down a literal welcome mat as the final touch.

His brothers had left the site a while ago, each of the parts they'd been working on already complete. He was usually the last one to leave whatever they were working on at the time, as he insisted on doing all the final checks before handing over the place back to whoever owned it.

Since those final checks had been done before he'd stepped outside, he was more than satisfied to call it a day for today. It was only 3PM, but there was bound to be a few things he could get done back at the ranch before treating himself to a rewarding dinner.

Pulling away from the house once everything had been packed back into his truck, he couldn't help but think who might be moving into the place his parents had planned to rent out. Mr and Mrs Jameson, an elderly couple, had sadly passed away earlier this year and had left the property to their closest friends, his parents. Neither had any children, much to his sadness, and they'd been family friends for as long as he could remember. He was beyond thankful they'd left this place to their parents, it was a lovely gesture, except for when they got into the place to do it up, it needed a whole lot more than doing up.

Part way into stripping out the old plasterboards, floors and such other things, a local youth had come by, obviously to check out the house to see what was going on, only to accidentally set alight while exploring. Turns out the foolish youth had decided it was a good idea to smoke right next to some chemicals they were using to clean a part of the house, not that he knew what those things were. He'd apparently dropped the half-smoked cigarette right onto the chemicals, causing the whole place to go up in flames.

Of course, his parents weren't happy about what had happened, as they'd already sunk a small portion of money into starting the refurbishment, only to have it literally gone up in flames. That being said, they knew the youth didn't mean to set it alight and was only curious as to what they were doing to the place, so they didn't press charges. People often explored abandoned places around these parts, simply to satisfy their curiosity. So it wasn't like he was doing wrong by being there. At the end of the day, the youth had actually proven useful when he'd volunteered to help out when they decided to build a new home from scratch. So, all's well that ends well.

Showered, shaved and refreshed, Ralph relaxed on top of his bed at his place as he let the mild Texas heat naturally dry his body, clad only in a towel around his waist. Hands resting behind his head, his eyes were closed as he savoured a moment's peace after carrying out a few jobs around the ranch before heading home.

It didn't last long.

His phone began to vibrate from the bedside table, bringing him out of the lovely scene he was playing through his mind as he relaxed.

I knew it was too good to be true.

As her picked up his phone, he saw the name of one of his brothers on the screen. Much to his relief, it was a text message instead of a phone call. People knew he was far more comfortable texting than he was speaking on the phone. Just one of his quirks.

He tapped on the phone and brought up the message.

Reed: Yo, Bro. You coming to Lock, Stock & Barrel for a drink? I'm buying!

Lock, Stock & Barrel was the locally run 'bar'. It was more of a communal café turned karaoke bar turned watering hole for the whole community of Dripping Springs. He often met his brothers there once a month or so for a regular drink, usually more frequent if they've been on a harder job and were in need of refreshment for a hard day's work.

He didn't really want to go anywhere tonight, but at the same time he didn't like letting any of his brothers down, even for something as small as catching a drink together. They always made time for family as each believed it was precious and should cherish it while they could.

He typed back his reply.

Ralph: Sure. Give me an hour & I'll meet you there

Reed: Sweet! Just Ryder, you & I tonight.

Ralph: Great. See you later.

It never took him long to get ready to go anywhere, he just wanted a bit more time to himself before he'd be in the company of two of his boisterous younger brothers. He wasn't old himself by any means, twenty-eight was still considered young for a man. It was just that it seemed his younger brothers had a hard time leaving the late teen phase behind.

Smirking, he got up and set to his task of getting ready to go out.

Ralph arrived at the Lock, Stock & Barrel just over an hour later, walking through its double doors which were designed to look like old western saloon doors, maximised to fit the whole doorway instead of just half.

Inside, he instantly spotted his two brothers over by their usual corner spot at the back of the place. They were pretty hard to miss even if they weren't tucked away, as all the men in his family possessed impressive height which was often used to their advantage. Not wasting any time, he quickly made his way over and filled one of two vacant seats, sitting beside his younger brother, Ryder.

"Hey man, glad you could make it." Ryder patted his shoulder, flashing him a dashing smile that would make any man or woman go weak at the knees.

He had a good relationship with all of his brothers, but he'd always been closer to Ryder, the second born after his own arrival. They'd gotten into their own fair share of hijinks over the years as each of their brothers made their arrivals, creating memories he'd always be able to look back to in great fondness.

"Hey. How's it going?" he asked.

"Meh, slow day. Fixing fences mostly, took longer than planned with just the two of us." Ryder said, gesturing between himself and Reed, their younger brother.

He raised a brow at them both.

"What about the others?"

"Two are on a run into Austin for more supplies, don't know about the other. He's bound to be milling around somewhere on the ranch doing his own thing." Reed shrugged.

Their youngest brother had not long returned from an extended stint at college, after having to take a year off half way through due to health reasons. He'd been down with a serious virus for most of that year, making the recovery period a hell of a long one. While he did help out on the ranch as his older brothers did before him, he did sometimes go off and do his own thing without telling anyone. As long as whatever he was doing was safe and legal, they trusted him and left him too it.

Picking up the drink Reed slid his way, he took a generous slug from it before returning it to the table. "He'll pull right, you'll see. After all, you all did." He smirked.

"Yeah, yeah. So, how's it going with you big brother? Everything finite now with the Jameson place?"

"Just finished it earlier. I need to give Pa the spare keys for the new owner. When're they arriving again?"

"Was supposed to be today, but since we were running just a day late, they're staying at the B&B until tomorrow." Ryder piped up. "Ma called me earlier to tell me."

There was still nothing that gave him a clue as to who the new occupant had been. He was even more surprised when his Pa had someone lined up for the place so soon after they'd started the second re-build, and that the then potential new occupant would be willing to wait three months or so until they'd be able to move in.

I know I wouldn't be as patient.

"Well boys…" Reed clapped his hands together, bringing Ralph back into the moment. "This calls for a celebration. You still buying the rounds Ry?"

Ryder sighed. He really wasn't upset about paying for drinks, he just liked to appear put out.

"Yeah. Yeah I am. Go on, order what you want and I'll get it added onto my tab. My treat."

He hadn't even finished his first drink and they were already calling for more. None of that was happening tonight. Slugging down the rest of his small pint, he shook his head.

"Only one more for me, I'm driving home and I have an early start tomorrow. One more's my limit."

"Nonsense!" Reed stood up, "You're going to have a drink with us and I mean a proper drink, no arguments. We've worked hard on this build and you've been grumpier than usual lately so it wouldn't hurt for you to loosen up once in a while. I'm not taking no for an answer so you better drink up and have a good time." he flashed them both a grin before ducking through the moderate crowd, reaching the bar like a pro.

So much for big brother authority.

Soon enough, Reed was back at their table with a tray of their signature favourite beers.

"Cheers, to another successful build!"

Ralph and Ryder raised their glasses, albeit reluctantly in Ralph's case, joining Reed's in a toast to their latest project completion. Their glasses met with an almost angelic clink, signaling the start of a night in which he could never have imagined the outcome in a million years.

Little did Ralph know now, it would be the start of the best thing to have ever happened to him.

CHAPTER THREE
~ Robinne ~

Never has a person ever wanted to stay in a bed more than Robinne did right now. If the world ended right this moment, she would happily tell it to wait whilst she soaked up the bliss of laying here in this bed. Granted it wasn't *the* most comfortable bed she'd ever slept in, but after hours of exhausting travel, it was pure heaven.

Or at least, it would be.

Something was poking her. Again.

What the…?

Not only was she being poked, but something extremely pesky to her in her slumbering state, was also nudging her shoulder.

"Honey...rise and shine…"

Honey?

No, her name was Robinne.

Wait a minute. Only one person had called her honey since she'd arrived here.

Mrs Jenkins.

"Good morning honey. I didn't want to wake you but if I didn't, you wouldn't have enough time to sort yourself out before Joe swings by to take you to your new place."

"Mmm...no no, that's alright." she said sleepily, sitting up and stretching her arms above her head.

She couldn't be mad at Mrs Jenkins waking her up. If her own mother was still alive, she could imagine her waking up her teenage self on the weekends. Mrs Jenkins was only being kind, and a good host to boot. She needed to thank her when she was ready to leave, kindness should never go unnoticed or unappreciated after all.

Before she was able to think about anything else, the most delicious, most mouth-watering smell filled her nose, waking her up fully. Mrs Jenkins didn't miss her piqued curiosity, smiling as she bought over a tray of food from somewhere behind her.

"I normally leave the complimentary breakfast outside of guests' rooms but, I thought it wouldn't hurt to bring it into your room. Once I knew for sure that you were decent."

You're far too kind, Mrs Jenkins.

"This is...wow, thank you! It looks so good!"

"No trouble honey. You finish that all up and come on down when you're washed up. I'll have Joe here for you in a jiffy."

As quickly as she must've come in, Mrs Jenkins left. Robinne looked back down at the miniature feast on her lap, feeling immensely grateful.

Damn it looks good.

She only hoped it tasted as good as it looked.

It was.

Robinne didn't waste any time getting washed up and put together after eating her delicious breakfast, as she was more than keen to settle into her new place. She placed the tray neatly outside of her door for someone to collect when they were ready, then grabbed her cases and carefully made her way back downstairs to check out.

Down in the lobby, she could see the ever happy-go-lucky Mrs Jenkins chatting to someone on the phone. Whoever it is, she could see that they'd been able to turn her cheeks to turn that 'rosy apple' colour everyone in books writes about, the kind of colour you go years after falling in love with 'the one'.

If that ever exists in the first place.

She wasn't one to shy away from anything romantic, she just had *the* most God-awful luck when it came to the opposite sex and belief in true love. Although, it was mostly her fault. She was raised by adoptive parents who chose to brainwash her with those typical high school-ish type of movies, showing how perfect a time you could have in the 'best years of your life'. There were too many expectations for her to live up to, to experience, causing herself to be let down at every single one of them.

While others her age were experiencing the first 'love' of their life, she wasn't. When others her age were churning through boyfriend and girlfriend after boyfriend and girlfriend, she wasn't. At the time when prom came around and everyone was bringing dates and arriving together in a stretch limo, she went alone. By no means was her life a sob story like a few others she'd known about, but she'd wished she'd at least experienced some of the 'basic' things a high school teen goes through.

Not that this was the time to rehash those times.

Spotting her standing at the bottom of the stairs, Mrs Jenkins quickly finishes up her conversation before rushing over to bring her bag close to the check-in desk.

"Sorry about that! I was just telling Joe you were ready for him to take you home."

Home.

Was anywhere home for her right now? She was just going by the seat of her pants in regards to her life right now, no specific direction in site. No specific route or plan.

Focus, Robinne!

She smiled sweetly back at Mrs Jenkins, stepping up to the desk to sign out.

"My offer still stands, anything I can do for you in return for the best night here, for free, you just name it and I'll return the favour."

Sliding the guest book towards her, Mrs Jenkins shook her head.

"I don't need anything right now honey, though I'll keep your kind offer in mind. I can tell us small-tower tendencies are already rubbing off on you." she winked.

Grabbing the pen off the desk, she couldn't help but laugh. Maybe it was. Just maybe.

"Deal." she signed her name out and set the pen back down. "Well uh...I guess there's nothing more to say right now other than well, thank you. I had the best stay, even if it was for one night. I'll leave you a good review. If you have an online profile that is."

"Oh yes! We most certainly do!" Mrs Jenkins beamed. "Nothing fancy like that Advisor Trip thing..."

Bless her.

"Trip advisor." she politely corrected.

"Yes that. We have a comments book just on the side table there. You're more than welcome to leave a comment before J--" before she had time to finish, a loud horn honked twice from close by.

"Goodness! I love that man more than anything, but he's either really early or really late. Ten minutes he said, that was more like five if that. Tsk."

It wasn't really that big of a deal, but she didn't want to be rude and say anything. The woman clearly was trying to be a good host and for all it was worth, perhaps even a possible friend.

In a way, it made Robinne smile. This wouldn't happen back home. The mild chaos of this woman was the kind of different thing in her life which she needed. She hated anything that usually was full of unnecessary drama or fuss. This however, this wasn't so bad. If it was someone other than Mrs Jenkins, maybe it would be a different story.

Not that I plan to find out anytime soon. I'm happy with just her for now.

After leaving her comment in the book, she turned around to retrieve her suitcase to take out to Joe. Only, it wasn't there. Where had it gone?

Looking around the lobby, she couldn't see hide nor hair of her two suitcases.

Where could they possibly be?

"Over here ma'am." a deep, yet warm voice called out to her.

Heading out of the B&B towards the direction of the voice, two sets of eyes were watching her from the sidewalk. One belonged to Mrs Jenkins, leaving her to assume that the other pair of eyes belonged to none other than the lovely woman's husband, Joe.

"Robinne, honey, this is my dear Joe."

Joe extended a well-worn, calloused hand, holding it out to her in polite

"Pleasure to meet you ma'am. I'm sorry we couldn't have your place ready for you when you landed yesterday, finishing touches took longer than expected." he looked rather sheepish, guilty almost.

"Don't worry about it." she smiled as she gently shook his hand, finding his grip firm yet comforting. "Your wife was kind enough to give me a room for the night. Free too! I'm too grateful to be anything else."

"That's my Cassie for you." he beamed. "Always helping those in need."

Whilst she wasn't exactly 'in need', she deeply appreciated the kind hospitality of the pair in front of her. So, she wasn't going to start arguing.

Seeing that she was in somewhat of a confused, not sure what to do sort of state, Mrs Jenkins ushered her towards the truck's passenger door.

"Now you just go on and get up into that truck honey, Joe will take care of your case for you. Won't you Joe?" she said, as if she didn't know her husband would do it without a kind prompt.

Joe simply chuckled to himself, already picking up Robinne's case. "Yes dear."

Aww.

Soon after saying a quick goodbye to Mrs Jenkins, Robinne and Joe were well on their way to her new place. As they left the centre of the small town, Robinne watched the quaint scenery give way to a beautiful landscape she could only have ever imagined coming up with in a book. Where she did do her research on what the town looked like before she came her, the online photos didn't do the place justice as seeing it in person.

Happily content with the scenery rolling by the window, she turned her head ever so slightly to get another look at Joe, now that she had the time and opportunity to do so. He wasn't a small man by any means, she estimated him tipping the average 6 foot mark, and he looked to be in a decent shape for a man of advancing years.

Must be good genes.

Very good genes.

"So...how're you finding life here so far?" Joe said, interrupting her thoughts. "I know you've not been here all that long and all but, I hope everyone's been kind to you. We don't get new people very often. Hoping the first-time homes will stop that. A little side project of mine."

She was happy that Joe was the one to first break the silence. It wasn't uncomfortable by any means, she just always found it hard to start a conversation without making it awkward.

"Good, thank you." She smiled. "Everyone's been more than kind. I've never experienced anything like it. Especially your lovely wife. Mrs Jenkins did so much for me yesterday, I must think of some way of repaying her somehow."

Chuckling, Joe shook his head.

"She won't accept anything in return honey. I know my wife too well. She'd help every homeless person, wandering soul or otherwise if she could. I'm not stopping her believe me, but she'd run out of juice trying to save every last person. That's what I love about her. Though I wouldn't change who she is for the world."

If that didn't give her the slightest spark of hope that there might be something to love after all, she didn't know what would.

"She's lucky to have you too Joe."

Joe just gave her a knowing smile, he knew it.

Oh Joe, you lucky devil you.

Clearing his throat, he turned his eyes back on the road ahead.

"We never really did discuss it over our email correspondences, what made you chose the United States? Seems like an awful long way for a first-timer so young to move her whole life to start over here, if you don't mind me saying so."

She was expecting this subject to come up at some point, just not so soon. Nonetheless, she felt she could confide somewhat in this kindly man.

"Just…life. I didn't have a great deal back home, in my personal life or work life. I had more than others and for that I was grateful. I didn't feel…complete. I was barely making a living to keep a more than basic flat…uh…apartment, over my head and I just wasn't happy. I'm usually not the risk-taking type, so it was a huge thing for me. I just happened to see your ad before I was about to close my laptop and give up hope of finding somewhere new where I felt I could finally give my life the jumpstart it needed, you know?."

Joe was ever patient listening to her talk, never once did he try to interrupt her or make her stop talking. A true gent.

He nodded his head, motioning with his hand for her to continue, somehow knowing she wasn't quite done.

"I didn't really have a destination in mind as such. As long as I laid my head where I was able to speak the language, eat the food and have a roof over my head, I knew I would do me fine. So, that brings us up to where we are now, sitting in this truck talking about me. Not my favourite subject, if I'm honest." She nervously laughed.

Joe reached over and patted her hand in a fatherly-type gesture, clearly understanding her intention.

"Say no more, I'm just being a nosey parker. I know you know I did a background check on you, just to make sure you were who you said you were, as I do for anyone I do business or work for. It's nothing personal. I've always been nosy, as my wife will no doubt confirm for you sometime"

If I ever get to meet her again.

Which seems very likely in a small town such as this.

Thankful that the conversation had turned away from being about her, the two settled into an easy conversation as Joe drove them towards her new home.

Soon enough, Joe pulled his truck to a stop right outside Robinne's new home. Her first true home as an adult, not counting her shoebox of an apartment she left behind.

There was no other word that she could think of to describe this place other than perfect. Here stood before a home not usually seen build in America on the whole. The home looked to have been made from the most beautiful combination of bricks and stones, creating a unique design she instantly fell in love with. In the centre of the front of the house, stood proud a door of the deepest brown, almost reddish colour with an oval window at its centre. It also pleased her eye that either side of the stunning door, were two sides to the house that were symmetrical in every way from the windows to the size of the rooms obviously within. This house seemed like it was almost designed with her *exactly* in mind.

"Joe…I…wow…" she was stunned, which was a new feeling in itself for her.

"I know." He smiled. "Here."

In the palm of Joe's hand sat two brand new shiny silver keys.

Oh my god, this is really happening!

With a giddy smile, she gently took the keys from Joe's open palm, clutching them tightly in her own.

"I still feel like I'm dreaming. It just doesn't feel real. Well, it does but, I just feel like I should be pinching myself."

Joe merely chuckled, not at all phased at how she was acting.

"It didn't really hit me either when I first owned a home when I was a young man. My old man, he left me a shack of a property when he passed on, said in his will if I could do up the place within a year, it'd be mine. I couldn't hire on no one, all the work had to be done by my own two hands. Oh I got it done within the year alright, but, it didn't feel like a home. At least Not until I had the love of my life right beside me when I went to sleep and when I woke."

Listening to Joe, she completely forgot why the two of them were here in the first place, until a hand on her shoulder brought her out of her thoughts once again.

"Anyway, enough about me."

Robinne held up a hand, smiling softly at him.

"I'm more than happy to listen to you any time. You've shown me great kindness and for that, you'll always be welcome to join me for tea to sit and chat. Drop by any time and I'll always welcome you with open arms. You and Mrs Jenkins both."

"Now I'm certain I made the right choice in accepting you." He beamed before cleared his throat and straightening his posture. "I'll take you up on that tea offer later. As for now, let's get you inside so you can settle in." he placed a key in her palm and went around to get her bags out of his truck.

The weight of the key in her hasn't wasn't as heavy as she expected it to be. It wasn't a key that was tying her to one place, or a key that signified finality. No, it was a key as light as a feather which was opening the door, quite literally, to the first of many new opportunities.

Time to open the first door hopefully of many yet to come.

Placing the key in the door, she turned it and opened the door as wide as it would go. Stepping just a little bit inside the hallway, Robinne took in all that was before her. Directly ahead of her was the grandest dark wooden staircase she'd ever seen carved to perfection. This staircase looked like it belonged more in a grand manor back home in England rather than in the middle of Texas. Yet, it suited where it was in a quirky sort of way.

Either side of the hallway and staircase stood two tall, curved archways where doors would've been, clearly missing as a modern feature of homes today. Open-plan.

To the left, she saw what she could see being used as a living/morning room. From what she could see from where she stood, no other rooms led off it. She was already envisioning it as a cozy living space.

This.Is.Awesome!

Looking to her right, she saw another spacious room around the same size. This one however, she could clearly see had another archway at the back leading elsewhere, perhaps to a kitchen.

"Right..." Joe said from behind her, depositing her bags beside her just inside the front door. "What do you say to a grand tour?"

As much as she'd love for Joe to show her around, he's done enough already for her. She couldn't possibly impose on him further.

Turning to Joe, she placed a hand gently on his shoulder.

"I couldn't possibly ask you to do that. You've done so much for me as it is, I couldn't even dream of asking for another favour. Besides, the longer I take to explore this place, the longer I can drag out the excitement of seeing each new part. I'm sure Mrs Jenkins would love your company. Not that don't, I'm just sure she'll love you with her as much as you want her with you." Her cheeks reddened a little, feeling like she's digging herself more of a hole just to avoid potentially offending him.

Patting the hand on his shoulder, Joe chuckled at her trying her best not to dig herself deeper.

"Don't worry, I know what you mean. I think I will get back to my wife after all. Might man the desk and do some chores for a while. She deserves an afternoon off, she works too hard." He stepped outside the door, turning back to face her. "Just holler if you need anything. My cell number is on the kitchen counter on a notepad. Take it easy now." He said with a friendly wave before hopping back into his truck, driving away from her place.

Robinne watched him drive out of view before she closed the door to the outside world.

Taking a deep breath, she took in all that's happened to her up until this moment. As of just over twenty four hours ago, her life was so different. Now, here she was. Her life still as different as ever, but in the best way possible.

At least I hope it will be.

Pushing off the door, she moved the cases closer to the stairs, not quite ready to take them up. She had exploring to do downstairs first.

Seeing that the room to the left of the hallway was for sure going to be the living room, she headed instead for the archway at the back of the other room. A kitchen decked out to the nines greeted her on the other side, clearly having been done to include new equipment in keeping with the quaint, cottage-like feel of the whole place.

Walking to the back door which lead out from the back of the kitchen, she was pleased with the view she was met with previously in the pictures she'd been sent via Joe in email. She'd fallen in love with this view right away, not imaging for one moment it'd be hers until this very moment. Lush greenery she was never blessed with back home met her happy eye, with what appeared to be a slow-flowing river peeking out between the trees.

Ah, Heaven.

She could explore more of the outside later on as despite the rest she had the previous night at Mrs Jenkins' B&B, she was starting to feel the effects of jet lag come over her again.

Closing the back door and making sure to lock it behind her, she headed back through the kitchen and into the hallway. Deciding to unpack her suitcases later after she'd done more exploring, she ascended the grand staircase to the second and top floor, leaving the cases where she'd moved them to.

As she climbed the stairs, she recalled part of the conversation she'd had with Joe on the way over here. He'd made it clear that the home was a re-build of what was once called the 'Jameson place'. According to the information he'd sent to her, they'd had a terrible accident with a fire of some sort, deciding to re-build the damaged houses from scratch. Not something she'd be able to do, so she mentally applauded everything she saw.

At the top of the stairs, she paused when she heard a noise she wasn't expecting to hear in a supposedly empty home, coming from one of the rooms on this floor.

What on Earth…was that the heating pipes? Plumbing? Racoon? Why now?

Groaning, she started to take slow steps towards the rumbling noise, wishing she should've had an object up with her for protection. Just in case. Then again, why would she in the first place? It wouldn't be normal to creep around your own home wielding a potentially deadly-ish object.

Putting her hand on the door handle of the room emitting the mysterious noise, she readied herself to face whatever was causing it. Taking a deep breath, she nodded to herself.

Opening in 3…2…1

"AHA!" she yelled into the open space.

What greeted her was *not* what she was expecting at all, as sprawled face-down in the middle of the room, was a man.

A *naked* man at that.

What was a naked man doing inside her house?

"OI!" she removed one of her shoes, flinging it at the muscular-buttocked man on the bedroom floor. She was surprised her shout entering the room didn't wake him in the first place, as it doesn't take much to rouse her, being the light sleeper that she was. Though on a second glance, the bottles of alcohol around him soon answered why he didn't.

Her shoe landed right on one of his globe-shaped cheek, mildly stirring its owner.

"Huh…" the man said, beginning to stir.

She bent down and slipped off her other shoe, hurling it in the same direction as its right-footed partner, landing successfully on the other muscular cheek.

"Who are you and what the Dickens are you doing in my house!?"

She stressed every word, very agitated to have a stranger, a naked stranger at that, in her home.

These things only usually only happen in the movies, aren't I the lucky one?

The mysterious man groggily stood up on wobbly legs, not all that indifferent from Bambi on ice. Normally, Robinne would find this kind of thing funny, as people brought this on themselves after a night's drinking, but she was in no mood to enjoy the hilarity this time. She was feeling the jetlag, she was tired, and she wanted to identify this man then get him out.

Preferably dressed.

"Ungh…" the man groaned, placing a hand to his no doubt throbbing temple, totally unaware of his state of undress.

Since she had no more shoes to throw at him, she crossed her arms under her chest and waited for him to answer her. He appeared to wobble in place for a second before finding the best version of his footing that he could manage. After a minute or two, it appeared that he'd just about registered that someone had spoken to him. Slowly turning around, his sleepy, hungover eyes spotted Robinne's form standing on the other side of the room.

"Wha…?"

Robinne rolled her eyes.

Great.

He was evidently in the stage of his hangover where words were yet able to make the journey from brain to mouth to complete a fully coherent sentence. Guess she was going to have to get tough with this guy, hangover be damned.

"I *said,* who are you and what the Dickens are you doing in my house?" She repeated her earlier words to him, only a bit louder this time, hoping to get them through his brain.

Or lack thereof.

The message seemed to get through this time as the man winced at her louder tone of voice.

"Sleeping?" he said, looking around at where he'd been laying down.

"No…no I wasn't…where am I?"

Seriously?!

"IN MY HOUSE!" she yelled this time, clean out of patience.

Covering his ears, the man winced again, turning back towards her with his face masked with annoyance at being shouted at.

"Yes yes…" he waved his hands about, "I just don't know how." he lowered his arms back down to his sides, clearly trying to work it out.

She didn't have all day to stand around and wait for him to eventually figure this out, as he was already pushing her patience to its limit. It did however, amuse her that he still didn't notice the state of his undress now that he was awake. It clearly wasn't his first concern. Nor was the fact that he was speaking with a stranger in a place he clearly didn't recognise well.

Oh how I'll remember this moment if ever we cross paths again.

Highly unlikely, she hoped.

Walking as close as she'd dared to this rather annoyingly near-perfect specimen of a man with his textbook abs and muscles, dusting of chest hair and GQ-like features, she bent down and picked up one of the many bottles which had outlined his former sleeping form on the floor.

"Maybe this will give you a clue you drunkard!" She waved the bottle between them. "Clearly the reason why you're here in the first place might be escaping your befuddled brain right now, but what I'd like to know is why you don't even have anything about you to cover your…" she looked briefly down at the rather uplifted appendage which separated the remote space between them, "…modesty. Up to speed now? Or do you need me to repeat it again to you, perhaps slower so you'd understand?"

Feeling ten times better for getting it out of her system, she released her grip from the bottle she was holding up to his eye-level, letting it drop onto one of his two bare feet.

"Fuck! Fuck! Fuck! Fuck!"

It was highly amusing to see this man literally hopping mad in front of her, who wouldn't be amused? However amusing as it was though, she turned and headed for the door, turning back to face the man at the last moment.

"When you're ready and suitably dressed, if you can find anything to cover up your modest…modesty, you will join me downstairs where I will find out who you are and get you out of my house. Are we clear? Good." She sweetly smiled, all for show of course, leaving him alone in the room still holding his foot.

"Huh?" the man said as he slowly lowered his foot back to the floor. "What mod…" he cut himself off short. Looking down at himself, eyes met his naked flesh, not instead the clothing or at least underwear in which he was expecting to see instead. "Woah!" he cupped his saluting privates, shielding himself.

"No point doing that now I've seen everything!" Robinne called back to him as she slowly descended the stairs.

He groaned. "Wonderful." He muttered.

Men…

Robinne simply couldn't believe what her eyes had seen upstairs. Then again, she wasn't expecting to see anything here in the first place. At the very least, she would've expected to have something like a stay or feral animal hiding away somewhere, not a man.

Muscular feet soon descended the staircase, followed rather obviously by a pair of deliciously sculpted calves. That's about where Robinne allowed herself to let her eyes wander to, as next in her eye level would be something she wasn't in a hurry to see again any time soon. His footsteps were as light as a feather for a rather tall, built man, which is why she never noticed him coming down until she physically saw him.

As she'd asked, he'd thankfully covered up before joining her downstairs. What didn't expect however, was to see what he actually came downstairs in or rather, wrapped around his tapered hips.

Are those…my curtains? So not going to ask for them back…

The rest of him soon followed until he was standing with her on the ground floor.

"Cat got your tongue ma'am?" he said, smirking at her.

Crossing her arms over her ample enough chest, she quickly put her wall back up.

"Hardly. You'd be lost for words yourself if a woman came down your steps in a pair of bedroom curtains" she cocked her head to one side, returning his smirk. "I don't believe it's your colour at all."

Shaking his head, he struck a rather garish pose.

"I think I work it well."

Yeah, don't you just.

She couldn't help but roll her eyes at his attempt at re-breaking the ice with her, seeing as the first try upstairs didn't go so well.

"Not the point. The point is you owe me a new pair of curtains, because I'm buggered if I'm putting *those* back up again."

Now it was his turn to look bemused. "Buggered?"

"Yes, buggered. English phrase mate, get used to it. You'll be hearing it a lot around me I'm afraid."

He chuckled at her remark.

"I don't exactly plan on being around you a lot after this, no offence. I don't even know or remember how I got here after all, hence why I'm sans clothes and underwear and donning this rather fetching number instead."

"Stop trying to make 'fetch' happen…" the line slipped out before she could stop herself.

Raising a brow, he placed his hands on his hips, clearly trying to hold back the smirk threatening to break free on the right side of his devilishly chiselled jaw.

"Did you just 'Mean Girls' me darlin'?"

He seriously didn't just try to southern charm me…God.

Walking as close to him as she safely dared to get, she used her full five feet eleven height to square up to him as best she could. Not quite such an easy task seen as he seemed to fit the strapping 'over six feet tall' category. It was like David going up against Goliath.

"First of all, so what if I did. Second, I'm not yours or anyone's 'darlin', I'm a free woman starting her life over here in the United States. Arriving here to find a man in my new home, who doesn't even remember how he got here in the first place, wasn't something I'd planned on so, I'd like you to take your curtain-clad behind out of my house pronto. I don't particularly care how you make that happen, but you're going to make it happen. Okay?"

He held up both his hands as a friendly gesture.

"Message received loud, clear and understood." He lowered his hands.

Letting out the breath she'd unknowingly been holding, she nodded.

"Good."

It was out of character for her to rant at anyone, let alone a stranger. She had no idea why she'd gone off at him like that, despite her claim of being travel-weary and burdened with jet lag, it was still no excuse to be rude.

"Good" he repeated.

"I'm assuming there's a phone around here somewhere you can use, please do so and hopefully when I come down, you'll be on your way. I would say it was a pleasure to meet you, but I think I'd be speaking for the both of us when I say that wouldn't be the case. Good day to you." She swiftly grabbed her suitcase, deciding now was the perfect time to change her mind and unpack while he made arrangements, she ascended the staircase he'd come down not long ago, leaving him standing alone in her hallway.

Lord almighty.

Hearing the front door close not long after she'd gone upstairs, Robinne let out the breath she'd been holding in. She knew that he knew she knew it was wrong to go off on him like that, her grandma would have her backside across her knee if she was here today to witness her rudeness.

Despite her not wanting to run into him again, she knew deep down she'd have to find some way of apologising to him, she owed him that much at least. Even if she did meet him under now rather amusing circumstances. At least in her point of view anyway.

Sitting down on the top step of the stairs after coming out of her bedroom-to-be, she rested her elbows on her knees, perching he chin on her open palms. This was supposed to be all so simple. Then again, she should've known that nothing would ever go simply.

It was too foolish a thing to hope for one thing to go simply.
What does?

She should've seen this coming though. The more you try to avoid doing something no matter if it's big or small, eventually you're going to end up doing what you set out to avoid. It was exactly like the time she said she'd go on that no chocolate diet. What happened the very next day? Yep, Mother Nature came cruelly knocking on the door one whole week early, causing her to crave into her special stash of 'monthly' only chocolate. Yes, she had a specific stash of her favourite chocolate for the worst time of the month, sue her. Every woman's allowed to indulge during that time.

Bringing her thoughts back to the present again, she started thinking about what she was going to do next, now that her unexpected visitor had finally left. She could unpack her bags, clean up the alcohol bottles in her bedroom, or flop where she was until something stuck out to her the most that she needed to do. One thing was for certain though, she'd be adding 'avoid handsome men' to her list of things to avoid while starting over in her new life here.

My list.
My list!

Racing back upstairs into the room she'd placed her bags in, she hoped she'd remembered to pack it, as she never went long-distance without it. You never knew when you had to add something spur of the moment onto the list. She'd made the list in the first place to keep her head on straight and her priorities true. People had lists for things all the time, hers was just a little unconventional than most.

Grabbing her carry-on bag which held her journal, which inside it sat *the* list. Unzipping the bag, she pulled out said journal and opened it wide. Page after page she turned, yet all she was met with was her own writing. No list.

NO!

Where is it?!

My list!

She distinctly remembered putting it in here, so where the Dickens was it?

Thinking back at what had happened to her so far and where she'd been, she could only have opened he carry-on bag back at Mrs Jenkins' B&B. There was no other possible place for it to be as she hadn't been anywhere else.

With yet another weary sigh, she reluctantly decided to search for the list the next day. If it was lost, then it wasn't going to go anywhere but the place in wherever it had got lost at. Though the list was very precious to her, it wasn't worth a trek anywhere just to find it, especially after she'd just left. In any case, if Mrs Jenkins was as kind as she'd seen her be so far, she'd probably see Joe again before the day's out with her list.

Hoping that was the most likely case, she closed her journal and put it back in her bag. Unpacking can wait, everything can wait. She just needed a moment to relax and decide her next move. Again. Walking over to her stunning view of the back of her property from her bedroom, she sat down in front of the sliding doors leading out onto her luxuriously designed balcony. She didn't want to be outside just yet, she was content here.

This is home now.

Despite what had happened today, she found herself smiling.

Huh…he actually had a nice butt, come to think of it.

I'll be dreaming good dreams tonight.

CHAPTER FOUR
~ Ralph ~

Never in his life was he ever kicked out of someone's house, especially for something he knew wasn't his fault. At least, he thinks it wasn't his fault. He couldn't quite remember. What he could remember though, was how much of a handful the woman he'd just encountered was, whom he could be certain was the new owner of the house.

"She better be damn grateful for what she's living in, after all our hard work." He muttered, currently lingering in the shadows behind the huge tree on the front of the property, just about hidden away in case anyone should pass by and see him in his current state of dress. Or rather, lack thereof.

He wasn't an exhibitionist by nature, other than sometimes doing work around the ranch without a shirt, which wasn't completely uncommon for any rancher to do. Standing here now with only a bedroom curtain round his waist, minus any form of underwear underneath, was the closest he'll ever get to being 'naked' in public.

Thankfully, he'd been able to reach one of his brothers at the main ranch house while he'd been left alone downstairs while the new owner scampered up the stairs faster than a squirrel up a tree. It wasn't a phone call he'd ever expected to have to make, as he was usually the one who picked up one of his brothers, so they were bound to get a kick out of their big brother in a bother.

Well, there was a first time for everything.

While he stood there contemplating just how he was going to explain to his Ma and Pa why he looked the way he did when he got back to the main house which was closer, to borrow a spare set of clothes, a rumble of a familiar engine came from behind him, getting ever closer to his current position.

Less than a minute later, a truck did in fact pull up relatively close to where he stood and honked its horn twice, evidently giving him the signal he needed to come out of his place of hiding and get inside. He peered around the side of the tree trunk, just to make sure it was someone who was definitely here to pick him up. Peering at the driver, he instantly relaxed at the sight of his younger brother, Ryder, who from even this distance away, looked as if he had the beginnings of a smirk on his face.

Oh, wonderful.

Checking left and right one more time, he came out from his hiding spot and dashed as quickly as he could into his brother's truck, slamming the door a little harder than necessary.

"Rough night?" Ryder said from beside him.

Ralph turned his head and threw a piercing glare at his brother, not amused by his question one bit.

"Alright, alright." Ryder chuckled, pulling away from the sidewalk and headed off towards the ranch. "I wasn't in favour of this prank but Rol made me drive him out here to get you back for that prank you pulled on him."

"That was *two months* ago!"

"Yeah, but he never forgets. You know that. Besides, he threatened to tell Ma about what I did the last time I was hungover."

He smirked, despite his mood.

"That was a doozy."

"Don't remind me. So, how'd things go down? I promise this'll stay between you and me."

He relayed the events, not leaving a single thing out to him.

"Well...I bet it was a heck of a welcome to America for the girl." Ryder chuckled.

"I'll say. It'll be a bit of luck for me if I don't run into her any time soon." He muttered, leaning his elbow on the passenger door's open window. Thankfully for him, it would only look to others as if the day's heat had gotten to him, rather than what was really going on below the window where no one could see.

I'll probably end up running into her anyway, hopefully with better results.

"You might. Anyway good news for you, Pa went with Ma to the B&B to help out with the morning work, so you don't have to worry about explaining to or sneaking around them."

Thank heaven for small mercies.

"Awesome."

Ryder got them back to the ranch, pulling up beside his own truck which Roland must've used to get back here last night in. "By the way, what happened to my clothes once I was stripped?" he said as he unbuckled his seatbelt.

"I believe they're in your old room."

He nodded, "Thanks."

A short while later, Ralph was thankfully dressed in the spare clothes he'd kept in his old bedroom's chest of drawers, having decided against going for the clothes he'd worn last night which disgustingly reeked of smoke and booze. Tossing said clothes into the washer, he turned to speak with Ryder who'd come to sit at one of the kitchen island stools.

"Got anything planned for today?" he asked as he walked over to the coffee machine, slipping in his favourite flavour.

"I've got to run into town to pick up a few things, that's about it. I got up earlier this morning and got quite a bit done, the rest can wait till tomorrow." Ryder replied, sipping his own beverage of choice. "You?"

Ralph leaned his lower back against the counter, arms crossed casually.

"Paperwork, mostly. Pa asked me to double check a few things. Might look in on Glory Days, see how she is what with it being almost time."

Glory Days was their prized breeding mare who was expecting her second foal. She'd sadly lost her first when they'd had a terrible storm last year, thankfully being able to conceive a second foal without any issues. Hopefully they'd manage to keep it that way until she was ready to birth her little one.

Ryder nodded, "Sucks about the paperwork bro, but, we all have to do it." he stated, rising from his seat. "Well, no time like the presence, I'm off." He gave Ralph a pat on his shoulder as he put his mug in the sink, the coffee machine finishing up brewing as he placed it in. "Catch you later."

"Alright, later."

"Oh and Ralph?"

He turned and looked over his shoulder, carefully pouring his own coffee. "Yeah?"

"Take it easy on Rol when you see him, don't want Ma or Pa catching on about what happened to you last night." Ryder chuckled, turning on his heel and heading towards the front door.

Ralph groaned.

That kid's going to get one hell of a payback someday.

Picking up his mug of steaming coffee, he shuffled off towards his father's study to complete at least a few hours of agonising paperwork, which he was assured would put him to sleep if not for the coffee in his hands.

Thank heavens, again, for small mercies.

CHAPTER FIVE
~ Robinne ~

After she'd been able to shift her unwelcomed, unexpected visitor, Robinne had actually managed to get a lot done in the few hours after he'd left. She'd taken her bags upstairs, unpacked them, explored the house and set up her laptop and other writing essentials. She'd arranged for her other items, the few they were, to be delivered here by a moving company from Austin. They should arrive within the next few days.

I hope.

Putting her hands on her hips as she stood in her bedroom, planning on what she'd put where, her stomach grumbled loudly.

"Guess I got to go shopping huh?" she said, rubbing her stomach. It wasn't like she didn't have a decent breakfast thanks to Mrs Jenkins, but working always did work up a hunger with her. Besides, if she was still back at home, it would be right around dinner time.

People say that talking to yourself is often the first sign of insanity but personally, ninety-nine percent of the time she only got decent answers from talking to herself. The other one percent? Not so much. Utter drivel really.

Making her way downstairs, she checked herself in the mirror by the doorway one last time before doing the standard check before leaving the house.

Phone, check, Wallet, check. House keys, check.

Everyone does this check before they leave the house, as it was a sure-fire way to make sure you never left the house without the essentials. Most of the time.

Locking the door behind her, Robinne started to walk back the way which she remembered Joe driving her earlier this morning. The wind whipping around her hair as she leisurely walked down the road. She thankfully remembered to walk on the right side of the road, literally, the 'right' side. The last thing she wanted was to be walking on the path of incoming traffic because of her anglicised brain forgetting that they drove on the other side of the road here. She's seen many a people on those dashcam programmes back home when they drive 'accidentally' on the wrong side, claiming they're not used to driving on foreign roads when they perfectly know well that where they're going, they do.

Idiots.

Then again, she'd have to get used to driving on the right side of the road when her car came. In her tight budget that was her move, she just had enough money to find a cheap truck which like her stuff, was also being delivered from Austin. It should be arriving sometime later this week, luck be on her side. Even then, she's only on a provisional licence here until she took the U.S. driving test. That was a thought for another day though.

One thing about she knew about Texas that for sure fit the stereotype, is the enormity of everything. Everything was truly bigger in Texas, especially the expansiveness of the sky. In all directions she turned her head around to look at, it was just simply so vast.

Her pondering was interrupted with what sounded like horse hoofs in the distance. Looking to her right and squinting her eyes, she covered her eyes with both of her hands as she spied in the distance, a lone rider was perched on top of a horse. From where she stood, she couldn't make out if the figure was man or woman but whoever it was, they were tall and were not afraid to work a horse fast. She could never go near a horse, let alone get on top of one. Horses were one of her many flaws she wasn't afraid to admit. They absolutely terrified her.

Turning her head away from the direction, she carried along the road towards town. She needed to stop getting distracted. Then again, being here was all about figuring herself out and beginning a new life, maybe being a little distracted by this and that wasn't so bad a thing after all.

You just keep telling yourself that girlie.

She eventually made it into the centre of the small town, making her way back towards the main street. Stopping under the shade of one of the store awnings, she paused to see what was going on before her eyes. As a budding writer, she had a habit of stopping every now and then to take in things around her, hoping that something would pop up and serve as inspiration for a scene, be it a character profile or an idea for a book. Anything could stir up her imagination, so she couldn't miss the opportunity to observe the new town properly this time without having anywhere she needed to be urgently.

One thing she loved about the Americans, they made the best out of the good weather which face it, was a lot better than English weather for the majority of the time. Today's weather seemed to prove her theory just right as the main street was out in full force with people, even for a weekday. It wasn't near as busy as her home town city centre on a Saturday morning, but she'd have a time of it getting down one side of the pavement for kids running around their families, people of their golden years sharing a cold drink sat on cute vintage chairs, and men going about their daily business even on the weekend. No rest for the wicked, she assumed. Ranching life couldn't be an easy one.

"Are you lost ma'am?" a voice called out to her.

Turning around and looking down, she was met with the kindest eyes of the sweetest elderly-looking gentleman she'd ever seen. He couldn't have been more than 5"5, aged with soft wrinkles she assumed contained many,

many memories and moments from a life well-lived. His hair was sparse on his head but from what little there was, its soft silver colour glinted in the sun shining down on them.

"N-no, not lost no. Just enjoying the view."

His face lit up with a broad smile.

"Ah, not a local I see. Well, welcome to Dripping Springs, young lady. The name's Niall Locke, but you can call me Niall. What brings you into town on this fine day?"

"Oh, I'm just looking to get a few things for the fridge, plus a few necessities. I just moved here, as you could tell." She laughed, "I need to get a few things I couldn't have shipped over or brought in my luggage." She said with a nonchalant shrug.

"Ah." Niall nodded, saving her explaining everything to him. "Oh!" he clicked his fingers, "You're Robinne! Of course you are! You moved into the old Jameson place. Joe said you'd be arriving pretty soon. How're you finding your stay so far?"

How many people have heard about me?

"It's been lovely so far, everyone's been so helpful and kind. I can't fault a thing."

"Good to hear! Very good to hear. Now before we forget, as I have a tendency to go off-track a bit, what things are you looking to purchase today?"

Digging a list of things to buy from her bag, she scanned her eyes down said list for what she'd intended to purchase on this excursion.

"Fridge food, non-perishables, toothpaste, shampoo & conditioner, shower cream & other bathroom items, deodorant, perfume, skincare items, bottles of water, medicine cabinet items, period items…" she mumbled the last few items on her list, Niall didn't need to know about those.

"I see. You really do need almost everything but the kitchen sink don't ya? Well, you've come to the right place. I just so happen to be the owner of the biggest store, which really isn't all that big after all, in town containing most of what you're looking for. Come right this way with me, ol' Niall will look after ya."

I can't exactly tell him no.

Nor can I tell him I'm not much of an extrovert, or 'people person'.

I'm more than happy to do things under my own steam as much as possible before needing help.

Then again, the sooner I can get these items, I can get back to the sanctuary of my new home.

Niall walked with her to the store in which he must've come out of before coming across her. He grabbed a trolley or rather, a 'cart', from inside the entrance of the store, gently guiding it into her hands before walking them under the A/C unit and into the store itself.

"Now, you look like a bright young lady to me so I won't need to explain how a store works." He chuckled to himself, "You'll see how easily things are marked out for you to find. At the top of every aisle as you can see, are what each aisle contains in them. You only normally see these in large superstores, but I think it makes the whole place look nicer. Anyway, each aisle has little subsection headers so you can easily find smaller items not listed above. If you can't find what you're looking for, you can find me at the checkout desk and I'll be more than happy to help you out. Okay?"

"Yes. Thank you so much, you've been a great help."

"Anytime, see you in a short while!" Niall headed off with a wave, walking over towards the checkout desk.

Okay, let's do this.

A short while later, she had most of what was on her list piled into the trolley, which was becoming harder to manoeuver with each new addition. She was by in no terms a weakling, but even she had to admit that she was getting close to being unable to move the trolley without assistance. Only a few things from her list weren't available, she'd order those in later at some point. Nonetheless, she was pleased that she was able to find as much as she did without having to go elsewhere.

Making her way over to the checkout with her loaded trolley, Niall was there as promised. Putting down the magazine he was reading, he perked up. As busy as the main street looked before she came inside, today was not the day that many people needed something from his store it seemed.

"Well that sure didn't take you long! Did you find everything you needed alright?" he started checking out her items as she put each one up on the counter.

"Mostly. Just a few things I can easily order in, it's not a problem."

"Great! Glad to be of use to ya. We're a small town so I try to stock as much as I can into this place, even so, there's bound to be a few items here and there that not many people have use for, so I don't stock it."

"Understandable." She nodded in agreement.

"There's just one thing…" Niall started to say.

Oh no…what is it?

"How are you going to get all that back with no vehicle?" a deep voice said behind her, making her jump.

She turned around to come face to well…chest, with a man the size of a great redwood tree. He wore a white Stetson.

So that's really a thing, men in cowboy hats.

Yes!

She marveled at the sight of such a beast of a man up close. Thankfully for her, she never went gooey at the sight of such a man like this, she just wasn't used to being so up close and personal with one. Men like this did really only exist in books after all.

"Mornin' to you young Ryder." Niall said from behind her back.

The beast of a man, Ryder, tipped his hat at Niall's greeting.

"Niall." He turned his eyes back to Robinne. "You still haven't answered my question little lady."

Question? Oh, question!

Little lady?

"I was going to dr...ah shoot!" she cursed to herself.

Ryder chuckled, clearly knowing her predicament before she did.

"Exactly. So, how'd you like a little helping hand?"

She blinked at his offer.

"I don't even know you. Wait, how do you even know that I don't have a car parked outside?"

"No truck parked out front beside mine, and I know most folks around here and the cars they drive. Plus you're new to town so if you had a ride, it would be parked outside and I wouldn't recognise it, so I'd know it had to be yours." He said smiling, very pleased with himself. Yet, not in the typical cocky way you'd expect a handsome stranger to be. No, he had a kindness about him.

"Touché." She admitted.

A throat cleared behind her. Niall was done checking her items out. Turning around, she got her purse out to pay.

"How much do I owe you?"

"That'll be $40.95, tax has been added automatically for you."

"Oh, thank you!"

Niall smiled.

"So, what'll you say to Ryder's offer?"

"Huh?" She blinked.

Niall gestured to the brown bags he'd packed full of her items.

"Oh! N-no, I can't impose on anyone else. Everyone I've met has already helped me out a great deal. I'm sure I can make a couple trips back home on foot..."

Robinne never got to finish her sentence before four of her many bags were lifted off the counter by Ryder, her own literal white stetsoned knight.

"Nonsense, I couldn't sleep tonight knowing I did nothing to help you out. Allow me to give you a ride home and if you really feel like it later on, I can call in a return favour someday. How'd that sound?"

It actually sounds pretty good.

Deciding not to be any more stubborn than she naturally is, she nodded in agreement.

"Thank you, I kindly accept with your added offer. I intend to return it someday though." She nodded again, this time with a reluctant smile.

She still had to get used to accepting help from others, as well as people now actually coming up to talk to her, instead of what she was used to back home which was being completely ignored by strangers that is.

"Great! Grab those last two bags and we'll load up and get you home!" Ryder said with a spring in his step as he turned to head out of the store.

Niall chuckled again from behind her.

"Those boys don't stop with the good deed doing. Not that it's a problem. They just have a hard time saying no. Anyhow, don't want to keep him waiting now. It was a pleasure to meet you Miss Robinne, hope you grace me with your lovely presence sometime soon!" he opened the door to the store for her to pass through.

Such a kind old gent.

Placing a soft kiss on his aged cheek, she nodded at his statement.

"You too! Thank you so much for your help! Have a good day!"

Leaving the store with a wave at Niall, she headed over to the only truck parked outside.

Woah...

"A beauty huh?" Ryder said as he leaned on the side of the truck. "2018 Chevrolet Silverado 1500 in 'Red Hot'. Worked hard for this beautiful gal. What do you think?"

He's asking me what I think of a truck?

I don't really know what to say.

C'mon, you have to say something!

Making her way over with her bags, she stopped just before the truck to admire it.

"You're lucky to have such a truck. This year's model too."

"Know much about trucks?" Ryder asked as he took the bags off her, placing them with the others in the truck bed.

Shaking her head, she had to admit the truth.

"Not a thing. Then again, I don't need to. I know a beautiful thing when I see it."

"Spoken like any true native. C'mon, hop on in and I'll take you home."

Ryder headed around to the driver's side of the truck, the side she normally would get into back home. Getting used to the way things work in America was still new to her, which of course they would be, at least until they become as second nature as doing things back home was.

It was easier than she thought getting into the high truck, thanks to the step on the side.

A blessing for the shorter girl I'm sure.

Once seated in the huge yet comfy seat, she buckled herself in and looked at Ryder, who was now seated in the driver's seat and buckled in like her.

"Do you need the address to my place? Or do you know where it is already?"

Smirking, Ryder turned his head in her direction.

"I'm invoking the right to feign ignorance here and say I'd like your address please. Even though I know who you are and where you're now living, since I was one of the people who renovated your place."

"You were?"

"My brothers and I do a little work on the side like this when we're not too busy on the ranch. We get to help out people while keeping busy at the same time."

"Makes sense."

Ryder pulled out of the parking spot with ease, thanks to handy dandy reverse cameras and the screen within the central console. Though she suspected he'd do alright without them, he seemed skilled when it came to vehicles and how to handle them.

"So, I'm sure Niall talked your head off in there."

She shook her head. "He did speak a bit more than I'm used to, but it was no bother."

"Yeah? Not everyone would say that."

"Why? He's so sweet."

Ryder shrugged.

"Not everyone wants to be talked to about everything under the sun every time they go in the store. Folks around here are content 90% of the time to listen, it's just the odd occasion you get the 10% wanting to get in and get out fast-like."

Kind of like me then…

"That's awful."

"I guess, but like I said, it's just the minor 10%. Sometimes folks are more that 10% than 90, but it doesn't happen a great deal."

"That's good then."

Ryder seems like quite the talker too.

He headed back out of the main street in the direction in which she'd walked in. How she wished he'd been near her house in the first place, so she didn't have to learn the hard way just how far it was back into town. It didn't seem far when she rode with Joe.

You live and you learn.

Thinking about what she was going to place where when she got home, she suddenly remembered something major she'd left off her list.

"Oh no!" she creed out.

Ryder looked at her briefly before returning his eyes to the road head of them.

"What's the matter?"

"I forgot! I don't have my fridge or freezer connected to the mains! I meant to get that sorted before I went food shopping! I don't know how to do that sort of thing yet."

Ryder instantly relaxed back into his seat, shaking his head while a smile formed on his face.

"Thank God, I thought something was seriously wrong there for a second."

"A disconnected fridge and freezer isn't a problem? I got frozen goods in some of those bags in the bed of your truck!"

"Not a problem." He flicked on a turn signal, turning the truck around in the world's quickest U-turn.

"What're you doing?"

"Taking us to my place."

A handsome stranger taking a girl back to his place to help her out? No!

This is exactly the sort of thing that happens in those badly written cowboy romance novels. I can't let him take me there!

"I really can't let you do this. It then *would* make me a total burden to you. I'm sure there's things that you need to do right now other than to drive me here there and everywhere."

Ryder shook his head.

"Not really. Believe it or not, today is one of the rare days where I have some time to spare, which is rare for a rancher. Helping you out is what I'm happy to do today. It would be an insult to how my Ma raised me if you refused my offer." He threw a puppy dog look Robinne's way, clearly aiming to guilt-trip her into conceding.

How can I resist that look?

Oh who am I kidding? I can't. Dammit…

"I'll only agree if you let me owe you another favour. I don't like taking the liberty of others for free."

Ryder chuckled at her, amused at how dang sweet she was.

"Oh alright, if I must."

She nodded.

"Great, now that's settled. Homeward bound it is."

Settling down in her seat, Robinne turned her attention back to the rolling scenery outside of her window, wondering what else this day could possibly bring her way.

Half an hour later, Ryder pulled onto a short dirt road which she assumed lead to the ranch home he'd spoken about. On the short drive here, she learned he owned his own place but worked on his family ranch. She'd of course never been to a ranch before and she never thought she'd ever actually be visiting one yet, here she is.

"Home sweet home. Or should I say 'ranch sweet ranch." Ryder laughed, amused by his own joke.

Pulling around one final corner, his ranch came into view.

Robinne was in great awe when she saw the main house in front of her, as it was more than she was expecting. Not that she was expecting either a mansion or a rundown shack, she was just surprised generally at how beautiful the home was.

"Now I don't want to be rude here but, you don't get out much do you?"

She shook her head. He was right, she didn't.

"You wouldn't be rude, it's the truth. I'll confess, I'm a bit of a recluse. Happy in my own bubble. No, I'm just…this place…wow."

"Maybe I'll give you a tour in a little while if we have time. For now, let's get your stuff inside and into the fridge. Don't want it to spoil now do we?"

"R-right!"

They both got out of their respective sides of the truck.

"Oh and one more thing." Ryder started to say from his side of the truck at its bed.

Before he could continue his sentence, Robinne turned in the direction of what sounded like heavy footprints heading her way. Only, they weren't the type of footprints she was expecting. This sound had two more feet than the human she'd expected to be heading her way. Instead, what was heading her way was what looked like to be several pounds of wet, muddy dog.

"Aaah!" she cried out, failing to protect or get herself away in time in order to avoid being caked in the same mud as the boisterous dog.

"BUDDY! NO!" The shout coming from Ryder was in all vein, as the dog had already decided to greet Robinne up close and personal, jumping up at her front, covering her in the same mud as it. Ryder quickly wrestled the dog, appropriately named Buddy, off of her.

Looking down at her front, she realised that this was something she did not picture happening today either. Why would she?

"I'm so sorry! Buddy here is the best dog a man could ask for, but also the worst ranch dog a man could ask for. He's more likely to want a cuddle than to do what ranch dogs do."

"No kidding." She said in good humour, as there was no point getting mad at what Buddy did. It wouldn't get her any cleaner at this point.

With Buddy now under control in Ryder's arms somewhat, he himself looked up at her with a look of guilt on his face.

"I'm guessing you don't have a spare change of clothes with you, do you?"

"Uh…no. Sorry."

"Nothing to be sorry about little lady, it's all this mutt's fault here. Tell you what, go on up to the main bathroom which is the last door on the right, and I'll go find something for you to wear while you clean up. Least I can do for what's just happened to ya." Sounding so sincere while he held the muddy Buddy still, she'd be rude and stupid to refuse his offer.

Not bothering to argue, she nodded.

"Sounds like a plan. I won't be too long."

"Take as long as you need. I'm going to give this one a bath and get your clothes washed. Leave them outside the bathroom door and I'll leave some clothes for you to change into."

"Got it."

It wasn't too hard finding the master bathroom Ryder described to her, after all, the big clue aside from the directions had to be the 'bathroom' symbol on the outside of the bathroom door.

Must be if guests visit or something.

Shutting the bathroom door behind her, she was left looking at the most grand décor of a bathroom she's ever seen in her entire life. Ryder in no means came across as a poor or rich man, but he or whoever did the décor here spared no expense in the end result wow factor. The ceiling instead of being flat, was softly curved. Not quite a full semi-circle shape, not slightly bowed. Just right. The colour scheme of the room matched most of what she briefly caught of the house décor on her way up, a cream which was more of a gold hue, teamed with the deepest, richest wood trim, cabinets and general bathroom furniture which under the bathroom downlights, shone a beautiful chestnut brown. To each side of the room spreading the entirety of the two walls were two giant mirrors, mirrors so big that this had to be inspired by the room of mirrors at the palace of Versailles. At the top of each mirror in uniform rows hung short, equally spaced golden lamps, adding yet more light to the downlights in the ceiling. Towards the end of the long master bathroom, she could see a bath. To either side of the bath were two arched doorways, one leading to a wet room shower, the other holding toiletry supplies. Walking up to the bath, she could see that it was designed with as much dedicated detail as the rest of the bathroom, as she had to step up a single step to even look down into the enclosed tub.

She could spend all day marvelling at this miniature Versailles, but she didn't want to hold up Ryder for more than she had to. So much to her dismay, she decided to forgo a bath in the decadent tub, choosing the quickness of the wet room shower instead.

Leaving her clothes outside of the door as instructed, she darted back to the shower, naked as the day she was born. She wasn't much of an exhibitionist, not that anyone was even around to see her right now, but the act of being stark naked in a stranger's house gave her an oddly strange yet satisfying thrill. Others may not think so, but this was something she definitely had to save to write about later in a future story. Someone would surely find this amusing in a story.

A little under twenty minutes later, all the muck that had managed to seep through her clothes somehow, had all thankfully been washed off and gone down the drain to where it belongs. It certainly didn't belong on her body, despite Buddy thinking it did when he put it there, intentional or not.

"Now, Ryder said he'd leave clothes for me outside the door. I hope to God it's something not too tight-fitting." She said, turning off the shower and stepping out onto the oddly warm floor. "Huh, under-floor heating too? Fancy." She made her way over to the door, leaving wet footprints in her wake. She'd clean it up with a towel once she'd brought the clothes inside, there wasn't a rush to towel up right this moment.

Reaching forward to open the door which thankfully opened outwards, the door handle came away from her, as did the door, the second her fingers touched the metal of the handle.

"What the…"

There wasn't any time at all to cover up remotely one inch of her body before she came face-to-chest with someone she'd never expect to see again.

"Well hello there. Returning the favour are we?"

The naked man from my place!

Oh no…

CHAPTER SIX
~ Robinne ~

If there was a moment where a human being could die from embarrassment, it would be this very moment. All of Robinne's limbs didn't seem to want to move, her brain too failing to compose any sort of response to who was standing in front of her, running his eyes up and down her body approvingly. Never in a million years did she think she'd be seeing him again, let alone like this.

"Don't hurry to cover up on my behalf darlin'. I'm rather liking these turn of events." The former naked man from her bathroom smirked.

"Wha?" she said, finally managing her brain to get her mouth to say something.

Cover up damn it!

When her brain finally engaged, she snatched up the towel he held in his right hand, stepping back in order to slam the door shut in his face.

This time, lock it woman!

Thinking that she wasn't going to run into anyone up here when no one looked to be around, she didn't even think twice in stopping to check to see if the door had a lock. Why wouldn't it? A grandly-designed bathroom such as this one wouldn't skimp on the small things such as door locks. Flipping the lock closed as soon as the door was firmly shut, she let out the surprised breath she'd been holding in.

That man…he…it…h-he was the one from my bedroom! The naked man from my bedroom!

He's here! Why?

Why is he here?

And why did he have to see me like THIS!

Two swift yet gentle knocks rapped on the door, which was now at her back.

"Since you're occupying this bathroom, I'll just go use one of the others, shall I?" she could tell he was smirking on the other side of the door, just by the sheer tone of his voice.

Jerk.

Why didn't you do that in the first place?

Well, there was no point in her putting on the towel now. She was only going to put it on to get the clothes from outside of the door anyway. One thing did puzzle her though, why weren't the towels in the bathroom? There was a perfectly good storage area for them, so why not put them there? It must've been a wash day or something.

Oh right, the clothes!

Unlocking the door and slowly opening it outwards once again, she peered out to see that the coast was clear, this time with the towel against her front to protect her modesty. Pointless really when it's already been seen, but she could do without it happening for a second time.

There as promised right outside of the master bathroom door, was the set of clothes Ryder said he'd leave for her. It puzzled her further as she took them in and closed the door, locking it once again, why the 'naked man' handed her the towel and not the clothes. Perhaps he really was enjoying seeing the tables turned, seeing that she was now the naked one instead of him.

A turn of events indeed.

All of it is irrelevant to her now, as she doesn't want to see him again to even find out the answer. She was going to dress into these feminine clothes, which she hoped wasn't left by an ex of Ryder's, and she was going to find him and forget the whole sordid incident. After all, there was nothing worse and more cliché than dressing in a former flame's clothes. Not that she has before, it's just a cliché hate of hers. One of the many.

As she dressed, she found it harder than expected to forget the look on the 'naked man's' face as the door came away from her hand. It was clear to her that it was much a surprise to find her there as she was to see him again. She supposed neither of them expected to see the other again in a month of Sundays. Yet, here she was, thinking about it and how embarrassing it was.

So much for avoiding a dramatic second-meeting cliché, well done Robinne.

Donned in the thankfully close-fitting to her size clothes, Robinne left the bathroom in search of her new friend and grocery store hero. He said he'd be washing her clothes, so it'd be a safe bet to say he'd be in the kitchen, orr the 'washroom', she had to get used to the way Americans set out their homes. The washer and dryer was most often in a separate room close to the kitchen, rather than actually in the kitchen like back home.

Going back the way she came, this time with a little more time to spare to look at the décor as she walked, she could hear two male voices somewhere close by. They weren't talking overly loudly, leading her to the assumption that they didn't want to be heard. Yet by the tone of the voices and gruffness accompanying one of the two voices, she safely could guess this wasn't a good type of conversation.

"You didn't do anything to piss her off, did you?" one of the voices said as she drew closer.

"Didn't need to, she could do that all by herself." The other voice replied, this one making her spine stiffen.

Definitely that naked jerk.

"Why didn't you check to see if the door was locked before you went in? Surely Ma didn't raise you to be that stupid?" Ryder asked.

Stopping just outside of what she assumed was the washroom, she leaned against the wall to listen to what Ryder and naked man were saying. Normally she would think it rude to eavesdrop, but this was different.

"Because little bro, I didn't expect anyone to be in here. Last I checked you were off running errands in town, Ma's at work, Rowan and Reed are helping Pa mending fences and Roland was out doing God knows what. So I assumed it was safe to the damned master bathroom without assuming someone was inside."

He kind of has a point there…

Ryder sighed.

"From now on, check ok? That's all I'm asking."

"Why? It's not like she'll be coming back here again. She'll be out of our hair once you've played maid with her clothes."

"What's she ever done to you?"

"Why're you playing white knight for her?" Naked man retorted, sounding more pissed off with every reply.

"I'm no white knight, never have never will be, but we were raised right. Man or woman, if someone needs help, we help them. I had to go into Niall's for something when I saw her stuck with all her groceries and no way to get them home, so I simply offered her a ride. Her appliance not working wasn't her fault, it'll be fixed and I'll do the good and right thing of getting her home safely. I'd do this for anyone, not just because she's new to town and single. I don't know why you've got such a stick up your ass about her, but pull it out and treat her right. Besides, she looks like she could use a friend."

I do? I didn't even see that about myself.

Naked man echoed Ryder's earlier sigh.

"Look, I'm sorry man. It's been a rough week and it got shittier the other morning when I woke up buck ass naked in her new bedroom with her brandishing a shoe at me. It was like a switch flipped inside of her and she couldn't get me out there fast enough. Why I don't know, but when I opened that door to find *her* buck ass naked instead of me, I couldn't help but find it amusing just a little bit. Who wouldn't?"

"Any decent gentleman in the state of Texas?"

"Yeah, right."

Ok, I knew I was out of order by not letting him explain himself, I'll admit it. He didn't have to act like such a jerk yesterday or today.

I know I'm not much of a people person, but I'm reasonable if people are cordial to me.

"You're right though…" Naked man continued. "…I should at least apologise for being so crass to her just now. My shitty week doesn't mean she should bear the brunt of my mood."

Huh, so he CAN be nice after all.

"You'd be doing the right thing bro. See, Ma didn't drop you on your head as a baby after all."

"Fuck off dude." Naked man said with a laugh.

Two pairs of booted footsteps came towards her, reminding her swiftly that she had to move if she didn't want to get caught. Making it halfway across the kitchen before she heard the washroom door swing fully open, she turned to see the two men coming out of it, joining her in the vastness of the kitchen.

"Ah, Robinne. All done up there?" Ryder approached with a friendly smile.

She nodded, trying to best convey that she'd just arrived instead of her trying to escape her eavesdropping position. "Yes, thank you. The bathroom was very uh…lovely. I really appreciate you letting me use it." she said, avoiding naked man's gaze.

Ryder waved a hand between them, "Nonsense, it's nothing. Your clothes should be done and dry in just over an hour. Think you can hold it out here that long?"

An hour?

An hour in the house with the naked man?

Guess I have no choice here. I can't be rude.

Again.

"Sure! No problem."

Clapping his hands together, Ryder's charming smile widened. "Excellent! In that case, allow me to introduce you to someone." He reached behind him with his left arm, not taking his eyes or face off her direction. Pulling naked man from behind him, he brought him to his side with his arm now holding onto naked man's opposite shoulder. "Robinne, meet my bear on the outside but daft puppy dog on the inside big brother, Ralph."

Ralph.

So naked man DID have a name after all. Obviously, you ninny.

Why did it have to be such a nice name?

Darn it.

Ralph shrugged Ryder's arm off from around his shoulders, and extended a hand out towards her. "Let's start over shall we? As this dunce here said, the name's Ralph. Pleasure to re-meet you, *Robinne*."

She slowly raised her hand, slipping it gently inside his.

"Yes, nice to re-meet you too, Ralph." As her hand touched his, she let their hands keep that connection for the briefest amount of time possible. She wasn't a germaphobe, she just had her own reasons for not wanting to touch him for too long.

She could see by the look in Ralph's eye that he knew something that she didn't, and since she wasn't going to ask what it was, she would just have to resist the urge to scratch that itch, burying her curiosity back down deep within her.

Returning her hand back to her side, she saw Ryder give Ralph the slightest of nudges.

Uh oh, what now?

Ralph's broad shoulders physically relaxed, with him echoing the sigh she heard Ryder give in the washroom. "Look, I'm not the best with words, or actions for that matter. Thinking back, we both got off on the wrong foot yesterday, I'd like to set that right. How about we both grab a cup of coffee and start things over with a mutual chat out on the back porch? How'd that sound?"

For a moment, she was gobsmacked.

Maybe I should give him a second chance…

"Sure, that'd be nice."

Nodding, Ralph led her through the kitchen and out onto the back porch.

Woah…

Ralph paused beside her, him too glancing around at the site before him. "I know right? I love when I'm able to spend time back here."

She could see why. The home matched the front of the building in terms of the style of the build, it's what was added onto it that amazed her. The porch itself wrapped around the entirety of the back of the house, making it look as if it was going on forever. Lights seen on top of lamp posts in Victorian London hung from various points on the side of the house, emitting a comforting yellowish glow on the respective spots on the porch below. A table was situated in the middle of a brief stone-clad strip just before an endless sea of greener than ever seen before green grass. Around the table sat enough seats for which she would assume was every family member when all were here at one time, a big family by the looks of it. Most impressive of all though as she took a look to the left, was an outdoor stone log fireplace, reaching from the ground to way above the roof of the house. How grand it must feel to spend one night out here.

"You alright there crumpet?"

Crumpet?

She let his nickname for her slide, just this once. The fewer arguments the better.

Ralph must've since gone back into retrieve their drinks while she gawked at everything, as he now held two steaming mugs in his previously empty hands.

"You didn't look like much of a coffee person to me so, I got Ryder to whip you up a cup of tea, more of what you're used to y'know?"

That's…kind of thoughtful.

He handed her the mug with her tea in, to which she nodded her thanks.

Ralph sat down in one of the loungers situated here out on the back porch. Taking his lead as a cue, she took a seat on her own respective lounger, taking a sip of her tea. "Mmm, just how I like it."

Ralph nodded and looked back out at the view of the garden, which basked in sunlight on the hot Texas day. He looked a little lost as to what to say next, so she decided to break the ice, despite her reluctance to do just that.

"So…why'd you want to start over with me? Please, be honest."

He looked back at her when she spoke.

"I'll be honest, it was Ryder's idea. I tend to be a bit of a bear when I have a rough week, I mean, who doesn't? Yesterday didn't help. Waking up in a stranger's house I mean. I was out drinking with Ryder and one of my other brothers, one of which decided it was a good idea to get back at me for a past prank. Anyway like I said, it's been a bit of a week and I shouldn't have been rude to you, even though you did kick me out without letting me try to explain. I'm not a total ass, and I know when to admit when I'm bested I knew Ryder was right in me trying to make things right with you. Sometimes I feel he's the eldest brother instead of me." He chuckled, amused at the thought of Ryder being the mature one this time around.

Wow.

Maybe he's not such a jerk after all.

Putting down the mug at her feet, she turned to face him fully. "I'm not good at admitting when I'm wrong either, but, you're not the one in the wrong here. Sure it wasn't nice to find anyone, not you specifically, in my house, but that didn't give me the right to kick you out without giving you a chance to explain. Taking the decision to move here was huge for me, yet it was what I needed and it was done in rather a hurry so…after travelling for the first time and everything, the jetlag and tiredness got to me and you just happened to be the one I eventually took it out on so…I'm sorry."

He blinked at her, apparently not expecting that she'd apologise to him. She was much like him in that respect, a proud person when it came to personal honour.

Finishing most of his coffee, he set it down on the floor like she'd done and he extended a hand out to her. "Let's call a truce yeah? We've got our own reasons for why we treated each other the way we did and we've apologised, now let's move on and start over, yeah?"

Phew. Yes please.

"Deal." She shook his hand, looking into his eyes at the same time.

ZAP

The two of them sprang apart. Well, not quite literally sprang, but moved away from one another swifter than expected

What on earth was that?

Robinne felt as though the very Earth's sky itself had struck a bolt of lightning at their hands, spreading at the speed of light all over her body, causing her heart to run as fast as a horse at the Grand National.

Oh no…no. Not 'THE' connection…

It can't be…

Ralph was looking at her with a rather bemused expression on her face, not quite sure what happened or what she was thinking, but also not wanting to question the nature of what they'd both surely felt. They'd just both apologised and cleared the air between them, they didn't need to complicate things or apologise to each other again.

He cleared his throat, picking up his mug and downing the rest of its contents.

"So, uh…what's it like, you know, being from England?"

She returned his bemused blink, before realising that he was thankfully moving things past what just happened.

"Uh…much like what I expect feeling coming from America feels to you, minus having a disgrace of a toddler in charge though."

Ralph chuckled heartily.

"Can't argue with that. Though I have to say, I've never met an English person before. Nice accent you got there."

"Well, thank you. I'm not exactly a rare creature though, we do come out in the daylight and everything."

"Damn, and there I was about to get my garlic out."

"Smart arse."

He smirked. "Guilty."

Soon, they both finished their drinks with a relatively comfortable air of conversation between them. She found out from him that he was the eldest of five boys, known around town as the 'Jenkins Boys'.

Ralph Jenkins, damn he had a nice name.

She also found out that he was the one in charge of the ranch, placed in the position a couple of years ago when his father retired from the full-time position. On the side, he did the fix-up jobs as Ryder had also brought to her attention earlier. He'd also mentioned to her that his mother still insisted on working to give her and her husband some income, despite them having enough money to retire on.

That explains why she was at the B&B then.

He admired her for her willingness to work, he just wished she'd take on help to take a bit off her shoulders a little.

"Well, despite how things started out for us, this hasn't been that bad of a day after all." He piped up after a brief silence.

"No, it hasn't has it? Thank you for the drink." She lifted her mug in thanks.

He waved his hand.

"Can't take credit for yours, Ryder knows how to make drinks for us all in the mornings the best."

"Ah."

Standing up from his lounger, Robinne could see from her seated position just how imposing Ralph could seem to some, especially to kids. He could block out the very sun if he stood in the right position. If she thought Ryder was tall when she came across him in the store earlier, he had nothing on his brother's height.

If she was someone else in another lifetime, she would think she stood a chance with someone like him, totally ignoring the zap she felt earlier, that didn't mean anything.

Did it?

Shaking her head, she cleared the negative thoughts away. It wasn't something she was even thinking about at this point anyway, she'd just moved here. It was time to start a new life, which included no prior thoughts or expectations. A new slate, that's what this was.

"C'mon, let me take these back inside and let's get your clothes and see if they're done by now."

"S-sure!"

Getting back onto her feet, she handed over her mug to Ralph, being careful to avoid touching his fingers as much as possible.

They were just about to turn to make their way back inside when a familiar voice called out to them.

"Robinne! Ralph! How lovely to see you both here!" an older voice cooed.

Turning around to the direction of the voice, Robinne was very surprised to see who stood in the doorway leading out to the back porch.

"Mrs Jenkins?"

What on Earth is going on here?

CHAPTER SEVEN
~ Ralph ~

"Hello again dear." Ma said to Robinne, who currently looked as if she couldn't believe who was standing before her.

What's got her so spooked? It's only Ma.

"Ma, I thought you were working today?" He piped up, walking over and embracing his Ma in a gentle hug, placing a tender kiss on her cheek.

"Your father called in a favour, one of the girls came in to relieve me." She turned to look at Robinne. "What's the matter dear?" Mrs Jenkins said as she peeled herself out of Ralph's arms. "Are you feeling alright?"

He saw Robinne swallow and shake her head slightly. "Y-yeah, I'm alright. Thank you." She cleared her throat. "You're…you're Mrs Jenkins, from the B&B

"Correct." Ma smiled kindly, allowing Robinne to make the connection between her and him on her own.

"That means the men who fixed up my house were the sons you mentioned, which I discussed with…"

"Me, yes." Ralph interjected, as unlike his mother, he wasn't good at holding back.

Putting a palm to her forehead, he watched her inwardly groan.

"They're your sons. Joe's their dad. I'm officially an idiot for not putting two and two together. Urgh."

Oh Robinne, you're such a sweetheart.

Coming forward, he watched as his Ma placed a hand gently on her right forearm.

"Don't worry yourself about it, it's not something to worry yourself over. You know who's who now, so that's that. Now, you can tell me why you're here a little later, I rarely get chance to come back here and make lunch for all my boys, so I insist you stay and eat with us."

Robinne turned to face in his direction, almost as if she was silently asking if it was alright her staying for lunch. Of course, she didn't need his permission. He wasn't that sort of guy who gave women permission to do things on his say so, but that being said, the poor girl looked nervous enough being here with him considering what went down between them since they'd met so, he swiftly gave her a slight nod.

Robinne turned back to face Mrs Jenkins, putting on her biggest, friendliest smile, nodding her acceptance to her invite, "I'd love to, thank you."

"Excellent!"

"I will insist on helping in prepare it though, if there's anything I could do."

"That'd be nice, thank you dear. Ralph honey…" Mrs Jenkins turned to him again, "Go and get whatever you have to do, done, then wash up before you join us for lunch."

Ralph nodded obediently, giving his mother a quick peck on the cheek. If his Ma told you to do something, you do it. "Yes Ma." He didn't meet Robinne's gaze.

"Who's joining us?" Robinne asked.

"Just Roland, my youngest. Everyone else is workin' through lunch today."

Ma clapped her hands together, "Right. Well, shall we get to it dear?" She said cheerfully to Robinne.

"O-of course!"

With one last look behind her, she flashed Ralph a soft parting smile as she followed the older woman inside.

Damn, that smile could melt the coldest of hearts.

Just not yours right now, Cowboy.

Patience boy, patience.

Dragging his eyes away from where his Ma and Robinne had disappeared through, he made his way through the other back door, darting quickly upstairs to grab a quick shower before lunch was ready.

Finishing up not long later, Ralph turned off the spray of water he'd been standing under for the last few minutes, trying control his wandering thoughts he had no right thinking in the first place. Soft country music played in the background while he'd been washing, as he always loved having music on while in the bathroom ever since he was a little kid.

Grabbing a towel off of the towel rack which he'd re-stocked when he came up here, he crooned along to the latest song playing on the radio, while wrapping a towel around his waist. Padding over to his razor, he picked it up after filling the sink with warm water, lathering his face with shaving foam. He never shaved while in the shower, it just wasn't something he did.

"At least you're not completely naked this time huh?" a very familiar voice suddenly said to him out of nowhere.

Huh?

"Wha…ah, shit!" Ralph jumped at Robinne's sudden appearance in the doorway, as he turned his head too quickly at the sound of her voice coming out of nowhere stunning him, causing him to catch his cheek with the razor. "Now look what you've made me do. Why didn't you knock first or something?" He wasn't a nervous man by nature, but who wouldn't jump at someone's sudden appearance when you weren't expecting anyone to show up?

She rolled her eyes at him.

"I did. You're the one who doesn't, remember? Anyway, your music was too loud I suspected for you to hear me, so I just came in."

Cleaning up his graze, Ralph flashed her a mock-glare before patting his face down with a towel. "What brought you here anyway?"

"Your mum said to tell you lunch was ready. Want help putting your shirt back on?"

"Darlin', if I needed you to help me in any way with my shirt, it would be taking it off, not putting it on." He smirked. "Though I have to say, you do have a habit catching me without it on."

Well, he's not wrong.

"Excuse me, so have you!"

Ralph shook his head as he slipped his shirt back on over his head, clearly finished with freshening up. "Nope. I've only caught you topless, well, naked, once. You've seen me twice, therefore, you've caught me out one more than I've caught you."

Pushing off the doorjamb, she walked up to him and poked a finger square in the middle of his pecs. "That's beyond the point! I came up here to pass on a message and the message has been passed on so…I'll be going. Leave your smart mouth up here when you join us, will you?"

She started to turn around and face away from him.

Oh no you don't.

Ralph reached out and grabbed one of her wrists, holding her in place close in front of him, their respective chests mere inches apart.

"We could even the score you know, make it two-two. What do you say?"

Slowly, she narrowed her eyes at him.

"I say this." She pulled her wrist from out of his hold. "We agreed on starting a new leaf downstairs earlier, I'd like for you to remember that. Starting over again doesn't mean acting like this when you can clearly see I'm not comfortable about it."

"You're not comfortable with a little harmless…what do you call it where you're from, 'banter'?"

"That was not banter! That was flirting!"

"So you've got a problem with flirting? Why's that crumpet?"

She gave him another poke to the centre of his pecs, this time a lot harder.

Ow!

"First, you know my name isn't 'crumpet', its Robinne. Second, I *do not* have a problem with flirting."

He raised a brow.

"Oh yeah? Why're you so uppity about it then if you've got no problem with it?"

She outwardly groaned this time, rubbing the spot between her brows. "Listen, I don't want another argument, I've had enough of those to fill a month of Sundays. Just, come down for lunch okay? Put on some shoes while you're at it too."

Ralph chuckled, offering her a two-fingered salute of the nice kind as she turned and headed towards the door.

"Yes ma'am'."

"It's Robinne!" she shouted, her footsteps fading the further she distanced herself from the bathroom.

He chuckled and shook his head.

Clean, shaved (minus the bleeding this time) and dressed, Ralph gave himself a once-over in the bathroom mirror before selecting a pair of boots from the bottom of his bedroom wardrobe, slipping them on. Closing the door behind him, he made his way back downstairs with a spring in his step.

Wait. Am I looking forward to seeing her again?

Boy, you must be out of your mind.

Mostly.

By now, he knew whoever would be making it today to lunch would be gathered out on the back porch at the table yet when he got there, he paused just inside the kitchen, craning his head just enough to listen to his mother talking to Robinne.

"Robinne dear, this is my youngest son, Roland."

"Pleasure to meet you. I just got back from fixing up the appliances at your place." He could hear the smile in his brother's voice.

Tch, schmoozer.

"Oh? Oh! The fridge. Yes. Thank you! But uh…who…how'd you get in?"

He could hear in her voice that she wasn't completely at ease with someone else waltzing into her house, even if Roland was one of the ones who'd helped re-build it.

I wouldn't be either, to be fair. I can understand her unease.

"I used Pa's spare key. Here, it's rightfully yours now anyway."

Ralph peaked through the patio door blind to see Roland handing over the spare key to Robinne, who in turn looked somewhat relieved.

"T-thank you."

Deciding that his brother has had enough of Robinne to himself, he stepped out of where he'd been eavesdropping, clearing his throat as he approached the table.

"Getting acquainted, Roland?"

Two heads turned in his direction, both sets of eyes firmly locked on his sudden presence. Their hands were still connected from the handing over of the key, which Robinne noticed only when she caught his eyes glaring at the contact between her and his brother. She swiftly removed her hand, pocketing the key immediately.

That's right, no touching.

Roland leaned back in his seat, a cheeky smirk plastered on his face as he raised both hands. "No harm no foul." He smirked. "Why, are you jealous big brother?"

With a scoff, he claimed his usual seat at the table, a sandwich which his Ma had made sitting in front of him on a plate. "Jealous my ass." He mumbled, choosing to look out into the distance, so he wouldn't be tempted to see Robinne's reaction to his nonchalant staking of his claim.

Jeez, what's got into you all of a sudden Ralph old boy?

She's not yours.

Well, not yet.

No! She'll never be yours, you're not worthy of a woman like her.

She deserves better than you.

Out of the corner of his eye, it didn't seem at all like she was bothered by his actions. At least, not that he could tell anyway. Ignoring him, she returned Roland's earlier smile to her. "Nice to meet you too. I hope you enjoy your lunch."

"Are all English people as polite as you?"

"No, one of a kind me."

Got that right.

Roland chuckled, "I can imagine."

Ralph looked back around at them, once more sending a glare Roland's way. A clap of hands broke all forms of eye contact, as his Ma joined the three of them at the table, sitting in her own usual seat.

"Alright then, time to say grace."

Robinne blinked.

"Uh, who's Grace?"

He and Roland both shared a small chuckle between them.

His Ma simply patted her arm gently, not patronising her for not knowing something they did. "You say a little thanks to God, known as 'grace', for the meal before you start eating it. That's all dear."

"Ah, okay."

"Not what you usually do is it Robinne?" Roland asked casually.

She shook her head.

"No. I'm Christian but, I've never thought to say grace before. I guess it's more of a Catholic thing, since this is a majority Catholic state."

Roland shrugged, "Both do it I guess, but ma's always done it so…"

"Got it. Sorry Cassie, continue."

They all joined their hands together in prayer, ready to say grace. Robinne copied them, dutifully bowing her head as they all did. His Ma then proceeded to say grace. "Dear Lord, we are truly thankful for this meal in front of us, and for the lovely added company of Robinne, who's travelled thousands of miles for a new life. We are ever thankful for your tiny mercies, Amen."

"Amen" the boys chorused.

My own personal blessing.

Again, not YOURS.

As soon as grace was finished, he heartily tucked into the food in front of them. He usually ate a lot when he was with his Ma. In his younger years as a teen, he'd been able to pass it off as a 'growing boy' thing. Now? Now he doesn't care what people think about how much he eats. He likes food and he's a big man so, he needs it. Thankfully, the ranch work kept him in shape to compensate for his eating.

Robinne however, took a gentler, more paced approach. She looked as if she was tacking a monster challenge instead of just eating a sandwich. He supposed she wasn't used to just how much Americans eat, in portion sizes anyway. He'd heard they were smaller in England after all.

How do they manage?

Minutes later, a pair of quick-moving boots came through the house and onto the back porch.

"Ryder, honey. How nice of you to join us." His mother said cheerfully, happy to see another one of her sons. She stood up and embraced him as he came towards her. He was breathing rather quickly, so it was evident he wanted to make lunch on time, but failed to do so. Even if was only a few minutes.

"Sorry I'm late ma. I told Roland to tell you I wouldn't make it but, I wasn't needed any longer so…here I am. I tried to text but my cell died." He looked deeply apologetic. Classic Ryder.

"Not a problem honey. Sit down and I'll pull a sandwich out of the fridge for you." Patting Ryder's hand, he watched his mother get up only to be halted once risen.

"You made it, I'll eat and compliment it. Won't take me a moment to get it. I need to wash my hands anyway."

Ryder dashed back in the house half as quick as he'd arrived, with lunch resuming much the same as before he showed up.

"So Robinne, how're you liking your life in the U.S. so far?" Roland said around a mouthful of sandwich.

This earned him a gentle smack on the arm from their mother, scolding him wordlessly for talking while eating.

Robinne laughed and wiped her mouth free of sandwich crumbs, "It's been um…revealing."

He coughed around his own sandwich, very well knowing what she was talking about. Looking up after he'd recovered, he found a set of emerald green eyes fixed on his face. Having trouble holding back a laugh, he watched Robinne delve back into her sandwich to try and cover it.

Yeah, it's been revealing to me too.

The best kind of revealing.

"Oh? Well, hopefully it continues to be even more…*revealing*, from here on out. Things can only get better the longer you stay in one place." Roland smiled, taking a chug from his lemonade, flicking a knowing look his way.

Ass.

At the end of the table, his Ma happily sat there eating her lunch, not phased at all at the banter around the table. Being so used to their bantering as they'd grown over the years, this was a normal thing for her to hear, hence why she hadn't bothered to stop them.

"Indeed." She muttered, finishing her cup of tea, keeping her eyes anywhere but him

Yes. Indeed.

Lunch was finished as quickly as it was prepared, leaving everyone around the table with very satisfied and full stomachs. Wiping the crumbs from his own mouth, he watched as Robinne rose from her seat and made her way over to his mother. "Thank you for lunch Cassie, it was lovely."

Cassie turned to her and smiled. "You're welcome dear. You're welcome back here anytime you know that, right?"

Both he, Ryder and Roland turned in their direction, clearly intrigued at their mother's eagerness to want her around the ranch house again.

"Thank you Cassie! I'd love that." She smiled.

You'd love that huh? I know what else you'd love.

"Let me help you clear up." Robinne lifted her plate from the table, her mug in her other hand.

The three brothers shared a look between them, knowing what they must do. Ralph reached out, taking her plate and mug out of hers, surprising her.

"Allow us. You two made it, we'll wash up and get back out there." Ryder smiled, making his way back into the house, followed by a Roland, then himself.

Making his way back into the kitchen, purposely going last, he was able to catch his mother saying something to Robinne.

"My boys can be angels when they want to be. Wasn't always that way raising them though." She chuckled. "Imagine 5 boys under 5, all tiny balls of unstoppable energy, limbs galore and plenty of cuts and scrapes to go around. Oh they did get themselves into a fair share of mischief over the years, but, they're good boys. I don't know what I'd do without them."

A sense of wistfulness came over him as he remembered his childhood with his brothers. They'd had the best upbringing that they could possibly ask for, by two parents who'd move heaven and Earth for them without wanting anything in return. Someday, he hoped to be as good of a parent as his own were.

Like you'll ever be that lucky.

Setting to the task at hand, he started cleaning up the dishes and mugs from lunch alongside his brothers.

A little while later when all had been washed and dried from their lunch, Ryder turned to Cassie and Robinne from where he stood at the freezer. "Looks like your stuff has kept Robinne, when do you want to get it back to your place?"

Ralph now sat at the kitchen island, watching the exchange between the two of them.

"Oh! N-now would be great actually. I've imposed on you all long enough today."

"Nonsense." His mother piped up.

Roland had since vanished to wherever he had to be after washing up after lunch, leaving Ryder, Robinne his Ma and himself sitting in the kitchen.

"I'll drive you home." He said, letting his mouth run before his brain had time to think about what he was going to say.

Good going Ralph.

"Y-you will?"

"Yeah, I don't see why not. Your car's arriving what, tomorrow, right?"

"Yes."

"So I can drive you home and head into town for some supplies I need, kill two birds with one stone that way."

Plus, I get to be in your company a bit longer.

As much as he wasn't keen to make an ass out of himself with her in the future, he found it impossible to not want to be in her company, even for a little bit. He'd only just met her, literally, a day like a day ago, yet he was amazed at a desire deep within him which seemed to argue against his reasons for avoiding any time with her. The least he could try to do was not tease her, or flirt with her, or anything else for that matter. He just needed to talk to her. Polite, civil talk.

Polite and civil talk wasn't going to get you any closer to doing what you need to do, but what the heck. Go for it.

Flashing a smile his way, Robinne nodded. "Sure. Why not?"

Ralph nodded back at her, "I'll get your stuff loaded into my truck. Meet me outside in say, 15 minutes?"

"Okay."

Ralph with the help of Ryder, soon got all of her groceries and other items packed into his truck, honking his horn exactly fifteen minutes later on the dot.

"I'm coming! I'm coming!" Robinne called out as she closed the front door to the ranch house behind her, jogging down the pathway to his truck.

Hopping inside, she closed the door of the truck behind her. "Why the incessant honking? I'm here aren't I?" she asked.

"I like punctual people. Fifteen minutes is fifteen minutes. No more, no less."

Keep it nice, ass!

"Well either way, I'm here. I appreciate you giving me a lift back home."

"No problem. Just, don't touch my radio okay? Country rule number one, never touch a man's truck radio." He said as he turned it on, tunes filling the truck from what she assumed was his go-to radio station of choice.

"I thought rule number one of 'country' was to never talk about country?" she smirked.

Ralph smirked. "Smartass."

"Better than a dumb one." She retorted.

"Touche."

Perhaps this wouldn't be a bad a ride after all.

As they made their way out of the ranch's main road in and out, Ralph couldn't be more thankful that he was the one who'd piped up and offered her a ride home. It wasn't every day that he got to sit next to such a beautiful woman as she. Working out on the ranch seven days a week didn't leave him with much time or much of a social or love life. Only rare ass nights like the one where he wound up naked in Robinne's house, happened once in a blue moon and were very few and far between.

He was thankful that his buddies understood the responsibilities he now had as the head ranch runner, as it was split five ways between the five brothers, with each maintaining an element they specialised in. Ralph had final say on any matter that came their way, including finalising the important decisions which maintained and kept the ranch working smoothly.

Now and then though, his father still pitched in with the odd minimal task, like today when he was out helping the twins with the fence. His father had reluctantly agreed to early retirement after a heart attack scare, which turned out to be extreme exhaustion, much to everyone's relief, but the old dog refused to give up what he was still given permission to do by his doctor.

Ralph had a deep sense of admiration for the man, only hoping he could be half of who his father was when he was his age.

As he got lost in his thoughts, he was momentarily unaware that he still had a passenger in his truck with him. Sometimes when he thought about such things concerning family and life, those around him fade and it feels like it's just him, alone, connected to the universe and all its mysteries. That being said, he didn't completely forget about her sitting not even a metre away, considering the effect she had on him when she was near, an instant effect since he'd first set eyes on her.

Out of the corner of his eye, still keeping focused on the road, he could see her sitting there on the other side of the truck's bench seat, contently looking out of the window, stuck in her own world as the real world rolled by her.

A pure English rose indeed.

She'll make some man a very lucky one indeed someday.

He just wished that the man, whoever he turned out to be, would realist that fact and cherish her every single day. As he would, if she was his to cherish.

Shaking his head, he rid himself of thoughts that he had no right in thinking about. He'd cross that bridge if ever he got to it someday. Someday being 'a hope in hell's chance'. Gripping the wheel a little harder and flexing his hands around the leathery material, he knew he had to change the subject of his thoughts and break the silence in the truck cab, both daunting tasks in his mind.

Ralph wasn't one for small talk, in fact, he despised it. However, it looked like it was going to be the only way to pass the drive with her without absolute silence. Another thing he couldn't stand. Absolute silence wasn't so bad when he was relaxing alone, he just found it unbearably awkward when in the company of someone else.

"So…" he started to say. Robinne turned her head to look at him. "What do you plan on doing for work now you're here? After you've settled in fully that is."

Robinne looked conflicted for a moment, as if she didn't know how to answer his question.

"Don't want to talk about it?" he asked.

"N-no, that's not it. I'm just…I'm just not much of a talker when it comes to things about me. Never have been." She paused, collecting her thoughts so she could continue. "I needed a new start. That's the main reason. Judge me if you think 23 is too young for one, but it's what I needed to do. I need to find a job that will allow me to start my real dream job up as a side-job/hobby before hopefully someday, making it my full-time or main occupation."

"Which is?"

Her teeth lightly sunk into her bottom lip.

Damn, that's so darn adorable.

"Uh…a writer."

One side of his mouth ticked up. Thankfully, it was the side she currently couldn't see. "A writer huh?"

She nodded.

"I had an old buddy who used to write for a living. How did you get into it?"

She arched a brow high in his direction, her clear surprise at his interest plastered all over her face, not that she seemed to try and hide it in the first place. After a beat, she relaxed her brow and began to explain it to him.

"I've never really been good at anything, whereas most girls around me were good at several things, some even without knowing it. They breezed through exams, sports, applied makeup with impeccable ease. Me? Not so much. From the big to the small, there wasn't really anything I excelled in. That is, until I discovered how much I loved to read at a young age, and that I could do what these people have and someday write my own story. Stories, if I was lucky enough. Since I didn't really get lucky in the friend department, when I got the opportunity back in secondary school, I started writing proper stories."

"What happened next?" he asked, keeping his eyes on the road.

"Took English Literature at A-Level, that's the highest school qualification in the UK. I wasn't able to go into university to pursue any course that would get me into a job where I would write or edit for a living, so I started voluntarily doing a remote unpaid editorial course, since everything else I turned my hand to required money. Which I didn't have much of." She sighed before continuing. "I was undecided for a long time. It took me a while to decide to even pursue writing and editing as a career and even when I did figure it out, I was only met with criticism and how I'd struggle, rather than advice on how to help me get to where I need to be."

Ralph nodded, smiling to himself. He was genuinely enthused by her story, secretly hoping he'd get to hear more before they arrived at her place.

"I see. That's understandable. I'm just glad that for someone who hates talking about themselves, that you feel comfortable enough around me to talk about it."

A smirk pulled at one side of her mouth, a smirk that she didn't bother trying to hide. "Doesn't happen often, consider yourself a lucky man."

That I am, more than you know.

He returned her smirk, choosing then to change the subject, hoping she'll return to it more at a time where he doesn't feel like pressing his luck in case she clams up. "You know, if you find yourself stuck on what to do if you get too low on money, I'm sure Ma would find you something to do at the B&B, just until you got things sorted out. You could still write on the side if you decide against giving it a go as a full-timer. Plus, it'd be nice to know she's not working herself too hard y'know?" he shot her a smile, hopefully giving her some reassurance.

Leaning back in her seat, he heard the soft sound of her breath exhaling before her reply a second later.

"Your mom has already spared me so much kindness since I met her yesterday, you all have really. I couldn't impose on her and ask for a job without knowing her a little more. Could I?"

"You know she'll coerce you into it eventually, even in the short time you've known her."

"That's true." Robinne laughed.

"So will you at least consider it if she offers it to you at some point? Please?"

Why am I begging her? She'll take it only if she wants to, you can't force her!

"Yes. Yes I think I will!"

"That's the spirit!" He smiled as he turned the truck round a bend, heading towards Robinne's place, feeling lighter than he'd ever felt for longer than he could remember.

As he pulled into Robinne's place, he found himself finding it somewhat hard resisting that he had to say goodbye to her, for now at least. He was never going to let onto her at this point that he actually enjoyed her company, yet he didn't want to act like a puppy seeing the owner to its forever home for the first time. She'd have to make the first move. If she actually wanted to make any sort of move at all.

"Thank you for the ride home."

"You're welcome. Now let's get this stuff inside." He said in a faux urgent tone, hoping he'd convince her that he was keen to get a move on. Judging by the look on her face as he hopped out of his truck, he'd say he pulled it off. A little *too* well, by the look on her face right now.

"Oh…okay."

They equally shared carrying the load back into the house, making a few more trips than necessary since he insisted neither of them needed to see who could carry the most to outdo the other, as she'd suggested to him not long after getting out of the car. He didn't want to be a spoilsport, but he could see how tired she was getting as jetlag was no doubt rearing its ugly head for her once more.

Ralph helped Robinne put everything away where she wanted it to go, as she looked to be a woman after his own heart. Everything had its place. He didn't have a form of OCD, neither did he suspect did Robinne, he just knew how he liked things organised and wouldn't dare try to disrupt another person's kitchen, just because he liked things a certain way which was unique to him.

Standing up from putting a bottle of wine in the wine rack, he wiped his hands together, noting that was the last item from her grocery haul to be put away. "If you don't need me for anything else, I guess I'll be on my way then."

She nodded.

"Of course. Thanks again. I'll show you out."

Something's off. She's not so...forthcoming anymore.

I wonder what the matter is.

I guess I'll find out eventually. If I see her again, that is.

Walking back towards the front door, he was mentally scratching his head at what suddenly could have put the bee in her hypothetical bonnet. He hadn't been rude, crass or anything of the like. There was no reason he should be concerned with this, as they weren't that close enough for it to have affected him, yet it still did. There was a part of him that wanted to stop and grab her by the shoulders, turn her around and politely ask her what the matter was.

Sadly, he didn't do any of that. Instead, he watched her perfect butt as she unknowingly sashayed towards the front door, opening it for him as he came up behind her.

"Have a safe drive."

"Darlin', I'm the only danger that's out on these roads. I'll be fine."

"That's good to know, considering I've just ridden with you."

Oh honey, you'd know if you'd ridden with me.

Smirking, he stepped out onto the step on the other side of the open door. "You need anything, just give any one of us a holler and we'll come running. Or driving, whatever mood we're in."

He was blessed with Robinne's first laugh since he'd met her the day before, a sound that was more than welcome. A sound he'd make sure to re-visit just to hear again sometime in the near future.

"I'll remember that. Bye, cowboy."

Turning to walk towards his stuck, his smirk grew wider. "Bye...Crumpet."

"IT'S ROBINNE!" She called out to his retreating form.

As he walked the rest of the way to his truck with his back still towards her, he laughed heartily at how much fun it was to harmlessly tease her.

Oh how I'm going to enjoy this...

After an unplanned stop in town to pick up a few items, Ralph hopped back out of his truck at the family ranch, stretching his stiff muscles. He loved the fact that he was a tall guy at six feet six inches, but it did mean that he had to stretch out more if he'd been sitting or standing for any length of time. Basically, doing anything that wasn't lying down. Small spaces were not his friend and the truck he owned although it was just like Ryder's, wasn't built for the taller gentleman with tree trunks for legs.

He didn't get a chance to show Robinne around the ranch earlier when she was here, as she had to get home with her groceries. He supposed he could invite her out again here sometime to show her what they did and what they had to offer her in terms of a job, he just didn't want to come across as needy or encroaching on her independence, seeing as that's why she's here. To seek a new life. Still, he so wishes he had the opportunity to show her around soon. There was so much he wanted to show her, something different for her to see that she wouldn't have back home. The ranch was his and his brothers', and of course, his parents' pride and joy, so he wanted to show it off at any opportunity he could.

Why don't I just puff out my chest and bang my fists on it while I'm at it?

Walking around to the stables which were located just at the end of the grass from the back yard, which marked the start of the many acres of land that he and his family owned, he was met with smells that he'd grown up with all of his life. Smells in which the ordinary person would have their hand clamped over their nose and mouth from. There was no other smell on Earth that made him happier. Well, other than one of his mother's dishes perhaps. They were pretty darn amazing to eat when he craved a home-cooked meal.

As he entered the stables, his thoughts turned to a specific one every time he walked through the doors, despite there being a total of six men on the ranch, they currently only had four horses to use between them. He'd have to get around to rectifying that someday.

One of their mares died foaling, as did the foal itself. The stud who bred her was given away to another ranch who was looking to expand their current line of horses, wanting a purebred horse to produce a quality filly or colt.

From down the end stall, he could hear his own stallion, Second Chance, also known as 'Chance', calling out to him, knowing a sugar cube or two was bound to be coming his way. He couldn't resist giving him one just for being happy to see him. As he neared the stallion's stall, Chance's head was already bobbing up and down trying to get a glimpse of his owner.

He chuckled. "I'm coming boy, I'm coming." He said as he pocketed the sugar cubes he'd picked up upon entering the stables, unlocking the locks on Chance's stall door and stepping inside slowly. "How are ya my boy? Hm? What do you say to a quick ride down to see how they're getting on with the fence, hm?"

Chance bobbed his head as if he was agreeing with Ralph, a sign of an intelligent horse if he understood his or her owner.

"Alright then, let's get you ready."

He went to turn around when something pulled at the right hand pocket of his wranglers.

Chance.

Shaking his head with a smirk, he should've known better than to have hidden them from his wise best animal buddy.

"Alright boy, here you go." He gave Chance the two sugar cubes, leading him out of his stall afterwards and over to where he got all of his horses ready for riding.

After Chance was all suited and booted in his riding gear, Ralph for a man of his size, gracefully got onto Chance's back and headed out of the stables and in the direction he was told his brothers and father were now mending the fence in. It was a pleasant day for a ride, which both horse and man could tell as Chance had a pep in his step only seen when the weather was just right.

I bet Robinne would enjoy this.

Wait…what?

It seemed to him that it was impossible to go even an hour without thinking about the black-haired beauty. Who could blame him? He would say he's only a man but he knew in today's day and age, that there was no such a thing as 'only a man'.

Robinne was impossible to shake out of his thoughts completely, so the best he could do was busy himself with some work if there was some to get done, until he was alone later on in his bathroom where he could rid himself of any thoughts for the night.

Needing to kick that in sooner than later, he decided it was time to kick things up a notch with Chance, as riding harder and faster was the only thing, at present point, to clear his mind completely.

"Hya!" he commanded gently, spurring Change to go from a gentle walk to a leisurely canter. As the wind rushed over his Stetson, he savoured the feeling of how Chance glided across the land as if it was water. Not that a horse could glide across water in the first place. The horse was just so smooth to ride and was so powerful in his gait, he barely felt like he was on a horse at all if it wasn't for the obvious sign of a horse between his legs.

I know who I'd really like between my legs.

Ralph shook his head again.

"You've gone without for far too long Ralph old boy." Groaning, he spurred Chance on just that little faster, hoping the faster the ride, the faster the fetching little English rose would slide from out of his thoughts and into his 'to think about later' part of his brain.

A little while later thanks to the speed of his magnificent horse, Ralph slowed Chance down when he came across three familiar looking figures not too far from where he rode. Two of which were built similar to him, his brothers Reed and Rowan. The twins were the older brothers to Roland, the baby of the family. The other, smaller figure, belonged to his father Joe, who'd given a certain someone a place to live and a ride to said place.

"Hey! Need any help there?" he called out, waving his arm in a friendly greeting.

Three sets of sweaty faces turned towards him as they were mid-repair on part of the fence, which to his eye looked like an animal had bulldozed its way through it somehow.

"Hey son! We're almost done here actually, not much to repair today but I have to go slow."

"You know we don't mind that Pa." Reed said, holding his part of the new fence to go up.

"Yeah Ral, should've got here sooner if you wanted to play white knight." Rowan smirked. Ever the jackass, he always had a smartass remark to make about something.

He rolled his eyes.

"Real mature."

"I don't have to be, that's why they had you." Rowan retorted with a grin.

Shaking his head, he hopped down off Chance and tied the reins loosely to a stable part of the wooden fence that wasn't broken. "Seriously though Pa, I don't know why you didn't let me help the twins fix this, you're supposed to be taking it easy, remember?"

Joe motioned to the twins to slide the last part of the repaired fence part into place, grunting a little as he did so before he wiped his brow and turned to Ralph. "Son, I'm retired, not six feet under. I have all faith in you boys that you won't let me do any more than you know I can do so, don't worry. Please. If I felt it was too much, you'd be here instead of me." He laid a hand on Ralph's shoulder, pride shining in his eyes.

Pa...I just care about you.

Deciding it wasn't worth an argument, he nodded, clapping his father back on his own shoulder.

"That's my boy. Now, how's it goin' with Miss James?"

Reed and Rowan chose that moment to walk up and stand either side of their father. "Yeah Ral, how's it going?" they said in unison, ever the stereotype of twins.

Just when I'd gotten her out of my mind for five minutes...

"It's going…alright." He knew he sounded hesitant, but it was pointless trying to lie to his Pa, the man always knew when he was lying.

"Ooooh, something happened!" Reed smirked.

Jackass.

"Well, yes and no. Yes something did happen, but nothing either of your two horny brains were thinking of!" he mock-glared at them.

When he didn't get a ruse out of any of them, he continued. "I suppose you would've heard it from Ry eventually. Okay, so I woke up buck ass naked at the Jameson place, no clue how I got there in that state, to which I later learned the truth. Anyway, Robinne was dropped off I assume by you Pa, where she found me in my undressed state. She sent me out onto the street with only a bedroom curtain to protect my dignity. Ryder picked me up and took me home. He then later encountered her in town where she'd forgotten she didn't have a ride to carry her groceries. Long story short, she ends up back at our place, slips in mud and showers in my master bathroom where I enter, unbeknown to myself that she's in there. Naked. Ryder then rips me a new one while cleaning her clothes, ma invites her to stay for lunch which afterwards, I dropped her home."

He gave nothing away on his face as he finished telling them the story, as he wanted to see how they'd react first. He soon got his answer.

Unable to hold in their combined laughter for any longer than they had to, Reed and Rowan doubled over holding their mid-sections, enjoying very much so Ralph's adventures over the last twenty four hours.

More reserved, Joe simply chuckled and removed his gloves. "Can't say that life's ever dull, son."

"No, you certainly can't." he mumbled.

He put his hands on his hips and looked up at the picturesque sky, waiting until the twins' laughter died down. Meanwhile, Joe milled around picking up light objects to be thrown away, and tools to go back into their toolbox. A short while later, the reprieve came.

"Oh man, I've not had a good laugh in ages! Who the hell needs comedians when we have you Ral." Rowan wiped the laughter tears away from his dark chocolate eyes.

"C'mon boys, enough with the jokin' around. You've got other jobs to do, leave your brother be." Joe said as he walked past all three boys, heading on over towards the truck parked not too far away.

Ralph felt a hand clamp down gently on his shoulder. It belonged to Reed.

"Listen man, I heard she's been through some tough stuff, go easy on her yeah?"

What the hell?

Why does he care?

"What's it to you?" he asked, intentionally sounding somewhat protective.

"We've all been through things, doesn't make it easier when someone's on our ass trying to make life harder, y'know?"

"Yeah, I know. It's just uh…it's not going to be as easy as that."

"How come?" Rowan piped up.

"What did you do?" Reed chipped in.

Sighing, he pulled out a now crumpled piece of paper from his back right pocket. He wasn't sure why he'd kept it in his pants. Yet, he did.

"When I was kicked out of her place, I had to make a phone call to get a ride home as you know." He opened up the paper further. "I went over to the phone to make the call, which I did, and rather than face her wrath again, I was going to leave a note on the notepad by the phone thanking her for letting me use her phone. On my way out, I saw this on the floor and naturally, I thought it was mine, carried in from the truck or something from when I'd left to meet Ryder yesterday. When I got home later on and undressed, I dug this out as I forgot I'd taken it. It's a list of things she doesn't want to do now that she's been living here."

The twins blinked, not quite sure where this was going.

"So?" Rowan asked.

He handed the piece of paper over to them to look at. "I started to tick things off. My plan was originally to get her back for being so darn rude to me when she kicked me out without letting me explain or apologise. Only, when she appeared at the house with Ryder and with what happened in the master bathroom, I had my doubts I could go through with it. It was only supposed to be harmless, I wasn't going to go out of my way to upset her or anything. I just wanted to prove that sometimes, the things you try to avoid happening aren't so bad after all if you just let them happen."

Reed gave him a look, not quite a critical one, but it was a look nonetheless. "That's somewhat fucked up dude. You want to do that for her but you didn't tell her you took this?" he said waving the piece of paper in front of him.

Ralph rubbed the spot between his eyes. "I didn't think it through, I admit. I just wanted to roll with it and see where it went. I didn't plan on seeing her again so soon. I certainly didn't take into account she could be emotionally fragile."

"Didn't Ma or Pa give you that clue when they told you she'd be moving here? We certainly got that message when we all did her place up."

"Yeah well, I clearly didn't." He sighed.

"No shit." Rowan said, taking the note from Reed and gave it back to Ralph. "What're you going to do now? Your intentions are always good, you just have a funny way of going about it."

Ralph put the note back in his back pocket.

"Honestly? I don't know. She can't find out I took the note so, don't either of you tell her."

The twins zipped their mouths up using their fingers.

"I'll leave it be for a while. This time, I'll seriously give it some thought into telling her about the note, or at least my true reason why I took it. I just hope she understands when I tell her."

"Wise move big brother." Reed smiled.

A horn honked from behind them, making all three boys turn around.

"Looks like it's time to go. C'mon Reed, let's get the rest of our shit done so we can enjoy an early afternoon beer."

"Amen to that. Later Ral."

The twins both finger saluted Ralph as they made their way around him, hopping up into their respective seats in Joe's truck. The truck after they were both safely in and strapped up, pulled away in the opposite direction Ralph came in.

Ralph made his way back over to Chance as he watched the truck disappear out of sight, feeling slightly guiltier than he did when he first arrived. One back on top of Chance, he gave his mane a scratch before looking out at the view of the land in front of him.

"They're right, aren't they boy? I've got to do right by her."

Chance bobbed his head once.

"Since when did you become such a wise one huh? C'mon, let's get you home."

Kicking his heels gently once more into Chance's side, the two headed off back in the direction they came in from the ranch.

Let's just hope I don't fuck things up even more.

Famous last words Ralph, famous last words.

Ah, Hell.

CHAPTER EIGHT
~ Robinne ~

Opening up her eyes on a brand new day, her first thoughts of the day immediately went to a certain southern cowboy who'd plagued her thoughts until sleep claimed her last night. Ralph had given her a lot to think about during their talk as he drove her home yesterday. The whole point in her moving here was to discover who she wanted to be, what she wanted to do in life and to do something completely outside of her comfort zone. Definitely a big fat check on that last one. Moving here was something from outside the outside of her comfort zone and so far, it wasn't as bad as she thought.

Okay so she didn't exactly plan for what happened in the last couple of days, who would? She was thankful her and Ralph had decided to put things behind them and start a new leaf.

Ha! That makes two new leaves for me now.

She had yet to meet the other two of the five Jenkins brothers, which she was told earlier yesterday were the twins, Reed and Rowan. There wasn't a great hurry inside of her to meet them, as it would happen as and when, but if they're anything like twins are always written to be in the books she reads, they were bound to be a handful.

Putting all thoughts about anything Jenkins to the back of her mind, she thought instead about how she'd started the day for once. She was NOT a morning person. At all. Moving clear across the ocean wasn't going to change that, no matter how much she wanted this brand new start. Mornings were the one thing she knew she was always going to hate.

The view from her balcony had been beyond anything she could describe, it was just the most beautiful reinforcement that she'd made the right choice in moving here, the sunrises were spectacular. It almost made up for her grumpy mood when waking up first thing.

If only mornings started a little later in the day, they wouldn't be so bad.

Knowing that sad reality would never be, she flopped back onto her bed, which thankfully had been delivered along with all of her other belongings she'd shipped over here, in the late afternoon after Ralph had dropped her back home. She'd lounge here for a short while, at least until she was less of a grump. She'd started her day right after that, with a lovely cup of tea. A cup of tea always saw that things got off to a not so bad start.

Lounging around was only pleasant for as long as the novelty of it remained. Which in her case, didn't last long today. She'd caught a nap early yesterday evening after everything had been moved in, which thankfully for her combatted the slight feeling of jetlag which had snuck up on her. As a result when she went to bed that night, she was able to sleep through the night with minimal interruption. Now, she was awake and itching to get her 'lazy day' off to a start.

Setting to her new morning routine, she'd cleaned up in the bathroom before changing into her comfortable, baggy clothes for the day. Seeing as she wasn't expecting to see anyone today, it really didn't matter how she dressed. So, she dressed in her go-to round the house clothes. Putting her night clothes back on the freshly made bed to use again tonight, as she always made sure to wear clothes at least twice before washing them, she headed downstairs to make her first breakfast in her first home.

Happily munching on her breakfast, she could only think of one thing that she definitely wanted to get done today. Sort out her books of course! When she'd been looking at the house and when she'd been in talks with Joe, she'd only requested one part of the house to be completely built from new to fit her, once she'd for sure secured the place. A floor to ceiling bookshelf.

It was her dream to one day have a mini-library in a house she planned to own. However, seeing as this was a house being given to her for pretty much nothing at all, her request would do her for now until should a day come in the future when she would be able to expand to the mini library. She'd spotted the majestic built-in bookshelf when she'd fully explored the place yesterday, though she hadn't been motivated to fill it. Until now.

Just as she was about to head to where she'd placed the book boxes, her phone went off in her pocket.

Who could possibly be contacting me? I haven't given out my number yet…

Opening up her phone, there was a text there from a number she obviously didn't recognise.

'*Hey crumpet!*'

RALPH!

She couldn't think why he'd be texting her, or how he'd even managed to get a hold of her number, but she intended to find out. Nicely.

Robinne: Hi Ralph. How did you get my number?-

Ralph: Asked mom for it from your B&B check in info

Sneaky…

Robinne: How can I help you?-

Ralph: You don't have to do a thing darlin', I just wanted to apologise to you

Robinne: For what?

Ralph: For not inviting you to our family cookout this weekend. Ma insisted & I totally forgot to say something to you

Inwardly and outwardly, she sighed.
Family.
I-I'm not family.
She hesitated to reply to him. He didn't know her reluctance to talk or participate in anything family-related. He didn't know about her past and what went down with her own family, and sure as hell wasn't going to tell anybody about it any time soon.

Yesterday was a rare occurrence where she actually felt comfortable around people she didn't know all that well. They'd made her feel so at ease and not so much as like an outsider, she was able to relax and banter a little with the Jenkins boys as well as with Cassie and Joe respectively.

Of course, she didn't HAVE to admit anything to Ralph, she just had to make the reason for not wanting to go a very good one. As the whole family would no doubt be there this time, she also had to make the excuse not sound like an insult to anyone she hasn't met yet.

Taking a deep breath and exhaling slowly, she knew exactly what she wanted to say.

Robinne: Thank you so much for the invite, it was so sweet of you to offer. I'm just a little swamped right now with unpacking & other stuff, maybe next time? –

Smooth…real smooth.

Ralph: Aww c'mon, you know you want to. I'll even throw in a few 'bangers' for you ;)

His attempt at using a British term of phrase brought a genuine smile to her face. It filled her with happiness to know that he could be sweet when he wanted to be.
You've still only known him for literally only a few days, give it time girl!

Robinne: Wow check you out, using my lingo to sweet talk me into accepting. Good job.

Ralph: Did it work? I'm on the edge of my seat here!

She laughed to herself as she replied to him.

Robinne: Nope

Ralph: Darn, guess I gotta try something else. Okay, how about if I come round and help you unpack, you'll be free on the weekend to attend the cookout? How about that?

She sighed. He wasn't going to give up, was he?
This is outside of my comfort zone, exactly what I wanted to experience. So why am I hesitating?
Ralph.
It has to be because of him. Has to be.
Taking a deep breath, she reluctantly agreed to his proposition, already knowing she somehow was going to regret this down the line.

Robinne: Tell you what, I'll unpack and I'll come to the cookout. You do your…cowboy things & I'll see you Saturday? –

Ralph: Works for me crumpet, as long as ma has you here, I consider it a small victory for me.

Robinne: Arse

Ralph: Yes, I have a nice one at that ;) So good of you to remember. See you Saturday!

Robinne: See you. Oh and by the way, it's Robinne. Not crumpet.

Ralph: Got it…crumpet

Robinne knew he wasn't going to stop calling her that any time soon, so she let it slide this time. Maybe forever, if he was lucky.

She wasn't feeling a hundred percent okay with going to the cookout exactly, but she figured she'd be able to stick next to Ryder or Cassie and feel as she did yesterday.

"If only there was a miracle medicine to take away anxiety." She said to the open space, eliciting no response from anyone or anything.

Putting her phone back into her pocket, she decided not to think about the cookout until it was closer to the time, as it was only Wednesday and the cookout was on Saturday. There was plenty of time to keep her mind occupied between now and then.

If only it wasn't filled with one person in particular as much as I'd like…

Saturday came quicker than Robinne had expected. She'd always found that the things you weren't looking forward to, or were nervous about, came around far quicker than the things you look forward to. The cookout/BBQ at Ralph's family ranch was due to start at 7, as all things seemed to do. Dates, meeting friends, cookouts, in all the books she read, 7 seemed to be the time everyone always manages to agree on.

She sighed.

Guess this is one cliché I can't help but let happen.

Oh well.

Can't back out of it now.

She stood in front of her wardrobe an hour before she was due to be at the cookout, hair already done in her usual go-to lazy carefree waves with minimal makeup applied to her face. Nothing she owned was classed as 'fancy', and she wasn't all too sure that fancy was the right choice for a cookout, she had to think country attire.

I don't own anything country attire-ish. You know, cowboy boots and such.

People were bound to judge her no matter what she wore, as she'd found out several times in the past, so, she decided to go with something that's always made her feel good. Her lucky red dress. This dress was the sort of dress that you'd wear on a lovely summer's day with sun out, sporting a glass of something freezing cold in your hand while gazing out over a water at sunset. Very appropriate for the climate she'd moved into. Even if it was hotter than the one or two occasional summer days back home, it was appropriate none the less.

Yes, I'm very specific in the things I know I like, sue me.

Taking the dress out of her wardrobe and slipping it off its hanger, she knew the dress would fall just below her knee with a bell-like shape protruding from the waist, though it would normally fall lower on a shorter woman than herself. Being tall sometimes had it drawbacks, or perks, depending on how you look at it.

Small, black flowers were dotted around the material of the dress from top to bottom, including the wider shoulder straps holding the dress on her shoulders, which she needed thanks to her more than generous chest. Again, sometimes a blessing sometimes a curse. Red on black was one of her favourite colour combinations, and this dress made her feel like an oversized ladybug. Yes, she liked ladybugs, people have liked stranger things than them before.

Robinne was definitely not one of those girls who spent hours getting ready, she was very minimalist in that sense. Simple things seemed to work for her rather than the crazy makeup looks she's watched on YouTube. She'd end up looking more like Coco the Clown, rather than a sensual maiden with a tropical gradient eyeshadow. A simple swipe of mascara and an application of foundation and setting powder was literally all she needed. She'd definitely be any man's dream, not having to be bogged down with so much makeup you could swim in it.

Not that men are on the table right now.

Definitely not.

No.

In no time at all she slipped on the dress, picked a pair of shoes to go with the outfit and selected her go-to perfume she never went without, her one guilty pleasure in the fragrance department, Calvin Klein's 'Eternity Night'. She'd made sure she was able to get some ordered to her new home if ever she needed more, to which she was delighted she would be able to. Win!

Now with a little over half an hour before she had to be there, she decided it would be a wise move to get on the road now, as things were further away here in the States than back home. Half an hour should be plenty of time to leave a little later if you had to, even with traffic. Here, because things were simply further away and much, much larger, it was bound to take longer to get to and she hated being late. Decision made, she grabbed her purse, phone and keys, she made her way downstairs and out the front door.

She was also excited at this being the first opportunity to drive her new truck since it arrived along with her belongings earlier on in the week. Having not needed to go anywhere until now, it sat idle on the spot on the pavement outside her house. Other than giving it a full explore now that she had it with her in person, where it was parked was where it stayed. Until now.

Turning around to lock up her front door, she was sure she was able to hear the throb of an engine coming from behind her. Turning in the direction of where the engine was coming from, she was surprised to see a familiar truck pull its way off the road and down onto her drive.

What's Ryder doing here?

As the truck pulled to a stop and its driver hopping out, her curiosity only grew as to why he was here in the first place, as she'd arranged to drive herself to the cookout so she could learn the roads better now that she had a car.

"Hey!" Ryder called out as he made his way over to her, pulling her into a friendly hug.

"H-hi. Um…I don't want to be rude but…what're you doing here?"

Ryder chuckled, stepping back from their hug.

"I'm only here on the orders of my worryguts of a big brother. He wanted me to come by and take you to the cookout. He claims that driving on Texas roads towards sundown aren't safe for new drivers from out of the country. I call bull on it but, you know."

"He does know it doesn't get that dark that quickly in July, right? I mean, he IS the local one here, not me." She laughed.

"Guess not." Ryder smiled. "So, shall we?"

He offered her his elbow, a gesture still practised in many parts of Texas as an act of a gentleman.

"We shall." She returned his grin, walking to the passenger side of the truck and being helped inside.

Sitting bedside Ryder as he drove them away from her place and off in the direction of the ranch, she was glad that she felt so comfortable around him. As she'd grown up, she always did feel more comfortable around men than women. Her first best friend of eleven years was a man, and her latest best friend before he found his boyfriend, was also a man. Obviously. She didn't hate women or their company, there was just something that put her at ease and stamped out her inner anxiety. Which she had a lot of.

There was just a feeling in her gut that the two of them would become fast, firm friends. If they weren't already.

Though it wasn't getting remotely dark by any means when they made it to the ranch house, the light in the sky had most certainly dimmed, bathing the house in the most beautiful light she'd ever seen. The house itself looked almost exactly like the dream home from her childhood fantasy. Well, to her it was a fantasy, even though it was just a dream reoccurring several times over the years. Never in her wildest dreams did she ever imagine she'd see it materialised in the real world. These things just never happened.

At least, not in my case.

"Home sweet home." Ryder said as he put the car in park.

"Who's actually coming to this cookout?" she said, trying to hide the nervousness in her voice as they got out the truck, walking onto the pathway leading to the front porch.

"Well, all five of us boys, Ma, Pa, Hannah, Niall and most likely Buddy. That dog may be a ranch dog but wherever meat or food is concerned, you'll bet your bottom dollar he'll be around somewhere." He chuckled.

Hannah? The lady from the bus, Hannah?

Huh, small world in big Texas.

"Nervous?" Ryder asked as he turned the doorknob to open the door.

"That obvious huh?"

"Just a tad. C'mon, you'll be just fine. You've met us all at some point. Well, aside from the twins. You'll hear them before you see them so, it won't be as much of a shock as it is to most people who meet them." He laughed, opening the door and holding it open for her to go in first. "After you ma'am."

She couldn't help but smile, he was too kind for words.

"Thank you." She stepped inside the front hall. "I'm also pretty sure this is where I say 'I'm too young to be called ma'am', right?"

"And I'll say 'it's a southern thing'." Ryder said as he closed the front door behind them.

"Fair enough."

"C'mon, let's go see everyone. I'm starving."

"After what I saw you eat the other day at lunch, that doesn't surprise me."

"Smartass." He chuckled.

A pair of boots announced that someone else had joined them while they were enjoying their friendly banter as they came in from outside.

"You called?" the voice to the owner of the pair of boots piped up. It was a voice that could only make Robinne feel like she'd had something fluttering around inside her stomach, while also trying to quash that self-same feeling at the same time.

Ralph.

All six plus feet of him now leaned on the bottom of the staircase, watching the two of them with sceptical eyes.

Huh. He thinks there's something going on between Ryder and me.

Hah! He's jealous!

Why would he be jealous?

I'm SO getting to the bottom of whatever is going on in that mind of yours Ralph Jenkins.

"Hey bro. What's up? Why aren't you out back with the others?" Ryder asked, dropping his keys into a woven dish on the door just inside the table.

"Can't a man go take a pee now and then?"

Robinne felt her cheeks warm up. The subject of pee isn't what made her cheeks flush, it was the brashness of him admitting what he'd been doing that did it. She was no dainty flower, but she thought he'd have some decorum around a lady at least. Maybe Cassie was the only lady that was given that privilege.

Ralph made his way towards them, stopping just in front of where they stood.

"Glad to see you made it in one piece." He said to Robinne.

She blinked. "Why wouldn't I?"

"You've driven twice now with this lunk and he hasn't crashed. That's got to be a personal best for him." He smirked, crossing his arms across his chest again, which was still amazing to her considering how muscular his arms were. She did have a weakness for muscular arms.

Stop!
No thinking about his arms!

"Yeah yeah. Okay so I crashed out one time on a date with a girl years ago." Ryder looked her way. "He's never let me forget it. Like ever." Ryder mock-scowled at Ralph.

"Whatever. I'm going to eat." He said, clipped and apparently, amusingly rattled. Well, to her he appeared so.

Robinne and Ryder turned to look at each other, both as equally as surprised as the other at Ralph's behaviour. Shrugging in unison, they shared a secret smile at his expense, heading out on back towards where the family and friends gathered on the back porch for the cookout/BBQ.

"Robinne!" a warbled, older voice crooned at her. As soon as she came through the double doors, the woman she'd first met when waking up in Dripping Springs came towards her at amazing speed for her age. Whatever age she was.

"Hannah!" she went willingly into the older woman's outstretched arms, the two of them sharing a friendly catch-up hug.

"It's so good to see you again! I'd wondered what happened to you after we parted that day. How have you been sweetie?" Hannah asked, her hands still holding Robinne's with care and comfort.

She smiled.

"I've been great, thank you, Hannah. So much has happened but it's not been too bad. I'm still getting used to the way life is out here. I'm so grateful you pointed me in the right direction that day. Thank you."

Hannah gently patted Robinne's hands which still remained between the both of hers.

"Always a pleasure to help someone in need."

"Yes, I'm getting that as the vibe around her." She laughed softly.

Ryder had since left Robinne's side, heading on over to share a brotherly hug with each of his siblings who were now congregating around the BBQ grill, with Joe at the helm cooking all of the food while wearing an amusing apron which read, 'I'm the head cook in this house, and I have my wife's permission to say so'.

Now that's funny.

"Hannah! Robinne!" Cassie's familiar voice called out to them. Robinne and Cassie watched as she made her way towards them from where she'd been sitting on a lounger, spotting another familiar face following her. It was Niall, from the store in town

"Good to see you again dear." She and Cassie shared a hug, as she did with Niall when he was close enough.

"So Miss James, I heard about the incident between you and Ralph. How's he treatin' ya now?"

Cassie turned to look at Niall, a quizzical look on her face.

"What do you mean Niall? Something happened between Robinne and my Ralph?"

Realising what he'd just did, Niall pulled on his not-too-tight shirt collar, clearly not quite sure what to say now that he'd let the cat out of the bag. Metaphorically a least.

Robinne's own heart begin to beat a little faster, nervous of what and how much she should tell Cassie. From what she'd heard of her raising five boys, Cassie wasn't unaware of just what one of her sons got up to. They might have thought they hid it well at the time, but she knew that Cassie knew exactly what they were up to, despite their best efforts. For now though, she decided to play it safe and keep things PG.

"Oh, it was just a little misunderstanding, it's all good now. We sorted out everything when I was here the other day, we're good. Promise."

Cassie turned back to look at her, her mother's eye giving her the onceover to see if she was telling the truth or if she was just covering for Ralph. Not that Robinne had a mother around to know what mother's intuition was like, but she did know that Cassie was as smart as a tack and knew if there would be something untoward in her words.

"Are you sure dear? If that boy did anything to upset you, no matter if he is my son, he'd get a clip round the ear for being rude to a sweet girl like yourself."

Phew. Crisis averted.

"I'm sure. He apologised, I apologised. We've moved on and started a new leaf." She smiled, waving her hand in polite dismissal.

Cassie once more patted her hand, seeming to have been thankfully placated by her words. "That's a relief to hear. Now go on with you, go sit down and I'll bring you over a drink. You look like you need one."

If only you'd know just how true that is.

She found herself a seat at the table she'd sat at the other day for lunch, finally feeling she was able to relax now that she'd put some of her stranger anxieties away for the night. Knowing two of them helped, she only now had to meet the last of Ralph's brothers, whenever they were going to turn up.

This isn't so bad.

I can do this.

Little did she know, it would be a lot sooner than she expected.

"Hey." A voice said to her left, startling her from her thoughts.

"Hey" A secondary voice said from her right, causing her to jump twice in under ten seconds. Looking both left and right, two sets of mischievous eyes attached to two equally matching faces looked at her with a grin on their faces.

"H-hi?"

"You're Robinne, right? I'm Reed, and that devil on your left is Rowan."

Oh, the twins. Of course.

Trust them to show up out of the blue.

Typical twin behaviour.

"Nice to finally get to meet *the* Robinne James who humiliated our older brother. We came over to thank you." Rowan said.

Famous? Thank me?

"W-why thank me?" she asked the two of them, as she was not quite sure as to who'd be answering her.

"Mr. Serious never gets humiliated. The story we managed to bribe out of Pa was hilarious! Wish I was there to have seen it." Reed smirked.

Robinne arched a brow as this was news to her. She thought that family usually kept things close to their chests, especially so when it was something of this nature that people didn't usually like to repeat.

He must've told someone after all. But who? It didn't really matter, as she was more curious than anything as to who he'd let it slip to. She'd have to find out. Jus to satisfy said curiosity.

"Are you boys harassing the poor girl already? She's not been here for five minutes." Cassie said, reappearing at the table with a drink in each hand, handing one off to Robinne as she sat down in her seat.

"No Ma." Rowan said, kissing her on her cheek.

"No ma'am." Reed said, planning a kiss on his mother's other cheek.

Cassie patted each boy's arms, "See that you don't. Now, go help your father and set the table would you please?"

"On it, Ma." The twins said in unison, leaping up from the table and setting to their task.

"Don't mind them, I'm sure you were pre-warned about those two rascals."

She nodded, sipping on the drink she was thankful was lemonade. She forgot to tell Cassie she really wasn't much of a drinker. There wasn't any particular reason as to why that is, she just wasn't. Though it did irk her when people expected some marvellous reason why she doesn't drink. It was truly fascinating how people easily accepted someone who drinks, never asking for a reason, yet when you don't, you're judged. Strange.

"They just startled me, but I'm alright. Thank you."

Cassie nodded, sipping on her own drink. "So, what really did happen with you and Ralph?"

Coughing on her drink, she wiped her mouth before slowly turning her head to look at Cassie.

"You know…don't you?"

"Hard to get much past a mother of five boys and one grown up one." She laughed, "I trust you Robinne dear. I know you'd tell me about it if it really bothered you. I'm glad you made amends with him, I'd hate for you to leave things in a bad place."

She nodded.

"Me too. Me too."

Dinner thankfully went off without a hitch. Robinne was grateful to have been seated between Niall and Cassie, relieved of having to sit next to any of the boys. Especially one in particular. Take a wild guess as to who that individual could possibly be.

She wouldn't have minded being next to Ryder, whom she'd adopted as her new best friend but still, she was thankful she was granted a brief reprieve of the younger males' direct company. At least for the moment.

"Excellent as always Pa." Roland piped up, patting his now full stomach after finishing his last bite of BBQ rib.

A chorus of 'hear hear' came from all point of the table as each person seated at it complimented Joe's rather excellent cooking skills. Even she had to admit with the small portion she'd consumed, it was a delicious meal. Normally she wouldn't choose anything BBQ as her go-to meal of choice, but she was glad she'd tried some home-smoked ribs and other meats that were grilled to perfection.

"You're all very welcome. I don't know what I'd do if I couldn't cook a decent BBQ for my nearest and dearest. Old or new." He said, looking at Robinne for the last remark. She lifted her glass to him, drinking back the last drops after the third top up of the night.

You'll need to pee soon, just you wait and see.

Everyone was excused to go their own ways after dinner, letting it settle in their stomachs before getting onto anything else they wanted to do. The twins carried everything inside to go soak to be cleaned up as and when, still making up for startling her earlier, having being lightly scolded by their mother. Joe and Cassie retired to a shared lounger, Ryder had vanished along with Roland, which left the pair of footsteps coming up behind her belonging to only one person. A very handsome person at that.

"Want to go for a walk? It'll settle dinner a little faster."

She looked up from her seated position, meeting the eyes of the man who'd spend far too much time invading her thoughts as of late.

She nodded. "Sure."

A little surprised at herself for willingly agreeing to spend more time in his company, she stood up from her chair and slid it under the table, wondering where Ralph was going to take her on their walk.

This should prove interesting.

Ralph ended up taking her on a mini tour of the part of the ranch closest to the house which comprised of the chicken coop, his mom's flower and vegetable patch and the stables where he'd introduced her to his horse, Chance.

The day had since fallen to a dark hue since their BBQ dinner had ended, no longer did the day shine bright, but night took over gleaming with all its celestial splendour.

As they came to the end of their tour, for the night at least, Robinne couldn't help but hear all sorts of bugs and critters as they started their night-time songs. People back home never usually heard crickets and insects alike unless they lived in the countryside. Being out here, hearing them now despite how perilously afraid of certain insects she was, she basked in the otherworldly atmosphere of the ranch at night-time. A complete change from the sound of vehicles and men returning home from the pub drunk night after night.

Which happened far too often, urgh.

Coming to a stop with Ralph close by, they stood out in the middle of the area between the barn, stables and utility shed, all of which were bathed in the light which hung from the end of the barn, twinned with the luminous presence of the full moon. "Did you enjoy your mini tour?" Ralph asked her, standing casually as he put his hands in his pockets.

"I did. Thank you for showing me around."

"You're welcome. I'm sorry I didn't get chance to show you everything, but Ma would have my hide if we're not back soon. I know it's not late but, she'd hate me monopolising one of her guests longer than she" He chuckled.

She waved her hand. "Don't worry about it. I'm sure if I come back, you can show me more."

An expression of delight crossed across Ralph's face.

He wants to see me again! He wants me to come back!

Wait.

Why am I excited about this?

Ralph was about to answer when a flash of light lit up the whole area as far as I could see, which was soon followed by a loud boom shaking the very ground beneath their feet.

"Uh oh. We weren't due a storm until next week. Looks like it came early, darn it."

She gulped, swallowing her clear nervousness of the sudden situation imposed on them. She was not a massive fan of thunder or lightening. In fact, she was downright terrified.

"C-can we go please. I-I can't be…I…hate, I hate storms?"

"Sure, c'mon."

Ralph gently cupped her elbow, intending to carry out her wish when not expecting it to, she felt a jolt of something powerful running up her arm, spreading over her body as he made contact with her skin.

Oh no…no no no!

It can't be…

It doesn't exist…it's, it's not real!

There wasn't any time for her to explain or cry out in protest against him touching her, as the storm from starting out as a faint sprinkle soon turned into an infamous Texas torrent of rain, crashing down on them in spades from the heavens above.

"Shit." Ralph paused, looking around. An expression of realisation spread across his face when an idea came into his mind. "C'mon, we'll hide in here until it passes."

Robinne felt herself being tugged towards the barn, somewhere they didn't get a chance to see before they'd planned to head back.

Guess I'm getting to see inside it now.

The two of them dashed inside of the barn as the rain grew even heavier outside, crashing on the tin roof now above their heads. It made it sound as if they were in the middle of a battle rather than in Dripping Springs. Not that she'd ever been in the middle of the battle, she just had an overactive imagination when trying to explain something. Curse of being a writer, she supposed.

Ralph closed the door behind them, sliding down on his back and onto to his bum, leaning back against the doors and panting a little from having to run them inside before they got too wet. Well, any wetter than they both were currently.

A sudden moment of panic came over Robinne as she too tried to catch her breath from having to act quickly. The thought that came into her head caused her mind to whirr, her balance to falter but at the same time, causing her legs to freeze.

A storm. A barn. Two people soaking wet…trapped together in a closed space until the storm passes.

Oh no.

No no no! I wanted to avoid this! I can't be stuck in here with him, I just can't!

Another one of her clichés, something that she didn't want to get herself into which she'd written down on her lost list of things to avoid, was getting trapped in a space with a man where certain things were bound to happen, no matter how much she tried to avoid it.

Not if I can help it, it won't!

Ralph might not know about her determination to live a book cliché-free life, to which he wasn't going to now. All she had to do was keep to herself, don't say anything that would provoke him, or look at him in a certain way which would make him want to do things to her, as she'd heard and read that that happened once too often.

She had to pull this off, she simply had to. For the very sake of her moving here in the first place. Only, that was easier said than done when deep down inside, somewhere within a volt with many locked locks, codes and security guards, she actually wished something *would* happen.

Shaking her head from dangerous wandering thoughts, she set neutral eyes on the panting man sitting on his butt on the ground in front of her.

Oh boy. This isn't going to be easy.

CHAPTER NINE
~ Ralph ~

By the way he felt and no doubt looked right now, you would've thought that he wasn't used to manual labour and long hours working on a ranch. He was used to all sorts of physical work that came with working and running a working ranch, what he was NOT used to and didn't like, was this sort of weather. Living in Texas had its moments when it came to the weather, especially when the weather was completely unpredictable. This being one of those moments.

The cold or bad weather always slowed him down. Usually with people it was the hotter weather which had that effect, but for Ralph, it was the opposite. He could work for hours in the sweltering Texas summer heat, no problem. Give him a day like this or when he was buried 3ft with snow, he was as useless as a fawn on ice.

Looking up from where he sat, he could see Robinne standing a short distance away with the most conflicting look on her face he'd ever seen since he'd known her. He wasn't aware of anything happening from their short dash form the ranch courtyard to inside the tiny barn they were sheltering in, but as he was getting to know with Robinne, it was the fact that she had many hidden layers of insecurities, anxiety and secrets. All of which weren't a bad thing at all in his mind, he just wanted her to feel comfortable enough with him to slowly trust him with what she's obviously kept inside for so long.

"Hey, everything alright?" He asked softly, carefully.

Speaking to her had snapped her out of whatever was currently running through her mind, her eyes connecting with his as she turned her attention to where he sat.

"Yes. Everything's fine..."

"C'mon crumpet, I know you better than that. Sort of. What's running through your beautiful head right now?"

She seemed to hesitate for a second before answering him, still unsure of just how much she was willing to reveal to him, despite their short time in each other's company since they'd met.

"You'd never understand."

"Try me."

You'll be amazed at just what I understand sweetheart.

She gave him a look before dropping her shoulders, exhaling deeply to calm the nerves he could see rolling off of her in spades. Whatever's going through her mind must really be troubling her. Before the night was out and hopefully while still stuck seeking shelter together, he was determined to ascertain even if in brief, what was truly troubling her. Once he set his mind on something, he rarely let go until he'd achieved his goal. This time wouldn't be any different.

"You might've picked up just a little bit that I'm not exactly…social. I have a lot of insecurities and anxieties, which include certain things I just don't want to do."

As I thought.

He sat there with one of his legs slightly tucked under the other, arms crossed as he waited for her to continue in her own time. A few beats later, she did just that.

"From a young age, I didn't exactly have the best luck when it came to making friends. In fact, I was bullied more times than I made and retained friends. I had the same four friends from the start of Primary School at age 4, right up until our last year together at eleven. No one else wanted to be my friend, they only wanted to pick on me and make my life miserable. I suppose that's where my social anxiety started. Not that I knew that at the time, as I was only a kid who knew nothing of the word." She took a breath before continuing on again. "So what did I do? I stuck my nose into a book from the moment I was able to read a full sentence in a book at age 4. It was my escape mechanism, a way of blocking out anyone who said or did anything hurtful to me. As long as I had my books, I knew I didn't need anything else. Socialising included. Skip to adult me from when I started reading more…advanced books. Most of those books turned out to be western, southern romance, cowboy books. In those books at some stage, there's always a situation where the two main characters end up much like we are now. Which sounds innocent enough, right? Wrong. Things always…happen, in those closed confined spaces. So me being me, I didn't want that to happen to me. Authors always wrote those scenes in relatively the same way, with the same words, actions and outcome, even if they put their own spin on it. I thought if I was that main character and if I was ever in that situation, I'd experience something more…unique. Something that if I wrote it down as a scene in a book, it wouldn't follow the same formula, the same structure. I didn't want a cliché experience."

Oh Robinne.

You're truly not alone, we're more alike than you know right now.

How brave you are for sharing this with me, how I wish I could thank you.

He listened to her speak for around another five minutes while she talked about things that he'd suspected she'd bottled up for longer than she should have had to. The poor girl clearly didn't get this opportunity very often in her life, which was why he was more than happy for her to let it all out here, with him, in this enclosed space where she'd suspected something would've happened. Which it hasn't.

His own past was littered with events in which like her, he wasn't able to confide in people to let the weight off of his conscience and his shoulders alike. Despite having four brothers, his parents and a good group of humble, hard-working buddies surrounding him, there were still things which he ended up holding close to his chest which weighed him down deeply. He'd often prayed that the good Lord would send him someone who he could share these things with. It looks like his prayers have finally been answered.

In no way was he about to interrupt her train of thought as she spoke, as this was what he wanted of her, for her to be able to let out as much out as she was willing to do. However at the same time, he didn't want her to say so much that she burnt out from offloading so much information. There would be plenty of other opportunities in the future, he hoped, that would give her the chance to talk to him again.

Clearing his throat, he rose from where he'd been sitting. Hit butt was so darn sore from the hard ground, but he wasn't about to go about rubbing it while she was here. He had SOME sense of decorum about him, much to contrary belief.

"Robinne, listen to me darlin'."

He walked over to where she had sat while in the process of talking, encompassing her legs with his as he put both of his hands on her shoulders. He was met with the pleasant, indescribable feeling he got every time he touched any part of her, clothed or unclothed. The only way to describe it if he really had to try, was wholeness. Completion. Touching her felt like the final piece of his soul connecting with the part of him that laid deep within somewhere. He only hoped she could feel it too, someday if not right this second.

"I know better than anyone on this ranch about worries, insecurities and anything of the like. I might not be the most expressive guy in the world, but that doesn't mean I don't have things that bother me or that I want to avoid. You don't have to explain yourself to me as much as you don't have to pour your heart out. If you want to say something to me, say it. I'd much rather you chew me out and be honest with me, than hide something from me and suffer in silence. No one deserves to suffer in silence, so, if you don't want anything to happen in here, it won't happen. I'm just thankful you're here with me now, opening up to me. It's a big thing to do no matter what people say." He smiled before he continued. "Just answer me this one thing if you will. Why are you so keen to avoid something happening here, in here with me?"

An unexplainable expression crossed Robinne's face as she listened to his every word, as if she couldn't quite believe what she was hearing. He could understand her confusion, as he himself had once been in a situation similar to her where he'd been able to pour his own heart out to someone. Only, his ending wasn't a happy one. He would make sure that unlike his, hers would be.

"Y-you really want to know?"

He nodded.

I really do, sweetheart.

After another short beat, she began to open up to him once more.

"I've not had certain…things happen to me in my life. Even now at my age, those things still seem to escape me. Even if it's just down to something small as a man holding a hand, kissing my cheek or going on a date with me, they still haven't happened. People always think that it's down to my choice, not wanting any of those things. It's not. Why would I chose that? I don't want much from life, just the simple things and to me, those are. Those things once too often are taken for granted when other people are lucky enough to experience them, they don't think about people like me who are never ever chosen by someone. We're not even someone's second, third or fourth choice. We're lower than the last choice if that's even possible. Year after year as each birthday of mine instead of being a happy, joyous occasion, instead marks another year of those things not happening to me. By aged 20, I thought I'd be in with some sort of chance of even getting one of those things, my first kiss for example. But no. Cut to three more years and I'm still in the same place as I was when I first started taking interest in…things, when I was 15. All those years and not one nibble of any kind. Who wouldn't think that something was wrong with them if that happened to anyone else?" she took a breath, years of what was weighing her down was now rolling off her in spades.

Before he could speak, she continued. "Now, I'm kind of…hesitant to experience those things now I've moved here. Because I've wished for those things, those stupidly simple things for years, I don't know what I'd do or how I'd react if someone actually took an interest in me. I wouldn't know what to think. The only time anyone' even remotely paid attention to me was when guys in school would fake flirt with me to amuse their mates. I can't help but think that if it happened to me now, no man would actually really mean it." she sighed. "I have a lot of emotional baggage with me, Ralph. Maybe that's why men are hesitant to get to know me beyond being a friend. No one would want to deal with all of me, all of what I carry. I don't just want things to happen to me that have happened countless time in books, as you can gather from what you know about me, I read more than the average girl. I'm a simple girl of simple needs, despite the heavy baggage and if these things were going to finally happen to me, I want them to be memorable, not something that follows the same pattern in books. Something that if I wrote them down myself, it would be memorable to the reader as well as me."

Understandable. I'd want the same if I was a woman.

This poor girl, she's kept it all inside and to herself for too long.

That changes now.

As much as she must come across as a complicated, emotionally damaged person to anyone else, he could completely understand why she wanted to do, or in this case, avoid, what she did. He'd had enough of his own bad experiences in the past he didn't exactly want to re-visit, he just didn't show it as much as she did now. Never again would he fully expose himself to anyone. Though with Robinne, who knows. It might happen again.

Keeping one hand on her right shoulder, he used his other hand to gently tip up her chin so she was looking directly into his eyes.

"Darlin', if I had met you sooner or in another life, you wouldn't have had to hold it in this long, keep things to yourself or go it alone. If you were my girl, I'd make all of your deepest wishes come true, even the tiny ones you think are insignificant. I'd do it. Want to know why? Because you deserve something special, because you are special. I've known you not even a week but from what I do know of you, I'm sure of that. You. Are. Special. In every positively possible way imaginable. You sass me instead of wanting to get into my pants, you aren't afraid to banter with me and damn girl, your accent could stir a fire inside the coldest of people. Like it did inside of me."

Well heck, who knew I could be such a Casanova.

Okay, more like a wannabe Romeo.

No girl has ever wanted to be wooed like this beauty before me. They all just wanted a quick wham, bam and thank you ma'am from the eldest Jenkins boy. Any Jenkins boy.

Robinne was different. She's well… Robinne.

Her eyes grew moist as he continued to look down at her, never breaking their connection for even a moment. The smallest of tears slid from her right eye, slowly cascading down her delicate, porcelain cheek. He wiped it away with his thumb, still holding he chin up with his hand.

"That…that was the loveliest thing anyone has ever said to me. Like, ever. I-I had no idea you…that you could be so…so sweet."

No, neither could I.

He smiled down at her.

"That's all on you darlin', you bring it out in me."

"I-I do?"

"Yes." He said, his voice growing breathy.

Robinne's cheeks grew a dusky rose pink beneath his hands, which were now gently holding either side of her face.

He swallowed.

"Say no if you don't want this darlin', because I can't hold back from giving you your first memorable experience for much longer."

She didn't say a word. A simple nod was his only cue that she was alright with this, that she wanted this to happen as much as he did.

Wasting no longer deliberating on what he should do, he bent down and brought his lips close to hers, a hairs width between them, giving her a last chance for her to change her mind.

She didn't.

In no time at all, he closed the gap between their lips. Soft, satiny lips met his own.

So this is heaven?

I like heaven.

A kiss was a kiss to him, how else could you describe a meeting of two lips coming together? That was, until his lips touched those of what he could only describe what a kiss from an angel would feel like. He thought he'd been kissed before, doing his fair share of kissing in return over the years, yet nothing compared to this very moment he shared with an extraordinary woman.

Though the weather continued to batter down above them on the shed roof as if the war of the worlds had come, all sounds slowly faded from his ears as the only sounds that became present in their little bubble of heaven, were the sounds of their lips, their mingled breaths, and their hearts beating as one.

He never really understood the meaning of the words 'time stood still', when he read them in a book, or heard them used in a movie or TV show. He did now. It's one of those moments where you don't understand something fully until you experience it for yourself, then and only then are you able to begin to describe it. In a way, he secretly wished that someone was capturing this moment of the two of them, even if he wasn't all too keen to see himself in a photo. This was a moment he would want to go back to time after time, for many years to come.

Standing here and kissing the sweetest ray of light he'd ever had the pleasure to meet, giving her her first kiss, he couldn't help but think back to how his very own first kiss took place. If it even counted as a real first kiss.

He was in eighth grade. It was the last day of the last semester of the year before summer vacation, with the next time that he'd be going to school, he'd be a freshman in high school. His Pa couldn't pick him up from school as he'd had to go to Austin for a business meeting with a few other ranchers, and his Ma was busy between running the B&B and looking after his younger brothers. They didn't pick him up every day, just on the days where it was too hot or too cold to walk or get the bus home.

The bus that took the kids home to the more remote parts of the town, away from the 'town centre', just pulled up. He was about to head to get on it when he heard a sniffling sound coming from somewhere behind him. Turning around, he'd followed the sound around the corner of the building, coming across Delilah Hamilton leaning against the building, sobbing into her hands.

Delilah was a girl in his grade that everyone liked. She was loved by everyone and never had a shortage of friends at her side, even at their tender age. He couldn't think what on Earth had upset her so much to make her cry like this, alone too!

He'd approached her slowly, as not to spook her.

"Delilah? Are you alright?"

Of course she's not! Fool.

Delilah raised her head looking in his direction, her cheeks stained by her salty tears. She hiccupped, wiping the current onslaught of tears away with the back of her hand.

"I-I'm…I'm fine." She sniffled.

Putting his backpack down on the ground, he came closer, pulling an unused tissue from out of the side of his backpack. Offering it to her, he cocked his head.

"You sure? Something must have upset you."

Blowing her nose on the tissue, Delilah kept her head down, refusing to meet his eyes.

"I'm sure. Thank you for coming to see if I was alright. You're a kind one Ralph Jenkins. Not everyone is as kind as you are."

He blinked.

She thinks I'm kind?

I didn't think I did anything more than what anyone else does around here.

He picked up his backpack again, putting it over one of his shoulders. "Well uh…I'm glad you're alright. I'm just going to…" he went to take a step back, if not for his body moving in the other direction instead of the way he'd intended to go.

For the briefest of moments, he felt something come into contact with his lips. The moment was fleeting as the feeling was over as quickly as it took his brain to register what was happening. By the time it caught up, Delilah was no longer in front of him.

Leaning around the corner of the building, he watched her as she walked away with her usual gaggle of female friends, all whispering and chatting in hushed tones among their laughter. He wasn't able to catch the entire conversation between the group as they boarded the bus he was supposed to be getting onto, but later on that week, he'd learned that she'd been dared by her friends, to kiss him.

It wasn't a big dare like pulling a prank on an unsuspecting individual that would leave a lasting traumatic effect, or even a public prank. It was a stupid game among a group of rather stupid, immature girls, which left him more bemused than mad.

He was less mad at the fact that his first kiss was taken away from him, as he never really put much thought into when it would happen and how. What he did have a problem with, was the fact that someone had played upon his good nature to get something out of him. He was always taught and raised to help those in need, regardless of if it was a woman or a man, he was raised to help both genders and someone had abused the result of his humble upbringing.

Never again.

He shouldn't really be thinking about his first kiss while he was giving Robinne hers, but he guess he could see why she wanted a memorable moment for her experiences in life. At least she wasn't being made a monkey of as a result of it. He could only hope that this moment between them, trapped in a barn, a small barn at that, with only the two of them existing at this moment in time was enough a memorable moment for her.

Bringing himself fully back into the moment, he slid his hands away from her face, down her slender neck, past her delicate shoulders and to her perfect to him shaped waist. He held onto her as he stepped as close as he could get, moulding their bodies together as perfect as God above designed them to be.

Her lips didn't need to surrender under his, because for once in his life, he'd met someone who was his equal. His missing piece. Her lips moulded to his own, mirroring the passion inside of him which was now coming out by the second.

If I died now, I'll have died a happy man indeed.
Lord, please don't actually take me now.

CHAPTER TEN
~Robinne~

Someone once said, 'happiness is an unplanned first kiss'. She never used to like that phrase until now. Now, she was a firm believer. As she'd written out what she wanted to avoid happening in her new life here, she should've known in some respect that by doing so, it was inevitable that they would all, or at least some of them, come true.

The kiss she was currently sharing with Ralph was indeed the most unplanned moment of her move here, and she was enjoying every moment of it. She didn't plan to be here with Ralph during a storm, in a barn, kissing him like she'd been starved of oxygen until he'd come along to give her some of his own.

Her mind started to wander as her lips remained locked onto his, a new thing for her. Since she'd never given much thought as to how her first kiss would happen, she never planned it out. She didn't actually have a written plan down as to how she would go about getting her first kiss, the thought was just always in her head though as to when the moment *might* pop up, and how she'd go about getting that kiss without letting on that it was her first.

At the ripe old age of twenty three, everyone else she had known in her life prior to moving to America, had already received their first kisses. Most of them taking the moment for granted, which often made her madder than she'd ever admit. Barely a piece of metaphorical string held her back from telling those people just how lucky they should consider themselves. Thankfully for their sakes, the string held.

Around the age of fifteen, she'd first began to develop an interest in boys, almost feeling kind of confused as to these 'feelings' she was the experiencing. After realising what she was feeling was completely normal, she assumed at some stage from that moment onwards, she would begin to experience a kiss here and there, holding a hand or two. But no, nothing of the sort ever happened to her throughout her adolescence.

It half killed her to watch everyone around her 'in love', or rather, what they thought was love. Valentine's Day was the worst. Eventually, she came to the conclusion that it just wasn't meant to be. So she focused on her school work instead, for all the good that did her.

When she finally became a legal adult in the U.K at the age of eighteen, the time seemed right to finally start pursuing a relationship. Well on the way to getting her first job, it felt like the right time in her life to do so.

After trying and failing to get any man's attention, she once more decided again to focus on bettering herself, thankfully gaining her first job.

Of course, the job wasn't anything to shout home about Working from home selling beauty products wasn't what she wanted to do, but it would earn her some money before she could really get down to do what she wanted to do. Write a book. Anything in publishing would do, but that was her dream job.

Two years later after the job had fallen through, she managed to get a full-time job in way of an apprenticeship at her local museum. Again, not her first choice. However, it would provide a chance for her to get her confidence back and get out there in a proper working environment, hopefully running into a potential relationship as she went.

Coming to the end of her apprenticeship a year later, there hadn't been as much as a nibble in the relationship world. By this time, she was sure that her past insecurities and anxieties were as true as she believed them to be. If there wasn't something wrong with her, someone would've been with her or at least interested in her. After all, she was almost twenty one when she finished at her first job, surely it wouldn't be much longer of a wait until she'd get into her first relationship?

Wrong. It would be longer.

As it currently stood, quite literally as she stood here kissing Ralph, she was staring down the barrel at being twenty four, with only now getting the very first hints of what she'd been dreaming about for years. She should've had it happen to her by now, except she knew she wasn't the sort of women men usually went after. At first, she blamed herself, thinking it was something about her that put people off. Now, she realised that she was wrong. She just had to wait for the right man to come along to make her feel that there wasn't anything wrong with her. Fate just wasn't ready to step in before now.

Fate was stepping in now. Big time.

Her hands instinctively went to his sides as their kiss continued to deepen, anchoring herself to him. He didn't try to press his luck and increase the heat, he waited for cues from her that she wanted it hotter, or if she wanted to sweet and soft.

With a last feather light brushing of his lips on hers, he pulled back just enough to look down at her with the most beautiful expression she'd seen on a man. She was a firm believer that a man had a capability of being described as 'beautiful', hours spent on Pinterest and Instagram confirmed that.

"Mmm. That was most certainly memorable for me, and it wasn't even my first kiss. Did I do okay?"

Oh boy, you did more than 'okay'. You did great.

She nodded, happy tears threatening to leak from her eyes.

"Perfect." She whispered.

Ralph pressed a chaste kiss on her lips again before he looped his arms around her middle, holding her close to him as he caressed her hair. Pressing her face into his chest, she felt as if he was protecting her from the storm outside. He couldn't actually protect her from Mother Nature, but she knew he would do his best anyway.

Never before in her life had she had the opportunity to seek solace and comfort in another's arms before, as she was usually only given the option to cope with things on her own, she was glad those days were over. She didn't like to rely on others for anything, even if those things were aspects of life that even the strongest of people needed sometimes. Yet at the same time, she secretly wanted to succumb to the very things she swore she'd never succumb to. If ever anyone needed to see a physical representation of the phrase 'walking contradiction', she was it.

Happily content at where she was, she saw no reason to move from his warmth any time soon.

"Thank you." She mumbled against his clothed chest.

"What for darlin'?"

She looked up at him, her face so angelic it would make an angel cry with happiness.

"For this. For making me so happy about being wrong for once."

He chuckled, placing a kiss on the top of her head.

"You're welcome. Guess it was worth making the list after all."

What... No... It...it can't be...

As soon as it left his mouth, she knew he'd made the most colossal mistake with her yet.

Robinne pulled away from him slowly, moving him to an arm's length away from her rather than flushed close together. Her expression changed rapidly from one of bliss, to one of confusion and brewing anger. She damn well knew what list he was talking about, as it was the only one she'd made so bringing up a random mention of a list wouldn't have made sense to her.

All the signs were there not to trust anyone else ever again, she knew that. Still, she let her foolish heart think that for once in her life, things could be different, that she'd escape the same hellish cycle of comfortability then betrayal. Alas, she was wrong for the billionth time in her life.

"Ralph..." she started to say, unable to complete the sentence.

He exhaled, his head dipping in shame.

"Let me explain. It's not what you think."

"Not what I think? Good God Ralph, I get that I'm not as educated or life experienced as most people would be my age, but I'm not blood stupid! How would you know about a list that no one on this planet knows about? How did you even..." the moment she knew what he'd done, he knew he'd blown his chance of explaining and apologising to her. "You have it...don't you?"

He nodded once, clearly ashamed to even say anything.

"You're unbelievable! Why would you even keep something like that which you know isn't yours? Any normal person would read it and throw it away! When did you…" she realised as she spoke, that the only time he would've picked it up was not long after when she realised it was missing.

The day we met…

Keeping her distance from him as best she could in this small space, she watched as the infamous list came out from his trouser pocket, safely nestling in his annoyingly muscular hand.

"You…you kept it with you?!" she fumed. "You've had it on you this whole entire time? All night?"

He nodded, devoid of finding an argument for his case as to why he has it, though she was starting to suspect, rather quickly too, as to why that was.

"All that crap about if I was your girl, the making it memorable, it was all a ruse to check something off my list, wasn't it? You wanted to be the guy to tick all my missing boxes of my list, as if that would make you some hero, some…some…southern white knight, here to cure all my problems. Go on, deny it! Deny that you were doing this for anything other than your own sick, selfish satisfaction. ADMIT IT!"

He doesn't really need to admit a damned thing, it won't make any difference. I won't ever trust anyone ever again.

"Robinne…" he made to move towards her again, only to be halted from doing so with a firm hand pushing against his chest.

"Save it. I already have my answer." She slid down off the hay bale, giving him no choice but to back up so she could stand. "Thank you for re-confirming what I've always believed in. I can truly never experience any happiness of any kind at all in my life. I'm just one big joke to the whole entire world, a way for people to use me to their own amusement. I'm really nothing other than some piece of worthlessness that gets fucked several times over because that's all I've been put on this godforsaken earth for." She moved around him and strode over purposefully towards the doors, pushing them wide open with all her strength.

"ROBINNE!" He shouted, knowing just what she was about to do.

Without looking back, she dashed out into the rain running at full speed.

"ROBINNE COME BACK!" she could hear Ralph yelling from behind her, but she wasn't going to stop. No way in hell was she going to him. He could go to hell.

Not bothering to look back as she made her way across the grass and into the house, she wasn't sure if Ralph was following her and quite frankly she didn't care. She was getting out of here and she was getting out of there right now, weather be damned.

There was no way that she could stay in this house, or around his family for another minute. Everything around here screamed Ralph, or reminded her of him in some shape or form. If there was one thing that she definitely didn't want being reminded of for the foreseeable future thanks to what she'd unfortunately just learned, it was anything to do with him.

Moving to a whole new country to start a brand new life was starting to look like a bad decision. She hadn't even been here for a week and things had already gone so badly wrong, how was the rest of her time here going to go if it started off like this? It didn't beg thinking about.

As she moved swiftly through the back part of the garden and into the house, she saw no sight or sound of anyone. She could only assume everyone must be in the living room or somewhere else out of the rain, taking shelter like she and Ralph had done not so long ago. Fine by her, she could make her escape without drawing too much attention to herself.

Ralph himself would no doubt make his way inside at some point, though she didn't really care when that moment would be. In a way, she hoped the rain would continue so he'd be stuck out there in the barn for longer than he wished to be, as he clearly looked like he wanted to chase after her as she fled from his company.

No such luck, buster.

You're not getting anywhere near me any time soon.

I'll make sure of that.

Never before in her life had she ever been a lucky person, though tonight, luck was for once on her side when she came into the hallway by the front door. She remembered Ryder had dropped his keys on the table by the front door when they came in, so she was able to snatch up his keys in a spur of the moment decision in her desperation to flee from the ranch by any means possible. No way was she getting stuck here or being forced to ask for a lift home, she'd feel obligated to tell people what had gone down between her and Ralph just now and no way in hell was she going to be telling anyone about this unless she had to.

This, she was keeping to herself. It was the only way to protect what parts of her heart she had left that weren't crushed to dust within her.

Taking one last, quick look around the entrance hall of the main ranch house, Robinne left via the front door, dashing once more through the rain and out to Ryder's rain-soaked truck. Having driven her truck since she'd got it earlier on in the week, she knew she'd be okay driving the truck back home. She wasn't completely familiar with the routes around the more remote areas of the town yet, though that was the least of her concerns. The top priority for her right now was to get the hell out of there and worry about where she'd end up when she got there.

Once inside the truck having remotely opened it before getting close to it, she buckled up, turned the engine and lights on just in time to see the front door bring wrenched open, with a familiar bulking figure filling the doorway backlit by the lights within the house.

Goodbye Ralph. Thanks for opening my eyes.

Taking care to use the reversing camera on the centre console, yet another new feature of the more up to date Ford trucks, she hit the gas to reverse and sped out of the driveway, just in time to see Ralph's huge form make futile progress and covering as much ground as his wet form would allow in an attempt to get to the truck before she left.

He didn't make it.

By the time he'd reached the spot where the truck had been parked when she and Ryder had arrived earlier that day, she'd already vacated it and had made swift progress in driving down the road leading out back towards the main road. Turning the truck around at the end of the driveway, she slid it into drive, instead of what would've been first gear back home, and booked it out of there faster than a bullet out of a gun.

Making sure to pay attention for any other drivers on the road as she put her foot as close to the floor as she dared, she had expected her heart to feel lighter the further she got away from the ranch. It didn't. If anything, she could feel her heart getting heavier as her mind started to work overtime, her thoughts going haywire and her anxieties coming out of their temporary hibernation.

Driving through the monsoon in which not so long ago she was protected from, she felt her tears now becoming one with the rain outside of the truck. The tears she'd shed within the very hour had been ones of happiness, of joy and hope. Not anymore. These tears were ones of extreme sadness, sorrow, broken trust and promises of what once could've been but will never be.

She had trust issues, they both now knew that. It wasn't new news anymore. She'd made her point clear as to why that was, as to how much it had meant to her that people treat her with open honesty and truth, yet he still lied to her. He had successfully made her look the biggest fool for thinking that anyone could treat her any other way than what people had always treated her.

Well for one thing, she'd re-confirmed one of her biggest past beliefs. She can't trust anyone ever again, and it was all thanks to someone she foolishly thought she could have the slightest hopes of seeking some sort of security, some sort of future with. Even in her deepest dreams.

Feeling like her heart was going to give out and break the last strings holding her down to this mortal world, she slowed down. But only enough to be able to safely drive in the rain, heading to a place she thought she'd be able to consider home.

If there was ever truly such as thing as home.

After what she'd have to guess was half an hour driving through the continual, monsoon-like rain, she suddenly realised that she was no longer driving towards the direction she'd known her home to be in. Not that she was driving towards her own home in the first place. Getting off the ranch had been her only thought. Only after leaving did she think about heading back towards home. Though that would be the first place Ralph would look if he decided to go after her, so she'd ended up driving anywhere to get her as far away from him as she could.

Eventually as exhaustion began to set in, she pulled over onto the side of the road and flipped on the truck's hazard lights, just in case anyone came by so they didn't miss her and smash into her. She might be beyond upset, but even in her current state, she knew she had to still be safe on the road.

Turning off the engine, the only sound that she was left with was the beating of the rain on the truck roof, the crash of the thunder surrounding her from every angle and flashes of lightening which bathed everything in a urethral light. Completely the opposite of anything she was feeling inside of her right now.

"Ralph you…you…I hate you. So much." She whispered, crossing her arms in front of her on the steering wheel, laying her head within them to absorb the wracking sobs that burst forth out of her.

Never again.

Never again am I ever going to trust anyone.

They're all liars!

Liars!

I just knew happiness wasn't meant for me. I…I just knew it.

Alone. I'm meant to be alone.

Always alone…

CHAPTER ELEVEN
~ Robinne ~

He smiled down at her.

"That's all on you darlin', you bring it out in me."

"I-I do?"

"Yes." He said, his voice growing breathy.

Robinne's cheeks grew a dusky rose pink beneath his hands, which were now gently holding either side of her face.

He swallowed.

"Say no if you don't want this darlin', because I can't hold back from giving you your first memorable experience for much longer."

She didn't say a word. A simple nod was his only cue that she was alright with this, that she wanted this to happen as much as he did.

Wasting no longer deliberating on what he should do, he bent down and brought his lips close to hers, a hairs width between them, giving her a last chance for her to change her mind.

She didn't.

In no time at all, he closed the gap between their lips. Soft, satiny lips met his own.

So this is heaven?

I

like heaven.

* * *

What met Robinne's cheeks now felt neither soft nor human, or smelled as divine as a certain human. In fact, what met her cheek now felt hard, course, and smelled…leathery?

Leathery?

Robinne groggily lifted her head, tired eyes reluctantly opening, gazing upon the steering wheel of a truck she knew didn't belong to her. The face of the man in her dream fading with every second she now remained awake in the darkness engulfing the truck cab.

Ryder's truck…

The man in my dream, it was…Ralph.

Sitting up against the comfortable driver's seat, all the events leading up to why she was where she is now, sitting on the side of the road in a storm, came flooding back to her. That's right, she'd been at the Jenkins' family ranch, eating and mingling with a few members of the family and their friends. After dinner, she was given a brief tour of some of the ranch buildings, including the barn. A place now burned into her memory. It perfectly explains why she'd just dreamed what she did.

Ralph…

He was the reason why she'd fled in Ryder's truck, and why she'd had to pull over to cry out the torrent of emotions that had unexpectedly come forth from deep inside of her. It was all his fault. All of it. Getting out and away from him was her only thought and priority, regardless of the consequences and unexpected monsoon currently thundering down on the truck and all that she could see. She hadn't been thinking clearly, she knew that now. Her not so smart decision to flee has left her sitting here, wondering what the hell to do next. Should she stay where she was and wait out the storm? Or should she continue on, now that she was a little calmer after her nap?

While she sat there in the darkness of the truck cab, the torrent of rain continuing to cascade down outside, a sudden pounding began on the driver's window right next to her head, startling her.

"Robinne!" a muffled voice called out to her.

Huh?

Someone's calling my name? Am I hearing things?

The knock sounded again, this time sounding more urgent. The muffled voice called out her name a second time, a little lounder than the last.

What the…

Turning her head towards the sound of the noise, her driver's door suddenly came away from her, pulling backwards to reveal someone she never expected to see here. Dripping wet and breathing somewhat heavily, Ryder's intense eyes stared back at hers.

"Robinne! Thank goodness you're alright! We've been looking everywhere for you!" he panted, leaning forwards into the truck cab so his head was shielded from the rain.

Leaning back slightly so he'd have some room, she looked Ryder up and down, assessing whether or not he truly meant it. Judging on how he currently looked, rain dripping and soaking every fibre of his being, she couldn't deny that he truly did mean it. Taking sympathy on him, she shuffled along the cab's bench seat until she was sitting in the passenger side, allowing Ryder to slide in to the driver's seat to take complete shelter.

Once settled and the driver's door was closed, Ryder turned to face her, his face only lit by the occasional flash of lightening from the never-ending storm outside.

"Ryder, why…how…you're here." She said, bemused.

Shaking the raindrops from his sodden hair, he nodded.

"Uh-huh. We all went out looking for you when we realised who booked it out of there so quickly."

She blinked.

"A-all of you?"

"All of us. Aside from ma, Hannah and Niall. We were all worried about you Robinne. You're not used to driving in conditions like this unlike us when we *really* have to. It's not like a rainy day in the U.K."

"No shit Sherlock." She mumbled, unamused. Yet, she was still grateful for their concern about her safety.

Leaning back against the passenger seat, she groaned and closed her eyes, taking a moment to absorb what Ryder had just told her about everyone searching for her. Everyone.

Still with her eyes closed, she asked Ryder a question.

"When you say 'everyone' is out looking for me, do you…do you mean *him,* too?"

With a serious expression plastered across his face, Ryder nodded. Confirming for sure the feeling she had within her gut, despite what went down between the two of them in the barn, he still went out to look for her.

Sighing and opening her eyes, she turned back to face Ryder.

"Why? You obviously know what happened between Ralph and myself, and that *he* was the cause of our falling out back at the ranch, why's he out looking for me? I don't get it."

No ounce of irritation came from Ryder's eyes as he began to explain to her the reason why the last person she'd expect was also out looking for her. The way he'd become somewhat of a friend to her in the short time since she'd come to town, there was no way he could be mad at her.

"He wouldn't *not* go looking for you, regardless of the reason why what happened between the two of you, happened. He's not doing it out of obligation *because* of what happened either, he's concerned about someone he cares about and their safety. No matter what happened between the two of you, he certainly wouldn't want to hear that you'd ended up getting hurt, and I know for sure if it was the other way around, you wouldn't want him to end up hurt either. He'd do all in his power no matter the hour, day or night, to find you and make sure you're safe. It's also safe to say that he'd be the last person you'd want to see, so if I know my brother, which I'm pretty sure I do very well, if he did find you, he'd make sure *someone* would get you somewhere nice and dry, warm and cozy. Sure it would sting his pride a little that he didn't get to play hero all the way through, he'd put you first, even if that meant him keeping his distance so you wouldn't be upset. In no means is my brother perfect, hell none of us are. We've all messed up plenty here and there. That being said, even if he was an ass of the highest order tonight, he'd still run into a burning building for you if that meant you'd be safe and the clothes on his back would be burned." He smiled kindly at her. "Does that answer your question?"

Does it ever.

She truly struggled to find the words to say after such a heartfelt, brotherly speech. If she didn't feel more for Ryder than the new friendship they'd recently formed, she was sure she'd be a pile of gooey mush on the floor of his truck right about now. Whoever would complete Ryder someday would be one lucky woman indeed.

Needing no words at all, she nodded her head. He'd managed to answer her question and then some. She was still plenty mad and hurt at what had gone down between her and Ralph, but she was tired and she just wanted to get out of this storm and into her bed.

"Alright." Ryder smiled kindly her way, pulling his mobile phone from out of his pocket.

"Who're you calling?"

"I'm not. I'm just firing off a quick message on the family group chat thing we got goin' on, just letting them know I've found you safe and sound, and so that they can all stop searching and go on home."

She leaned back into the truck bench once more.

"I feel so bad everyone's out looking for me in this weather. I wasn't thinking when I took off but you guys, you all have a steady head on your shoulders. The thought that I've put people at risk because of my stupidity is--"

A hand to her left forearm stopped her short.

Still without an ounce of irritation on his face, Ryder looked at her with a kindness akin of a father looking down on a daughter, a face full of compassion and understanding.

"I'll be havin' none of that now sweetheart. None of us do anything we don't want to do, and you can trust my southern honesty on it."

"I thought it was 'southern hospitality?'"

Ryder gave her a friendly wink.

"That's what everyone writes about. We're also brutally honest. Just, don't give away our secret."

She laughed heartily at his goofiness.

"I won't, I promise."

"Excellent!" he reached down to the keys, starting the engine of the truck and bringing light back into the cab.

She blinked, arching a brow in his direction. "What are you doing? Surely it'd be safer to wait out the storm than drive through it?"

Like I know the right thing to do in a storm anyway...

"I texted one of my brothers to come pick up the truck I drove up in, in the morning. Since you drove off in my truck, it only makes sense for me to take you back to mine in it."

"T-take you back to...to your place? Why?"

"Since you drove in the complete wrong direction to your place, mine's much closer and it'll give ma some comfort to know someone's with you tonight. Don't worry, I won't try anything. I have a feeling a certain someone would break my arm seven ways to Sunday if I did. Not that I would but, his imagination has always been vivid." Ryder chuckled as he pulled the truck from its spot on the side of the road, to back onto the road itself, heading in the direction towards his home.

Ralph would hurt Ryder even after what happened between us?
The man truly is complex.

After ten or so minutes of driving through the still persisting monsoon, Ryder thought he should be the one to break the silence. By no means was it uncomfortable, he just had this feeling in his stomach that Robinne could use some distraction from her thoughts, if anything from the lost look on her face was anything to go by.

He'd never been the type of guy to never know what to say to a woman when she was upset, in fact, he was quiet the listener, therefore, he knew what to say in return. However, he didn't know Robinne as well as some of his other female friends. He was still figuring her out, despite having a pretty good idea of who she was in the time he'd known her so far.

Keeping his hands firmly gripped on the wheel, he let out the breath of air he didn't realise he'd been holding in for as long as he had.

"So uh…" he cleared his throat. "You're not the only one to get lost y'know. When I was 15, I took pa's truck out for the first time without anyone with me. I thought I was ready y'know? I'd passed my test and I'd not long got my licence. Thought I could drive all proper and adult-like because of it." he chuckled to himself, recalling the memory. "Taught me a lesson it did."

Seemingly interested in his story, Robinne's head turned somewhat in his direction, her lost expression slipping ever so slightly from her face. "How so?"

Two words. Better than nothing.

"Well, kind of like tonight, I chose the wrong sort of weather to go out on my first solo drive as a newly qualified driver. Before while learning, I at least had pa and uh…him, with me. They'd quickly act if I wasn't fast enough. So when I was on my own that night, I wasn't able to act fast enough when an escaped horse from a neighbouring breeding ranch bolted in front of my truck during a storm. I swerved quickly, hoping to and successfully avoiding hitting said horse, but I wasn't quick enough to react and avoid putting the truck into a ditch. I should've hit the emergency break or turned the wheel the other way or something, fact is, I was going too fast for the wet road. Rookie mistake, one that cost pa a lot of money to fix."

"Why did you even go out that night?"

"Same reason every cocky young man does." He smirked, "I was going to show off to my then girlfriend that I'd gotten my licence."

A small smile pulled at the corner of Robinne's mouth. "What happened after you binned it?"

Ryder turned the truck down the gravel path which lead to his place. "I made the call of shame."

"Call of shame?"

He nodded.

"I had to call my pa to come collect me. We didn't have a tow company at the time, we helped each other out if we ever had car issues. He came to collect me and you can bet your bottom dollar he tore me off a strip for being so foolish. I deserved it though."

They shared a laugh together, to which he was relieved to hear hers.

"I bet you got into trouble for that."

He nodded again. *I sure did.*

"Pa made me clean out the stalls all day for a whole week. I don't think I ever got rid of the stench from the previous day before I had to go out the next day and do it all over again." He chuckled.

Ryder brought the truck to a gentle and steady stop around the back of his house. Robinne would be in for a shock when she saw the front of the property, but he'll get around to showing her that soon enough.

"Home sweet home."

Turning the truck off, he turned to face Robinne, who wore a more contented expression on her face. He guessed she was just relieved to be anywhere but alone right now.

"Nice place." She said, unbuckling her seatbelt. "Must've cost you a fortune to build."

He felt a small surge of pride that she liked his house, his home. It did take a lot of manpower to build, and though it was somewhat costly, it would have cost a lot more if he'd bought a house like this already built in its place.

"Thanks. Yeah it did cost a dime or two to build, in manpower that is. The wood, most of it, was from other buildings that we've lost to storms and bad weather around five years ago. Rather than have it burned or left around, I offered to take it of the town's hands and used it to part-build this place."

Robinne nodded her head in approval, filling his heart with even more pride than he ever thought possible. He'd never bought one of his female friends back to his place before, he'd never even thought about doing so, so her praise made all the hard effort worth seeing how she looked at it now.

Rain continued to thunder down outside, with no sign of it letting up than it did earlier when he'd found her. Clapping his hands together, he sat up in higher in his seat. "C'mon, let's get inside and get something warm inside of us."

Chance would be a fine thing.
Not with Robinne though!
No. Definitely not, Ralph would kill me.

Darting around to the passenger side of the truck, he opened her door and quickly ushered the two of them onto the small deck outside the back door of his weathered timber cabin home. He reached into his pocket for the set of keys which unlocked the front and back door, selecting the back door key which opened the back door with ease, letting them both inside. Closing the bad weather behind them.

He shook off the fresh droplets of water that had fallen on him since their exit from the trunk, making him only a microscopic bit drier overall. He seriously needed a chance of clothes and a warm shower.

Makes a change from a cold one…

He put a hand on Robinne's shoulder. "Go on upstairs if you want to use the bathroom, I'll get the drinks started for when you come down. Then I'll go shower and join you back down here. Sound good?"

She nodded. "I won't be long."

"Take your time." he called to her retreating form.

Sighing, he rubbed his forehead.

You've got a lot of making up to do Ralph.
A hell of a lot.

Ryder's home is way more beautiful than Robinne ever imagined a bachelor's place to be. First of all, he wasn't living in some sterile, modern, grey-clad one-bedroomed bungalow. That's a one floor house back home. No, he lived in a house he'd built with his own two hands, and it was stunning!

Not that I didn't like my own place, it was stunning in its own right. However, this place is architectural bliss.

He shared similar furniture to what she'd seen at the big ranch house during her few visits there, assuming they've all gone to either the same place, or the same person, placing the items in both of their homes. Either way, the stunning red tartan pattern of the sofa material really stood out to her. The couches themselves were encased in darkened wood, obviously stained to give the place a bit more of an older feel to the place. By older, she meant from the 1800s, not the taste of someone in their older years.

The rest of the living room space was just as charming as the tartan sofas. On one side of the room taking up the main focal point of that wall, stood a grand stone fireplace, complete with logs ready to burn. The fireplace itself was a sheer masterpiece. It was made of some stone that Robinne clearly wouldn't know the name of, with different coloured stones creating a grand structure. Usually, using so many colours often took away from the beauty of whatever had been created, not this fireplace. Somehow, the miss-matched nature of the fireplace stone placements worked. A landscape painting completed the fireplace perfectly, hanging just so above it.

Completing the look of the room was evidently touches of Ryder's own style, making the space unique to his taste. A massive mahogany table was situated in the centre of the space, large clearly for when more than one of his family members came to visit. The same could be said for the four massive armchairs that looked like you could get lost in when you sat in one. Both screamed family gatherings and memories by the fireplace. It was not, however, any of these things along with the odd furniture piece here and there that caught her eye the most. It was the biggest window and view outside of it that she'd ever seen in her life.

Woah…

Imagine you were standing right in the front row of a cinema screen, looking up at the screen and marvelling at just how big it really was compared to where you normally sat to watch a film? Yeah, that came pretty close to what Robinne was seeing right now.

What met her eyes as she walked as close to the wide window, which spanned the whole of that side of the living room, was a crystal clear, high-definition, picturesque view of a lake.

Holy cow!

His house is a lake house! Go Ryder!

Or rather, it would've been a picturesque view of a lake and surrounding woodland area, if not for the storm that was still raining down on them, not letting up in the brief time that had lapsed since coming inside.

"Not bad is it? Even with the weather." Ryder's voice said from beside her, bringing her back into the present moment.

"Hm?"

Ryder nodded his head towards the window, answering her question. "O-oh! Yes. Yes it is."

Chuckling, Ryder placed both of their drinks down on two separate coasters on top of the coffee table, placing a hand on her shoulder. "I'll give you a proper tour of this place a little later, if you'd like. Shame I can't say the view is nice right now what with the storm and all, but once it's clear, it'll be prettier than a postcard." He beamed.

Robinne laughed, not doubting him one bit.

"For sure. I'll just go and dry out a bit, now. Couldn't help myself getting distracted with this view, I was like a moth to a flame."

Plopping down into what she assumed must be his go-to armchair, Ryder's smile never left his face as he listened to her praise the view.

"Understandable, I often find myself passing the time just standing there too."

"I can see why. I won't be long."

"Take your time." she heard him call, making her way across the living space, going at a gentle semi-jog up the stairs to locate the bathroom so she could towel off a little.

All towelled off and ready to head back downstairs, Robinne paused. Now that she wasn't occupied even with the menial task of patting dry her hair a little, her mind started to wander back to the events of the night, those which lead up to her standing here in Ryder's bathroom.

Perhaps I'm being too rash about this. Overreacting.

No.

I'm not.

He knew EXACTLY what he was doing when he chose to lie to me, yet he still chose to carry it out and not tell me he'd taken my note.

There's never NOT a reason to tell someone the truth, no matter the excuse that may come into someone's head. So why…why did he hide it from me? I'm not some guinea pig to be tested to see how I'd react!

How dare he!

Robinne was skipping past all the chronological stages of grief, as she'd gone from upset when she was in the truck on her own, right to anger where she now stood. She'd never been one to always go the path of others, or to go the 'right way' of things naturally, so it didn't surprise her one bit that she was as mad as hell right now.

Shaking her head, she was determined not to let this get to her too much, until a time when SHE was ready to deal with everything. Placing the towel into the hamper by the door, she left the bathroom to head back down to where a lovely warm drink and Ryder awaited her.

"So…" Ryder said as she joined him back on the living room chairs, sitting into one opposite him with a clear view of the still stormy lake beside them. "How're you feeling? Do you want to talk about, you know, what happened. Back at the ranch."

Robinne flicked her eyes reluctantly to meet Ryder's gaze. She knew he would broach this subject at some point, she just hoped it would've been a little later than this. Picking up her mug, she exhaled, reclining back into the big comfy chair and allowing it to feel like it was giving her a big hug from behind. She needed that comfort right now, without it being from a human being that is.

"Do I have to?" she grumbled, sipping at her drink, delaying her response a little longer.

"Only as much as you want to say. I'm not going to force you to say anything you're not ready to yet. Trust me, ma raised us to respect people's reluctance to open up. As frustrating as some people, like my brother, could be." He smiled, putting his own drink back down on the coffee table.

Keeping her hands firmly gripped around the warm mug, Robinne decided there wasn't much point in putting off telling someone, even a little bit, about the truth. Ralph was bound to have to have told someone anyway, with how she swiftly left the ranch house.

"I'll start from the beginning, if you don't mind."

Ryder nodded, "Wouldn't have it any other way."

She laughed, he was right after all.

"Okay, well… When I first came here, I made a list of all the cliché things I wanted to avoid when I started my new life here. These were things I'd read several times over in books, moments authors had written about several times as their go-to used phrase for a situation, moment, feeling, description etcetera. I didn't want to feel or go through anything like this, I wanted something…unique to happen, if it were to happen to me at all. Maybe something along those lines, but I didn't want to experience the typical things written about so much, I could pretty much predict an outcome, result or have the obvious pointed out to me. For example, every man is always written in a book as some sort of 'Greek God' or 'Adonis'. Always! Can't anyone think of some other way to describe a man? I know that's really irrelevant to how I'd experience something, but if I was going to meet a man, I didn't want that thought coming into my head. I wanted to see a man other than how people have always written a man to be, not all men are like that. Am I making sense?"

Ryder nodded. "So far, yes. Go on."

She continued after another sip of her drink.

"The list was full of these examples, such as the cliché 'zap feeling' when touching hands, the guy kissing the girl first, things like that. Somehow though, the list got lost. So, I let it go. I know what I want to avoid so, I didn't think much of losing it. After briefly panicking that is."

Ryder chuckled, motioning her to continue as he finished the remainder of his own drink.

"Cut to last night, when Ralph and I were in the barn together. Don't give me that look!" she wiggled a finger at a smirking Ryder. "Nothing indecent was going on there. Much. We were taking shelter from the downpour, when he saw the opportunity to be the first man to uh…to…t-to kiss me." Robinne could feel her cheeks go pink without even having to look at them. "I made the mistake, before the kiss happened, of opening up a little, to him. I wanted to be honest with him right from the beginning, including telling him the fact that I'd never been kissed before because I wanted it to be…memorable." The last word escaped her lips on a sigh.

"Was it?"

"Was it what?"

"Memorable."

The blush Robinne knew was on her cheeks, grew even warmer. "Oh, yes. It was. However, that's beside the point. He wanted to be the man to give me that memorable experience, and I didn't see why not. I trusted him to make it exactly how I'd dreamed my first kiss to be, and he delivered. Afterwards, after he uh…he kissed me, saying 'guess it was worth making the list after all'. He knew he'd slipped up when mentioning said list, as no one knows it even existed. There was no doubt in my mind as to which list he was referring to. The very list I'd lost."

Finishing the last of her drink, she put it back down on the coffee table, joining Ryder's now empty mug.

"I'd come to trust him, like I've come to trust all of you in the short time I've known you all. He knew how fragile my trust is, I've been screwed over, metaphorically, so many times, especially by those who've become the closest to me, and I didn't want that to happen when I moved here. It was one of the reasons I chose to move, among others."

Leaning forward, Ryder now wore a concerned expression. "Then what happened?"

"I said to his face that all he'd said to me leading up to the kiss was a ruse, a way of getting to check something off my list without me realising what he was doing. He didn't deny it. He tried to explain, probably, his reasoning for doing what he did, but I wasn't having any of it. In the moment I realised what he'd done, any ounce of trust I had left was gone."

Robinne realised now as she explained to Ryder, the remaining glimmers of happiness within her, had burned down to withering embers. She in no way had gotten over what had happened at the ranch, despite Ryder's efforts to comfort her here in his home. Yet, any remaining part of her which held onto happy feelings, dwindled rapidly with every word she uttered.

"It might not seem like much to anyone else, or anyone who's come to know me, but it is. To me. I might be overreacting, yes, but when something upsets me like *really* upsets me, it's usually something like this. Something which hurts me to the core. Well, what's left of it." she exhaled, fully sunken into the cozy chair.

Remaining silent for most of what she had to say, aside from telling her to continue a couple of times, Robinne watched as Ryder silently got up out of the chair he had acquisitioned, coming across the short space between them to sit in the chair directly beside hers. Reaching over, he took both of her hands in his, holding onto her like a big brother comforting his little sister.

"Nothing and I mean, nothing, about any of what you just said is insignificant in any way. Hurting someone isn't on no matter if you're hurt in a big or small way, if your feelings are hurt, that's what matters. Not what others may think of you. I've known my brother, well, all my life, and I know he like the other two, myself included, can be asses from time to time. Still, that fact doesn't give us any right to intentionally hurt someone else, regardless of how well we know them, we were raised better than that."

Never having had any siblings around her growing up, Robinne was entranced and in awe of Ryder's brotherly efforts to comfort and console her. Yet, she still didn't know how to respond to it. Being shunned by most people around her would do that to a person.

Before she could even think about how to respond, Ryder continued.

"You've already offloaded a great deal tonight, and if I'm right, there's probably a whole lot more to the story, right?"

Robinne nodded.

"Which you'll tell me in time I'm sure. Even if it isn't me, I know a very wise woman who's always willing to lend an ear. Ma'll worm it out of you even if you don't intentionally mention it, I'm sure."

She laughed, she could see Cassie doing this with her.

Stroking his thumb on the back of her hand, Ryder smiled at her. "Now, I don't know about you, but I'm pretty beat. There's no way in hell you're going back to your place tonight, I'd have my hide felt if I even tried, so you've got a few options. One, you can sleep in the guest bedroom until I can take you home tomorrow. Or two, you can sleep in the guest bedroom until I take you home tomorrow, which will it be?"

Laughing and tired as hell, Robinne removed her hands from Ryder's and gave him a hug, leaning back into her chair wearily afterwards. "I don't think I have much of a choice, now do I?"

Chuckling, Ryder shook his head.

"Nope. Now, go on with you. Go on up and use whatever you need to. I'll be puttering around down here for a bit, need to get a few things done."

Putting a hand gently on his forearm, Robinne smiled wearily.

"Ryder Jenkins, how the Dickens aren't you taken already?"

Patting her hand with his own, Ryder spared her a somewhat forlorn smile, while standing up and collecting their mugs.

"Guess the right girl just hasn't seen the me they want to see yet. Still, I'm happy to help a friend who truly deserves looking after."

I don't know about that, but thank you.

Not stopping to wait for her to answer, Ryder began making his way out of the living space, heading towards the kitchen, leaving Robinne to make her way to the guest room in her own time.

Someday, you'll find her Ryder. When you do, she'll be so lucky she'll count her blessings for you several times over every day.

Admittedly, Ryder was right about her being tired. The weight of the day's events had more than caught up with her, so she wasn't going to argue or fight against staying a night in the guest room. Her unexpected host for the night was busy washing dishes, while also listening to a country radio station on his kitchen radio when she passed by on her way upstairs, so she silently bid him a fond goodnight and made her way upstairs quietly.

The guest bedroom of Ryder's place was as lavishly and homely decorated as the rest of his home was. It wasn't made clear to her if many people had stayed in said guest room, but those who have should feel very privileged they did indeed. The bed in the middle of the far wall was grand in its own right, she'd never seen one so big well…ever! Ever read about those princess-style, four poster beds with the canopies on them? *This* was one of those beds, much to Robinne's delight. She'd always wanted one of these beds, now was her chance to sleep in one, even if it was just for the one night.

A small chandelier hung from the centre of the ceiling. Not too big as you'd might think a chandelier to be, but just right to fit the decent size of the room. The light within its centre shone just-so on the chandelier crystals, giving it an almost heavenly angelic, yet royal feeling, complementing the princess feeling of the bed below. Around the room were various dark-wooded pieces of furniture, all of which completed the look and overall cozy décor of the room, topped off nicely with scattered paintings in various shapes, sizes and content, around the room. She wasn't a girl who was big on art, however, these paintings were lovely and obviously reflected the owner of the house and suited the room well.

Sorry Ryder, but I'm stealing some of these ideas for my own room…

She'd get a chance to better look at the room tomorrow after she'd had a decent night's sleep. All she wanted to do right now was jump onto the massive bed, burrow under the covers and let all the worries of the day melt away with the onset of slumber soon to come to her. However, realising that she didn't plan on ending up here today, it dawned on Robinne that she didn't have anything with her to change into for the night.

"I suppose I could ask Ryder if I could borrow something…" she muttered to herself. Cracking the door open, she paused when she heard something other than the crooning voice of the radio coming from downstairs. Walking into the upstairs hallway, she paused just before the top of the stairs, listening to the two voices below.

It was evident and clearly obvious one of them was Ryder. The other, she wished she didn't know all too well.

What the hell…

"Just let me in God damn it! Let me see her!" Ralph's voice carried through the house to her, dripping in desperation.

"You know that's not going to happen, Ral. You fucked up big time."

"How would you know what happened?"

Robinne heard Ryder exhale, clearly torn between keeping what she said to him, private, and admitting the truth to his brother. He went with the former, surprisingly.

"What she told me tonight will stay between her and I, and what happened between the two of you which she didn't tell me, will stay between her and you. All I'm saying is, I'm the one who found her, listened to her and am giving her a bed for the night. The guest bed, and that's exactly all that's going to happen tonight. She's not in the mood to see you right now, brother. You know that. She needs time and as her friend, I'm going to see that she gets it."

No words could express how grateful Robinne was right now. No one had ever stood up for her and took care of her as much as Ryder has done tonight and on other occasions before. She knew they'd always only be friends, but considering all friends she had in her life left eventually for various reasons, she was truly touched that he was willing to forgo the brotherly connection between them both, to put her welfare first. She'd never ask him to do it in a million years, but she was starting to see what best friend material was truly made of.

Some may still find it a bit odd to have a man as a best friend, even in today's world where so much more is becoming widely talked about and accepted more than ever, but not to her. She had no problem what so ever considering a man her best friend, especially someone like Ryder. In fact, she welcomed it.

Shaking her head from her wandering thoughts, she resumed listening to the rich voices below her.

"Hell…I know." Ralph sighed. "I'm just…I'm just glad she's okay. I know I fucked up tonight, yet when she sped out of there, all I thought about was her safety. Even as ma chewed me out, I wanted to go out and search for her."

Why? Why would you go after someone you intentionally hurt?
It makes no sense.

"I'm not going to lie to you Ral, she's more cut up than fruit in a blender. That said, she's physically fine. Listen, go on home and trust in me to get her home safely tomorrow, okay? You have my word."

Peering over the top step of the stairs, she watched as Ryder reached out and put a hand on his brother's shoulder, who stood just out of sight on the other side of the door they'd come in when they arrived earlier.

"Yeah. Yeah I'll um…I'll do that. Goodnight. Um…tell her I said…never mind. Night." With heavy footsteps, Ralph she could only guess, headed back to however he arrived here, confirmed seconds later with Ryder closing the back door.

The weighty feeling that laid heavily on her chest upon hearing Ralph's voice, immediately vanished upon hearing the door close. Robinne never realised she was even feeling as tense as she was, until the feeling of relief washed over her like the biggest wave at a beach on a summer's day.

Why did you have to come Ralph?

Wasn't my running away from you a big enough clue that I don't want anything to do with you right now?

"It's safe to come out now Robinne." Ryder's honey-coated voice called up to her from below.

Huh…

Slowly standing up with her hand gripping the top of the staircase for support, she looked down at Ryder leaning against the wall at the bottom, meeting her gaze half with amusement, half with understanding.

"How did you know I was here?"

"Darlin', I built this place with my own two hands. I know every sound this place makes. Besides, your door was open."

Oh. Oops…

"Not to mention…" Ryder smirked as he continued. "I could see the top of your head poking up over the top step out of the corner of my eye." He chuckled.

Ah, hell.

"Yeah, stealth ninja isn't currently listed in my set of skills on my CV."

"Your what?"

"CV. Résumé to you guys."

"Ah." Ryder nodded, clearly not expecting any further explanation.

Walking carefully down the stairs as her wobbly legs would allow her, Robinne joined Ryder at the bottom, stopping level to his height on a step on the stairs.

"This may sound *so* rude of me but, why did you defend me like that? Why did you turn him away? He's your brother. An ass of the highest order but still, he's your brother."

Ryder tucked each hand under the opposite arm, remaining in his casual stance against the wall, back against it while facing her. "That he is, yes. However, I also know when right's right, and wrong is wrong. He was in the wrong, clearly."

"Got that right." She mumbled.

"Anyway, neither of you need to see the other tonight, despite what my idiot brother thinks. He needs time to think about what he did. As for you, I know I don't know you all that well yet but, I have the feeling you need time on your own while in the company of an ear who'll listen to you. If that makes sense."

A laugh escaped Robinne as she listened to Ryder. He was exactly right.

"Do you know what? If you weren't such an understanding, emotionally in tune, rare gem of a guy, you'd make a gal a really good sister BFF."

Robinne's remark earned a full-blown belly laugh from Ryder, a pleasant sound to this otherwise awful end to the day she wish she could forget.

"If you say so. I was just raised by a wonderful woman who taught her boys to show their emotions, rather than to 'be a man', whatever the hell that means these days. You don't have to be a man to be tough or brave, strong or to lead. Man or woman, you can do it I say."

"True that. How'd we get to this anyway?"

Ryder gently poked her right shoulder blade. "I believe you started this."

"Oh sure, blame the foreigner."

"Ah c'mon, you'll be one of us in no time. You'll see."

Robinne playfully rolled her eyes, as there was no way she was ever going to shed her inner or outer Brit, they'd just have to adapt to her level of awesome in their own time.

A second later, a yawn Robinne didn't know was there, escaped ungracefully from her lips, which prompted another kind smile from Ryder's face.

"Go on back up with you, I think we won't be disturbed for the rest of the night. I'll make us a special breakfast tomorrow morning before we head out, okay?" Ryder came over and gave her a brief hug before turning her in the direction to head on up back upstairs, giving her a gentle nudge up a step.

Robinne nodded, not arguing at all. She was tired, and that bed hadn't stopped calling her name from the moment she left the room.

"Goodnight, Ryder."

And…thank you.

Ryder simply tipped his imaginary hat to her, heading back to where he must've been when interrupted by his brother. Robinne herself made her way carefully back upstairs and into the guest room, closing the door behind her with care.

Once the door was closed behind her back, she inwardly cursed, suddenly remembering why she was leaving the room in the first place.

"Clothes. Bloody hell." She groaned, putting her palm to her face.

I suppose I could…sleep naked.

Ryder won't have to know. Well, kind of. He knows I don't have any clothes with me,

Stopping her own thoughts mid-thought, she went over to the chest of draws on the far side of the room pulling open a drawer, hoping to find something within here to wear.

"He must provide something for guests. Surely…aha!" she cried out in triumph. Upon opening lucky draw number three, she came across what was evidently a pair of male pyjamas. Not that it mattered to her, she was just glad she was able to find something after all without having to bother Ryder again. He'd already done enough for her as it is.

Slipping out of her clothes and into the slightly baggy on her body male pyjamas, she put her clothes in an unladylike pile on the chair next to the chest of draws, before gleefully jumping full bore onto the princess-style bed.

If anyone saw her now, they'd certainly deem her certifiably crazy or at the least, borderline childish. She didn't care about that either. The little things had always mattered most to her so enjoying one night in a bed like this, she was determined to enjoy it however the hell she wanted.

Her enjoyment was short-lived, as but a few moments later, she was interrupted by a louder than expected buzzing sound, coming from somewhere within the room.

What the…

Oh! My phone!

Never one to be on her phone much, she'd completely forgotten the fact it must've fallen out of her jeans pocket at some point. Probably when she was undressing just now. Then again, she was much more focused on belly-flopping on the bed than anything else.

Sitting up, she looked over at where she'd undressed and low and behold, on the floor was her phone happily buzzing away. Deciding not to put off whoever was calling her, she got up off the bed and retrieved her phone, only to pick it up just in time for it to ring off.

"Bloody hell."

A second later, a notification popped up informing her that she had one voicemail to listen to. She clicked on said notification, hoping to listen to it and dive under the covers for the final time that night, not intending to come out any time before morning. Once more, someone 'up there' must have decided that this wouldn't be the case, as the voice that played in her ear was one she'd not long heard downstairs.

'Robinne, darlin'. Its um…it's me. It's…its Ralph. I didn't expect you to pick up, I wouldn't if I were you. I don't deserve even a second of your time right now, but darlin', please just listen to this. Please. I don't need to point out the obvious, I don't want to hurt you any more than I already have. If I've fucked things up for us for good, please let this be the one time I'll get to say this to you. Sorry won't even cut it close, and I

don't expect you to take any lesser apology than the highest of which you deserve. I don't know what that is yet, but I'll spend however long it takes to figure it out, while I give you space. I know we've not spent the longest time together. In fact, I wish I had spent more time getting to know you before I royally put my foot in it. You've spent more time with my brother than you have with me, lucky guy. Anyway, I called to make a promise to you. I promise from the very bottom of my Texas born heart, that I won't step a foot near you, come within spittin' distance or even make contact with you, at all, until you're ready to see my ugly mug again. There's a whole lot more to you than I thought was ever there to discover, which doesn't really say a lot about me, but I'm holding my hands up here and admitting I was wrong. Darlin', what I feel growing inside of me isn't something a person feels for another friend, and I wish I had the chance to say this to your face and maybe someday, I will. For now, know that I mean every word of this voicemail from the stubborn, stupid, asshat of a cowboy I am. Until I get to lay my eyes on the other half of me again, please take care. Look after yourself. Spread your heavenly light to those who deserve to receive your love, warmth and so, so much more. Until we meet again, goodbye Robinne. I'm sorry."

Three beeps rang loudly down the phone, signalling the end of the lengthy voicemail message. No words or thoughts entered Robinne's mind as she robotically lowered the phone from her ear, allowing it to bounce onto the pile of clothes below.

Without knowingly doing so, she found herself the next moment, sitting on the side of the mattress. Knowing he wasn't able to see her to know that she was safe, Ralph must have waited until he'd left Ryder's place to leave her a message of what he wanted to say to her in person. He said so in the voice message. Neither was she expecting such a passionate, heartfelt and genuine promise, apology and plea all in one from someone who'd just ripped her very being in two.

Laying down on the bed, she grabbed the overly plump pillow, burying her head within it. Soon enough, her body was wracked with sobs she had forced down deep inside her when she woke in Ryder's truck. Crying had always been her outlet to off lay any stress or pent-up emotion when no one was around for her to offload the tension onto. Yes Ryder was downstairs, but she was in no state of mind to move from the very spot she'd collapsed into.

Seeing as the tears didn't look or feel like they were going to stop any time soon, Robinne clutched the pillow as tight she could against her weary body, holding on for what would be the longest cry of her life since the last man who'd broken her heart.

She held onto the pillow for dear life, as if it were the last thing that was holding her, connecting her to the very Earth she lived on, right up until the moment her mind, body and soul decided to put her out of her misery, granting her what she could only hope was a peaceful slumber.

Damn you Ralph Jenkins.

Damn you…
At last, she was granted the blissful darkness.
Peace.

CHAPTER TWELVE
~ Robinne ~

Dragging his ass out of bed was easier than he imagined it would be, considering how late he'd gotten home last night, how little sleep he had, he was downright impressed with himself. He had no right to be, of course. Considering what he'd done to someone who'd come to mean so much to him in such a short time, he deserved all that was thrown at him in return.

Saddling up his trusty horse Chance, he glanced on over to the barn which was situated across from the stables, over to where his colossal ass of a mistake took place not even twenty four hours ago. He could bet his bottom dollar that he wasn't the one who was thinking about it the most, but his conscience be damned, he couldn't get it out of his mind if he wanted to.

He hadn't gone back in there since he followed Robinne's more than hasty exit, he'd asked one of the twins to lock it up and take care of the chores that required going into there, today. He was as ready to enter into there again as Robinne was about seeing him.

Robinne.

Never before had he physically ached for someone in anything other than a primal need to work off some extra energy, or just getting off with someone because he was honest in admitting he was horny. He wasn't any different than any other male his age, or any male in general for that matter, but he also wasn't a tail chaser. He'd had a few meaningful relationships in the past, yet none of those he could see lasting or making it to a lifetime commitment. He did have a few go-to women who he'd call up if he ever got *that* desperate in needing release, but he wasn't like his brothers when it came to using those women for booty calls. No, the few, and by few he literally meant two, women, that he called, were also on call for other things other than sex. If he needed a date to something, he'd call them. If he needed a plus one to an event, he'd call them and vice versa. They were two of his good friends, and treated them with the upmost highest respect as he'd do his buddies.

So why did I go ahead with my foolish idea knowing Robinne would eventually find out?

Because I'm stupid, that's why.

He's not too 'man enough' to admit when he was wrong, or when he did the more than occasionally stupid thing. In fact, stupid was a common theme among his brothers. He just never thought he'd be lumped in with them more so than not. On more than one occasion did he have to bail or make amends for something one of his brothers had done, with the pleasure of tanning their hides going to Pa, of course.

Mounting Chance, he guided them out of the stall and the stable, out into the beginning of what would no doubt be a long day. The sun was just beginning to rise over the horizon, marking the official start to the day for any rancher nor only here in Texas, but across the whole country wherever a rancher laid his hat. It was in any rancher's blood to rise this early, even when not on a ranch. If you didn't rise early, you weren't a true rancher. Period.

As he rode Chance out of the back end of the house property towards the path leading to back pastures, he couldn't help but think back to the events of the night before after he'd watched Robinne speed off out of the driveway in Ryder's truck. What happened shortly after had greatly surprised him greatly.

* * *

Ralph, standing with his mouth agog at what he was seeing, witnessed an upset Robinne booking it out of his parents' drive as if her own house was on fire. How had it got to this so fast? Things seemed to just…escalate, way beyond what he thought the consequences of his actions would be, should ever she find out what he'd done.

"What on God's good Earth is going on out here?" his Pa's voice called out from behind him, filled with deep concern and confusion.

Turning, he reluctantly met his father's gaze with what he knew was a guilty expression plastered all over his own face. He might be nearly thirty, but he turned instantly into a teenage boy full of guilt when he had to admit something to his father.

Exhaling, Ralph raised his lowered, shameful head.

"Robinne, Pa. She left."

"Why would she leave?" Joe said, raising a curious brow. "Did you do something to upset her?"

Nothing snuck past his father, even if it was something painfully obvious. He had to come clean, no use trying to cover this doozy up.

"Could we do this inside? I don't want you getting sick in this rain."

"Son I was out in many a rain when I was your age, a little drop won't do me no harm. Come on now, let's go into my study so we can talk."

If there was one thing he admitted about his father, is that no matter what he'd done, he wouldn't receive any anger off of his father. He wouldn't be shouted at or physically rebuked for anything he got up to, the disappointment from his father, even if it was just a look, was enough to make Ralph realise what he'd done and see the error of his ways. He had a feeling tonight would be no different.

Once inside his father's study, he sat down in one of the chairs opposite the grand desk his father used to go over the ranch finances and other such things which required a huge desk such as this. He and his father were soon joined by his mother, whom was also sporting a concerned look much like his father's own.

"What's going on sweetheart?" his mother softly asked him, sitting down in the chair next to his own.

"I think that's what the boy is about to explain, my love." Joe said as he sat in his chair at the desk, giving him a commanding presence within the room. "Go on son, tell us what happened."

Rubbing the bridge of his nose and using the back of the chair on his own back for support, he began to tell them a play-by-play of what had happened at the barbeque earlier tonight.

"I might as well start from the beginning. Things would make more sense that way." He cleared his throat. "When I helped finish off Robinne's house, we must've gone to celebrate or something, I don't really remember. Next thing I'm aware of, something hits my uh…rear end, and I wake up with no clothes on in Robinne's upstairs bedroom."

His father's expression didn't change as he began his story, whereas his mother, her cheeks pinked as she was no doubt picturing and imagining what I was like for Robinne to find him like that.

He continued.

"After a brief, and rather heated conversation, she asked me to leave. I wasn't going to argue, as even though I had no idea what I was doing there I had no intention to stay. I phoned for a ride when I noticed this piece of paper. It was a list of some sort. Things were written on there that she didn't want to experience or have happen to her when she started over here. My intention was to prove her wrong. Not in the malicious sense, mind you. I thought I could show her that not every cliché is a bad thing, but something that can be tweaked and made unique to her so she can feel…special. I didn't want her to know that I was doing these things for her, because she'd feel reluctant to go through with them if I had told her I found the list and what I planned to do. So, when I got home I went about planning just how I could carry out each thing without her knowing. Only, I didn't get too far into the list before I inadvertently blarted it out in the barn last night."

"What were you doing in the barn with Robinne?" his mom asked softly.

"Not what you two are thinking, I'm sure No, I was giving her a tour of the close buildings on the property when the heavens opened. The closest building which wasn't completely locked up for the night was the barn. I got us inside and we sat for a short while, sheltering from the storm which still hasn't let up, and she started opening up to me. I thought this would be the perfect opportunity to give her, her first kiss, without things getting too heated as they often do in ranch barns. Pa." He directed this and a smirk at his father, who'd caught more than one of his brothers on more than one occasion, in said barn with an amorous female. "So, I kissed her. All in good name I swear to you both. Nothing about that kiss was about simply striking a thing off her list. It may have started out that way when I first picked up the list, but after kissing her, it wasn't any longer."

Ralph paused, rubbing his temple this time.

It became so much more…

"After the kiss, I stupidly asked her if it was worth putting on her list about her first kiss cliché. Instantly, she knew what I was on about, to my surprise that I'd actually asked her. To say she was even upset instantly is a serious understatement. She seemed…destroyed, emotionally. I chased after her when she suddenly booked it out of the barn, but she was too fast for me and she got out of here, somehow using Ryder's truck. That's the whole story."

His father who had been silent throughout his explanation of the series of events up until now, leaned forward, elbows resting on the desk which supported his clasped hands under his chin, looking at Ralph with deep and intense eyes. Much to Ralph's surprise, he didn't look disappointed as he was expecting him to. In fact, he wasn't sure what his father was thinking.

Well, this is new…

What is he thinking?

His thoughts were soon answered.

"What do you intend to do to set this straight, Ralph?" his father asked, his tone giving nothing away as to what he was really thinking.

Uh oh.

No judgement, no disappointment…this is new.

What's he thinking? I wonder…

Sitting back up, Ralph gripped the arms of the chair, the decorated ends digging into the delicate flesh of his palms. "Honestly, I need to think on it tonight. I already rushed into many a bad decision, I don't want to do it again. If I can help it."

A hand touched his right arm gently. Turning in its direction, he saw his mother looking at him with the same concerned face as what she entered the room with. It was hard for Ralph to know what she was thinking either. He wasn't even sure he really wanted to know.

"I see." His father said, rising from behind his desk. Ralph turned his head back to his father, who now stood at the window looking out on the storm still raging on outside. "Cass, dear, make sure Hannah and Niall have a room each for the night upstairs, I don't want them driving home in this."

"I wouldn't dream of it either. Come join me after I settle them in, I'll run you a bath before bed." His mother kissed his father on the cheek tenderly, a love of youth still ever present in her eye after all their years of marriage.

That is yet another thing he admired about his parents and their marriage, no matter how many years pass from the day they got married, the same spark of love remained as if they were 25 forever. He hoped he was as lucky as them to have the same someday, but with his current actions with Robinne, he was unlikely to keep a woman if he treated them like that.

Marriage to Robinne wouldn't be bad at all.

Wait.

Why am I thinking about marrying her? What does this mean?

Do I…Am I…?

"Ralph." His father's commanding voice called out to him, bringing him out of his daydream.

"Yes?" he answered without hesitation, as he was only called his name by his Pa when he knew he meant business. Usually he was 'son' or 'my boy', today, he was Ralph, and he was in trouble.

"You're to stay here tonight too, in your old room. In the morning after you've completed what needs to be done, you're free to do what you need to do. Am I understood?"

Ralph nodded.

"Yes Pa. Thank you."

His father nodded, not needing to say anymore. Ralph bid his Pa a goodnight, quietly leaving the study and closing the door shut behind him. He wasn't quite sure how to deal with his Pa when he was like this. Non-judgemental. When he was mad, angry or disappointed in him, he knew how to act and what to do to make amends.

Well, they do say you learn something new every day.

This is THAT something new, and I sure am learning.

Not wanting to confront any of his brothers, for at least tonight, Ralph swiftly made his way up to his old bedroom. He hadn't stayed in his room since he'd turned twenty one, the self-same day his parents gave him the keys to his own place, proclaiming that now he was a man, he was entitled to the things left to him in his grandfather's will. The same applied to his brothers when they turned twenty one respectively. For him though, he was the first to leave home being the eldest, so he'd been the one away the longest. As the baby of the family and having only recently turned twenty one, Roland was the newest Jenkins son to receive his key. He was still in the process of moving out, as he's been busy building Robinne's place, so his stuff was all over the place as Ralph made his way into his bedroom.

Laying on his old single bed, hands behind his head while staring up at the ceiling, Ralph had no idea how much time had passed since he'd entered the room. All he knew though, was that he now knew what he was planning to do to start making it up to Robinne.

However, before he could think about how he was going to go about executing his idea, more than one voice sounded like they were coming from just outside his room somewhere in the hallway. Since he'd already resigned himself to not sleeping much tonight anyway, he leapt up off the bed and yanked open his bedroom door, sticking his head out in the direction of the voices.

Two pairs of concerned eyes met his own. His younger brother Ryder and youngest brother, Roland, were both speaking out in the hallway. At least they were until he'd interrupted them. They didn't look pleased to see him once they'd turned to see what had interrupted them. Then again, he wouldn't be pleased to see his own reflection right now, so he totally got why he was getting the look he was from both of them.

"What's going on out here?" he gingerly asked.

Both brothers put their hands on their hips, shoulders rigid, a stance well known for being less than impressed with someone. They clearly would've heard from either his Pa or Ma what's gone down by now.

"We're having a discussion. Sorry, did we wake you?" Ryder spoke first, his voice oozing sarcasm. Not unusual for any of them really, but this time, he knew *why* his brother sounded that way.

Damn.

Exhaling, he emerged from his room enough to lean dejectedly against the doorjamb. "You both know I couldn't possibly sleep right now." he swallowed. "What's going on out here?" he asked softly, hoping to get a less frosty response this time.

Dropping his hands from his hips, Roland turned to face him.

"We're going after Robinne."

We? Who's we?

The statement, despite him asking what was going on, still surprised him, making him literally stand up in attention.

"Why? Has something happened to her? Is she okay?"

Before he could advance towards them, Ryder held up his hands, indicating that he wasn't to take another step.

"Slow down there partner. I said we, as in Rol and I. You're not going anywhere."

He knew his hands were balled into tight fists, but that wasn't his soul focus right now. Robinne was.

"Why do you get to decide what I do? You're not the boss of me, you're my brother, and as far as I'm aware of, we do things together around here. Or did you forget that?"

Roland went to take a step forward towards him, his own head turning in his direction to face whatever was going to come his way. Or he would have if Ryder hadn't put his arm up across where Roland was about to walk, stopping him in his tracks.

Ryder came to stand in front of him instead.

"I get why you're acting like an ass right now, however that's no excuse for you to talk to us like you've got a stick up where the sun doesn't shine. To answer your question yes, Robinne is fine, as far as we know. We, and by we I mean Rol and I, plus the twins if they're able, are going to go look for her because she's not used to driving the roads in these conditions. YOU are not going anywhere because you're not thinking straight, you're more prone to making rash decisions and the last thing we need is you getting yourself hurt in the process. I'm only going on Pa's orders, and from what I heard of your talk, you've been confined to your old room till things are settled. Am I right?"

You damned well know you are.

Inwardly and outwardly sighing, Ralph's shoulders slumped with the fact that he couldn't deny what his brother was saying. He *was* right. Sometimes, he felt and knew for sure that his younger brothers, despite himself being the eldest, knew better than he and were way more mature on more than one occasion. Like now, for instance.

For the billionth time since mucking things up, he rubbed the bridge of his nose before meeting Ryder's gaze again, Roland watching on from behind him still.

"Look, I'm sorry. That word and its meaning won't mean jack to anyone at the moment but, I am. Just, go out and find her and please, make sure she's safe. Look after her. Both of you." He directed to the two of them, turning back towards the doorway to his bedroom.

"Ralph", Roland's voice called to him, stopping his stride. He turned his head and looked over his shoulder. "Yeah?"

"We got this, brother. We'll let you know when we find her. We'll take care of her." Roland nodded to him, a silent vow passing between the two of them.

Returning his nod, he reluctantly retreated back into his bedroom, closing the door behind him.

Time crawled by slower than a snail's pace as Ralph waited for news from at least one of his brothers, that Robinne had been found safe and sound. He hated cooling his heels when he could be helping, or doing something productive to contribute to the overall effort. Yet, he understood why he had to sit this one out. Even if it meant taking orders from his younger brother, he knew when to hold back when it was necessary.

Rain still continued to cascade down outside his bedroom window, rattling the windows themselves within their very frames. There wasn't one part of him right now that wishes he could've done something to prevent Robinne being out there, all of him wishes it was him instead. Nothing could change anything now, yet he still foolishly held onto a small hope that it would.

Somewhere within the somewhat empty house, he heard a door open and slam closed, interrupting the sad train that was his own thoughts. Sitting up bolt upright, he waited a moment to try and hear who had return, secretly hoping that whoever had, that they're brought Robinne with them. None of the muffled voices coming from downstairs sounded remotely like a woman's, not one.

Where are you Robinne?
Please be okay.
Please.

A knock sounded at his door, followed by the self-same door opening ever so slightly. "Ralph, son. Could you come out here for a moment please?" His father's unmistakable voice asked him. He daren't say no, so he got up off his bed without hesitation, joining his father out in the hallway.

"What's going on Pa? Is everything alright? Did they find her--" he stopped short when his father raised a single hand in between them, indicating that he should stop his bombardment of questions.

His father lowered his hand again, a calm expression permanently etched onto his face with what looked like rain coating lightly every inch of his exposed skin and now damp clothes.

So Pa had been out there too…

Inwardly, Ralph sighed. He didn't like the idea of his Pa out in this weather as much as he didn't like the idea of Robinne being out in it, but as mentioned to him many times before, his father was a tough man and he'd lived through many a Texas storm. He wasn't a novice by any means, which means he knows when to call it quits. It gave him some sense of comfort as he prepared for his father to continue.

"Everything's fine. We found her. It was Ryder, actually. Found her on the side of the road. Smart girl to have pulled over rather than carry on driving without assistance. Last I heard, she followed him back to his place where I believe she's taking shelter from the shitstorm outside."

Thank you God.
Thank you.

Nothing could describe how thankful, yet relieved he was. He'd already resigned to caring less about himself, but as of right this moment, he allowed a momentary lapse and thanked whoever was above that she was safe, and that he'd been granted a chance to someday make things right again.

"I'm…I'm glad."

"So you should be. Now, I'm beat. I'm turning in for the night." His father patted his shoulder, casually walking around him towards his own bedroom. "Oh, by the way." He looked over his shoulder at Ralph. "Don't do anything rash. Do what's right."

No other words were exchanged between them as his father made his way into his bedroom, no doubt to shower and join his wife in snuggling down for the night. He wished he could do the same right about now, having someone to hold in his own arms for the night. However, that wasn't going to be the case for what he knew would be for quite some time yet.

Before he could even think about sleeping, there was something that he needed to do. He had to simmer down the desire inside of him, the desire which physically craved to see that Robinne was truly safe, even for just a second. Without any further ado and with perhaps the same haste as she, Ralph fled the house, jumped in his own truck, and headed towards his brother's place.

I'm coming Robinne. I'm coming.

To say that once he'd arrived at Ryder's place, that he would be met with a less than happy demeanour from his brother, would be one of the many underestimations added to his list recently. Though he didn't physically say what he was thinking, being so close to Ryder in age gave Ralph the ability to read his brother better than any of his others, and what he was currently reading wasn't anything worth recommending to anyone else.

"Just let me in God damn it! Let me see her!" he demanded, his voice dripping in desperation.

"You know that's not going to happen, Ral. You fucked up big time."

"How would you know what happened?"

Ryder exhaled.

"What she told me tonight will stay between her and I, and what happened between the two of you which she didn't tell me, will stay between her and you. All I'm saying is, I'm the one who found her, listened to her and am giving her a bed for the night. The guest bed, and that's exactly all that's going to happen tonight. She's not in the mood to see you right now, brother. You know that. She needs time and as her friend, I'm going to see that she gets it."

"Hell...I know." Ralph sighed. "I'm just...I'm just glad she's okay. I know I fucked up tonight, yet when she sped out of there, all I thought about was her safety. Even as ma chewed me out, I wanted to go out and search for her."

Ryder exhaled, leaning his body against the doorjamb.

"I'm not going to lie to you Ral, she's more cut up than fruit in a blender. That said, she's physically fine. Listen, go on home and trust in me to get her home safely tomorrow, okay? You have my word."

His brother reached out and put a hand on his shoulder, Ralph stood just out of sight on the other side of the door, catching the full force of the icy wind and rain on his back.

Thank you, brother.

"Yeah. Yeah I'll um…I'll do that. Goodnight. Um…tell her I said…never mind. Night." With heavy footsteps, Ralph made his way back over to his truck, climbing straight inside as he'd left it unlocked from when he'd arrived on the property.

The door to Ryder's placed closed the second he got inside his truck.

"Guess he won't be watching me go then." He muttered to himself, expecting nothing less than a less than sarcastic reply from himself in return he was sure.

Coming up with not even a sarcastic response to his own statement, Ralph fired up the ignition, put the truck into reverse, turning it around until he faced the gravel path in which he was now leaving down.

He was extremely disappointed that he didn't get to see even a glimpse of Robinne, not even a whisper of hair or the tip of her finger. After all, that was the whole point in which he'd come out here in the first place. If he knew he'd be turned away at the door, he wouldn't have made the journey.

Yet you came anyway, you hopeless fool.

His brother had every right to turn him away, he thought as he drove back down the now slightly flooded gravel path, his father did warm him that Ryder was taking care of her. Who knew he'd pull the whole big brother routine with her, on his own big brother!

At least he could rest a little easier knowing she was actually alright. Not that he'd ever doubted the word of his father in the first place, but he was always the sort of guy who liked to physically see things himself to be more than somewhat calm, content or relaxed.

The weariness of the night's events finally started to creep up on him as he made his way out of the end of Ryder's property. There was only one place he could think of, besides his home or the main ranch, where he could sit a spell and take the time to reflect. A place he'd always gone to when he needed to do some serious thinking and recoup without interruption.

Decision made, he headed for his infamous spot.

Why did his neck hurt? Why was he so cold? Was that…was that…drool? With quite a bit of effort, Ralph managed to prise his eyes open, his face still plastered against…a steering wheel?

Oh, right. The river…

In no time at all, where he was and why came back to him quicker than a horse to brand new hay. Sitting up in a more natural, less painful position, he stretched out all the bunched up muscles from his previously uncomfortable slouch.

He'd parked up at the river, the place he'd always find himself ending up at when he needed to be alone. Or when he needed time to think. Hard. No one knew that he came here, not even his parents and they knew everything about him and his brothers. Including several things he had no idea how the hell they knew about.

The river in question he'd pulled up at, was the self-same river that flowed directly behind Robinne's place.

Robinne…

Glancing out at the storm which never seemed like it was ever going to end outside of his truck window, Ralph ran a hand slowly down his face. He didn't mean to fall asleep in the place he was supposed to be doing some serious thinking. Though he suspected it hadn't probably been a long a sleep as first thought.

Before he could debate the fact any further, a light vibration came from his front right pants pocket. Fishing it out as fast as he could, he picked up the call without stopping to check who it was calling on his caller ID.

"Hello?!"

"Sweetheart, where are you?"

"Ma."

Of course, it was his mother. The little bubble of hope within him, burst. He was foolish to think a miracle just happened, where instead of his mother who was calling, it would be Robinne. Not that he didn't regret his mother calling. Ever.

"Sweetie, I know you left. Where have you gone to?" concern riddled her voice.

"I'm on the way back from Ryder's place, Ma."

Technically, he wasn't lying. He was on the way back, he'd just, taken a little unannounced detour.

"Well, please hurry on home. Be careful, of course. Just, come home."

"I will, Ma. I'll be there shortly, I promise."

"I love you, Ralph."

"Love you too, Ma."

His mother hung up the phone, ending the brief call between them. Cassandra Jenkins was a woman of few words when it came to ordering around her sons, even with a motherly touch. If she told you do so something, you listened. Or else you wouldn't be fed that night.

Starting up his truck, he pulled away from his private spot and headed for the warmth of the main ranch house. He'd do his thinking in his old bedroom when he'd made it back through not only the storm outside of his truck, but when the one inside his own heart had calmed down too.

Ralph arrived back at the main ranch house not long after he'd finished on the phone with his mom. It wasn't clear to him upon getting out of his truck, if anyone in the house was up watching him come in, as there weren't any lights on giving anyone from within away.

Once back in his old room and still in his clothes, he laid back down on his bed in the same position he'd been in before he'd spoken to his brothers in the hallway. On his way up, he didn't encounter anyone else from his family, meaning his suspicions about them being down for the night when he arrived, were confirmed. Hannah and Niall would've been out like a light after being shown their rooms, he knew they were early to bed these days anyway, even when they weren't staying at the ranch.

None of that mattered much to him at the moment, including how tired he was. Sleep could wait. There was one more thing he had to do. Fishing his phone out of his pocket for what would be the final time tonight, he sat up, pulled up Robinne's number, and hit dial. As he predicted, his call went straight to voicemail. Taking a deep breath, he began his message.

"Robinne, darlin'. Its um…it's me. It's…its Ralph. I didn't expect you to pick up, I wouldn't if I were you. I don't deserve even a second of your time right now, but darlin', please just listen to this. Please. I don't need to point out the obvious, I don't want to hurt you any more than I already have. If I've fucked things up for us for good, please let this be the one time I'll get to say this to you. Sorry won't even cut it close, and I don't expect you to take any lesser apology than the highest of which you deserve. I don't know what that is yet, but I'll spend however long it takes to figure it out, while I give you space. I know we've not spent the longest time together. In fact, I wish I had spent more time getting to know you before I royally put my foot in it. You've spent more time with my brother than you have with me, lucky guy. Anyway, I called to make a promise to you. I promise from the very bottom of my Texas born heart, that I won't step a foot near you, come within spittin' distance or even make contact with you, at all, until you're ready to see my ugly mug again. There's a whole lot more to you than I thought was ever there to discover, which doesn't really say a lot about me, but I'm holding my hands up here and admitting I was wrong. Darlin', what I feel growing inside of me isn't something a person feels for another friend, and I wish I had the chance to say this to your face and maybe someday, I will. For now, know that I mean every word of this voicemail from the stubborn, stupid, asshat of a cowboy I am. Until I get to lay my eyes on the other half of me again, please take care. Look after yourself. Spread your heavenly light to those who deserve to receive your love, warmth and so, so much more. Until we meet again, goodbye Robinne. I'm sorry."

Hanging up the call, he let his phone drop to where it would stay for the rest of the night, on his bedroom floor. He didn't care if it had broken or not, cracked the screen or not, when he himself was breaking in two with every stupid decision he made. There was only one thing he hoped for right now, and that was he wished he hadn't made another one by leaving her that voicemail.

Groaning, Ralph cracked his eyes open for the second time that night. Turning his head towards his bedroom window, he could still see nothing but pitch black outside, indicating that not much time had passed since he must've fallen asleep.

The clock beside his bed displayed 2:30AM, confirming his slumber was only brief, as he'd arrived back at the house a short while after 1:00AM. Knowing he was in for a night of restless sleep, he decided to make the most of this moment of temporary consciousness.

Soon seated in the dark at the table in his parents' kitchen, he held a glass of something stronger than water between his hands, rolling it gently back and forth, not having touched a single drop yet. It was a highly unlikely thing that he would actually touch any of it before he wound his way back up to bed, but things could change.

A moment later, his thoughts were once again interrupted by the sudden switching on of the kitchen lights, illuminating the dark cloud which had fallen over Ralph's world since Robinne's departure. Looking up, the small form that was his mother, stood by the kitchen doorway, her hand still lingering on the switch she'd just flipped on.

"Sweetheart, what are you doing down here on your own in the dark?"

"Just thinking, Ma."

"You mustn't worry yourself so much." She said as she came towards him, holding her night robe together with her right hand, placing her left on his shoulder.

Easier said than done Ma.

"Easy to say when you're not the sort of person who makes these kind of colossal mistakes."

"Oh sweetheart, if only you knew. Just because I'm your mother, doesn't mean I haven't been guilty of a thing or two."

He smirked.

"You must enlighten me one of these days."

"Maybe. Maybe. Now, what's that handsome head of yours thinking about. Humour me." She took a seat beside him.

The smirk vanished from his face the moment she asked him to humour her. She was the last person he wanted to snap at because of this, yet he knew if he tried to put it off, she wouldn't relent unless he'd confided in her. Just another reason he admired his mother, her tenacity.

"Yeah, Ma. *Her.* I don't deserve to feel the way I do. I wasn't the one who got hurt, I *did* the hurting. Yet, I feel as I'm being split in two. I've only known her a short time but...I've come to care for her. In more ways than a friend should care for another. I wanted to get to know her better, do things for her, I just...messed everything up in the process. She came here looking for a new life free of hurt and deception, I gave her both in spades." He hung his head, defeated.

A small hand belonging to his mother, touched his forearm, radiating gentleness and comfort.

"Sweetheart, where I do believe what you did is wrong, and yes you'll atone for it in your own way, but the way you're feeling now, it shows you're genuinely feeling remorse for your actions. If you felt sorry for yourself and only for yourself, that instead would be wrong. You're a smart young man, Ralph, we've raised you right. You've got a smart head on your shoulders and aside from being your mother, I can clearly see in your eyes that she genuinely means a lot to you and that's why you're feeling this so much. If you felt sorry for yourself because you want to make things right so you didn't, she wouldn't mean a dot to you. It doesn't matter if we've known someone for a hot minute or a lifetime, if we hurt them and regret it, we know they mean something more to us than just accidentally hurting a stranger in the street and apologising for your actions. It only took one foolish action to put the brakes on the start of your friendship with Robinne, yes. However, you have a *lifetime* to make it up to her and make things right to hopefully produce a place where the two of you want to be. Okay?"

Woah. He knew his mother was a wise woman, though just how wise she was became truly clear to him just now.

Pushing his glass away from him, he stood up out of his chair and planted a soft kiss on his mother's cheek. "Someone should give you a medal or something Ma, your advice is truly worth gold."

His mother smiled fondly at him, patting his hand.

"When you're a parent yourself someday, you'll see for yourself."

A parent huh? A child with Robinne does sound appealing.

With one final peck to her cheek, he bid his mother goodnight and headed back to his bedroom, feeling a little lighter than when he'd first come downstairs.

Settled back in his room, this time inside of his bed, Ralph let his eyes close for what would be a short sleep before he had to get up at sunrise, his heart a little more hopeful that he could actually set things right for the person who truly deserved it.

* * *

Thinking back on it, the events of last night after Robinne had left, combined with the lack of sleep, in a way were worth it. She'd been found safe and well, she was being cared for by his brother, he'd spoken to his parents respectively and eventually came to a rational and realistic way to set right his wrongs with Robinne. It was just a shame that it all had to happen for him to learn his biggest life lesson yet.

Beneath his strong thighs, Chance moved, eager to get going at a faster pace than the two of them were currently going down this slightly drier path. The weather had well and truly gave the Earth a good dose of rain, which was good for the plants and such things of the like, it just made getting around a little more difficult if your main mode of transport was a horse.

Guess I'll be giving this boy a big clean-up when I get back. Whenever that'll be.

"Alright boy, let's see what needs to be done then shall we? He-yah!" gently kicking Chance's sides, the two set off at a faster pace through the muddy ground, heading for the ranch's furthest border fence and pasture.

CHAPTER THIRTEEN
~ Robinne ~

Sundays had never been Robinne's favourite day of the week. She hated them even more than everyone collectively hated Mondays, if that was possible. It was. Even more so considering what she went through the night before. Remembering it the second she opened her eyes was torture of the highest order. At least it was for now.

By now, she was sure that at least Ralph's parents would've known what went down or at least, more than just one of his brothers. Minus Ryder. He would've known about it one way or another, a backwards perk of sorts for him being adopted as her new best friend.

Speaking of Ryder, it must be him who'd created this delicious smell which was the only thing that was tempting Robinne to peel herself out of this more than comfortable bed. Of course it was Ryder, no one else lived here and by her own intuition, no one would dare try and come near her until a suitable amount of time had passed since the incident. She hoped.

Wasting no time in diving into her thoughts for longer than she had to, she stripped out of the clothes she'd gone to bed in, folded them up on the bed, dressed in her clothes from the night before which had been left just outside of her room when she'd come back from washing her face, and made her way downstairs to meet face-to-face with what was creating that mouth-watering smell.

She wasn't disappointed by what she was met with.

Happily munching away on his own breakfast, Ryder had cooked up what could only be described as a modern day replica of a medieval feast, which was currently spread out across the entire space of his kitchen island counter. Minus a few spots where his and her plates were situated.

"Mornin'. Sleep well?" Ryder asked with a mouth full of food.

"Good morning." She blinked, sitting down on the stool waiting for her. "I…I slept ok. Thank you." Picking up her plate, she piled on a modest amount of food to start off with. "This looks incredible. You didn't have to do all of this just for the two of us."

Ryder shrugged.

"Habit. I'm used to cooking up at the main house for everyone when we get together, it's a hard one to get out of when it's just me here on me own. Or rather, when I have a friend or two here on the odd occasion."

"Do you have many friends join you then?"

He shook his head. "Not as often as I'd like but, you know, they've got lives of their own. I'm just happy they still come round when they do."

She nodded, tucking into her food. "Well…" she swallowed a mouthful, "I'm thankful for this. Though I don't know how much of it I'll be able to eat. I'm not that big of an eater."

"No bother. Most of it can be re-heated or eaten cold. Eat what you can." He smiled, chugging down the rest of what she assumed was coffee in his cup. Americans did love their morning coffees, after all.

They ate the rest of their respective breakfast amounts with admirable comfort, much to Robinne's relief. Ryder never brought up the events of the night before, including any of the words that they'd spoken to one another. Another thing she was silently grateful for. It was as if he had a spy inside her mind that told him she needed space to figure things out, with him giving her just that.

"So," Ryder started to say as he and Robinne began to clear things away. "I've got to head on over to a buddy's ranch fairly soon, he needs an extra hand for an hour or two. Would you be wanting dropped off home? Or would you like to join me?"

As much as she would love to say yes and join him at where he had to be that morning, she decided to go against it and stick with her new home. She could get on with whatever she wanted to do. Or not. Whatever took her fancy. There wasn't much she was in the mood for right now.

"Thank you but, I think I'll go home. If that's alright with you, I don't want you to think that I don't want to be around you."

"Not at all, it didn't even cross my mind. I feel the same, I'm more at ease when I'm in my own home too." Ryder finished washing up their plates before turning to her, "I'll meet you out by my truck in 10?"

She nodded.

"Sounds like a plan."

Gathering what few possessions she came with, Robinne met Ryder out in his truck ten minutes later, hopping up inside and strapping herself in.

"What do you do on this friend's ranch? Is it much like your parents'?"

Ryder started the truck engine, reversing it out of its parked place and onto the road leading out of his property. "Almost. We're more cattle-based and he's more of a horse breeder. One of his ranch hands had a family emergency, so he called me in to help last-minute."

"Does this happen often?"

"Not really. His hands are usually very good at not needing outside help, as there's plenty of them with it being a breeding business. These things happen sometimes, so it's no bother to pitch in if I'm needed."

"What about your family ranch? Won't they be short without you?"

He shook his head, eyes focused on the road.

"Not for a few hours. Sundays don't tend to be busy days for us, as we get most of the smaller jobs done before the weekend so if something bigger comes up, we're able to deal with it rather than put it off."

Granted she wouldn't understand everything there is to know about ranching, she was impressed at how much dedication went into this line of work, this way of life out here. Not many people back home would be willing to work past five on a weekday, let alone through the weekend. These were the types of people she wanted to capture in her future books. People who were genuine, real and hard-working. Not people in unrealistic situations which seemed to be able to take more time off work than normal.

Robinne and Ryder fell once more into an easy and comfortable conversation as he drove them back towards her home once more. They talked about everything from the buddy of his he was going to do work for, to what her plans were for the following week. With it being Sunday, there wasn't much she was going to do today, unlike Ryder.

Normally back at where she used to live in the U.K, Sundays were a day to just laze about and do whatever the hell she wanted to. Not here they weren't. It seemed to be that people still got up and did things instead of letting the day go to waste. Perhaps she should do the same.

If only I could think of something to do.
Something that won't make me think of a certain cowboy…

Robinne said goodbye to Ryder when he made it to her place, making a quick U-turn and heading back towards the direction his buddy's ranch must be in. She would always be grateful for anyone who gave her a lift back home, though she wished she had more opportunities to drive her truck other than into town. After all, what was the point of buying something if you were barely going to use it?

Fishing her keys from her trouser pocket, she could see there was something sitting on her doorstep even from the bottom of her front garden.

That's odd, I don't remember ordering anything.

Walking up to her front door, it was evident that this wasn't something that could be ordered, by her or by anyone else. Unless amazon or some bespoke company started delivering their items via a…picnic basket? She didn't think they'd be around these days, what with so many things coming and going, new trends and what not. Some things just tended to vanish, fading into the past. Guess this wasn't one of those items.

Bending down and picking up the basket which upon holding it, was much heavier than she'd first anticipated. She leaned her ear towards it, thankfully hearing nothing coming from within. The last thing she wanted was to be left with a doorstep baby. If that sort of thing still happened…

Not that she wouldn't look after a baby if it DID happen, it just wasn't something she'd know how to go about dealing with right now.

Satisfied that whatever was inside the basket could wait until she was inside, she let herself into her house, with some effort, what with having to hold onto the heavy basket with both arms. She dropped her keys on the tablet just inside the doorway, by the notepad and hall telephone (yes, she had a telephone. So what?), making her way straight through to the kitchen to free her arms of the heavy weight within them.

"Good Lord." She huffed, placing the oversized basket on the kitchen counter. "Maybe I'm just out of shape. I need to start running again." She muttered to no one but herself.

Removing the tartan ribbon that was woven around the handles of the basket, which was the only thing keeping them together, she opened up the lids. On top of what looked like tissue paper, sat a yellow rose. A note laying beside it. Picking up the note and leaving the rose behind, it soon became clear as to whom the basket was from thanks to said note. It read:

Robinne. I promised I'd leave you alone until such a time that you could begin to see my face again. This is me, keeping that promise. Please accept this basket as a parting gift, until we meet again. I'm sorry.
~Ralph.
(P.S. Yellow means friendship – something I hope to earn again someday)

Despite the fact that she wasn't currently at present speaking a word, if she was, she would be sure as eggs she'd be stumped for words. Well, she was. Sort of. Ralph was the last person she'd expect something like this from. Yet, here it is and here she was, speechless.

There was no way she was able to thank him for doing this. Not that she would on the basis of what he'd done to her. Still, they'd both made it clear to the other in some way, that until she was ready and ready to make the first move, he'd back off. Which meant no communication.

Ack! Why do things have to be so complicated?

Setting the note and rose aside, she peeled off the few layers of tissue paper to reveal whatever goodies or items laid beneath. Much to her surprise, what she came across was not what she was expecting. To be fair to herself, she wasn't expecting any of this at all so, all of it was unexpected.

In this unexpected basket was an array of British food, snacks and drinks. Obviously his aim here, at least with the food and drinks, was to give her something that would connect her with where she'd come from. Giving her a sense of something familiar in this otherwise foreign world. At least, that's what she assumed it meant. Yes, the note might've provided *some* idea as to his intentions but as she'd learned in the short time she'd known him, anything could be possible where Ralph was concerned.

Literally, anything.

Deciding she would go into more of this later, she packed the tissue paper, the rose and the note back into the basket, returning to her original plan of taking her mind off of a certain cowboy. Which had almost been corrupted thanks to the rather irritatingly tempting basket.

Damn you Ralph. Damn you and your hidden sweet side!

A little while later after unsuccessfully trying to get Ralph's irritatingly sweet gesture out of her mind, Robinne set aside her laptop and got up from her position on the sofa. She'd decided to delve back into her freelance editing work, while she continued to search for a more resourceful work source. Unfortunately, even getting back into something she really enjoyed, failed to occupy her mind enough to forget what she'd set out to forget.

Just as she was about to go get herself a drink from the kitchen, she was halted mid-stride through her foyer by the sound of the doorbell.

I didn't realise I even had one of those...

Cautiously approaching the front door, Robinne looked into the peep-hole which she'd listed in her small list of specific requirements as her home was being re-built. There's no such thing as being 'too cautious' where someone's safety was concerned.

Satisfied that it was no one sinister on the other side, she undid the security chain and opened the door. Stood on her front step was a small, yet sweet-looking old lady, carrying something in a dish that was topped off in foil.

"Hello, can I help you? Do you have the wrong house?" she asked politely, not wanting to offend the poor woman.

"You're Robinne? The new owner of the Jameson place?"

"Uh, yes. I am. How can I help you?"

The woman took a step forward, pleased and placated that Robinne apparently appeared to be the person she'd intended to see. "You don't need to do anything for me dear. I'm Georgina, Georgie to my friends. I run the local library, and I just wanted to welcome you to the neighbourhood. I live not too far away. Wanted to let you settle in before the world and its wife started showing up on your doorstep."

She'd heard and often read about this sort of thing in many cowboy/western books. People would mass-make food items and deliver them to new people in town/people who've had something tragic happen to them and such other events of the like. Secretly, she'd always wanted this to happen to her, minus anything too tragic, but back home no one ever did this sort of thing. Everyone was sadly all too consumed in their own lives to think of someone else. Here though, things were thankfully different.

"That's true." She chuckled.

"Anyway, I just stopped by to give you a little something I whipped up to you know, welcome you to the neighbourhood."

Georgina handed over the foil-covered dish, placing it gently in her arms. "It's my own chicken casserole, made fresh this morning. I do hope you eat chicken. I thought I'd go with something safe, you know? Unless you're a vegetarian. You're not are you?"

She shook her head, offering up a friendly smile to the very sweet and thoughtful woman. "No, I'm not. This'll be perfect for tonight's dinner, thank you so much. It's very thoughtful of you."

Georgina waved a hand, "No need to thank me, it's what we do around here. It's a pleasure to do something for such a sweet girl."

Though Georgina didn't know Robinne well enough to determine her 'sweet' yet, the sentiment still struck her with all the warmth of what she assumed it would be like to be loved by a grandmother-type figure. Her own grandmother sadly had long-passed, leaving her with nothing but a few fleeing memories now and then.

Stepping back, she held the dish away from the doorway so Georgina could step inside. "I insist on at least offering you a cup of tea as a thank you, if you'd like to join me."

"Thank you dear, I'd love to. But I have to get back to the library, I'm here on my lunch break and I don't want to leave Sandra alone for too long."

"Does it get busy around this time?"

"Oh, no. She's just got a little boy in part-time day care she has to pick up just after lunch. Single mother, a lot of responsibilities."

She nodded, understanding where Georgina was coming from. "Fair enough. Thank you so much again for this casserole, I can't want to tuck into it."

"A pleasure, have a nice day now!" Georgina called out as she made her way back down Robinne's front garden, hopping into a tiny little car and pulling away, driving back in the direction of town centre.

Stepping back inside her house, she made a mental note to stop by the library at some stage to thank Georgina and hand over the casserole dish after she'd finished eating its contents. By the looks of it, she wouldn't be getting through it any time soon, Georgina had cooked up enough to feed her for a week if she portioned it out right.

Shame there aren't more people like Georgina in the world.

Robinne placed the casserole in the fridge where it would be fine until dinner time tonight. She hadn't had a home-cooked meal in such a long time, it would be a welcome change. Not that she was an advocate for change. Where most would go with the flow and the saying that 'change is good', she'd rather stick with the familiar and the comfortable. Nothing wrong with that.

If there was one thing she really did hate, it was people who tried to make her feel like her beliefs were wrong. Everyone had the right to believe in what they wanted to, even if it was wrong. Yet, whenever it came to her and her own beliefs, for some reason people always seemed to deem them wrong or socially unacceptable.

For example, change. For the majority of people it seemed, they welcome change and condemn anyone who doesn't share in their like-mindedness and train of thought. There's nothing wrong in being a part of a minority, no matter what aspect of life it's in. At least not to her. So when those within the majority say to her that she 'must' accept and embrace change, she fires straight back at them with something along the lines of 'I don't *have* to do anything I don't want to do'. They certainly wouldn't change their views to what hers were, if she asked them. So why should she?

Everyone has the right to say, think, do and live how they want and with Robinne, her chosen way of life is the road of comfortability and the familiar. If that wasn't what others wanted in their lives, she just didn't understand why they didn't keep to themselves instead of potentially upsetting someone else? It truly boggled her mind.

Of course, there were things that were inevitable to change, she accepted that. She wasn't 100% against change on the whole, but as much as she could keep the same and what felt comfortable to her and her anxieties, she would. She just wished that others could leave her to beliefs as she left them to theirs. Then again, not everyone thought the way she did or was considerate. A shame, really. If more people thought about being a bit more considerate now and then rather than outwardly seeking people out to upset, the world would be a percentage closer to a better place.

Yeah, and pigs fly.

Walking out of the kitchen and heading back to the living space to resume a spot of freelance editing for a little while longer, her stride was halted by yet another ring on her doorbell.

"Who could that be…?" she muttered, wandering over to the front door and opening it once more.

This time, there was a middle-aged man at her door. He too carried something that resembled a home-cooked meal in his hand, topped off with yet more tin foil. "Hello there ma'am." He removed his Stetson, bowing his head to her slightly in an old-time southern gentlemanly manor.

"H-Hello. How can I um…how can I help you?"

God she sounded so rude! She hoped she didn't come across as such to the poor man. Unfortunately for her, she was just awkward by nature, even more so when meeting someone for the first time. The level of awkwardness from her would break any scale.

Shaking her head, she turned her attention back to the man currently on her doorstep.

"You don't need to do anything for me ma'am. The name's Wade. Wade Stephens. I run the local timber company. It was my men who delivered the wood used to re-make this house." Wade beamed with pride.

She smiled softly at him, genuine thankful for his input into what was starting to feel like a real home to her, not just a place she'd simply moved to.

"Well, thank you, Wade. The boys did a wonderful job with this place and not without your timber."

"Mighty kind of you to say so Miss…uh. I'm sorry, your name's escaped me again."

"James. Robinne James."

"Ah yes, that was it. Forgive me, a lot to do and not enough space up there to remember it all with." He said, tapping the side of his head, chuckling at his own predicament. "Anyway, I'd heard we've been given the greenlight to stop by and welcome you to the neighbourhood and our little town, now that you're somewhat settled in."

"We?"

Wade nodded. "Most of the community. Those of us on the welcoming committee anyway. Not an official committee, just a small number of us who rally around those new to town when it happens."

"How lovely. Thank you for stopping by. I've just had Georgina from the library stop by not too long ago as a matter of fact."

"Sounds about right. She's usually the first but then again, none of us would dare stop her from being otherwise." He smirked. "This is for you anyway, from me and the wife. Not sure if you eat much American food but, my wife's peach cobbler isn't anything but delicious. Though I am a little biased."

Wade handed her the dish he'd been holding the entire time he'd been standing to her, chatting away with her on the doorstep. The cobbler was heavier than it looked in his hands, which could only mean there was a hefty amount for her to eat too.

Not that I'm complaining or that I'm ungrateful. I just…don't know where I'm going to put it all. That's all.

"Anyway I won't hold you up." Wade's voice said, bringing her back to the present. "Welcome to the neighbourhood Miss James, don't hesitate to call on me or my wife if you ever need anything. Have a good day now!" he tipped his hat to her, beating a contented retreat down her garden, not unlike Georgina had done so a short while ago.

She waved a friendly goodbye to Wade as he strode off down the street, heading back inside when she couldn't see him anymore. Closing the door behind her, she lifted the foil from a corner of the dish, inhaling the surprisingly deliciously sweet smell of the cobbler within.

"Hm, not bad at all. I might actually enjoy this."

Much like with change, she rarely took the opportunity to try new food or drinks. She knew what she did and didn't like so no matter how many people tried to convince her to eat other foods or drink other drinks, she wouldn't do so until she was ready. She might come across as very stubborn, she wasn't. Like everyone else, she did her own thing and wasn't afraid to do so. This time though, she was pleased she'd accepted Wade's wife's food, it would make a nice little treat after Georgina's casserole.

The two visits from two of Dripping Springs' kindest residents, set the precedence for the rest of her morning and into the early afternoon. She'd lost count of how many people had stopped by after the tenth food-related item had been dropped off at her place.

So much for a 'small' welcoming committee.

By the time the last person dropped off their welcome meal/food item, she felt as tuckered out as if she'd been doing a twelve-hour shift at a retail store during the Christmas season. She'd been there and done that for more years than she'd cared to, having no intention to return to it or anything of the like.

Her fridge was now so full of well-wishers' gifts, that there was only the small odd space where she could still see all the way through to the back. Standing and looking at it all, she couldn't help but feel both grateful for their thoughtfulness yet worried for her stomach at the same time.

If she lived with another person or two, consuming all of this before it went to waste but seeing as it was just her, she definitely had to consider freezing some of this until she was ready to get around to it.

"Looks like I won't need to be cooking for a while." She said, chuckling to herself as she closed the fridge door, plopping down on a stool at the moderately-sized kitchen island.

She had to think of a way to thank all of these people who visited her, even though pretty much each and every one of them refused to accept anything off of her in return. It was just escaping her as to what she could do for them all. Not to mention how she'd deliver whatever she came up with as a thank you, as she had no idea where most of these people even lived.

Oh well, I'll cross that bridge when I get to it.

At least all the activity had taken her mind off Ralph for the morning at least.

Urgh…after all that, he STILL creeps in somehow!

Deciding on the only way she thought to push him from her thoughts once more, she up and grabbed her keys from the front hall, seeing a spur of the moment trip into town was exactly what she needed. While she was there, she could also look for ideas on how to thank people for the gifts, there was bound to be something there that would spark some sort of idea from within her.

As she drove into town, she couldn't help but think about something that had failed to creep into her thoughts until she had a moment alone to truly do some deep thinking. She wasn't a natural around people, there was no doubt about that. Yet, she'd encountered more people today than she'd ever done in her short time here so far. Not once did she freak out, stumble over her words or make anyone feel awkward. At least, she hoped she didn't.

This was a huge step for her. One of the many reasons she moved here. Doing things outside of her comfort zone was a big to do thing on a thankfully non-existent list. One list was enough and look at where that had gotten her after all. No more lists for her unless they were absolutely necessary.

Feeling rather pleased for herself, she saw no reason as to why she couldn't pick up a little treat while she was here in town. It seemed like a good idea right up until the moment she remembered all the items she'd got yet, waiting to be tucked into.

A blessing and a curse indeed.

Pulling her truck into a vacant parking space outside one of the stores in the main part of town, she saw that the small town centre was just as busy as it was when she'd been here earlier this week. People milled around in clothes which she'd only could be imagine were deemed 'church clothes'. It wasn't uncommon for small-towns like these ones in Texas to be a part of a church-going community.

She'd never given it much thought as to whether or not she'd be attending church while living here. Thought it had been made clear by more than one of her visitors this morning that she'd be welcome to any activity within the community, she didn't want to step on any toes or take attention away from anything, simply because she was the new girl in town.

There was plenty of time to think about this though, she thought to herself, stepping out of her truck and closing the door to. She could always give Cassie a ring and ask her what she thought about the matter. Though, that would mean word about her would get back to Ralph somehow, it was inevitable what with her being his mum. She wouldn't hide things from her son and Robinne couldn't blame her.

Locking her truck, Robinne walked onto the pavement, taking a moment to look at the shops that lined each side of the charming small town main street. During her trip here earlier in the week, she didn't take the time to stop and properly look at exactly what Dripping Springs had to offer, as she was too concerned with getting her stuff and getting back home.

By the looks of things, the small town actually had a lot to offer. Much like the Tardis from Doctor Who, it looked small on the outside but on the in, there was much, much more.

From what she could see, without having to walk further down the street, stood your typical shops. Plus a few which she'd have to come back again to check out further. There was a coffee shop; a hair salon, vet clinic, the library Georgina mentioned she worked at, Niall's shop, gift shop, ice cream shop, clothing & antique shop. For a small town, this already blew her mind in a big way.

Hoping inspiration would strike her while she was here, Robinne decided to head into the clothing store in the meantime. It was often said that inspiration struck at the most unexpected of times. She hoped this was one of them.

'Susan's Springs' looked to be a chic/vintage/boho sort of clothing store. At least that was her impression upon walking inside the small yet, cozy lady's clothing store. She could only guess by the name of the store, a woman called Susan either owned it or was the store's namesake. Either way, the name suited well with the name of the town. Which she suspected was it' intended purpose.

Since no one came out to greet her as she walked in, she assumed whoever owned and/or worked at the store was busy or on their lunch break. So, she decided to take a look around herself, so not to bother anyone if they were busy or on a late lunch.

Five or so minutes into looking at the locally made clothes, she felt as though eyes were watching her. An odd feeling considering she still didn't know anyone as well as she knew Cassie and her family, even with all her visitors earlier today, she was still a stranger to most people in town.

Even if they all seemed to know my name, age, blood type.

Okay, maybe not those last two. It just feels like it.

She'd been debating on whether or not to get the shirt currently on a hanger in her hand, as she'd been deciding between it and one near it. It wasn't a major life decision but seeing as she didn't do this sort of thing usually, she had to choose right. After all, despite clothes shopping not being her thing, she was a believer in supporting small businesses and that always trumped her reluctance to splurge on clothes.

Deciding on the shirt currently in her hand, she turned around to head to the counter to pay when instead of striding across a clear path, she came face-to-face rather abruptly with another person.

"Oh, I'm so sorry!"

The poor woman she'd run into stepped back, appearing to brush off dirt while sporting what appeared to be a very sour expression on her face, as if she'd smelled something bad and got stuck that way. Maybe it was her resting face, as Robinne's own often looked like she was mad about something. Nevertheless, she should've apologised too.

"Are you alright? I didn't hurt you did I?" she asked the woman, hoping this would elicit some sort of response from her.

Not sure I really want one if she can't even say sorry...

Straightening up from brushing absolutely nothing from her pristine-looking clothing, the woman eventually acknowledged her and met her eyes. Steel-blue, cold as ice eyes met her own thankfully warmer green ones.

Yikes! This woman could scare the pants off a naked mole rat. And they're naked!

"You didn't ruin my outfit, so that's something at least."

There was always that one person out there that was just snippy and rude for the sake of it, and it just so happened that Robinne ran, quite literally, into one of those people. Nine out of ten people you meet are thankfully pleasant people, it's just the one percent that ruin a perfect ten. This woman was certainly in that lesser category.

"You're that English girl who got herself lost in the storm last week, aren't you?" the woman asked her, clear snide undertones running through her rather irritatingly nasal voice.

Lost? That's a new one on her. Last time she checked, she willingly drove away from the ranch.

There was bound to be the odd person who got it wrong at some point, not bothering to check the facts before their mouths ran ahead of what she assumed was their brains.

Not rising to this woman's obvious yet pathetic bait, Robinne straightened her own back, looking down at this woman from her for once thankful height. "If you mean I'm the English girl who left the company of the Jenkins' the other night to go home then yes, that's me. I moved into the old Jameson place. Who do I have the pleasure of addressing?"

If there was one thing the people who raised her taught her, it was not to get mad at people, but to get even. Getting mad at people never solved anything. However getting even, well that was way more satisfying both morally and personally.

The woman flipped her hair back, "Delilah. Delilah Hamilton." She took a step forward, trying to square up to Robinne's height and failing miserably. "I'm glad I caught you anyway, I've been meaning to speak to you."

She blinked. What on Earth could this rude woman want?

Without giving her time to respond, Delilah ploughed on.

"You don't need to worry about hanging out with Ralph anymore. Now that I'm back we're going to be picking things up where we left off and I heard he did a number on you anyway so, I'll be doing you a favour. You're off the hook."

Off the hook? Ok, this lady's going down!

Robinne was about to throw it down with the woman who clearly thought she ruled everyone's lives around here, when a woman came hurrying out from somewhere out back, coming to a stop when she saw the two of them together in the middle of the store.

"Spreading your hate again Delilah? When will you ever stop pushing your nose where it's got no place being?" the woman said disapprovingly, putting her hands on her wide hips.

"When people finally learn their place in this world. I'm outta here. You just lost yourself a very valuable customer."

Delilah thankfully departed from the store, taking her air of vileness with her. Robinne physically relaxed, her shoulders dropping back to a much normal place than before.

"Good riddance." The other woman in the store muttered, turning her full attention to Robinne. "Hello dear, how can I help you today? Other than turf the trash back out onto the street?" she laughed. "I'm Susan, I own this place."

Ah, as I suspected.

"Nice to meet you Susan. I'm Robinne. I moved into the old Jameson place not too long ago."

"Oh, the lovely girl from England!"

"That's not how *she* described me just now."

Susan waved a hand, clearly used to dealing with people like the delightful Delilah. "Don't pay attention to her. She's been sour ever since the day back in high school in which…ah you don't need to know about that. I talk too much."

The two of them shared a mutual laugh which for Robinne was a relief, relieving the tension left behind from the woman who could give the Ice Queen a run for her money.

"Now." Susan clapped her hands together. "Are you just getting that one item? Or are you browsing for more?"

Since this woman had defused a potentially violent situation, she decided to go against her own 'beliefs', deciding on getting as many clothes as her budget would allow.

"Tell you what. Why don't you help me pick out a basic seasonal wardrobe? I think I seriously misjudged my clothes packing moving here." She smiled, crossing her fingers behind her back.

"Ooh I'd love to! I know exactly what would suit a lovely young lady like yourself! Come this way, Aunt Susan will help you out."

Oh I bet you will.

My purse will cry at me for this though. She won't be happy at all.

CHAPTER FOURTEEN
~ Robinne ~

If there was one thing Robinne hated more than anything first thing in the morning, was the morning itself. She'd made her hatred for the start of the day pretty clear several times before, yet they still happened. She was usually a grump until she got her first cup of tea of the day inside her. For others, its coffee but for her, tea was the only way to go.

Dragging her pyjama-clad butt downstairs and into her kitchen, she just about filled up the mug with water to make her tea, when the front doorbell rang unexpectedly.

It's a Monday morning! Who with an ounce of sanity in their heads would disturb someone at this ungodly hour?

Not many people would call 8AM an ungodly hour, as often she read that Americans tended to favour getting up at the absolute ass crack of dawn, but she wasn't many people. Early on in life, people had learned the hard way not to disturb her too early, as her inner bear often tore off heads with no mercy or aesthetic, if disturbed too early. In bed or otherwise.

It doesn't exactly come across as friendly. Despite that, she doesn't mean to offend anyone if caught in one of her early morning moods.

With the doorbell continuing to ring, she supposed she should go and answer it, as it wasn't in her nature to be rude to anyone in any degree. If she could help it. Sometimes she did slip up, she's only human.

Since when has that been a genuine reason for anything these days?
Never, that's when.

Putting her cup down on the kitchen island counter, she made her way over to the front door, where the incessant ringing didn't stop until she as calmly as she could, opened the door.

"Hi? How can I help you?" she said, fighting back a yawn as she'd not yet fully woken up.

The woman on the doorstep almost looked as if she was beginning to regret her showing up here so early. She must look moodier to others than she felt she did. Not what she wanted to do at all. Her hatred of mornings and her moods never deserved to be pushed onto others, including this woman. She had to change this ASAP.

"Sorry, I don't mean to be rude. Not a morning person." She laughed, hoping to ease the tension. "I'm Robinne, it's nice to meet you…?" hoping the woman would give her name, she held out her hand for a friendly shake.

"Elaine. Elaine Barkley. Laney to my friends." She said, shaking Robinne's hand with a surprising amount of strength coming from such a small frame. Laney had to be no more than five feet four at a guess, yet the strength coming from her hand you'd normally expect out of someone at least Robinne's height or that of an average sized man. Guess you can't totally pin down a stereotype on everyone until you truly know them.

Laney from what Robinne could see of her as she stood before her now, looked like what people would deem 'mousey', being small with delicate features on a small form. Her hair wasn't quite blonde, nor brown. It was somewhere in the middle, what people would call strawberry blonde. From the looks if it, Laney too seemed to favour the little-to-no makeup look, as did Robinne. She liked the woman already.

"I'm really sorry to stop by first thing in the morning. In truth, I'm not much of a morning person either. Which is odd when I own the bakery in town, it doesn't seem right to have a non-morning person have to get up early every morning to bake for the day's customers." She laughed.

"Not at all. After all, what is normal these days?"

"True. Anyway, I came by to give you this." Laney held up what looked to be a small paper bag with her bakery's logo on it. "I heard from Susan what went down yesterday between you and dreadful Delilah."

"Dreadful indeed." Mumbled Robinne, agreeing with Laney's statement.

"Indeed. So, I thought you could use a little pick me up. Nothing like this is ever too naughty for a Monday morning. It's my latest creation. I hope you like caramel. It's a caramel cupcake with gooey caramel right in the middle under all that vanilla frosting."

That might sound sickly to someone else but, my God, it sounds divine to me!

Robinne graciously accepted the bag off Laney, offering her a sincerely kind smile. "Thank you. It's most kind of you, even though you really didn't have to. Believe it or not, I wasn't upset at what she said. I was more stunned that she had the nerve to seek me out to warn me off uh…someone. Even though I have no um…intentions towards him anyway."

Liar.

"Don't worry, I understand where you're coming from. She did the same to me when she thought I had interest in Ryder, Ralph's younger brother." Laney said, her tone wistful.

Something tells me you're still into Ryder, Laney.
I can see it a mile away.

Laney continued. "She's only interested in sinking her claws into any one of those boys. Foolish girl thinks they're full to the brim with money, just because they own a successful ranch and cattle business. The city messed with her head, full of idiotic ideas she is. Doesn't she know that there's no real wealth in ranching anymore?"

She shrugged.

"I wouldn't know. Not from around here." She laughed, "Don't really know how the whole ranching thing works exactly."

Laney face-palmed, only just realising her mistake.

"See? Early morning brain."

Sharing another laugh together, Robinne could see how this woman would easily make friends and be equally admired by them, she was simply adorably funny. Unlike what she thought of herself. According to a former friend of hers, she wasn't funny at all. Only funny-looking.

What does he know?

Nothing! Not anymore.

Robinne put the cupcake bag on the table inside the hall, stepping back with the door. "Would you like to come in for a quick drink before work? I don't know if you're anything like me but, I like a good cuppa first thing. I've just made myself one. I can whip you up a quick cup if you'd like?"

Laney beamed, nodding enthusiastically.

"I'd love to! Thank you! Sorry for the intrusion." She hopped inside, glancing around at the front hall décor as Robinne closed the door behind her.

"Beautiful, isn't it?" she asked Laney, coming to a stop beside her.

Laney nodded.

"Very!"

Robinne stepped around her, making her way slowly towards the kitchen while waving for Laney to join her. "Let's get you that cuppa!"

Catching up behind her, Laney followed.

"I just love how you say that!"

She laughed, appreciating how honest this woman was. In the short time since meeting her at her front door, she was loving how she was growing on her with every minute that passed.

For a short while, the two sat at Robinne's kitchen island while sharing more than one cup of tea between them. She'd truly found a kindred spirit in Laney, finding much of herself in this slightly more outgoing woman. They'd talked mostly about the town, with Laney filling her in on the local culture, goings on, events and such other things of the like.

Robinne was incredibly grateful for this, as she was not one to pry, so she'd gathered a wealth of information without having to stick her nose into people's businesses.

Laney set her cup down, turning to her. "Thank you for the lovely tea. I don't think I've had that type before.

"You wouldn't have done, its English tea. I ordered some for myself when I moved here." She smiled.

She felt Laney put her hand on her forearm. Turning to face her, she saw her giddy with glee. "You must tell me where to order some. I'm hooked"

Nodding, she flashed her a smile. "I will, I promise."

Laney clapped her hands together, standing up from her seated position on the stool. "Awesome! Thank you".

There was something about Laney right this moment, Robinne noticed. She was obviously genuinely enthused by the tea they'd just shared, but she could sense there was something else on her mind in which she was hesitant to approach her about.

"Is there something you want to ask me, Laney?" Her smirk appearing, failing to be kept at bay.

"How did you know?!"

"I can hear it in your voice." She winked. "Go on, ask away."

Laney clasped her hands together as if she were begging, looking up at her with the classic puppy dog look. For a grown woman, she still retained that child-like presence which Robinne found simply adorable. Where others would appear childish and that would be that, Laney made it work for her.

"Please don't be mad at her, but I ran into Cassie yesterday after I spoke to Susan. She told me you might be needing temporary work until you find something you really want to do. Or if you hit it off with your books."

"I haven't actually written one yet."

"Semantics." Laney fired back. "Point is, she asked me to offer up the chance of working for me temporarily, saying that she would've offered a place with her but she didn't want to put anything your way that would remind you of Ralph until, you know, a time where you're ready to see him again."

There was no way of knowing what Laney was going to say to her, though she wasn't expecting that. Sure, she had thought about what she was going to do to earn a bit of extra money, though she didn't expect Cassie to still be thinking of her. Especially since what happened a few days ago. Though, she should really know Cassie enough by now to know that she'd still think of her, no matter what happens.

She's an angel right here with us on Earth.

I can't refuse her kindness. It would be rude of me.

Though she was somewhat perplexed at the initial offer, it soon dawned on her that there were people out there who truly did care about her. It didn't have to necessarily be in a romantic way for it to matter, but they did. Cassie, bless her, was one of those wonderful people.

Pushing a lock of hair away from her eye, she softly exhaled. Turning towards Laney, she squared her shoulders and nodded her head. "Alright, I accept. I'll happily do whatever jobs you want me to do at your bakery. Especially if one of the job perks is testing out new recipes like this one here." She said, picking up the wrapper of the cupcake and putting it in the bin.

Laney looked equally as surprised as Robinne felt when the notion was proposed to her, clearly not expecting that she would agree and fold to it as easily as she did.

"Y-you really mean it? Oh this is going to be so awesome!"

Americans really like that word, don't they?

Robinne nodded, moving their cups into the sink to be washed at some point. It wasn't imperative that they be washed right this moment.

"I've no doubt it will be." She meant it. As anti-social she considered herself, she wasn't afraid to admit that she was looking forward to this opportunity, and the chance of trying something new. "When do we start?"

"We could start you off with a half day today, if that works for you? Just to see how you'll get on and if you like working at the bakery."

"Oh I don't have any doubts that I'll like it, I just hope you're prepared for the odd broken, squashed, smashed or smooshed thing here and there."

Laney waved a hand, a smile once more on her delicate face.

"Nothing I don't already do myself. As long as you make sure I don't catch anything on fire, we'll watch out for each other's backs."

Robinne chuckled, "Deal. Let me just go and change out of these rags and I'll meet you outside in say, fifteen minutes?"

Nodding, Laney got up and gave her a swift hug, before she happily walked with a spring in her step towards the hallway. "This is going to be great!"

Oh for sure. For sure.

When Laney said she'd put Robinne to work, she really meant it! It wasn't backbreaking work as working on a ranch would be, for example, but by the time lunch rolled around, she had a newfound appreciation for people who literally spent all the day on their feet.

She wasn't given a specific job title while on her half day work experience, testing her to see if she could really make the cut, but she assumed it would be something like an assistant.

If bakeries had assistants…

"How're you holding up?" Laney said, coming out from the back of the bakery with a fresh load of cakes to put in the display counter.

As soon as they'd arrived here earlier, Laney soon went to work doing what Robinne assumed was her usual morning routine before the bakery opened. Soon after, she was put to work assisting her with whatever she needed help with, whether that be passing her a bag of flower, sweeping up the mess or arranging the counter display, whatever Laney said, she did.

It was more the persistent back and forth movements that had worn her out a little, rather than the workload. Though she did have to pat herself on the back metaphorically for sticking it out and not pulling a sickie to go home. Even if she wanted to call it quits, which she didn't, she still owed her being here to Cassie. So quitting wasn't even an option.

"I'm good, thank you. Not really used to work other than on a desk in an office but, this is a surprisingly good change."

"Good, I'm glad. Let me just flip the sign to 'closed' and we can talk about where we can go from here."

Laney had already explained that she often did that when she took her lunch break, so not to leave people milling around the shop without being attended to. It did surprise Robinne that only Laney was the single person running this bakery, as she'd assumed there would be at least two or three. There was no doubt left in her mind that she was more than capable of running things on her own, still, it surprised her at first.

They'd been blessed with a dribble of customers here and there during her small stint working with Laney, as this even being a small town, was bound to have most of its residents working hard during the day. Leaving them only able to come in around this time to fuel up before heading back to work. This reminded Robinne not to hold Laney up too much while they talked, as she didn't want to deprive her of a lunch time customer or two.

Besides, she'd already made her decision.

"Okay then…" Laney said, sliding into the seat opposite her in the booth-style seating arrangement. "Hit me with it."

There was no use lying to her, or tricking her for that matter. Honesty was the best policy in her book and she wasn't going to keep Laney in the dark for a moment longer.

"If you'll have me, I'll take the job."

Laney didn't look surprised at this. It was as if she knew what Robinne's decision was before she did. What Robinne didn't know, was that while she worked and helped Laney in the shop, Laney herself kept a secret side-eye on her. Watching her. What she saw was a woman enjoying a different pace of life, something that occupied her mind and gave her focus. She knew by just watching Robinne that she would say yes. She hoped at least.

"The pleasure is all mine."

The two of them shook hands, grinning like two best friends who'd known one another longer than half a day. Besides Ryder, Robinne could easily see Laney become as close as a best friend to her as she could imagine. Having the easier time trusting men over women, at least until recently, it would be interesting to see how much more she'd connect with Laney while working with her.

Maybe this won't be so bad after all.

* * *

He promised her he would stay away from her until she was ready to see him again, to which he fully intended to carry out no matter how much he itched to go round and see her, or call her up and ask if she was okay. He was going to have to settle on catching glimpses of her from a distance. Or in this case, from the cab of his truck.

Ralph had completed his usual Monday morning routine of checking the ranch inventory lists, checking on the cattle and figuring out what was needing to be done that week, when his stomach protested that it needed to be fed. He happily obliged its demands, driving into town and deciding to indulge himself with one of Laney's famous sweet treats.

He knew she closed around lunch time, but he hoped he'd caught her before she'd had a chance to shut the shop for her break. Even though he hadn't made it in time before she closed temporarily, he was rewarded with the unexpected sight of his favourite, and only, English rose.

What was she doing here?

Of course, he knew that she had every right to be here, or anywhere else in the town for that matter, it was just that his heightened male curiosity got the better of him when he caught the two ladies shaking hands as if they'd just agreed on the deal of the century.

There was nothing stopping him from waiting here until she'd made her next move, whatever move that may be, just as there was nothing stopping him from entering the bakery while she had vacated. Except for his promise. Nothing would give it away to her at a later date that he'd been there around the same time as she, except for if Laney told Robinne about his stop. Though he knew if he asked her, Laney would keep it to herself if she really had to.

His stomach grumbled as it reminded him of why he'd come into town in the first place. To be fed.

"Patience. You'll get what you want soon enough." He patted his stomach, hoping to placate it soon.

Movement at the bakery in the corner of his vision caused him to look up from the moment with his stomach. Robinne in all her perfect beauty was exiting the shop, a smile on her face as she headed towards her truck, which was parked not too far away from the bakery.

He felt his heart kick up into high gear upon seeing the look on her face, as he wanted to be the one to put it there. Knowing he'd caused her more heartache than a smile on her face, soon tore away the fleeting joy in his stomach at seeing her so energised. Instead, it was replaced with deep regret.

Soon, her truck did a U-turn and started back in the direction in which her house was in. Whatever she was doing at Laney's shop was her own business, not his. It just meant that for a while until he knew exactly for sure what was going on, his irritated stomach would have to go without doughnuts for a while.

Damn it…

* * *

Considering how her day started, with her crabby as hell and cursing at whoever had created such a thing as mornings, the rest of Robinne's day seemed to go surprisingly well. For a Monday too!

After coming home from her half a day stint at Laney's bakery, she'd hopped right back on her laptop now full of beans, and got as much freelance editing work done and out the way as she could. Putting in her notice to anyone still interested in hiring her to edit their work, that it would be done in her spare time and still completed to the highest level of perfectionism, now that she'd be working elsewhere during the day.

She'd come to an agreement with Laney, that she'd be working a full day on Friday to get a hang of how to close things down at the end of a working week there, starting part-time work as of Monday the following week. Robinne would be working Mondays, Tuesdays, Thursdays & Friday's, giving her the middle of the week and weekends off to do whatever she needed to do, which was beyond kind of Laney. Then again, she wouldn't have offered those days if she wasn't able to accommodate Robinne's other commitments.

From there, the day had wound down nicely, with her finishing it off with a movie she'd been meaning to watch, courtesy of her free Netflix trial. Topping the night off with a soothing bath and a book in bed.

If there was one thing she really liked to do in life, albeit not being as glamorous as other things people enjoy, it was snuggling down in bed at the end of the day with a book. Call her what you want, judge her how you want, this was what made her inner and outer being happy and she wasn't going to change that no matter what anyone said or thought.

Midway through the book and thankfully not too late at night, her stomach rumbled. Despite eating from one of the many dishes she'd been given by the welcome committee, she still found herself hungry and the most inopportune moments. Even though she was only midway through the book, she still had to fight hard the urge to continue on. At least until the next chapter.

Her stomach however, won the battle this time. Setting her book aside on the bedside table, she grabbed her robe and padded downstairs and to her kitchen, flipping on the light as she entered.

She wasn't up for eating a big meal, not at this time of night anyway. A small snack would get her through until morning where she could perhaps have a more sizable meal to start her day.

"What to pick, what to pick." She mumbled to herself, opening and closing various cupboard and not particularly fancying anything within them.

Since when has it been so hard to pick food?

Since now, apparently.

She was about to give up and go back to bed without anything to eat, when she suddenly remembered something that had been left quite literally on her doorstep when she came back early Saturday morning.

Ralph's basket.

Before leaving with Laney to go to her bakery, she'd tucked the basket into the pantry. Not planning on touching it until well, until now, when she had a craving for a small snack. Apparently her subconscious wanted something from her homeland, something that Ralph had picked out for her.

She'd done so well to keep her mind off of him for most of the day, relishing in the work at the bakery which had been the main contributor. Now as she stood picking one item out of the basket, it was inevitable that her thoughts would of course cast upon him. Momentarily at least.

As much as she wanted to stay mad at him and throw the basket away for the hell of it, simply because of what he did to her, the food didn't deserve it. She'd managed to convince herself to keep it for their sake.

You're acting as if the food is alive. You fool.

Admittedly, she was a fool. A contented fool now, thanks to the divine biscuity goodness she was munching into on her way back up to her bedroom, plopping down on the edge of the bed once there.

Letting out a moan of pure satisfaction, she forced her mind to purge all thoughts of the man who gave this savoury goodness to her, focusing singularly on said food item alone.

It worked for all of two seconds.

Damn you again Ralph. Damn your Wrangler-clad hyde!

CHAPTER FIFTEEN
~ Ralph ~

Time for a rancher was never available by the big load. There was always so much to be done and always so few hours within the day and week to get it all done in. Yet for Ralph, by the time Thursday had rolled around, it felt like it had taken a millennia to get there.

He knew why. It was because there was a lacking presence in his life which had slowly and unbeknown to him until it was too late, had become the core element to what he thought about for most of the day. Now that's been taken away, his mind had been given a chance to think and wander far beyond what was comfortable with him. He didn't like it.

Keeping a promise had never been so hard before. Then again, whenever he'd had to keep a promise before, it had always been for a good reason. Not for the benefit of anything. This time, he damn well knew what the benefit was for and he was having a hard time reining his thoughts in from it.

Robinne.

He thought it would be easy keeping his mind off of her since seeing her at the bakery earlier on this week. He was epically wrong. Not even putting in extra hours on the ranch was enough to quash those thoughts until a time where he was alone in his own home to do so. He was in deep. Deeper than he'd ever been with anyone since…*her*.

Entering the main house kitchen, he gave his head a mental shake as he sat down at the table to enjoy some of his mother's delicious cooking for today's breakfast. She'd invited him to join her and his Pa this morning, having enough time to cook for whoever wanted to join them before she headed off to the B&B.

"Morning baby boy, what'll you have?" Cassie said from the stove, cracking another egg into the frying pan.

No matter how many times Ralph told her not to call him that, albeit politely, she still called him her baby boy. Being the oldest of her five sons didn't seem to enter into the equation either, as she'd always maintained that no matter how old he or any of his other brothers got, they'd always be her baby boys.

"Whatever you're cooking up Ma, it smells delicious."

"I wouldn't do anything less."

He chuckled. "No, no you wouldn't."

As he grabbed the mug which had been placed in front of him while he sat down, his Ma piled up a decent-sized amount of breakfast onto his plate, sliding it onto the table for him to eat.

After she grabbed a plate of her own, with a much smaller portion size than his own, his Ma joined him at the table.

"How've things been with you sweetie?"

"Good thanks, Ma." He said, taking a bite of a hash brown, moaning in appreciation at how delicious it was as it melted in his mouth.

The two of them settled into a comfortable silence as they both tucked into their respective breakfasts. Ralph did always enjoy his Ma's cooking, there was just something about it that no other food never truly ever came close to being as nice, as warming. Even Ryder's cooking, and he wasn't a half bad cook thanks to his Ma teaching them all how. Making sure that they could well look after themselves when in their homes, or with families of their own.

As if I'll get that any time soon…

A few more minutes of silence surrounded them as they continued to eat, until his Ma brought up something he'd been working so hard over the last few days or so to forget. The very thought that would be on his mind twenty four hours a day if he wasn't working so hard to keep busy. Her.

"I know you've been wondering what Robinne was doing at Laney's bakery on Monday. Am I right?"

He blinked, completely dumbfounded at her scarily accurate guess. "H-how did you…"

"How did I know?" she laughed softly, "I saw Laney after she told me she'd seen your truck pulling away after Robinne had left. She stopped by to deliver me some of her foods for the desert menu. Figured that's why you left rather than coming in to talk to her."

He slumped back into his seat, half-deflated in the fact that someone, namely Laney, had spotted him. Especially after he thought he'd been super sleuth-like. Then again, a big truck which easily identified its owner, probably wasn't the best thing to go about in if you didn't want to be seen.

Though he didn't go into town in the first place under stealth, he certainly wanted to get out in it. Failing miserably.

Thank God I'm not a Navy SEAL or something, I wouldn't make it past basic training.

Holding his hands up, he admitted defeat.

"Guilty as charged." He sighed. "I was going to get a doughnut or something from Laney's bakery when I saw her inside with Robinne. Curiosity got the better of me when I saw in there, I wanted to know why. I know she's a little shy around people so, I stopped where I'd parked to see how things played out. Rather than go in and ask. See, I couldn't anyway."

"Because of your promise?" his Ma interjected.

He nodded. "Exactly. Wait, how'd you know about that too?"

Reaching over to pat her hand on his forearm, she offered him a warm, motherly smile. "Honey, you should know that nothing stays secret for long in a small town. Besides, I was passing by your father's office door when you and he were speaking about it. I heard you tell him about the promise. Don't worry, I'm not offended you didn't come to me about it."

Somehow, he managed to feel as if he was a child again, being scolded for something he'd managed to get out of his Ma after his Pa had told him no. He'd done that a few times, more than a fair few times, as a kid. As did most of his brothers when they got old enough and caught onto the idea.

"Sorry Ma." He leaned over and gave her a small kiss on her forehead, clearing away his now empty plate at the same time. "I…I just wanted to actually keep that promise with her. When really, more than anything, I wanted to go into there and talk to her. Or not. Just being in her company would be more than enough to satisfy my soul but, making her happy means more than making me happy." He sighed again, slowly feeling a lead weight come off his shoulders. "I get the feeling that not many people have thought of her or her feelings much, or if ever. Call it a gut feeling, but I just feel that she's been screwed over one too many times and I just put the final nail in the coffin. Well, no more. If there's going to be someone who's going to restore her trust in people, showing her that not everyone's out there to use, abuse, deceive her and toss her away, it's going to be me."

He turned when he hadn't heard a peep from his mother after a minute or so after he'd finished his impromptu speech. What he didn't expect to find when he did turn around, was his mother standing there with watery eyes her hand pressed to her mouth.

"Oh Ralph." She came towards him, sliding her arms around him and embracing him in a motherly hug. "I knew I raised you right. You mean well sweetie, even if you have a funny way of showing it sometimes."

"Who's got a funny way of showing what, sometimes?" His Pa said, striding into the kitchen to get his own breakfast.

His Ma detached herself from around his middle, walking over to her husband and pressing a kiss to his cheek. "Your son. Like you he means well, but he's got your tendencies to go about it in a funny way."

Puffing his chest out, his Pa looked at his wife with a mixture of a faux dented pride and pure love. He knew his parents never harboured any ill will against one another, no matter what happened between them or in their lives. If anyone was the epitome of true love, it was them. "I don't know what you mean, Cass dear."

"Sure you don't" she winked, patting him on his chest. "Now sit down and I'll fix you up some breakfast."

"Who am I to say no to that?"

"A wise man." His Ma muttered, heading on over to fix up another plate.

"Darn straight."

Ralph chuckled, shaking his head.

Nicely done, Pa. nicely done.

After fixing up a plate for his Pa, his Ma joined him back at the table once more. "Anyway as I was saying, Robinne was down at Laney's because she was getting a job. See, I would've happily offered her one at the B&B, but I thought I would remind her too much of you."

"Makes sense." He nodded.

His Ma continued. "So I spoke to Laney and managed to talk her into letting Robinne work for her until she secured something she really wanted to do. Your father kindly let her have the old Jameson place for no rent at all."

Putting down his fork, his Pa pointed his fork their way as he spoke around a half-eaten mouth full of food. "That's because it's not rented."

"It's not? How?" he asked, confused as to how this could be.

"Well, long story short, I ended up with the property as a way of thanks for looking after the Jameson's, seeing as they had no kids of their own. So technically, the deed is in my name for the house."

"Doesn't that mean she's not actually living in a house she owns? Since it's in your name and not hers?"

His Pa nodded, though on his face was a sneaky smile, one he saw as a kid when he and his Ma would be planning a surprise while trying not to let on that they were doing so.

"So, what, you're not going to tell her this like, ever?"

Shaking his head, his Pa finished what he was eating before continuing. "I did a background check into has a I do with anyone I rent out a house to, just to make sure for our own security that they're who they say they are. In doing so, I found out a little bit about her history. Nothing sinister, I promise you, but she needed a break. Breaks don't come easy in this world so, I thought till at least she got on her feet, found what she wanted to do etcetera, I'd keep the deed in my name and sign it over to her when she's found her sea legs as it were."

Ralph was dumbstruck but in the best way possible. He knew his father had a heart of gold, though he continued to be surprised when he occasionally did things like this. Pushing the boundaries of what a normal person would do so that someone else could have something instead.

He could only hope that he'd grow into half the man his father had become. Who needed a hero when people could have a Joe Jenkins? One thing for sure, he was one damned lucky son.

"Won't the poor dear be mad at you when she realises that the home she's making wasn't hers for all the time up until you tell her?" his mom piped up.

His Pa shook his head.

"No my dear, she won't. I can't be one hundred percent sure of course, though when I do tell or rather, reveal the truth to her, I have a feeling she'll see why I've done it rather than withholding truth from her. After all, we know she has trust issues with people being dishonest with her, but this is a more of a belated moving gift so to speak, not deception." He smiled, patting her hand tenderly.

Seeming placated, his Ma stood up and cleared her own plate and mug in the sink. "As long as you know what you're doing, I'm behind you."

Turning to face him, his Pa shot Ralph a wink before finishing his breakfast, adding his plate to the sink before pressing a kiss to his wife's cheek, departing for wherever he had to go to this morning.

Soon, his mother departed for her usual run at the B&B. She did have help every now and then but usually, she ran things herself, seeing as it was just a small little place. Not one of those big, corporate deals he'd stayed at in Austin when he'd visited on business with his Pa. They never did have the same feel as his Ma's place, though he was biased about that.

Just as he was about to head off to start his own day, he heard two pairs of booted feet come down the hall and enter into the kitchen. Reed and Roland walked in and planted themselves down at the table, each grabbing a mug and filling it to the brim with the leftover coffee. It was highly unusual to see one of the twins without the other, as they often did things as much together as possible. Only on rare occasions such as these did he see one without his partner in crime.

What was even odder to Ralph, was seeing Roland here in the first place. He never saw him in one place for too long. Ever since he returned home from college, he'd been caught goofing off and playing hooky. He pitched in at the ranch when he really had to but other than that, he was flitting about the town here and there doing God knows what, keeping himself entertained until someone reined him in.

"So, what brings you two here today? Especially you Reed." He asked, crossing his arms across his chest, casually leaning back against the kitchen counter.

Reed playfully flipped him off. "Can't we just stop on by to see our favourite older brother?"

"No. It usually means you want something, or you want to ask me something. You especially are more curious than a cat."

Roland smirked behind his mug, choosing to stay silent for the moment.

Clicking his fingers together, a big grin crept onto Reed's face.

Busted, little brother.

"Nothing gets past you eh Sherlock?" he chuckled, "Nah we just stopped by for a coffee and to invite you to the monthly poker game night tonight at Luca's place."

Ralph inwardly groaned. He wasn't for or against gambling, it just seemed that this month's game came around a little quicker than last month's did. Though this time last month he didn't have a beautiful British bombshell in his life, completing him while he complicated things.

Maybe a game or two might take my mind off of her for a little while.
It's worth a shot.

Unfolding his arms, he nodded. Pushing off the counter he headed towards the back door of the kitchen. "Count me in."

"Yes!" Reed and Roland chorused, reaching for a high five between them as Ralph shook his head, pushing open the door and heading to get his jobs done for the day.

Later that day, Ralph pulled up at the bottom of Luca's drive. As others would be there too thanks to the poker game night, he didn't want to block them in with his truck.

He and his buddies had met Luca years ago when he came to town lost. Luca wasn't a native to town, as made obvious by both his name and his Italian accent. He'd been looking for another small town but had missed his turn off, resulting in him driving into this down asking for directions. He'd been searching for the place where his mother had come from, before visiting Italy where she'd met his father and never returned.

Silly fool was following a Satnav which was showing him the wrong place to go, as another town had the same name and he'd been given the wrong state's co-ordinates. After that, he and his buddies ran into him one night when he came to town at the local bar, taking him under their wing. From that day on, he never left.

Ralph will never fully understand the reason why Luca stayed, as he assumed he would've wanted to carry on and seek out his mother's hometown, but whatever reason for him saying was, he was glad. Luca was a real stand-up guy, with all of the guys agreeing that they felt they'd known him a lifetime rather than a mere ten years.

He often escaped back to Luca's when things got a little bit too stressful between him and any of his brothers. Where he was a man who liked the solitude of his own home, sometimes it was nice to escape to a friend's place who had an open home for anyone who needed it, temporarily or otherwise.

Stepping out of his truck and heading up the drive to Luca's house, he could see a greater number of trucks gathered than usual on one of their monthly poker game nights. Usually, it was the five Jenkins brothers, if Roland joined them, the two Roth boys, Luca, Grant from the auto shop and Drayton from the aptly named 'Big D Ranch'.

Since it wasn't usually the same ten guys every month, as not everyone could make it on a monthly basis, it was potluck as to who would actually be attending tonight. By the looks of things, it seemed to be the usual group of guys based on the trucks and vehicles parked as he stepped up onto the front porch.

On game nights, Luca kept his front door open for people to let themselves in, so Ralph strode right inside the front hall, calling out to let them know that he'd arrived.

"Hey!"

Luca emerged from the kitchen with a huge grin on his face. It wasn't often that this guy didn't sport a smile, yet he always managed to make you feel at ease with it when you saw it.

"*Buona sera* my good friend!" his accent coming out strong and prominent.

The two embraced in a bro-hug as if they'd been friends for longer than their ten years. It was a strong embrace between friends as close as he was with one of his brothers.

"How late am I to the party?

Luca shrugged. "Not late at all. You're the fourth. Come on in, I have drinks ready for you."

He followed Luca through to the back room where they usually held their poker game and as usual, an array of food and drinks had been laid out ready for the players as they arrived. Coming from Italy and a family of renowned traditional cooks, they were more than blessed whenever they came over that they'd be guaranteed a good spread.

If only I had his cooking skills, I could do something for Robinne.

The thought of her stopped him as he came into the room behind Luca. He was here for the soul purpose of trying to put her out of his mind so he didn't break his promise and go see her, not to think about her at every turn. It was proving hard, but he was determined to give it his best shot.

Three pairs of faces turned to look at him once he returned to his senses. His brother Ryder, Reed and Roland were there, all tipping their drinks up to him as he joined them with his own.

"Good to see you make it." Reed piped up.

He sat down, raising a brow at him.

"Why wouldn't I? I said this morning I'd come."

"Yeah but, you had the whole day to change your mind. I was sure you would."

"Meaning?"

Reed shrugged. "As I said, I just thought you would."

"Well, I'm here so, you can quit your yapping."

Ryder and Roland chuckled behind their glasses, which looked to be filled with something stronger than beer.

"I hope you two plan on crashing here tonight. I don't want to have to explain to Ma and Pa why you two were found doing something idiotic under the influence."

Roland rolled his eyes, ever the rebel of all the brothers.

"Relax man, we're crashing. No need to go all commanding on us."

He took a swig of his beer, pointing a finger at Roland.

"Don't forget, I am the eldest and you're not twenty-one yet. I could easily tell Ma and Pa about your drinking and playing with us tonight, but I won't if you do what I say. Understand?"

He didn't respond, other than with a grunt as he slumped back in his chair.

Ryder and Reed did well to keep to themselves as he chastised their youngest brother. Thankfully, he didn't have to do that to him often. Though he just wished that Roland would fall into line sooner rather than later. Whatever had happened while he was away at college had changed him. Once a mild-mannered polite young man, was now a sassy and back-talking one. Maybe it was his age, as he remembered each of his brothers going through a similar stage. Either way, he hoped it would come to an end soon.

All four of them fell into an easy conversation, with Roland mostly listening, while Luca played ever the good host as each of the remaining players arrived in drips and drabs, with Grant filling the final and tenth place at the table.

"So, what's everyone been up to lately?" said Drayton, dealing out the cards around the table.

"I don't know about anyone else, but I do know someone who's been up to something with a certain someone as of late." Drake Roth smirked, flicking his eyes over in Ralph's direction.

Uh oh…

"Oh?" Drake's brother Brant asked, turning also to face Ralph. "Do tell buddy, do tell."

I knew tonight would be too good to be true.

These guys are worse than the town gossips.

Oh well, no use denying it, they'll only find out eventually.

"What do you guys want to know?" He sighed.

"As much as you want us to know." Drayton replied, fixing his own hand before looking up.

Ralph looked at his own hand, not giving anything away on his face as to its strength. The game continued as he began to explain to all of them.

"Depending on what each of you knows, I'll start from the beginning. The five of us built up the old Jameson place, and I had the misfortune of meeting its new owner buck naked, thanks to two idiot brothers of mine. A series of unfortunate events then occurred, where either she or myself were lacking in some or most of our clothes, running into one another when we least expected it. Skip ahead to the weekly BBQ at the main ranch house, where it rains heavier than I've ever known it to. Thinking logically, I got us into the barn to take shelter. We got to talking as you would do, with her revealing quite a few things close to her chest to me." He swallowed, knowing what he was going to have to say next. "I messed things up big style between us, just as I thought we were getting closer in knowing one another."

"What did you do?" Luca asked carefully, keeping one eye on the game at all times.

Ralph rubbed a hand down his face. "I confessed to her that I'd taken a list she'd made before coming here. Things she didn't want to happen to her. I stupidly thought if I could make them happen, in a positive way, I could change her mind and make experiences that she previously thought as bad ones, into good ones. Memorable ones for her. I just went about it in an arse about face manor."

After a beat of no one saying anything, perhaps not quite sure as what to say, the one person who'd been silent all this time, finally spoke up. Rowan, Reed's twin, leaned forward, setting his current card hand on the table.

"That's messed up brother. What the heck made you even carry it out in the first place?"

The rest of the table laid their cards down too, with Ryder winning the first round of the night.

"Honestly? As I've mentioned to anyone else who's talked to me about this, I don't know. Other than what I just mentioned about trying to do something nice for her."

"Funny way of going about it." Grant mumbled.

He sighed for the millionth time that night.

"I know, I know. Nothing can be done about it now. I've already had a dressing down, even at my age, and I've even made a promise to Robinne directly saying that I won't go near her until she's ready to speak to me again. I don't know when that will be or how long it will take to get there, but I'm willing to wait and atone for what I've done to her."

He felt a pat on his right shoulder. His brother Ryder, the person other than him who was closes to Robinne, gave him an approving nod. "I hope you go about things the right way this time, for her sake more than yours."

"Damn straight." Quipped Brant, the others around the table smirking at his remark.

Luca clapped his hands, bringing the table's attention back to the game.

"Now, *amici*, do I have to cut you all off or are you going to play nice and leave the poor guy be *sì*?"

"*Sì amico*." They called out in unison, doing their best Luca accent replications as they could.

Sharing a laugh between all of them, they got back to the game and much to Ralph's relief, dropped the subject about him, Robinne, or him and Robinne collectively.

Though he wasn't feeling much for playing anymore, he shoved his desire to bolt down deep inside of him and did his best to get his head into the game and the next hand that was currently being played. The least he could aim to do was win at least one hand before he decided to fold, chicken out and call it a night.

Though I'm not exactly sure how confident I am in my poker skills thanks to the topic that's just been discussed.

Great, just great.

Ralph managed to hold onto that thought for little over an hour before he felt it was right to call it a night. His head wasn't exactly in the idea of being here tonight, but he thought he'd give it a go for the sake of his brothers coming personally to invite him around that morning.

"I think that's me done for tonight boys." He said, folding his hand and collecting his winnings. Thankfully, he'd managed to win a few hands this last hour to call it worth coming for the short while he'd been here.

"Too late to stay out old man?" Roland sneered, playfully mocking Ralph's senior years over his own.

Ralph gently smacked him upside the head as he got up out of his seat, "You mind your mouth boy, or the next time you actually put your ass to work at the ranch, I'm going to give you the hardest jobs to do to make your ass as sore as can be."

Snickers were heard around the table as for the second time tonight, Ralph put Roland back into line.

"See you around buddy, don't be a stranger now." Drayton said, shaking Ralph's hand as he passed by.

"I won't. Laters man."

He made a point of bidding temporary farewell to everyone at the table who wasn't related to him, with saying to those that were that he'd see them bright and early tomorrow morning to get a head start on finishing things before the weekend work starts.

Luca was the last one to see him off, walking with him to the front door.

"Hey, listen Ralph, I'm sorry those guys ambushed you tonight. I told them not to mention it but, you know what it's like getting them to listen to anything any of us say."

Shaking his head, he clapped his hand on Luca's shoulder. "Think nothing of it, you're right. They're like a bunch of kids when one of us is in some kind of trouble with anything or anyone."

Luca chuckled, nodding as he knew that all too well.

"Drive safe, *fratello*."

He and Luca shook hands before he made his way back down to his truck, sliding into the cab with mixed emotions. He was glad he was out of there away from talk he was trying to avoid, yet he wasn't any lighter for talking about it. Feeling conflicted didn't even come close to how he could describe how he was feeling.

Turning the engine on, he wasted no time in pulling out of where he'd parked, heading for the sanctuary of his own home.

* * *

Back in Luca's, the rest of the boys resumed their game after the unpredicted departure of their friend.

As Luca sat back down at the table, Drake started shelling out the next round's cards. Unbeknown to Ralph, they all shared a single thought as from what he'd told them tonight, they pretty much knew what was going to happen in the end.

"So, how long do you reckon until the two of them finally get together?"

Reed smirked, "A month. No more."

"I say…six weeks." Rowan chipped in.

Brant held up both of his hands, "Let's make this official. $20 says they'll be an item before thanksgiving."

"Two months." Grant placed his own $20 on the table.

The rest of the guys made their own bets as to how long it would take Ralph and Robinne to patch things up and admit their feelings for one another. It didn't really matter as to when it happened, what each man knew sitting at that table, that it was going to happen. Period.

CHAPTER SIXTEEN
~ Robinne ~

August 31st 2018 (Friday)

Before she knew it, a month had flown by since Robinne had received the gift basket and note from Ralph, promising her that he was going to stay away from her. And keep his promise he did. She'd seen no sight or sound of him, even in such a small town as Dripping Springs.

In a way, she secretly hoped that in some way she would run into him, just to catch a glimpse of him. Even for just a second. Though, she really saw the fact that she didn't, as a sort of blessing in disguise. If she did see him, she knew in her heart of hearts she wouldn't be able to resist asking him how he was. No matter what he did to her.

No one else had mentioned him to her for that matter, over the last month. She knew everyone in town pretty much knew one another, yet they stayed silent on that one particular subject she assumed for her own sake. There were a few times in which she'd bumped into Cassie, one of Ralph's brothers and a few of his friends she'd had the pleasure of meeting, still, none of them mentioned or even hinted at how Ralph was.

Guess they're all in on the promise now too.

They had to be, there wasn't any other explanation which could come close to explaining why the entire town of Dripping Springs had kept quiet. Nonetheless, the month had crawled by and she'd managed to resist even using her phone to text or call him and to her, that was something of a feat.

Back home when she'd had a falling out with a then friend, it wasn't usually too long until one of them offered an olive branch of peace and they made up. Only on the odd occasion did things just naturally slide back into place with neither party apologising to the other. Usually, if neither party made the first move, often the friendship would just fizzle out.

She had one friend years ago, who was often under the thumb of her mother. When she means 'often', she meant completely. If she was exaggerating, she would go so far as to say that the girl wasn't even allowed to blink without her mother saying so. She was that meek and mild, she didn't even bother to utter a word against her, even if it was something she deeply disagreed with. She'd go along with it because her mother was that psychotic, she'd make her pay for it if she didn't.

Juliet had been her best friend for around three years while she struggled to make friends, the two of them finding a kinship facing the same issue. She'd invited her round to her house countless times, met her in town on weekends, hung out with her every break and lunch in school, even went to the cinema on occasion with her, as she was only allowed to see Juliet when her mother gave her permission. There was so much she could do with her that she was restricted against, all because of Juliet's mother.

One day at lunch in school, Juliet mentioned to her that she'd been after this DVD for a while but was unable to get it, as the cost of it was too high from any store in town. So, as her friend, Robinne decided she'd save up and get her the DVD off eBay or Amazon for a reduced price, giving it to her friend as a gift 'just because'. No reason behind it, other than the fact that she wanted to see her friend happy. So, that's what she did.

Only, Juliet's mother didn't see it that way. In her mind, there had to be some other reason as to why Robinne had given her daughter this DVD with wanting nothing in return.

What happened next was completely and utterly bizarre. As Robinne at the time was wanting to do something different, which was in learning how to play the guitar, she was given an electric guitar from Juliet, on behalf of her mother and father. Mostly her mother. As a way of making things 'equal' after she'd given her daughter the DVD. This was bizarre, but by far it wasn't the most bizarre thing to have happened yet.

Around the time Twilight's third movie instalment, Eclipse, was due to come out in the cinema, Robinne decided she wanted to go see it, as she'd missed seeing the other two in cinemas. Because Juliet was her best friend, she wanted to take her along with her to see the film. So, as a mark of respect, she decided to message Juliet's mum on Facebook, asking he if Juliet was allowed to come and see the film with her. The reply she got in response, and there were two of them, were not what she was expecting. Again.

If Robinne remembered correctly, the messages she was sent went something along the lines of: *Juliet can't always come out with you to places like the cinema, we're not made of money and she has to buy a completely new wardrobe for our upcoming holiday this year. She doesn't have time to always go out with you, so I'd appreciate it if you'd stop asking her out all the time. ~ Also, you are not permitted to see my daughter outside of school any more. Juliet is only allowed to see you during school times from now on. She will see you in September, please do not speak to her until then. Please give back the guitar before the start of the school year, as it's very valuable and we would like it back.*

All Robinne did was ask her mom, politely, if her friend could come see a film that *she* was paying for. She never made any of her friends pay for a cinema ticket if she was the one who invited them out to see said film. It was made quite clear to Juliet's mum that this was the case, though it didn't seem to make a blind bit of difference.

Her friend's mom was the very definition of psychotic. Pure and simple. No matter how many times she'd explained that she gave the DVD as a gift and would pay for the cinema ticket, wanting nothing in return or expecting her to pay, it went in one ear and straight out the other. On top of that, wanting a guitar back that had been given to her as a gift prompted the question as to why they'd given it to her in the first place, if they wanted nothing for it.

Because her friend's mum was as sane as a man in a padded cell, that's why.

It had ruined Robinne's summer that year, as she was looking forward to her and Juliet going into their second to last year of secondary school. A year where they had control over what subjects they'd take, and where more would happen that they could take part in together. Alas, it wasn't meant to be.

She never did speak to Juliet again after that, as her friend had no backbone to tell her mum that she still wanted to speak to Robinne. Till this day, she'll never know if her former friend did want to still speak to her, though she didn't really care. All she ever wanted to know was why Juliet never disobeyed her mum, even in the smallest way that wasn't disrespectful.

There wasn't much point worrying about it now, it's in the past and that's where it was going to stay. Only on occasion like today, as she was cleaning Laney's bakery tables at the end of the day, where she had a few moments to think about things like this. She'd soon put the thought behind her once again, not to come out again any time soon.

"Phew!" Laney said from somewhere behind her.

She turned around to see her friend and boss turning the sign over to 'closed'. The bakery was often left open to a later time on a Friday, to give people enough time to grab a snack at the end of the working week before they'd head home. As most of their customers were ranchers, they weren't always able to come in the middle of the day, as most people usually do.

"Glad to be done for the day?" she asked Laney, finishing up wiping up the table.

Laney nodded. "You can say that again. I never thought that seven would ever roll around."

Robinne laughed, plopping down on the booth seat. "Why didn't you ever hire someone else to work with you before I came?"

"Never seemed like I needed it at the time. I'm glad I decided to take someone on in the end, even if you aren't staying forever."

"Oh I don't know. It looks like I'll still be here for as long as you're willing to have me. I still haven't found something that I really want to do yet. I thought I'd have some sort of clue by now." She said, mentally and physically deflated.

She felt Laney slide into the booth beside her, gently placing an arm across her shoulders. "You'll find it, I know you will. After all, there's that saying isn't there? When you stop looking for something, you'll find it." she blinked. "Or something like that."

Robinne couldn't help but laugh, Laney was a funny woman. She'd grown closer to her in the month she'd been working for her. They'd texted most days of the week and often met up for drinks at the café when Robinne wasn't working and wanted to get out of the house. She was glad that she'd found a comrade besides Ryder, who she considered her best friend since moving here. They'd texted themselves a few times, asking no more than how the other was.

It was evident he was adhering to the promise made by Ralph to her, so she had to respect that.

"Anyway, since it's the end of the week, I thought we could go out and do something tonight."

She blinked.

"Out? As in, out out? Or just out into town?"

There was a difference, to her at least.

"Out out." Laney smiled. "I know this great little place just on the outskirts of town just off the interstate. It's a themed place, as you have to dress in such things as cowboy hats, boots and such." She waved her hand about, as if to indicate other items of the like.

"Aren't those things what people wear around here anyway?"

"Mmm, I suppose. Though it's only really the cowboys and ranchers who usually wear those sorts of things every day."

"There's a difference?"

"Between what?"

"Cowboys and ranchers?"

Laney smirked. "Oh yes. Any man, or woman, can be a rancher. But it takes a true gentleman or lady to be a cowboy. People think all people of states like Texas who work on ranches are all cowboys by default, but much like the title of a gentleman, it's something earned. Not given."

Woah.

I never knew Laney could be so deep.

Well, it goes to show you can't judge a book by its covers.

"I…I don't know. I'm not one for…you know, going out of a night?"

"How come?" Laney prised.

She shrugged, "Never have been. No one I knew back home went out late at night as they all worked, and the people I did know who went out always went somewhere where I didn't want to go. So, I just stayed home."

"Well, I promise you I can change that. This place doesn't charge to get in and how about this, when you're ready to leave, we can leave. I won't make you stay till any specific time. Let's test out your social water wings shall we? Just this once?" The puppy dog eyes came out then. If there was something she found hard to resist, it was people who used the puppy dog eyes.

She held her hands up in surrender.

"Okay, okay, I'll go!"

Laney beamed. "I knew you would! Now, go on, scoot off home and be ready for seven. I'll swing by then and drive us there."

Why is it always seven?

Later, Robinne was getting ready for when Laney planned to swing by to take her to wherever this place was. She said it was off some interstate, or highway or something, though she still would have no idea where those were. Thankfully, she'd learned where most of the local roads led to and what they were called, but forget anywhere outside of the town. That was still an undiscovered and unexplored territory.

Remembering what Laney said about this place's 'dress code', if that's the right way to describe it, she manage to scratch an outfit together thanks to her purchases at Susan's Springs nearer when she'd first arrived in town. She was currently sporting a pair of fitted jeans, a white vest, which was partially covered with a blue plaid/tartan shirt, a pair of cowgirl boots which had been made here in town, all topped off with a cowgirl hat, putting a cap on her long, wavy black hair.

You don't look half bad for once old girl.

She left her bedroom after feeling satisfied that her outfit would do, not bothering to put on a stitch of makeup, she made her way downstairs and into her kitchen, deciding on a cup of tea before heading on out. There was still plenty of time left before Laney was due to pick her up, as Robinne always made sure she was ready on time when going out with people. If there was one thing she didn't like, it was not being ready.

Soon enough after finishing her cup of tea, two friendly honks of a horn came from out front of her place. Laney was here. Taking a deep breath, she left her cup behind in the kitchen, grabbed her keys from their usual place, and locked up her front door before making her way down to Laney's truck.

Another thing she'd learned since moving here, pretty much everyone owned a truck. She didn't want to stereotype every southern person with owning one but so far, the stereotype seemed to be winning. If it wasn't a Nissan, it was a Dodge, or a Ford, or even a Chevrolet. She had a pretty good ideas to why the people of the south seemed to prefer the truck to a car, but that was a thought for another day.

She hopped up into the passenger side of Laney's truck, slipping on her belt before turning to greet her friend.

"Hi."

"Hey. You look great! Loving the hat and boots, are they Susan's?"

She smiled, nodding. "Yes, how'd you guess?"

Laney pulled away from the pavement, heading in the direction in which this place must be located. "Everyone goes to her for clothes. Well, at least the women. We do have a bigger clothing store but, we like to support our own first and keep the smaller businesses running."

"I'm the same." She said, turning her attention to the road. "Shame not everyone shares the same thoughts as us."

Laney nodded.

"Nervous?" she asked a short while later, driving the two of them past the 'Welcome to Dripping Springs' sign.

Oh only like, A LOT!

Robinne thought she'd done a pretty good job at keeping her inner thoughts from leaking outward, guess she was wrong. Though she wasn't as nervous enough to visibly shake, there were always other ways in which people could tell and pick up on nervousness. Laney obviously had.

"Yes, I am a little. I might seem like I'm over the whole 'meeting people for the first time' thing, I'm not. I just make things so…awkward. When I meet people, I have this amazing ability to turn any situation into an awkward one, which usually results in me embarrassing myself or saying something stupidly inappropriate, thus embarrassing myself further."

Laney laughed, nodding her head, clearly understanding Robinne's plight.

She continued.

"I don't know how I do it, I just do. Do you know what? I even manage to do it mid-conversation with someone I've known for a while. It just…happens. Some people are charismatic, some social. Me? I define awkwardness."

If there were ever a truer statement spoken from her own mouth, then she was a monkey's aunt. She'd heard it from more than one person on more than one occasion. Specifically, one of her latest former friends. He made it pretty clear that she was awkward, unfunny, over-sentimental and such other things of the like.

Yeah well, what does he know?

Nothing.

"I was the same as you, you know."

"You were?"

"Oh yes." Laney nodded, "Still am sometimes. It's not as noticeable but when I first came to town with my parents as a kid, I was forever making things awkward. Especially in my teen years when we were all finding ourselves. Where some girls flourished and looked absolutely flawless, walking about as if they were mini Queens of the world, I was there, awkward as hell and proud of it."

She blinked, stunned at the latter part of that sentence.

"Why were you proud of it?"

Laney turned and met her eyes for the briefest of moments, "Because I knew someday, one day, it would all change. I just had to wait patiently for that day." She turned her eyes back to the road, turning the truck onto the highway.

She wasn't quite sure as to what to say. Where she silently applauded Laney for being proud of one of her past insecurities, it boggled her mind that someone in fact *could* be proud of it. For her, when she'd had one of her insecurities opened and exposed to the world, more than anything she just wanted to shrink back and hide until people had forgotten about it and her.

Since she was four years old and well into her mid-teens, she'd been aware of things about her that people didn't like, pointed out on a daily basis to make fun of her, so she just can't imagine no matter how hard she tried, being proud of something that caused emotional or physical distress. One thing she had to remember, was that she and Laney were two different people. What worked for Laney might not work for her and vice versa. No two people were the same and although they shared similarities, there were bound to be things which differentiated them. This being one of them.

At the end of the day, which ironically would be upon them in five hours, she was happy that Laney could be proud of herself for something like that, hoping one day she could hopefully come to think the way she does.

They settled into an easy conversation as Laney drove them towards this bar, she thinks she remembered her calling it, with every mile passing, she became more relaxed and for the first time tonight, thinking that she might actually enjoy this night out after all.

A little under half an hour later, Laney turned the truck off a junction (off-ramp to Americans), taking them down a small road leading to the place in question which she'd been told about earlier. Though she didn't know what to expect, she certainly wasn't expecting to see what she was currently seeing right now.

"Am I seeing what I really think I'm seeing?"

Her friend beamed across at her from across the truck cab, parking up in the car park. "I knew you'd like this place! I thought of taking you here the moment we met."

Robinne turned away from her friend to look at the place in front of them. No way in a million years did she expect to see something like this smack-bang in the middle of Texas, in the middle of nowhere. What looked to be placed here right from her home country, was an English pub. Or at least, as best created to look like one. It was if she was right back home at one of the pub she loved to escape to on weekends, a small-town place where she could get some reading and work done.

"Laney…it's amazing" she beamed.

"Well what are we waiting for? Let's treat you to a slice of home"

Home.

It wasn't my home anymore. Here, here is my home.

Still, a toast to the old days won't hurt.

They left the truck and ambled on inside the pub, with Robinne being just as stunned to see the inside as she was the outside. Whoever had taken the time to design this place, had truly done their job town to the pinnacle of perfection. If she didn't look outside and see Texas staring back at her, she would've taken this place for jolly old England itself.

Never mind that England wasn't so jolly at the moment, what with all the bull that is Brexit but still, some part of her was glad that she was still able to have some slice of home, here in Texas.

Laney waved to the man behind the bar who was currently pulling a pint for someone, with him nodding his head back as the two of them made their way over to a table in the back corner.

"Do you know him?"

Laney nodded, "Yeah, that's Mike. He owns this place and often works at the bar most nights of the week."

She gave her friend a look, trying to assess if there was something else going on between them, or if they were just acquaintances. Though, her friend wasn't as daft as she herself was, she soon saw through what Robinne was trying to do, shaking her head in reply.

"The answer is no. There is nothing between Mike and I. We're just friends."

By the look on her face, Robinne could tell that Laney meant what she said. Unless Laney was a fantastic actress, she had no reason to doubt what was just told to her.

Robinne was a good judge of whether or not people were lying to her. Well, she is now. After saying goodbye to her former friend, she became more cautious with people and paid more attention to what people were saying to her. Thus, her newfound skill of being able to pick out the truths from the lies. She liked to think she was able to do so anyway.

"Evening ladies." Mike said as he approached them, a friendly smile on her face. "What'll it be?"

Laney looked up at him and returned his smile, holding the drinks menu in her hand. "I'll have my usual please, Mike. But you've got your hands full with this one here." She teased, nodding to Robinne.

Mike arched a curious brow, looking between the two of them. "Oh?"

"You see, she's from the very land your wonderful place is based on. You'll have to pull out your best guns to impress her."

Robinne waved her hand, a little embarrassed at being put on the spot like that.

"Oh, no. N-no. I don't need to be impressed by anyone. I-I'm truly happy with whatever you'd recommend. I don't want to be any trouble."

Mike chuckled, putting his pen and pad into his pocket, crossing his arms loosely over his wide chest.

"So you're the British beauty everyone's been talking about back in Dripping springs. Well, it's a pleasure to meet you. As Laney here has probably already said, I'm Mike. Mike Harrison." He held out his hand towards her.

British beauty? No way am I beautiful.

She shook it, offering up her own friendly smile.

"Robinne James. I hope what you've heard about me wasn't too damning on my reputation."

Mike chuckled.

"Not at all. If anything, it's more about us looking after you, after what happened. We look after our own, old or new to town."

Why couldn't I have been born into a world like this back home?

Her cheeks flamed a little, flattered by his bold statement.

"Thank you Mike, that's very kind of you to say so. I'll have your house wine please."

Where she was normally more of a cider girl herself, tonight, she was feeling a little daring to try something different.

He nodded, "House wine it is. Ladies, I'll be back with your drinks shortly."

As he left, she could hear Laney's giggle from across the table.

"For as long as I've been coming here, I don't think I've seen him so charmed before. If things don't work out between you and Ralph, you might have a future there."

She shook her head, as that wasn't what she'd come here to look for. She was perfectly happy as she was, for now. Her top priority currently was trying to better herself and find something that made her happy, not seeking out the next hot-blooded male to keep her company. Or finally do the deed with her, as that could wait till another time.

Where most people would be unhappy at being in the smaller minority who hadn't slept with a man at her age, she wasn't. As she'd said to the few people she'd confided in about it over the years, she'd come to the realisation that she wasn't someone that people wanted to get intimate with, among other things. She'd resigned herself to a prospect of permanent purity, until Ralph.

Inwardly, she sighed. She was here to have a good time and to keep her mind off the cowboy with the dreamiest eyes she'd ever seen.

"Hey, Earth to Robinne." Laney said, clicking her fingers in front of her face, bringing her back into the moment.

"Sorry, I tuned out there for a moment. What were you saying?" she asked politely.

"I was asking you how you were getting on with your writing. You said you were thinking about starting your first novel, how's that going?"

Oh yeah, I forgot about that.

Mike came and dropped off their drinks, flashing them both a friendly smile before heading over to serve two people who'd just come through the door, leaving them both to talk alone.

"I've started planning it, and it's actually coming along really well. I made the mistake before of publishing a first draft, uncompleted once before ages ago and looking back on it, it was a horrid mess of a manuscript."

Laney nodded, "How come?"

"That year, I fell ill on January first. What a day to fall ill, right? New Year's Day of all days, when the start of a new year is supposed to be a new start. Anyway, I'd decided to write the book and publish it for a former friend of mine's birthday in June. Since he and I didn't work out as friends, I then decided to publish it on my then best friend's birthday, which I did. Promising I'd release the full story at a later date once my health had recovered." She took a breather, sipping at her wine before continuing. "I'd written the published manuscript while I was heavy with fever and full of delusion. Looking back on it, most of what I'd written didn't make sense and was full of major mistakes and errors. So, I abandoned writing for a bit until I was completely better. Which brings me to where I am now. This time, I'm doing things properly."

Laney looked like she'd heard the worst news in the world, or seen a puppy being hit by a car.

"Oh how terrible! I'm so sorry that happened to you! Please tell me you didn't go through this on your own?" she pleaded.

She wished she could tell Laney something different, but she wasn't going to tell her anything but the truth.

"I did."

It was then that Laney grabbed her hand and held it between her own, as if she were lending some of her strength, strength she wished she had at the time she was going through one of the worst times of her life alone.

"I wish I was there. No one should ever go through anything alone."

She appreciated how genuinely apologetic Laney was, as she too wished she had someone there for her.

"Thank you. I agree. But, I did it. My best friend at the time was deep in a relationship with her then boyfriend, so I didn't want to bother her too much by worrying her. As she had her own health issues to deal with. I did tell her I was in the hospital, twice, but I didn't say more than that."

"Was there truly no one else you could even call, text or anything?"

She shook her head.

"No one. The man I trusted and confided in more than anyone I've ever met, I had to say goodbye to back in the March of that year. I was almost tempted to unblock his number and tell him I needed him. It was one of the hardest things I had to do, but deep down I knew he didn't really care if anything happened to me or not so, I didn't call. My other friend was working, and he literally wasn't able to take time off during the day to come with me. He did call and ask how I was when I got out of hospital though, so I was thankful for at least that much."

Laney sighed, nodding.

"Well, it's over now and you won't ever have to worry about being alone ever again. I'll be there for you if you'll be there to me too, I don't exactly have a plethora of friends either. It would be nice to feel that I had someone who would be there for me when I needed them."

Oh you sweet girl, of course I will.

Robinne put her free hand on top of the ones currently holding her other one, "It would be my pleasure."

The two of them toasted to their brand new friendship pledge. Never before has she felt more grateful to be around another woman, as she often found it harder to trust women than men, but she sent a silent prayer of thanks to the big man (or woman) above for sending Laney to her.

For the rest of the evening, the two of them enjoyed pleasant and friendly talk from everything about their favourite books, to who their top five male celebrity crushes were. She felt as though the two of them were catching up on missed time talking about thing she would've talked about with someone while they were teens. Truth be told, she didn't really care. She was having a good time and that's what mattered.

By the time ten o'clock rolled around, they were more than ready to call it a night. Laney had stuck to only the one drink, as she was driving and she didn't want to be caught being over the limit, or doing something that would put either of them in danger. Robinne however, had more than one glass of wine and went over her usual limit when she drank.

Laney paid the bill for the drinks, insisting as because she invited Robinne out, she should pay for what they'd drank.

She thankfully was able to stand her own two feet when the time came for them to leave, albeit those said legs as being as wobbly as a new-born deer. Laney thankfully held onto her elbow as they began their exit from the pub, calling out a friendly and rather loud goodbye to Mike. He wished them a safe journey home and hoped to see them soon.

"Do you think you can get the door?" Laney asked her, struggling to keep her friend upright as well as negotiate the bustling crowd near the door.

"I-I think sho." Her words slurred, a clear sign she'd got even squiffier than she'd planned to.

She grabbed the hand of the door, trying to push at it.

"It's a pull door, Robinne." Laney said, the smirk evident in her voice, even with Robinne's back to her.

"I know…knew…t-that."

Moving her friends' hand off of her elbow, she squared her shoulders, preparing to give the door a good pull in her inebriated state.

One…two…three!

On three in her head, she yanked open the door at the same time someone pushed it open from the other side, causing her to lose her footing. Laney had stepped back as Robinne wobbled, thus resulting in her not landing in her friend's arms, but the big, muscular arms of a man who'd intervened instead.

"Woah there, darlin'. I got you."

A familiar, whiskey-toned voice crooned.

Oh no…no no no.

It can't be. Not here, not now.

Ralph.

CHAPTER SEVENTEEN
~ Ralph ~

When Ralph got the call from Mike to help him come shift some barrels, he didn't hesitate for a moment whether he should come and help him or not. He wasn't doing anything in particular, just lazing around his place after a full day's work. He would be a real douche if he didn't come out to help his friend.

Besides, Mike's usual barman broke his leg the other weekend from a barrel landing on his own leg while moving it. The guy wasn't overly strong and didn't really have a lot going on upstairs, so he didn't think to take his own safety into account when hefting a barrel down the basement stairs. Silly fool lost his footing and the metal barrel landed straight on his leg, breaking it clean in two.

Thank goodness Ralph knew better and knew exactly how to move them, as did Mike, who'd taught him how.

What he didn't expect upon arriving at the outskirts of town pub, was to catch in his arms the very person he'd been trying so hard, and succeeding, to avoid for the past month. He'd often heard of guys saying women literally fell at their feet, but this was his first time experiencing such an event.

"Woah there darlin', I've got you." He said as he caught her, hauling her gently back to her feet.

He could see Laney not too far away from her, standing just inside the doorway watching the scene unfold. Why didn't she try to catch her friend instead of him? Not that it really mattered, as he was secretly glad it was him and that he had the chance to have her in his arms again.

God she looks beautiful.

He'd almost forgotten just how good looking she was, for it not for the fact of his occasional dreams about her. He couldn't control that, though. Days where he wouldn't be as active led to nights where his mind was left to wander to things he was trying to not think about. Mostly Robinne.

Giving her a once-over from her head to her toes, checking to see if she was hurt by her fall in any way, the smell of alcohol reaches his nose. She reeked of the stuff. If it was visible to the eye, he was sure he would see it rolling off of her in waves.

How could anyone let her get like this?
Laney, it had to be her.

Robinne didn't say a word as he kept his hands on her shoulders, preventing her swaying body from lurching in any direction under its own steam. He looked over Robinne's shoulder to meet Laney's gaze.

"Let me guess, you let her get like this. Didn't you?" he might be coming across as harsh, but he wasn't. Not at all. He was just protective of Robinne, believe it or not.

Laney swallowed, reluctantly nodding and confirming his suspicion.

"I brought her out tonight to celebrate the end of the work week and to loosen her up a little." Her eyes told him another story that she dared not speak in front of Robinne.

He knew from what Laney was saying to him, that she brought his British beauty out to get her to forget him for the time being. Not that he could blame her for doing so. After all, he'd gone to that poker game to do the same thing. Except, he didn't go under someone else's demands. He'd gone under his own decision to do so. Robinne hadn't.

"Alright." He nodded.

There was no doubt in his mind that he was now going to be the one to take Robinne home, no matter how much she was bound to protest against the idea. Which was what was bound to happen.

He looked at Robinne once more, who just so happened to be looking a little peakier than she did a moment ago, before facing Laney again. "Listen, Mike called me to help move some barrels, but after I'm done doing that I'm taking Robinne home."

Robinne jerked under his touch, finally acknowledging something he'd said.

"Wha? No! You ish not doing dat! New way. N-no…no way."

Lord she's had a skinful.

It was then at that moment in which Laney came forward. Ralph moved one of his hands so she could put her own on Robinne's shoulder. "He's right, you should go with him."

He and Robinne sported the same bemused look, neither of them quite expecting Laney to agree with him, as usually women tended to stick together and pick their friend over a guy (or girl), no matter who was in the right or wrong.

"I'm not passing your place before I go home anyway, he will. I've got to stop by the bakery again, just to double check I've left enough ingredients out for my half day tomorrow."

It was a complete dud of an excuse, as he knew her well enough to know that she always made sure of this before she shut up shop for the day, but he doubted with Robinne in her current state, that she'd remember as such.

"C'mon darlin', I won't be long then I'll have you back in your nice warm bed and you can sleep for as long as you like."

She gasped.

"Walf Dekins!" she hiccupped. "Dew are nawt sweeping wid me! I knew yew wanted in my klick…nick…click…my panties!"

While that may be true in some respect darlin', I wouldn't take advantage of you.
He couldn't help but chuckle, shaking his head.

"I won't be sleeping with you darlin', you'll be sleeping solo."

She huffed, "Yeah, like always."

Laney scooted around them, fishing out her car keys. "I'll just be going." She turned around halfway to her car. "You be minding her Ralph Jenkins. Don't make me regret leaving her with you, or else."

Jeez, women can be scary sometimes.

He nodded.

"You have my word."

Seeming satisfied at his promise, Laney left them without saying another word. Pulling out the parking space and heading right on home, where he knew she was really heading back to.

This next hour or so was going to prove to be very interesting indeed.

Sighing, he guided Robinne back inside the pub, surprised that she was oddly compliant and not protesting against him. He sat her down in a booth near the doors, allowing her to soak in a bit of air while she waited him. Crouching down beside her, he waited until her glazed eyes met his own.

"I won't be long, okay? I'm just going to change a few barrels and move a few, then I'll be right back. Don't move from this spot, got it?" he said softly, not wanting to spook or enrage her. Anything could happen while someone was drunk, including unpredictable emotions.

"'Kay."

One word, that's either really good or really bad.

Not sure how to judge this one.

He got up and made his way over to the bar where Mike was currently wiping down the countertop.

"Hey man, thanks for coming by. Hate to ask you to come out this far but I was limited for options."

"So you called in your best one."

Mike chuckled. "You know it. Anyway, you know what to do."

He nodded, opening the door leading to the pub's basement. Pausing as he went through the doorway, he turned around.

"Hey Mike."

"Yeah?"

"Keep an eye on Robinne would you? She's not in the best condition right now."

Mike nodded. "Don't worry, I've had one eye on her all night. I've got this." He smiled.

At least I can rely on someone.

"Thanks man."

Turning back around, he made his way down the steps into the basement, beginning to check to see which barrels needed changing first. Moving then on to the ones that needed moving into place to be used next, putting the now empty barrels to be collected by the usual men who picked them up the following morning.

A short time later after huffing many barrels about, Ralph was finally done. He was used to working with heavy things on the ranch, so moving a few barrels here and there was nothing he couldn't do.

Ascending the steps, he closed the door behind him and checked back in with Mike, waiting against the bar until he'd finished serving a customer. The bar was now teaming with people, as what was usually the norm for a Friday night. He rarely came this way himself on a Friday night, except for the odd occasion where there were a larger group of them where they couldn't all fit into the smaller bar in town.

He looked over at where he'd left Robinne, making sure she was still there. Thankfully, she was. He knew he could always trust Mike when he said he'd keep an eye on her, but he still had a job to do and he wouldn't put it past Robinne to try and make an escape of some kind, even if it ended in failure.

"Thanks for doing that man. What do I owe you?" Mike said as he came over to Ralph.

He waved his hand, dismissing the notion.

"Don't even think about it Mike." He smiled. "Just sling me a free one for when I get home and we'll call it even."

"Done."

Mike slipped him his usual bottled beer of choice, tipping him a nod as he strode over to clean some glasses behind the other side of the bar. He tucked the bottle mostly into one of his front pant pockets, heading over to where Robinne had thankfully stayed. She was leaning against the side of the booth-style seat, her eyes closed as she sat there. He knew she wasn't asleep but damn his heart, she looked cuter than a puppy on a blanket.

Although I'm more of a cat person, thanks to Buddy, it doesn't really matter. She's too darn cute anyway.

He stopped just before her, resting his hands on his hips.

"Ready to head out?"

His voice must've startled her, even though he'd spoken softly, as she damn nearly jumped out of her skin. Taking a second to collect herself, obviously racking her brain as to where she still was, she looked up at him with those beautiful yet glazed eyes.

"Wha?"

Where she wasn't quite slurring her words just yet, Robinne didn't seem to be able to get the right ones out as they should sound. He himself has spent more than one time having a drink too many, not necessarily due to his own doing, so he knew that there were more than one type of drunkenness/tipsiness. She just happened to fit into the category where her words came out all jumbled.

He chuckled, crouching down holding up two fingers to her in the 'peace' symbol. "How many fingers am I holding up?"

Before he drove off with her, he needed to assess just how drunk she was so he didn't end up with her throwing up in his truck. As a cowboy and a rancher he was used to dealing with most things, even the more disgusting things, but one of the few things his stomach couldn't stand was vomit. He didn't know why and it didn't really matter, he just wanted to avoid the possibility if possible.

Robinne smirked, her nose scrunching up in the most adorable way he found hard to look away from, "Ha! I know what finger I want to show to you mister, and it's this one right he—"

He grabbed the hand she was about to raise before she could raise the finger in question, one he knew from various buddied of his flashing to him when he'd make a quippy comment here and there. Just the same as he'd done back to them when the situation was the other way around.

Smirking, he shook his head and held his hand out to her.

"C'mon darlin', I'll give you a ride home and I promise I won't even talk unless you want me to. Your decision."

There wasn't a doubt in his mind that she wouldn't take his hand, drunk or sober, she still had a head somewhat on her shoulders, and wouldn't willingly take his hand. He suspected she was still mad at him and to be fair, he's still kept his promise to her, as he didn't come here with the knowledge that she was too. That part of his mind could rest easy.

His suspicions were confirmed a second later when a very wobbly-legged Robinne got up from her seat, holding onto anything around her while her nose rose and stood proud in the air.

"I can manage myshelf, tank yew." She said, her words still slurring.

"Oh I've no doubt about that."

She slowly slid out of the booth, obviously trying to hide the fact that she was as helpless as a baby bird, trying her best to go slow and resist any sort of help from him whatsoever. As much as he yearned to touch and hold her again as he did when he'd first come in, he wasn't going to. Especially when she was in this condition.

The two of them slowly made their way to his truck, where he'd directed her to when exiting the pub. She almost got in the driver's side, clearly thinking in her current state that she was back at home in England, as he knew they drove with the other side of the car. He'd nodded to the passenger side, walking and opening the door for her while he let her get into the truck under her own steam. It took a few tries, but she got there.

Once he was inside the driver's side, he wasted no time in belting them up and pulling out of the parking lot, putting the bottle Mike had given him in the cup holder between the two of them.

Since she'd not said whether or not she wanted him to talk with her on the drive back to her place, he decided to keep quiet and see if she would be the one to talk to him first. It might seem like child's play, but he knew Robinne somewhat well and she'd eventually crack.

He didn't have to wait long.

"So, who was it who called you to come and get me? Laney? Mikey?"

Mikey? That better be her drunken way of saying his name, not a cute nickname.

"No one. Mike called me to move a few barrels for him."

She harrumphed. "You sure got de muscles for it."

Oh? So she's been ogling me during her time together? Interesting.

As much as he wished he could morally pump her for information, he was more than willing to hear anything she wished to confess while he drove them to her home.

"What were you doing there? Other than getting completely wasted."

She turned to him then, a look of abhorrence on her face.

"Dat is noon of your bus ness! For your infro…infro…information, Laney took me out. Girly night yew know."

He knew there was more to it than that, but he said nothing and allowed her to continue.

"Why'd yew have to take me back home any…any ways huh? I was perfectly fine wid Laney taking me home."

At least she was trying her best to not to slur or mispronounce her words, much. He knew when people were drunk, it meant one of two things. One, whatever they said was the truth and two, people just slurred a bunch of random things without it meaning anything at all. From the looks of it, Robinne was leaning towards the former.

"I'm sorry."

There was nothing for him to be sorry for, he just knew it was better to apologise than to antagonise anyone in anything other than their normal, natural state.

She nodded, "So you should bee. You know, buzz. Ha! Buzz!"

He held back his smirk, as much as he wanted to let it out and spread across his face.

"You know." Robinne said, swinging her gaze back to the road ahead of them. "I never thought that this would be how we would meet again. If ever." She sighed, her head lolling against the window. "I didn't think I could ever forgive you, trust you enough to want to see your face again. Yet, here we are. You hurt me bad, Ralph. Real bad. I didn't know when I first met you that day, when you were naked, that I'd ever start to even have the idea of possibly liking you. It was something I'd been set dead against happening when I moved here. It did, though. Boy was I glad that it did."

As she spoke, he knew that she was out of the drunken stages where her words were slurred, as she'd slipped into the talkative stage. Keeping his hands firmly on the wheel and his eyes ahead, his mind finally caught up with what she'd just said, the latter parts anyway.

She…she has…feelings for me?
This better not be the drink talking, because I'll remember this.
I want this as much as she knows she does deep down inside.

He was just about to open his mouth to respond when she spoke once more. So he instead focused on getting them off at the correct exit, pointing them in the direction of home.

"People haven't given me many opportunities to trust them before they've used me, lied to me and betrayed me. I've had more people deceive me than I have had being nice to me and do you know what? I still don't hate them. Do you know why? It's because I would never wish for something to happen to them like what's been done to me, no matter how much they did or how much it hurt. Once you've been screwed over as many times as I have, you think less about what happens to you and what you can do to stop it happening to others."

Been there sweetheart, I understand.

"Okay, so I was perhaps wrong in running out of there like I did, but it all came back to me. Every single thing that's ever hurt me, physically and emotionally, came back to me when you said you'd taken my list. You might not have known it, but in the small time since I've gotten to know you, you've become the most important person to me. Granted I don't have a lot of people in my life, you're still the number one person to me. So much I had to keep from you not because I didn't want you to know, it was because I was scared. Deep down, I'm scared. I'm scared to tell anyone anything because I don't want it to blow back in my face like it's done countless times before, like a vicious cycle. A never-ending one. I was terrified that if I told you that I'd even began to think I liked you, that you'd turn tail and leave me. I didn't want to come on too strong or even think someone as genuine as you could ever love someone like me. It just doesn't happen. The last time I confessed my feelings to someone, I was kept on a string of pointless hope for almost three years. I can't go back there again, I can't risk my heart. There's not much of it left, you know." She turned to look at him then, her eyes clearly watery even in the dim light that cast over the truck cab by the occasional street light.

Woah, I was right.
The poor girl's been on her own for far too long. Broken too often. Used as a play toy for the world and whoever came by.

Well, no more. From now on, I'll be her guardian angel. Even if she rejects me, I'll spend the rest of my life watching over her. She'll never be sad, used, or broken again.

I swear that as my life's mission, here and now.

Keeping one hand firmly on the wheel, he leaned and pulled out a tissue from the glove compartment, handing it to her. "Here beautiful, dry those lovely eyes."

Much to his surprise, she did as he said. She knew he heard every word, regardless of the fact it took a little booze to get her to open up to him, it got her there and he was grateful for it.

Wiping her eyes, she sat once more into the seat, her posture slumping from tiredness. She needed a good night's sleep and it wouldn't be too long until he saw that she'd get it. Taking the next left, Ralph turned the truck onto the final road that would lead to her own.

"Thank you for being honest with me, Robinne. Sorry won't ever cut it but, I needed to hear that and I am sorry. Just as a start."

She harrumphed again, "So why did you even use me in the first place? That wasn't a nice thing to do at all."

He nodded, "I know and I was wrong, as you've just said. I won't deny it wasn't wrong, nor can I say why I did it as I wasn't thinking."

She scoffed, "You can say that again."

"Yes well, when you're sober and had a good night's sleep under you and if you want to, we could meet again. Under your terms, of course. We could clear the air and if you think I deserve it, we can start again as friends."

Even though I want to be so much more than that, I'd start there for you.

Robinne scrunched the wad of tissue in her right hand, clearly mulling over his proposal. He didn't expect an answer straight away. As long as he got one, that was enough. He'd also come to realise as she spoke, that he was wrong about the types of drunk people there were. She didn't even come close to what he'd pegged her as. Yes she revealed some truths where she might not have sober, and neither did she say anything without it meaning anything, because what she'd said to him as he drove her home, was far from nothing.

She was a person all her own. There wasn't a category in the world that she fit into, as she was unique as he was. She didn't need to be defined or allocate anything, she was special. He just needed for her to see that.

He realised that, though she was somewhat drunk, there was enough of the Brit he knew and now realised, that he loved, in there, to know perfectly well what she was telling him. She was telling him because she wanted to. It was just that she wasn't used to handling liquor as he was. The very thought made him smirk as despite all the heavy of tonight's conversation, she made an adorable drunk.

"Tell you what." He piped up, bringing her attention back to his face. "Sleep on it and whatever you decide, I'll be happy with. Sound good?"

She seemed more at ease with this, like a weight came off her shoulders. A weight he'd put there since that night over a month ago in the barn.

"That…sounds good. Thank you."

He nodded, happy to leave it there. Shortly after, he pulled up outside Robinne's place, killing the engine before he turned to her. She'd begun to doze off against the window since she'd agreed to his proposition. Where he could happily sit here and watch her snooze until the sun came up, he didn't want to leave her in such an uncomfortable looking position.

Carefully as he could without waking her, he exited his side of the truck cab and made his way around to hers. Slowly opening the passenger door, he used his hand to catch her shoulder so she didn't fall out onto the floor. To his amazement, he managed to get her up and into his arms without her protesting. Only when in his arms did she realise what was going on, wiggling ever so slightly in his bear-like grip.

"I…I can walk, you know. Those funny things coming from my hips are legs, they're used to walking."

He chuckled, "Oh I'm well aware." He said, closing the passenger side door using his butt, before striding up her pathway to her front door. "Keys." He demanded politely.

"What?" Robinne blinked.

"Keys. I need them to unlock the front door."

"Oh!"

She looked around her before diving into her pants pocket, producing said keys. "Here" she held them out to him.

This isn't going to work.

"Reach to the lock and open the door, I can push it open from there. I kind of have my hands full."

"Hey!"

Realising what he'd just said, he shook his head, smirking at how what he'd just said had come across, even to her in her state. "Allow me to re-phrase, I'm rather occupied with the most delightful being in the world, who herself could open the door. Perhaps."

"Oh well, since you asked so nicely oh noble one."

I don't know about that…

Much to his relief, she managed to wiggle the key into the lock and push the door off the catch, allowing him to push it open with the toe of his boot, enough to get them through and into the hall.

Once inside, he slid her down his body and onto the floor. A move in which he both enjoyed and regretted simultaneously, wanting it so bad instead in a setting he could've made the most of it more. Sadly, he couldn't. After setting her on her feet, one arm still around her middle, he closed the door behind them.

"Now, what say we get you into bed hm?" he said, turning to look down at her.

Her eyes went from somewhat glazed, to what he called 'bedroom eyes', in a hundredth of a second. Appropriate for where he'd planned to take her. However, under the completely wrong circumstances.

"Now you're talking!" she said, winding her arms around his neck.

Jesus. This is going to be tougher than I thought.

Normally when he'd had the opportunity to be with a woman, this is where things would go a step further. Not today. He was a saint for restraining himself against the feelings of his belly, a title he'd wear with pride as long as he made sure she was settled in safely for the night. Even if meant he wasn't beside her.

"Not tonight." He said, untangling her arms from around his neck. Bending down once more, he scooped her up into his arms and proceeded to make his way upstairs.

"Do you do this often? Carrying women about as if they were your newly wedded wife?"

The topic alone with her here in his arms, would usually stop him in his tracks, if not for the fact that he was walking up the stairs where if he were to do so, would result in him losing his precious cargo. Possibly injuring them both. He chose to carry on up the stairs before answering her.

"No darlin', I don't make a habit of it. You're the first."

"Hmm, I like that. Your first bride."

Oh sweet lord.

If only.

Walking into what had been designed to be her bedroom by the looks of the obvious bed and basic bedroom furniture, he gently deposited her on her butt onto the bed before taking a step back, placing his hands on his hips. He looked down at her, assessing her current condition. She didn't look like she was any more close to throwing up as she was back at the pub, though he still needed to make doubly sure.

"How're you feeling? Sick? Dizzy? Anything?"

She shook her head, managing to stay sat up and looking up at him, meeting his gaze.

"Nope, nope and nope. I feel…okay. I ate too. No vomiting for me."

Thank God.

Since he didn't want to overstep his mark, he needed her to do the next step on her own. If she could.

"Great. Okay, I'm going to go downstairs to get something and I'll be right back up. Can you manage getting out of your clothes and into something…comfy, before I get back?" he swallowed. Imaging her in something even comfy rather than something sexy, was enough to make his thoughts wander. She'd even make a trash bag look appealing somehow.

She let out a soft laugh, a sound which reached deep into his heart and made his already wandering thoughts, scatter even further.

"I've been doing that ever since I was 8 years old. I'm more than capable, thank you. I promise, you'll like what you see when you get back." Her sultry voice crooned to him.

Rubbing the back of his neck as he turned towards the door, he exhaled. "I've no doubt about that." He muttered, striding out of the door and jogging down the stairs.

Downstairs in her kitchen, he filled a glass with water and another with orange juice, rummaging around her cupboards until he found some painkillers to add to the drinks which he'd placed on a tray. Getting her home had been easier than he'd imagined. What hadn't been easy, was having to keep a lid on his true thoughts once she'd revealed what she'd kept to herself, back in his truck on the drive here. That was heavy stuff he no doubt would be thinking about for hours yet to come.

He stayed downstairs for a little while longer, giving her plenty of time to get herself changed in privacy before he made his way back upstairs to her. Thankfully when that time came, she was dressed. She sported a rather fetching tartan pj night dress which just reached her knees, which was already testing his wire thin restraint.

Placing the tray down on her nightstand, he held his hand out to her once more. "C'mon darlin', let's get your teeth done and your face washed, then you can sleep for as long as you want."

"Mmm, that sounds appealing."

It sure does.

Soon, both her teeth were brushed and her face was washed. He'd managed to coax her into bed, assuring her that he wouldn't be joining her, tucking her in as if he were tucking in a child. Not that he'd ever done that, he was just making sure she would be comfortable before he left.

Stepping back to wish her a goodnight, he saw that her eyes were already closed and she was breathing softly in her slumber. The picture he was looking at, was one he'd hoped someday to be looking at each night for the rest of his days. For now, he took in this moment until he was able to see it again.

He scrounged around for a pen and something to write on, coming up lucky in her bedside drawer. Scribbling down a few words onto the paper, he restored the pen and pad to its rightful place, leaving the note beside the drinks and painkillers.

Before he could decide to do otherwise, he strode once more to the door, pausing to look back at her when over the threshold. She'd be alright until morning, eliciting no cause for concern for him to stay until then. He only allowed himself a brief glance back before exiting her home, closing the door behind him.

Normally, he wasn't one for believing in signs. But if tonight was anything to go by, he'd happily start. If this was a sign that they could finally start to patch things up, he'd run with it. Contented, he hopped back into his truck and crawled away from the sidewalk, looking forward to his own bed and full of lighter thoughts for the first time in what felt like forever.

CHAPTER EIGHTEEN
~ Robinne ~

Waking up, Robinne felt as if she had an elephant on her head. Not that she'd ever had one on there before, but if she even began to attempt to describe how she was feeling, that would be it. What had she done that would leaving her feeling like the living dead? If that were even possible. The thought escaped her as she peeled open her eyes, trying to focus against the blinding morning light. At least, she thought it was morning.

Urgh, what time is it?

What happened to me? Where am I?

Fighting off the feeling of fear that started to brew from the pit of her stomach, she used her weary limbs to push herself up into a sitting position. Thankfully to her and her back, she seemed to be on a bed. Meaning nothing sinister had happened. She hoped. Taking stock of her current condition as best she could, it appeared she was in…her night dress? Home, she was at home.

Oh thank God.

Looking around, her suspicions were confirmed when her eyes grazed upon her bedroom. What did escape her though, was how on Earth she got there. What had she done the night before that could possibly make her forget everything?

Groaning, she swung her legs out of bed, determined to find out the cause of her currently situation a little later when her mind was working better. As she was about to push herself up and out of bed, she spotted a glass of water, orange juice and some tablets on a tray on her bedside table.

Funny, I don't remember putting that there.

It wasn't her usual go-to drinks of choice when she came to bed. Usually she brought up a cup of tea with her and if she got thirsty through the night, she'd go down and drink a glass of water before returning to bed. Which is why it stumped her as to why they'd be there now.

On closer inspection, she saw a note tucked under the orange juice glass. Picking it up, she squinted her eyes to attempt to read what the note said. Thankfully, she was just about able to make it out. The note read:

Take the tablets & a drink.
I take it you're not used to drink so, I thought it would help.
Hope you feel better soon, come into work Monday. Take today off.
~ Laney

Laney? Why would Laney be…oh. Oh!

Scanning the note for a second time, she noted the use of the word 'drink'. Slowly, the word slotted into the missing space in her mind and the events of the night before came back to her. She'd gone out with Laney, much to her protest at first. Laney had taken her to an English-style pub, where they proceeded to chat and drink. And drink, and drink.

Normally, she wasn't much of a drinker and had always set her limit to what she was able to cope with. However, last night had changed her usual M.O. For some reason, she'd foregone her usual set limit and as a result, here she sat with the mother of all hangovers. Yes she was used to having headaches pretty much all the time, but this was in a league all its own. This damn near came close to a migraine, which she'd also suffered with in the past.

Taking Laney's note's advice, she took the two painkillers, swallowing it back with the orange juice. She wasn't much of a water-drinker, though she should probably start drinking more of it, as she'd heard it lessened the chances of getting a headache. Definitely worth considering, in her mind.

She set the note back on the bedside table after taking her tablets, deciding it was worth an attempt in standing up. She didn't do being ill or invalided, keeping busy was her usual way of pushing through whatever she was going through, and it was going to be what she'd be doing today too.

Eventually, she managed to get her lead-weighted legs to work, shuffling over to her chest of draws where her phone was resting nicely upon. Picking it up, she saw she had a few messages from Laney, asking how she was feeling this morning and one from Ryder. His as she read it, was merely asking if she was alright as apparently, Mike, the pub's owner and bar man, had informed him of her inebriated state.

She fired off a quick message back to him before deciding to give Laney a call, to thank her for what she assumed was her taking care of her when she'd returned her home last night. Dialling the bakery's main telephone number, she knew it was where Laney would be at 9:00AM in the morning, even on a Saturday.

On the third ring of her phone, Laney picked up the bakery main line.

"Hello! Laney's Bakery, Laney speaking. How can I help you?" her cheery voice echoed through the line, causing her to wince just a little.

"Laney? Hi. It's me, Robinne."

"Robinne! Hi! How're you feeling? I was worried about leaving you but, you didn't look like you'd choke or anything so…I'm sorry for leaving you anyway."

Oh bless her heart.

"Don't worry about it. I'm fine. I feel like I've been hit by a bus and then some but, I'm fine. Thank you for taking care of me."

"Y-yeah. You're welcome."

Something about Laney's tone of voice didn't ring right with Robinne, but she wasn't going to question it now. That would require brain power to do some top-level thinking and right now, she didn't have enough to even power a gnat. It could wait.

"Anyway, I called to say thank you for also giving me the weekend off. You really didn't have to do that."

Laney scoffed.

"Don't worry about it! I knew you wouldn't be in any condition today to work so…I called in help."

This revelation piqued her curiosity and then some.

"Oh? Who?"

"Luca. Luca Capriotti You don't know him, he's an old friend of mine. He had nothing to do today so, I called in a favour."

Unlike when she spoke to Laney about what Mike meant to her, when she heard her speak about this Luca character, she had a lighter more, contented tone in her voice. Something she'd definitely look into a little later.

"Well, if you're sure. Though don't even think about paying me still for this weekend. Donate the money from my pay to a local charity."

Laney laughed softly, "I thought you'd say something like that, so I went ahead and did so before coming in this morning."

If Laney and her bakery didn't work out, Robinne was sure she'd make a fortune in mind-reading. Or, she just knew her really well. Either way, the thought settled her as she didn't want to take money for work she didn't even do.

"You're a star. Anyway I'll let you get back to it, I'll see you on Monday."

"Laters baby!" Laney called, before the line went dead.

She shook her head, a smirk on her face.

"I should never have given her my spare copy of *Fifty Shades of Grey*." She mumbled to herself, setting her phone back on the chest of draws before she made her way, albeit slowly, to the bathroom.

A short while later, after taking her time to freshen up and get somewhat dressed, she found herself seated on her bedroom's balcony chair, watching the day unfold before her eyes on the land at the back of her house. She didn't spend as much time up here as she knew she should, as there were just too many rooms in the house she wasn't used to having, she tried to make the best of them all.

So far, she'd spent a significant amount of time flitting between her front room, kitchen, bedroom and back porch. Where she knew she had forever to use the other rooms and spend time in them, she still felt she had to do *something* with them. After all, people had worked so hard to re-build this place, it would be an insult not too.

She'd also been meaning to spend a bit of time down at the river running at the back of her property, but never got around to doing so. Looking for work and all the drama that had ensued since her arrival saw to that. Though with the weather bound to be changing with the time of year, as it was now September, she didn't want to risk getting into water that wasn't safe. Though she wasn't sure when the seasons turned for a place like Texas, it was better to play it safe than sorry.

The sound of a vehicle brought her out of her happy daydream. It didn't sound close and she wasn't sure if it was anywhere near her, but it was worth investigating. Just to give her something to do. Heading through her bedroom, she made her way to the top of her stairs where as it turned out by her doorbell ringing, the vehicle she'd heard just now must've been for her.

Opening her front door when she'd reached it, there was an envelope and tied to it, was a red rose. Usually as everyone knew, red roses symbolise the ultimate expression of romantic and abiding love. Red roses in themselves express loudly the feelings of beauty and passion, teamed with the not so common meaning of courage. Additionally, red roses are also known in some cases as meaning courage and a symbol of power.

In this case, she had a feeling it didn't mean any of those things. As she hadn't given anyone cause to give her such a token. Picking up the envelope, she disappeared back inside, just in case anyone was still hanging around after dropping this off for her. Setting the rose down on the hall table, she carefully opened up the envelope. What she came across once pulling it out of the envelope, wasn't something she'd ever expected to receive. It was an invitation to a ball here in Dripping Springs.

Were such things still happening these days?
The invite read:

You are cordially invited to:

Dripping Springs' 50thAnnual Charity Ball

Saturday Eighth of September 2018,
8PM until Midnight

Town Hall

This invitation admits one and optional plus one. We hope to see you there.

Well, this was a first for her. She'd never been invited to a ball before. A charity ball at that. Though the invite didn't specify what charity the ball was in aid of, she supposed those who've attended it would know who it was going to by now. As long as it was going to charity, that was enough for her for now.

She was genuinely surprised to even get this, as she'd not been a resident of the town for two months yet. It must be that all the town's residents got one and who could make it, turned up. This was the first invite now that she thought about it, that she'd ever received. Ever. She didn't even get an invite to prom.

Prom of year 11 in secondary school, she'd invited a friend of hers at the time to go with her. Rachael wasn't a 'friend' as such come to think of it, she was a girl she sat next to in Sociology class. There wasn't anyone else she could go with, as Juliet's mother forbid her from going. A no-brainer. Robinne really wanted to go with the guy she'd been crushing on for almost two years at that point, Sean. Alas, she wasn't even in his league and never even told him she'd once harboured feelings for him. Seeing as she knew she didn't stand a chance, she didn't and hasn't said a word to him till this day.

I've done it on my own once before, I can do it again.

Even if going to this ball would somehow end up backfiring in her face, she automatically decided she was going to go the second she finished reading the invitation. Would she want to go with someone as her companion? Sure. Would she like to go with some as her/their date? Maybe. One thing was for certain though, she could and would do it on her own. She'd take herself there, enjoy the night as best she could. Even if it meant bumping into certain people, she'd push past that. Especially if the ball would provide her with meaty writing material.

Oh yes, I'm sure it will.

She'd done plenty in her life on her own so far. It might sound sad to some, but if she left everything until someone was ready to go with her, she'd miss out on a lot. She did do a lot with her grandmother before she sadly lost her. If there was one person she'd felt more alike in her life, it was her. Her grandma was her hero and would cheer her on when she did things for herself, by herself. If there was one person she'd attend this ball for other than herself, it would be her grandma.

Grandma, I'll make you proud. I promise.

Seeing no time like the present, she grabbed her keys from their usual place and left her place, filled with determination to get herself the best kick ass dress that she could find. And afford. That part was crucial.

Having conducted a search for dress shops around the Dripping Springs area, she finally came across one just on the outskirts of the town, in the opposite direction to where she and Laney had gone to the pub the night before. Coming to think about it, she was feeling so much better than when she first woke up that morning.

Damn, those tablets worked a treat.

She parked her truck outside the small dress shop, tucked away between two other shops similar to it, both offering clothes of some sort. Hopping out of her truck, she looked up at the store to make doubly sure she'd arrived at the one. The sign above the store read 'Dresses for a Dame'. A long name by store standards, but memorable.

There was nothing that could brace for her for what she'd see when she got inside the store. Opening up the door, the sight before her eyes brought her right back to the day she went shopping for her prom dress. Dresses of evert shape, size, colour, fabric and style filled the small store so much so, that there was barely room for anyone more than two to three people at a time to move around in.

Thankfully for Robinne, there only looked to be two other people in the store with her, so she didn't have to worry about getting into anyone's way. Thank God. If there was another thing she couldn't stand, it was getting in someone's way. It was never intentional, yet people still got irritated when she'd apologised for her intrusion.

She was hoping she would be able to find herself a dress here today, as when she was a Susan's shop, she found clothes shopping difficult. Awkward, somehow. Which is why she was here now. Not that she had a lot of time to get a dress chosen away, as the ball was only a week away.

Stepping further inside the shop looking at the dresses, she was no more clued up as to what she'd want to pick than she was when she opened the invitation. When she'd picked out her prom dress, she'd walked inside the store with her grandmother and immediately saw the dress she'd end up with wearing to the prom. It'd been just hung back up from someone trying it on and not deciding upon it. So, *she* did. It was a classic prom dress. A long, poofy dress with a corset and plenty of what she called 'netting'. It was bright red and she felt like a princess. A princess still absent of her prince.

She was mid-thought when footsteps approached her, "Hello there, can I help you?" she turned to the voice which had approached her from her right. A kindly older woman with traditionally framed glasses greeted her with a kind smile.

"Yes, please. I'm looking for a dress for the um…charity ball." She said the last two words quietly. Why, she doesn't know. It just felt like something that wasn't meant to be shouted about.

The woman clasped her hands together, smiling even brighter.

"Oh how lovely! I was invited to the very first one fifty years ago when I was a mere scrap of a girl of fifteen."

No way is this woman over fifty! If so, I'm a monkey's aunt…again.

"Do you have any idea of the sort of thing you wish to wear? After all, it is a ball. You'll need something elegant." She pressed.

She shook her head, embarrassed. "I've no idea at all. I've never been to a ball before. Haven't bought a dress for seven years."

Next thing she knew, the women gently took one of her hands, patting it with her own. "No need to worry, I'll help you out. You're not local are you? I'm Bessie, Bessie Beaufort. What's your name dear?"

"Robinne James and yes, you're right, I'm not a local. I moved here just over a month ago, two at the end of the month. It's nice to meet you." She smiled.

"Nice to meet you too. Now, let's see about getting you the perfect dress."

An hour or so later after much discussion with Bessie, they'd narrowed down to a style of dress which she'd felt comfortable wearing, selected the colour, allocated a price range and finally, they came down to one dress which Robinne felt had been designed for her. She'd had a basic fitting with Bessie to get an ideas to how the dress would fit her, where it would need taking in or out, and how she felt while looking at herself in the mirror in the shop.

Bessie had taken the dress into the back to put Robinne's name on a tag, reserving it for her to purchase. As it turned out, she did have to come back to have the dress altered and much to her surprise, it wasn't to have it taken out. Instead, it was to take it in. She was a big-chested girl by nature, so it wasn't the norm for her to have things reduced so, this pleased her enormously.

After saying goodbye for now to Bessie, she was about to exit the shop when she heard a soul-shakingly shrill voice, very familiar to her too. Pausing behind a rack of big, poofy dresses, she leaned around them to see who the voice belonged to.

Delilah.

That witch of a woman form Susan's store was here! She couldn't blame the woman for following her because she wasn't, but it was an unpleasant turn of events. She didn't plan on running into her again any time soon, but what with the ball coming up, she supposed Delilah was also here to get a dress also.

At least I have my dress. Somehow I suspect if you knew I was here, you'd make it impossible.

"I know Karen, I know. It was a minor bump in the road last night, but it didn't show any promise of them rekindling their friendship again."

Who? Who won't be rekindling a friendship?

Delilah held a phone between her ear and her shoulder as she browsed the dress selection, speaking to someone called Karen. It must be a friend of hers, or a blind follower, as was the case with people like her.

Since she didn't have to go anywhere in a hurry, she decided to stop and listen in for a short while. Eavesdropping was becoming a bad habit of hers.

"I tell you something now Karen, I'm going to make him want me again if it's the last thing I do. We were the hottest couple in all of town once and we will be again. That British bitch doesn't stand a chance now I'm back in town. The moment Ralph sees me in my dress, he's going to fall head over heels in love with me all over again."

Oh good Lord, the woman's delusional!

Robinne had encountered more than her fair share of people like Delilah since being in secondary school. Countless times has she seen girls, and on occasion boys too, think for some reason that the ideas in their heads were what was going to happen. Usually, those ideas were absolutely bonkers and no on in their right minds would go along with their plans. Then again, look at the people making the plans, they *weren't* in their right minds.

Making sure she kept herself hidden, she continued to listen to Cruella's crazy planning, and happily ignoring the name she'd been called.

"No, I'm not worried about her at all. Last I heard, she's still not speaking to him and has no plans to until she's "ready"." Delilah scoffed, "Pathetic, really. Someone like her doesn't stand a chance with a delicious specimen such as Ralph Jenkins. You're speaking to someone who is."

Robinne rolled her eyes, having heard the same thing from countless people. It wasn't new to her.

"I'm going to rock up at that ball in the best dress and blow him off his feet. All thanks to her deciding that she wasn't having anything to do with him. She would've been invited to the ball by now. Sadie said she'd sent out all the invites for the Mayor and that bitch had been invited as she's new to town. Personally, I wouldn't invite her to wee on me if I was on fire."

That would make two of us…

Robinne had heard enough. She wasn't worried by this pathetic woman one bit. Not that she was competing against her for Ralph's affections in the first place, she just knew it wasn't worth fuelling someone like Delilah with even the slightest possibility that she might be. It was more than enough for her own personal satisfaction that Delilah didn't know that she knew what she was up to. She could leave this place with her head held high, worry and carefree.

Which is exactly what she did.

Leaving delusional Delilah to browse the dresses at the back of the store, she saw this opportunity as her one and only one to escape without being spotted. Delilah wouldn't know upon entering the dress shop, that the truck outside was hers, so she was able to slide into it and pull away without being stopped or called.

Driving away from the store, she couldn't help let the smile that had been waiting to break free, spread across her face. There was no way she was going to go up against Delilah in any way, she wasn't worth it. She could at least now though, be well prepared for anything that might come her way from the vile woman. She won't be expecting her to be ready for what was intended for her, but Robinne herself would be ready to show her and people like her, that she won't be kicked around anymore.

Come and have a go if you think you're hard enough.

Back at home and after many hours had passed, Robinne had decided once she'd arrived back at home, that she would get to work on writing the first few chapters of her first book draft. Having encountered Delilah back at the dress store, it had given her the necessary drive to get her to begin to write, having been given a bit of writing material to work with.

Where she wasn't going to write about Delilah, she was most certainly going to use some of her horrid traits as basis personality traits for her main antagonist. She had managed to get a lot of the planning out of the way, thankfully, so all she had left to do was get as much writing done before the ball in a week's time.

Usually when she'd written things in the past, she published the first draft of something she'd written, resulting in a really badly written and read story. Having learned from mistakes, she was now planning to have three drafts before publishing her work to Amazon's Kindle format. Someday, she'd love to have paperbacks and be published through a small, independent publisher but for now, she was more than happy to go through the Kindle format.

Before she came to America, she'd set up a few things to get her going once at a time she'd finally started to write, she could document her journey and hopefully pick up a few followers at the same time. Though she didn't expect to hit it big or gain a big following right from the off, she hoped that her debut book would at least get her a good footing in the door and get her name out there.

She'd registered and had been accepted into the Goodreads author's programme, and she'd made an Instagram account, her go-to social media platform of choice, where she would be able to post about her journey and give updates as to what she was up to with whatever she was writing.

So far, she'd only accumulated 20 followers with a few of her acquaintances from back home wanting to follow her progress. The few that weren't people she knew, were accounts which usually fished for followers. They'd follow you and once you followed back, they'd then unfollow you. Pointless in her eyes but sadly, it's just something that happens.

Wiggling her butt into where she had comfortably seated herself in her cozy front room, movie playing in the background on low volume, Robinne settled herself in for a good evening's writing.

Much later that night, after successfully writing a grand total of 6,000+ words, she decided at this point that it was just about a right enough stopping point to call it a night. On average 4,000-5,000 words were usually typed for an author creating a brand new story. She was pleased that she had gone over that average amount, as if for some reason she found herself unable to meet her writing target on any particular day, she had at least done more a day or two before to compensate.

Knowing she wasn't going to be making it upstairs to bed tonight, she grabbed the blanket she'd placed on the back of the sofa, pulling it over herself after moving her laptop to one side where it wouldn't be knocked. Writing always did make her tired, as staring at a screen for hours on end would do that to a person.

Laying down on the long sofa, she laid her head on one of the two cushions she'd purchased for it when she'd had her furniture come. Within two seconds of her head hitting the pillow, the weariness of the day started to fade from her body as she started drifting into sweet slumber, and a world free of delusional demons like Delilah.

Feeling her eyes close, she welcomed the sleep that had been creeping up on her for the past few hours as she'd been writing. Not needing to function on much sleep, she usually was able to get a lot done during the day but now, after moving here, she seemed to be craving sleep more than she used to. A welcome change, in her mind.

As sleep overtook her, she hoped that her dreams would be somewhat eventful and for once, free of a certain cowboy.

CHAPTER NINETEEN
~ Ralph ~

If it were not for his mother's initial begging that he would go, Ralph wouldn't be standing in front of the mirror in his bedroom, stood in a fitted tuxedo with matching azure blue bow tie. He hadn't intended to attend the annual charity ball this year, as proven in charity balls of the past, not all of them ended well for him.

Years ago, he'd had the pleasure of taking his then and only serious girlfriend, Delilah to the ball when they were both ten years younger. Well, he thought it would be his pleasure. After she'd kissed him that day on the last day of school of that year, he didn't plan on encountering her again. He didn't factor in the possibility she'd go to the same high school as him, thus leading him to think that by the time they were both eighteen that she'd changed.

He was wrong.

On the night of that ball ten years ago, he'd gone all out when he asked Delilah to go with him. She'd been thrilled, of course. As he'd blossomed from the gangly kid he once was when he kissed her, to a promising young man she could see using to her best advantage. Only, he didn't know that until it was too late.

After organising a special limousine for them to arrive in, buying her dress, paying for her nails and hair, what did she do? She subjected him to one of the most cliché things to ever happen to a man. He was waiting for her at their table after she'd said to him that she was off to the ladies room. Only, she never came back to their table.

Worried that something had happened to her, he'd gone searching for her. When passing the bathroom she'd supposedly gone into, he heard a muffled noise coming not far down the hall from a closet that was being used to store the coats of the ball attendees. Opening the door had revealed more than the truth to him.

His date for the night and then girlfriend, was more than wrapped around another young man. He didn't know this individual and he never planned to, he just shook his head and left, leaving her to finish what she obviously thought she'd get done without interruption. He'd left the ball right then and there in the self-same limo he'd booked for them, letting her find her own way back home.

Where he wasn't a cold and unfeeling individual, he was a sensitive one. Everyone usually has this image in their heads that men, southern men especially, were all rugged, muscle-bound and tough men. They weren't. Men were just as emotionally out there as much as women were made out to be. He was one of them. He was a sensitive soul and when you hurt him, it hurt deep.

He really thought he'd make a go at it with Delilah. Not once did he expect to change her, but he at least hoped that he could try and attempt a relationships and sort out the 'feelings' he had for her which as it turned out, was purely a hormonal response, no feelings attached whatsoever.

Cowboys had hearts that needed looking after, cared for and cherished. Not messed around with, which is what had happened to him that night. From that moment on, when he's been with the occasional woman for anything purely for anything but a relationship, he made sure that both of them were in agreement so he could release what needed releasing, and that the lady he was with would be treated right and he'd be treated right in return. He would never be used or use anyone ever again. Lesson learned.

"Daydreaming sweetheart?" his mother's voice called out to him, shaking him from his memory.

He turned around to see his mother standing in the doorway, dressed in a vintage-style gold dress, sequined and elegant befitting the woman wearing it. They'd all agreed to get ready in their respective homes, but he was the one who'd been tasked with driving his mother as his father was driving his younger brothers. The middle lot were making it to the ball under their own steam.

"Yeah, Ma. Thinking back to you know when."

"Oh honey, you shouldn't be." She said softly, her tone comforting. Coming away from the doorway, she came to stand in front of him, her hand coming to rest on one of his forearms. "She's never going to hurt you again. You know who you stand a better chance with, even with your slip up. She's your future and we both know it. Tonight you get a second chance with her, to re-start your future. I'm not speaking to you now as your mother, I'm speaking to you as someone who knows the truth and has all faith at what is meant to be. Go get your future, go get your girl."

He never failed to be in awe of his mother, she was one wise woman and then some. She knew just the right thing to say no matter if it was good or bad, she would tell you and things would be alright. They'd come right somehow. Now, he had no doubt in his mind that deciding to come tonight, much to his mother's request, was the right thing to do.

Leaning down, he placed a tender kiss on his mother's still smooth and wrinkle-free cheek, smiling at her with all the pride he hoped he could show that was stored deep inside his chest.

"Ma, thank you won't ever be enough. So let me just say this, I'm glad Pa fought for you because if he didn't, I wouldn't be thankful for this moment."

The two of them shared a gentle embrace, hugging one another until they really had to get hustling so they made it to the ball on time, with his Ma lightly and playfully scolding him for almost making her cry with pride.

Upon arriving at the town hall, he saw that the council members hadn't skimped on the decorations to commemorate the event. Where they weren't flashy or all 'Hollywood' as was often used to describe things of a glittery, shiny nature with lights that would dazzle any man or woman. The council usually did several things throughout the year in order to save up for the two annual balls each year. This one, the charity ball and the Christmas ball.

Ralph never understood why they had the two close together, it just seemed to work out that way. Sometimes they did hold the charity ball earlier on in the year, it just depended on what the town had going on and if something else needed bringing forward or sorting out sooner, as long as they held the charity ball at some point that's what mattered.

"Cassie! Ralph!" his father's booming voice called out.

Both he and his mother turned around to see his father walking up to them, flanked by Roland and Rowan, followed behind by Ryder and Reed. He wasn't going to lie, they made for an impressive sight. Six tall, six foot plus men plus his precious mother always made heads turn, and sometimes not for all the right reasons. Five budding bachelors made for shaky ground. Well, four if Ralph plays his cards right.

The seven of them made their way inside the town hall, handing over their coats to the coat clerk, heading down to where their invites would be checked. All the time he walked behind his Ma and Pa with Ryder to his right, he kept an eye out for the one person he hoped to see here tonight.

Since she hadn't got back in contact with him since he dropped her back home a week ago, he assumed that she'd forgotten that it was him who'd done so. Since he figured that was what was going to be the case, he'd left the note in Laney's name so not to upset Robinne in any way. In her mind, he was still carrying out his promise and he fully intended to still do so. So by leaving the note under Laney's name, he didn't go back on it.

After leaving Robinne's place, he made a call to Laney herself and told her what he wanted her to do. He told her or rather, asked her politely, if she would use a cover story in case Robinne called her. Which she did. Thankfully, Laney was in full agreement with him in his plan to keep Robinne happy and content, so she'd gone along with the white lie of her taking her home instead of him. As a result, Robinne had been given the day off and he'd begged Luca to step in for her. To which, he now owed Luca a favour whenever he chose to collect it.

A price he would gladly pay over and over if it meant doing the right thing for the woman he cared about.

It didn't look like she was here yet though. Until she was, he wouldn't fully relax. He'd try to enjoy the evening until he knew she was here safely.

"Mind on other matters, Ralph?" Ryder piped up from beside him.

He sighed. "More like who." He muttered.

Ryder's hand clapped his shoulder, holding him in a firm yet brotherly grip. "Don't worry, she'll be here. I also have it under good authority that she's coming alone. No date. No companion."

Whereas that did somewhat soothe his soul, it also meant that she was potentially going to be approached by other men who'll be attending the ball. Not that he could blame them, Robinne was by far the most beautiful person he'd ever seen in his life, he just wasn't prepared for someone else to come along and swoop her up. Not now that he was finally ready to make things right after all this time.

He swallowed, nodding his head. "Good to know."

Soon, his family were shown into the ballroom which was able to hold up to 500 guests at any one time. It had been decked out as lavishly and tastefully as the outside and hallway down to this main room had been. Seeing as it wasn't quite time for Christmas decorations and just a tad too early for Halloween, the decorations had followed a more appropriate 'country' theme. If that were possible to describe what he was seeing as.

Drapes, ribbons, table decorations and such other appropriate decorations of the like were all plaid/tartan, which most cowboys often wore around these parts. The colour scheme followed a traditional brown, cream, black white and red theme. It might sound like a bit of a mess but if anyone had ever attended a hoedown or a country-themed night at a bar, those were the colours often used as many ranches around the state used wood, so there was the brown. The cream was a neutral colour for any colour to lay atop it. The black, white and red were colours often worn at rodeo events, so that's where they came in. Basically, imagine a country-themed night just, magnified.

As they made their way to their assigned table, he noticed that Roland and the twins were rather silent. The twins usually had more to say than nothing at all, like what was happening now. He wasn't sure what to make of this or why this came to be, but it was none of his concern and for once, he was relishing in the niceness of peace and quiet. At least, until the charity auction got underway, that is.

Reed and Ryder chatted happily together as did his Ma and Pa, with his Pa pulling out a chair for his wife to sit down in before sitting down in his own. They'd be joined by three other people to make up their table of ten. Hannah and Niall were the two others joining them, as was the norm when they went to events like this, which thankfully wasn't often. The spare seat next to him? That belong to the person he'd hoped to see more than anyone else here tonight.

More and more people filled up the main room as time slowly crept by. It was doubtful that the full 500 capacity would be filled here tonight. He suspected it would be closer to 200-300, based on the amount of tables around the room. Niall and Hannah had joined them fifteen minutes ago, politely greeting everyone around the table as they sat down.

Just as he was about to give up all hope, the room fell silent and eyes turned to someone who'd just entered the room. Where the room didn't fall completely silent, it dulled down to a quiet murmur. He turned to see just who was causing such a reaction from the room. When his eyes met the person responsible, he could understand why everyone had gone as quiet as they did. His own reaction however, was not quite so silent, as he could swear his heart was beating so loudly everyone could hear its tempo.

The object of his every thought, breath and being stood at the entrance of the room, looking exactly how he'd imagine a deer in headlights would. He knew she wasn't one for being the centre of attention, hating all eyes on her, so he could only do the first thing that came to mind.

Damn the consequences.

Making his apologies to the table, he rose up from out of his seat, heading towards the very women whom he hoped would become part of his present, and his future.

As he made his way over to her, he got a chance to get a good look at her and the out of this world, pulse-racing yet heart-stopping dress she was wearing. He'd never seen a dress like it. Never mind the fact that he didn't see a lot of dresses anyway, this one just blew every single dress he *had* seen up until that moment right out of the water.

The dress was a colour that of a pale blue snowflake, or so he'd imagined a snowflake to be. Other than its common white colour. She'd opted for the lesser used but no less common option of a shoulder-less, strapless dress which came to rest and somehow stay resting above her chest. There was just the tiniest hint of cleavage, but nothing to be considered vulgar. The sides and back of the dress gave way to a cape-like veil which gave her this otherworldly, angelic, princess-like aura. It was laced with flowers dotted throughout the veil and parts of the long, floor-length gown which protruded from the corset-style part of the stress in which the veil was attached. If it were not for the thought of getting to her, he was sure his legs would've stopped working at the mere sight of her.

He knew that she often thought herself not worthy of being loved by a man 'like himself', but right now, he felt the exact opposite. Now, he wasn't so sure that he was even half the man worthy of the princess before him.

Just before he made it to her, her head turned in time to see him coming. Rather than looking angry, mad or any other emotion of the like, she looked…relieved, almost thankful to see him. A reaction he was more than happy to work with, if it was a promise of better things to come for the both of them.

Clearing his throat, he stopped just before her and bowed ever so slightly, holding out his hand. "Would you like me to escort you to our table? My mother has kindly placed you with us, if that's alright with you." He asked softly.

A look of surprise briefly flashed across her face before it was gone again, replaced instead with a look of thankfulness. Her shoulders squared, her nose rose ever so slightly and she seemed to stand somewhat taller after he'd addressed her. Which he supposed, she did. She must be wearing heels under that dress as she stood just a smidge taller towards his height, and he wasn't a small fella.

"I would like that, thank you."

Play it cool Ralph, play it cool. You got this.

He nodded, waiting for her to slide her hand into his. Once he had her hand safely in his own, he didn't miss the indescribable feelings flowing into him through their touch, it was a sensation he'd never experienced before. Making it easier on her, he transferred her hand to the crook of his right arm, leading her slowly but swiftly towards their table, avoiding the gaze of anyone else around them.

At their table, he patiently waited as each member of his family, plus Niall and Hannah, greeted Robinne once they knew that it was okay to approach her. Talk to her. They knew she wasn't fragile, but since she hadn't seen any of them since the night of the BBQ, he knew they were waiting for the okay so they could let her talk to them with ease rather than awkwardness.

Sitting beside her, he found himself in a somewhat nervous state, and he wasn't a nervous person by nature. He just wanted things to go as smooth as they could with her, he was making himself antsy with worry. His palms started to get a little clammy as he wiped them on his tux pants, hoping to return them to as close to normal as possible. Only when he got himself a little calmer did he date take a look at the stunning creature beside him, as no doubt just a mere glance at her would get his pulse back up racing in samba again.

"You look stunning tonight, Robinne." He said, whispering softly to her so only she would hear.

He watched as she swallowed.

She's just as nervous as me, the sweetheart.

I won't make her go through this for too long.

To be honest, I don't want to stay long either.

Ralph had already made a generous donation to this year's charity. All proceeds would go towards the local children's centre, sprucing it up just in time for the holiday season for them and their families. A cause he was more than happy to donate to.

"T-thank you. You don't clean up so bad yourself." She whispered back, her voice seductively breathy. At least, it was to him.

"Thank *you*." He smiled.

So far, so good. He knew that he was in for a long night ahead of him, as there was nothing more he wanted than to get the two of them out of there and into a setting where they'd feel more relaxed, less on display. As he knew this wasn't possible, he opted for the second best option and best solution for right this moment.

He took a chance, putting his left hand down between him and Robinne, clearing his throat for her to take note as to what he was doing. She looked somewhat stiff sitting there, needing to relax a little as much as he did. Thankfully, she noticed his hand and the look of thankfulness once more spread across her face.

As she took his hand, which was shielded under the table via the tablecloth, he knew deep down that they would be alright. By the very act of her placing her hand within his, willingly, it spoke a thousand words and the inaudible words that reached his ears were 'we're going to make it'.

Holding onto that thought and indeed holding onto her hand, he settled back into his seat just as the evening's festivities began.

* * *

CHAPTER TWENTY
~ Robinne ~

Seeing Ralph again was a lot easier than she thought it would be, considering the last time she'd seen him and been in his company, was the night she ran out on him at his family's BBQ. A million and one thoughts and feelings had been running through her mind and body leading up till today, sending her already overactive imagination from warp speed right into hyper drive.

She didn't know if he was as nervous as her, but if his demeanour was anything to go by as he sat beside her right now, holding her hand, he sure as hell didn't show it.

For the next hour and a half while they both endured the Mayor's lengthy speech about this year's charity in which all proceeds were going towards, plus a few other speeches from whom Robinne guessed were important members of the community. Since there were still people she'd yet to meet and places she was still yet to go to, she didn't know a single one of them.

Thankfully, the last thing that everyone had to listen to, while tucking into food that had been placed in front of them during the speeches, was a small video telling people in attendance, just how much last year's charity ball made a difference to their lives. Hoping that this year they could do the same for the people they were aiming to help this year.

The video ended with rigorous applause from everyone, herself included. She always did have a soft spot for helping people, especially the smaller charities which often got overlooked, though she wasn't always able to help as many people as she would've liked to. Curse of being unemployed and on low income, you weren't able to do as much as you'd like when everyone else was frivolously and stupidly spending their earnings.

Now with at least her earnings from working at Laney's bakery, she would be able to donate at least *something*, even if it doesn't match what she would imagine would be some impressive donations from tonight's efforts. She wouldn't underestimate anyone here simply because this is a small town. People in smaller communities in her experience often came together in a bigger way than larger communities. Not in terms of wealth, sometimes, but in the gestures they make and the overall size of the collective community heart.

This one? This was the biggest community hear she'd ever seen.

Throughout all of this, Ralph never left her side even once or let go of her hand. She thought he'd let go after a small while. Instead, he'd held on.

Even through eating their respective meals, he didn't let go even once. If this was anything to go by, it was a good sign of things to come.

Only when they clapped the video when it came to an end did he let go, obviously needing his hand to clap the other. As his hand slipped from hers, the continuous, indescribable feeling which had ignited when their hands touched when he'd come to rescue her from the glaring crowd, slowly went away. Leaving nothing but the faintest of tingles on her palm. A feeling she'd happily have for the rest of the night.

When the applause died down, the MC for the night's festivities announced that people were free to join the Mayor and his wife on the makeshift dancefloor. Dancing would no doubt be the main activity for the rest of the night, something in which she'd been dreading. As not being naturally inclined or able to dance, she fully intended to sit this part out.

That was, until Ralph stood up beside her, offering her his hand once more.

"Dance with me, then we can make our escape." He smirked, throwing her a wink for good measure.

I'd escape just about anywhere with you, Ralph.

"I'd love to. Thank you."

Ralph led her out onto the dancefloor where numerous couples had gathered since the MC declared it open to dancing, making them one of the couples dancing on the outer part of the floor. Now that she had a chance to look at him properly, away from the eyes of his family and family friends around their table, she truly realised how dashing he really was. In or out of cowboy gear.

The tux he'd either bought or rented out, fit him like a second skin. It moulded to his every curve, muscle and angle. Boy did he have a lot of angles. She'd never in a million years thought she'd see him in such an outfit, it didn't even come into her mind yet, here she was. On the dancefloor with the only human being to ever truly make her heart feel both as if it had stopped beating, and was galloping at tempo at the same time.

Ralph placed her hand on his shoulder and her other hand in his, while his other hand not holding hers, came to rest gently at her hip. He rested it in a respectful place, so not to come on as too strong, but in a place where he'd be able to guide them around the floor effortlessly. He was in for a surprise when she'd more than likely step on his feet, rather than suddenly become a swan of the dancing world.

Now there's a thought.

Before she knew it, she was dancing with the man who'd she'd spent the past month keeping her mind occupied from. As the month went on, she realised more and more just how much she missed him. Not that she'd planned to admit it to him until she was ready to see him, which he'd said to her that he'd wait until. Thoughtful, come to think of it. Thoughtfulness was one of his best traits, putting things like lying to her completely onto the burner. His good qualities as she'd come to realise, way outweighed his flaws.

After all, she had plenty of her own to match.

"You look like you're doing some hard thinking there darlin'." The burr of Ralph's voice broke through her thoughts. She looked up at him, her eyes wide and searching his own. His eyes however, seemed to have this magical quality all their own which she'd never taken the time to notice before. Kissing him back in the barn didn't exactly leave enough time to stare at…other things.

"You know me, it happens."

He chuckled. "That it does. I wouldn't change you for the world, Robinne."

The use of her name made her subconscious stand to attention. Usually, he'd call her 'darlin'', or even the ever odd nickname, 'crumpet. Using her real name and more than once obviously meant that he was playing things safe until things returned somewhat back to normal, if that was what was meant to happen. Who knows?

"I've missed you, Robinne. I want to make things right with you, if you'd let me."

It's not a case of if I'd let you, Ralph. Its will my heart let you.

She sighed softly, "Ralph, you hurt me real bad. I won't lie, I've missed you too. But I can't start things over with you again if you're going to do it again in the future. I don't expect you to be perfect because Lord knows, I'm far from it myself."

He shook his head. "I won't. I've been spending this last month thinking about how I can make it up to you, show you how I've truly changed and how I plan to go on from whenever you gave me the second chance. If you thought I deserve one."

She nodded.

"I think we both need a do-over. We've had time to cool down and get both our asses in gear, I think a second chance is exactly what we both need."

Judging by the look on his face, Ralph clearly wasn't expecting her to agree to his proposal. In truth, she was exhausted from trying to put him out of her mind, trying to move on when the direction she should be moving, is his.

"Well…woah…I…I um…I'll admit, I wasn't expecting you to agree. I think we still have a lot to talk about though. So, how about we dance to a few more numbers and make an early exit? I know the perfect place to go to talk." He smiled, a cheeky, mischievous one too.

He was right, they did have a lot still left to talk about. Why not do it now? No time like the present, as they say.

"Sure. What about donating though? It *is* a charity ball."

"I already donated a fair bit before I came. We're good."

"We?" she arched a brow, curious as to who this 'we' was.

He nodded.

"I was kind of hoping you'd be here tonight. So, I donated enough for the both of us."

"You didn't have to do that, Ralph. Let me pay you back."

It was at that moment during her protest, that he brought her flush against his body, moving them into the centre of the dancefloor alongside the Mayor and his wife. "Not going to happen, so don't even be stubborn about it because woman I know you will." He chuckled.

She wasn't one for pouting, usually, but she offered him up her best pout. He was right, and it happily irritated her for the fact that he knew that fact about her. She was stubborn, hella stubborn. She always did blame the fact on her grandma as she herself was a stubborn woman, thus resulting in why she was the same way.

"Hmph."

With another chuckle rumbling out from Ralph's chest, the two of them settled into comfortable pattern as they danced together, dancing to two more numbers before deciding to put their plan into place. As they danced, they'd decided upon leaving the ball together but leaving the room different times, so not to arouse suspicion from countless eyes that had been watching them the whole evening.

Clapping the second song that had come to an end, sung by the in-house band for the evening, Ralph took Robinne to one side of the room where he leaned down to her ear.

"Remember our plan?"

She nodded. "Got it. Meet you at the entrance in fifteen, I'm just going to run to the ladies real quick!"

With one last look at him, she exited the room as incognito as possible. Which considering she was in a snowflake blue dress was no easy feat without being noticed somehow.

Please don't let me regret this decision, I can't deal with it a second time.

* * *

As he watched Robinne exit the room, he didn't feel the uneasiness in his stomach as he did when he watched her flee from the barn and him in turn. This time, he felt a blossom of hope start to grow there, promising to turn into something that he could be proud of and won't have a chance at screwing up. He was determined to avoid that more than ever.

Little did he know that his moment of happiness was soon to be extinguished from the once promising flames burning within him. A blast from the past was just about to knock his legs from under him, one who he'd hoped he'd never have to deal with again.

"Hello Ralph." The shrill and all-too familiar voice said from somewhere beside him.

Who said the devil didn't exist?

Whoever it was, they were wrong.

The devil did exist, and she was standing right next to me.

Turning around, he faced the nightmare from his past head-on. He wasn't going to make the same mistake as he did ten years ago, so whatever she had to say to him or why the hell she was even doing here wasn't going to make a difference to his decision. He was going to get out of her presence as soon as possible and find the woman he'd intended to spend the rest of the night with. The women standing in front of him represented his past and he had no intention of going back there. His Ma was right, he needed to head towards his future and his future would be waiting for them at the town hall entrance, ready for them to re-start their future together.

"Delilah." He addressed her formally, coldly, feeding no emotion into his voice. She didn't deserve it.

"Aw, don't be like that Ralph. Aren't you glad to see me again?" she batted her terribly long fake lashes at him, making his skin crawl.

Is this woman mad or just pretending to be?

Why on God's good earth would I be happy to see her again?

Doesn't she remember anything at all from our last meeting? I sure as hell do.

"Frankly, no."

Delilah gasped, having the audacity to feign shock.

"I don't see why not. I called thinks off with that boy after that night, I left him to be with you."

"You were with me anyway! How can you leave someone you're cheating with to be with a man you're already with? That's just…barmy!" he said, rubbing his forehead where was sure a vein or something was about to burst. The nerve of the woman. The sheer nerve!

Even to someone who'd been rude or inconsiderate to him, Ralph never usually let his anger be known to them, choosing the path of inner peace instead. A calmer he was better than stressed out one This time however, he'd walked around with ten years of pent-up feelings, thoughts and emotions which he should've made clear on that night. Well no more. He was going to tell her just exactly what was on his mind and to hell with the consequences. He wasn't going to be rude about it, he was just going to tell her what had been deep inside him, festering unknown to him for a decade.

"Delilah, the night I found you in the closet with whatever his name was, broke me in more ways than your mind could ever imagine possible. You know when I feel I feel things deeply, and I was hoping to go in deeper with you, against the better judgement of what my head was screaming out to me. My heart wanted to follow the foolish hormones of a boy and chase a girl who had no intention of chasing me back. I was a fool, Delilah. A fool who was blinded by what I then that was 'beauty'. Never in a million years did I imagine I'd be getting the beast instead." He took a brief pause to breathe before continuing. "I wanted to do so much with you. I had plans, big plans. Ones that would've made you happy or so I imagined they would. Obviously, I wasn't even good enough for you to remain loyal to in the most primitive sense. I wanted to grow up and mature with you. I was going to return to the ranch and make a home for us there, a place where someday I hoped to have a family of our own where I'd work so you wouldn't have to. To me, you were my Queen. Silly me for picking the Queen of Hearts. That day I found you in the cupboard quite literally screwing me over, was the day that finally opened my eyes to just who you really were under all that fakery you plastered yourself in constantly. Do you know what? I should be thanking you, come to think of it. It took me ten years to find her but I've finally found the woman who's worth one hundred of the woman I thought you ever were. So thank you, Delilah." He picked up her hand, surprised she didn't wrench it from his own, and placed a sour kiss on the back of her hand. Letting it go a second later. "Thank you for showing me the path to my forever, good luck with your own life, you're going to need it."

With that, he took his leave from the room, heading in the same direction in which Robinne had taken not so long ago. Delilah for the first time in her life, stood as stunned as all the people around them who'd been privy to their conversation. He was past caring who'd heard him. In fact, the more people who heard him tell her how he felt at last, the better. He knew they'd be behind him, not her.

Now, go get your girl Ralph old boy.

He knew his family would understand where he was going off to, as no doubt each of them new the possibility of him talking to Robinne so his disappearance from the table wouldn't come as a surprise to any of them. To which he was thankful.

Striding out of the room and down the hall, he came to a stop just where the ladies' room was situated. He didn't know if she was still in there while he was talking to Delilah, but he'd wait here for a few minutes before heading to where they'd agreed to meet. As he waited there, he began to hear noises coming from behind him. Turning around, he noted the self-same closet in which ten years ago, he'd caught Delilah in with that weed of a man. Boy.

Feeling like time was repeating itself, Ralph felt himself being drawn towards the closet. Flinging it open, he'd never been gladder to be wrong. He knew Robinne would never do something like this to him, not after what had gone down between them both, but it was just the sense of déjà vu that had unsettled his stomach. The couple who were occupying the closet this time didn't seem to notice his opening the door, too occupied in their activities, so he closed the door and turned away.

That was too close. Too close.

Relieved to be putting another part of his past permanently behind him, he wasted no time in striding towards the meeting point where as he approached, he saw Robinne already waiting for him at. She turned to him just in time to catch the relieved expression on his face as he approached, making her eyes widen at the sight of him.

"Is everything alright? I was worried you weren't coming."

He put his hands gently on both of her cheeks, smiling down at her with his best megawatt smile. "Things have never been better, darlin'. Never been better. C'mon, let's blow this popsicle stand."

She blinked. "I don't get it."

He chuckled, sliding his hands down until he linked one of his with hers. "Doesn't matter, let's go sweetheart." Being careful of her footwear, he descended the town hall steps with her like a newly-wedded couple, handing over the valet ticket and getting them into his truck once it had been brought around. Pulling out of the town hall drive, he knew with every second that followed, that he was heading in the right direction with the woman who'd been sent to him, to save him.

Finally.

* * *

What wasn't aware of as they made their way out of the centre of town to wherever his ideal talking spot was, was that she'd heard every word of his conversation with Delilah. She'd put two and two together ages ago when she'd heard Delilah's 'plan' to get back with Ralph, realising that she was the said woman who'd burned him all those years ago. She had a feeling that the dreadful woman would be making an appearance at some stage, she'd just assumed she would be the target, not Ralph.

She'd gone to the ladies room as she said she would do, deciding to then grab her coat and head to the meeting point. Only on the way to the town hall entrance, she had a feeling in her stomach that something wasn't quite right, so she headed back to the main room where the ball was being held. She'd stopped just outside the doorway leading into the room, having heard Ralph regrettably answer his name being called.

From there, she'd heard every word and if her heart could get any fuller, she'd need to get a second one to put all the feelings into. Of course, she would never tell him she knew, it would be hew own little guilty secret.

"So, where are we headed?"

Ralph looked at her briefly before turning his attention back to the road. "You'll see. I promise I'm not taking you anywhere sinister."

She scoffed, smirking as she leaned her head against the passenger side window. "I wouldn't put it past you."

He chuckled, keeping his eyes on the road.

"You know, one day that sassy mouth of yours is going to end up paying the price sweetheart."

She turned her head to him then, her expression mildly serious. Mostly still sassy. "Better be worth the price."

The corner of Ralph's mouth hitched as he drove, clearly finding her attempt at seduction, or at least what she thought was seduction, amusing. She'd never been one to be good at flirting, as she always came across as awkward, but her attempts always warranted laughter. Usually at, rather than with her. Though she knew Ralph didn't mean it nastily like someone else usually did.

The rest of the drive to Ralph's "secret" location was met with a comfortable silence, with Robinne thinking while Ralph was driving, just how much the two of them were going to say to one another once they were there. She didn't have a doubt in her mind that things wouldn't work out, she just hoped that neither of them said too much to continue their second chance together.

When Ralph finally pulled up in the middle of nowhere, Robinne never thought that he was ever going to stop driving. From what she could tell after they'd left the 'Dripping Springs' city sign behind, they didn't venture further than the outskirts of the town. It was truly of no bother to her, as she was more interested in what the two of them were going to say, rather than where they actually were. She trusted Ralph, so that was enough to put any anxieties to rest.

Ralph turned off the engine of his truck once he'd parked up in what sounded like a gravel car park of sorts, taking a moment to breathe before he turned to face her. The awe-inspiring light of the moon outside of the truck provided the perfect amount of illumination inside the truck cab, so much so that they could see one another in the darkness in which surrounded them. As Robinne turned to look at Ralph, she was dumbstruck for a second time at how something as simple as moonlight added another layer to his breath-taking beauty.

Yes, men can be beautiful too.

"Okay." He started to say to her, finally turning towards her. "I don't know how to start this as I have so much that I want to say so, how about this? I want to get everything off my chest which I've been wanting to say to you since I pledged my promise to you, you can stop me at any time but if you don't, you can decide where we go from here. Okay?"

Sounded fair to her. She was more than keen to hear what she wanted to say. Almost as keen as she was for what she wanted to say to him but, she wanted to hear him first so she nodded, giving him the go ahead.

With another calming breath, he began.

"Okay so, let me first of by saying just how sorry I am. Sorry doesn't even begin to remotely cover what I need to do to start making things up to you but, I know I should say it anyway because I truly, truly am sorry. When I found your list that day, I had no intention or idea to carry out anything other than what I did which was read it when picking it up. Only a day or so later did I even begin to think about actually doing something with it. Again, I know that doesn't justify the fact that I did it but, hear me out. Since getting to know you, I like to think that I've gotten even the basics down as to what you like, don't like and what makes you up as a person. Even from the first moment of meeting you, I learned so much. Over the days that followed, I wanted to see you more and more but had no ideas to why or how to go about it without coming off as desperate. See, I'm not too good at the whole friendship/relationship thing. I mean, look at my choice in women."

Delilah, obviously.

"My soul intention was to show you that the clichés I'd learned that you hated so much, weren't so bad when someone who actually cared about you, cared enough to make them memorable for you. Hence why I genuinely wanted to kiss you in that barn and actually mean it. Which I did. We both know what happened next, I let slip that it was worth adding a cliché like a kiss in a close, romantic setting was worth it to make it memorable. Let me tell you this now Robinne." He leaned over and took both of her hands in his own. "I had *full* intention to tell you that I had the list, I swear that to you on my honour as a cowboy and my word as a gentleman. I had no idea when I was going to do it but I wasn't going to let it go on for longer than that day in the barn, I just needed long enough to show you that there are people out there who genuinely care about you and want to do things for you because of reasons scarily new to them, but in the best way possible. Again, telling you that I intended to tell you eventually doesn't come remotely close to clearing me of what I did. I fucked up and that won't ever change and I'll regret that moment for the rest of my life, but I hoped ever since I watched you run out of the ranch that day that I would get a chance, a second chance, to put right what I'd to my own fault messed up in the first place." As he spoke, he stroked his thumb against her hand, clearly nervous by both the fact that his hands were shaking, and that he needed to do something to distract himself against that fact.

She felt like her own hands were going to start shaking soon. This was turning out to be a bigger night than she'd ever expected and as of this moment, she was having a hard time keeping a lid on her already bubbling emotions. Still, she said nothing as she felt that he was nowhere near done.

He looked up from where he was focused on their hands, turning his attention instead to her eyes meeting her gaze head on, for what would become the most touching thing anyone has ever said to her for years as he continued to speak.

"I knew a simple apology would never do. People who think that alone enough are fools. So, I knew I had to do something to put you at ease so you could live somewhat happily considering what I did to you. I left you that voicemail so that you would hear in my voice that I truly meant I would leave you be until you were ready, not that I was calling to put my own mind and soul at temporary ease after upsetting you. Was it going to half kill me to stay away from you for as long as you needed? Oh hell yeah. Was it however worth it, knowing that I was putting you first? Again, oh hell yeah. Because I knew that someday when I was given that second chance, even if you decided to never want me in your life again, I would at least set things right with you and wish you well for the life I knew you deserved. The life you moved halfway around the world to get. In order to go about showing you how sorry I was, I knew I had to do things to make it up to you without you realising it was me who was doing them, to prove that I was *genuinely* sorry."

She blinked, stunned. "What do you mean? What things?" she said, her voice a feather-soft whisper.

He smiled softly at her, "Well, after I left you that note with the basket, I orchestrated a series of events which I somehow manged to get people to go along with. Willingly, of course."

She arched a brow, extremely curious as to what these things were. "Go on." She urged politely.

"The series of people calling at your door? Bringing you food and other such things?"

No way!

"That was "That was *you?*"

He nodded. "Guilty as charged."

"And the job at the bakery?"

He nodded again, "Guilty again. I wanted Ma to give you a job at her B&B, but she figured working there would remind you too much of me."

Understandable.

"Everyone in your family giving me a wide berth?"

"Me again. Sort of. Like with Ma, I knew it would be hard on you to be with any of them, given the fact they either knew me or were related to me. I didn't want you upset in any way, Robinne. I did everything I thought I was able, without overstepping my boundaries, to keep to my promise and to let you discover what you were searching for when you moved here. I hope you were able to find it." he said, his voice as genuine as he was.

Oh she'd found it alright. She'd found it and then some. Over the last month, she'd managed to get to know more people in the town, get outside of her comfort zone, get a job and get a good chunk of her first draft done of her brand new book. And it was all thanks to this man sitting here with her, holding her hand and promising her a better future. A future she could now see was possible between them.

Ralph had told her more than enough. If holding hands with him, feeling a pull she'd never felt before wasn't enough, she could tell by the tone of his voice that everything he'd just said to her wasn't false. Not one bit. It didn't sound forced, rehearsed or compulsory. These were his own words, words straight from his tender cowboy heart. A heart she wanted to take care of for the rest of her life.

There was plenty of enough time for her to respond to what he'd just told her a little later. For now, there was only one thing she wanted to do. Something that this time thanks to the air being cleared between them, would end better than it did the first time.

The expression on Ralph's face didn't go amiss as she decided on her next move. He looked as if he were expecting the worst news of his life. Imagine a scared lamb lost from its mother, he was pretty close to what she imagined what that would look like for real.

Time to put him out of his worried thoughts.

Moving his hands from hers, she moved herself so that she straddled both his legs on the driver's side of the truck cab, placing her hands on his face while being careful to pay attention to his expressions. As his face gave a look of complete and utter bemusement, there was no inkling of what he was thinking exactly.

Here goes nothing.

Leaning her head down to his, her arms naturally coming back to where they belonged around his neck, she pressed her lips once more against his own. This time and right in this moment, where it was just the two of them who existed on this magical planet called Earth which had brought them two together, she let her lips tell the story of what she was thinking. If her lips touching his could now speak, it would tell anyone fortunate to be listening to them, that the story they were telling was that this was just the beginning chapter to the story of the rest of their lives. The rest before, well that was just the prologue.

Bring on the next chapter.

CHAPTER TWENTY-ONE
~ Robinne ~

If anyone had told Robinne that a month ago at the Dripping Springs annual charity ball, that she would be sitting here on Ralph's back porch on her laptop watching the sunset, she would've pegged you for a fool. A madman at best. But, here she was, doing just that. Sunsets were always her favourite part of the day and here in Texas, they got a thousand and one times as beautiful as they did back home.

So much had happened since that night in Ralph's truck where she'd kissed him, her kiss telling him all that she needed to say at that moment until such a time she wanted to expand upon their words. Before she could tell him that, when they broke from their second first kiss, he did something she never saw coming.

He'd slipped off her shoes, threw them in the back of the truck and carried her down a small, winding gravel pathway, leading to the most beautiful cavern she'd ever seen. Granted, she hadn't seen any in real life so, this was *the* only and most beautiful one. Ralph had explained to her that this was a hotspot for any and all who wanted to get cool, hang out with family and friends or just come to take photos. Where he'd taken her was actually a place called 'Hamilton Pool Preserve in Travis County. Usually, you would have to come during one of the two reservation period times but, he pulled some strings to allow them to have the space to themselves for a brief period of time.

With it not being daylight, it was hard to see the cavern in all its beauty but nonetheless, what she had seen was worth it. Even what happened next was worth it. Ralph had the mad, bonkers suggestion of taking a late night dip. He'd made sure the bacteria levels were safe for them to do so. So, that's what they did. She was surprised she'd agreed to his crazy suggestion but, she never regretted it for a second.

Their respective clothes were left safely placed on a flat-ish rock, ready for them to collect when they'd finished swimming. Robinne was an excellent swimmer, so she had no worries about drowning. Ralph proved to be an excellent swimmer in his own right too, having confessed to her that he and his brothers, plus several friends over the years as he'd grown up, had gone swimming in more than a lake or two. So he was not a novice in any means.

They'd swam for at least an hour during their time there, talking about anything and everything under the sun thanks to the relaxed, romantic setting. She learned a lot about Ralph that she never knew, things that she never would've if she hadn't come out here with him tonight. Such as all the truth surrounding what Delilah meant to him, things he got up to as a kid, his likes and dislikes. Most surprising of all? Just how much he had opened his heart to her, confessing things she'd never pegged him to think or even feel. Things she'd cherish and keep close to her heart forever.

Just as their swim was coming to a close, they'd shared one final kiss under the moonlight, floating in the centre of the cavern's waters. Each kiss they shared unlocked the potential of more chapters to add to their lives, as their story was being newly written with each passing moment.

After leaving the cavern pool, Ralph donned her in spare clothing from the spare clothing in the back of his truck which he always kept in there, habit of being a cowboy. Always prepared. He'd then given her the choice of going back to his place or back to hers. Not wanting her to feel pressured in any way if he'd automatically taken them back to his place. Regrettably, she'd chosen her place. Though when being dropped off, she did offer to invite him in for a drink and a warm up before he headed off home.

He accepted.

It was around midnight when Ralph eventually left to go home, having spent the few hours after arriving at Robinne's place, talking to her, getting warm and sharing a few warm drinks with her. Neither of them had felt so contented and at peace with their souls for as long as they remembered. Both glad for their own reasons that they'd decided to give their 'friendship' a second chance. Though they knew that what was going on between them, was far from just being a friendship.

Robinne saw Ralph off at her door where before finally bidding her a goodnight, he'd tipped her chin up, left her a kiss worth a thousand promises before leaving her with '*Il mio*'. Which was Italian for 'mine'. She'd later learned why he'd used this, thanks to getting to know and meet his good friend Luca. Secretly, she'd thanked Luca for influencing his Italian upon Ralph, as she'd quite enjoyed the little phrase he'd used on her.

Going to bed that night, she'd no longer felt the sadness which she'd felt in going to bed alone every night. For that night, she was no longer a single woman. Her heart had finally been taken, she was no longer unlovable or a pawn to be used by anyone ever again. She'd found her forever and her forever wasn't far away on his family's ranch. Closing her eyes after sending Ralph a goodnight message, she just knew that things would never be so bad now that she'd had the other half of her heart finally in her life.

From that day on, things really kicked off between them. In the best way possible that is. Ralph took her to his place for the first time a few days after the ball, giving her a short while to get used to the idea that she was finally his and he was finally hers. He knew her well. He knew she'd need time and under their new start, they'd give one another some if ever they needed it, no questions asked. They spent the day goofing off around his house, with him showing her every room and giving her a grand tour of the place like his brother Ryder, which he'd built. He found it hard to let her go home at the end of the day, but he knew that their 'day' would come sometime. Sometime soon.

With the days that followed, they took one another out on a series of dates, proud of their new couple status. Robinne didn't want Ralph to be the one to always ask her out, as there were places which she still wanted to discover. So, she invited him out on dates to explore them. They'd agreed that things in this relationship should be equal. Where they wouldn't be an absolutely perfect couple and they knew things wouldn't always go swimmingly, equality would be the one thing they could always grantee would happen between them.

She'd also had the pleasure of meeting the rest of the brothers she'd never got to meet the first time around, introducing herself and getting to know them more alongside their big brother. Simultaneously, she'd also met a few of his friends other than the famous Luca, loving them all instantly and she couldn't help but to thank them for being great friends to her man.

My man! Eek!

Ralph also took it upon himself to open up to her more. She'd learned all about a cowboy's heart and as a result, she saw him come out of the shell he'd happily put himself in much like her own, telling her about the things that he'd never been able to trust a woman with before. She in turn had done the same. Where she wouldn't fully expose every single thing about herself to him or anyone else, she did feel like she could now trust him with the worst, including her anxieties, worries and doubts.

Life was finally what it should be. For them both.

Finally

"Daydreaming again?" a voice said behind her, startling her a little bit.

Ralph came out from the back of the house, joining her on the back porch beside her.

"Guilty as charged." She smiled, leaning into his side after moving her laptop onto the porch coffee table.

Writing had taken up a lot of her spare time between working for Laney, which she'd decided to keep going on with for now, and starting to help Ralph and the other Jenkins boys around the ranch. There was always something for her to do no matter if it was something small, or something big, she began to learn what they were more than happy to teach her and include her in.

"I told you, that's a dangerous thing to do." He said, kissing her forehead tenderly.

She sighed, smiling. "I know."

Ralph put his arm around her shoulders, snuggling her into his side as he joined in with watching the setting of the sun. "What were you thinking about?"

"Everything really. Especially Thanksgiving."

He chuckled, remembering very well that day and all its events. "Ah yes, now that was a day."

* * *

Robinne had been invited back over to the main ranch house for her very first Thanksgiving. She knew what the holiday was and what it represented, she just never had attended or celebrated one before. This would be her first. Not wanting to go empty handed, she'd asked Cassie just what she was supposed to bring, as she'd feel awful for just showing up to eat food.

"Just bring whatever you want to bring dear, we'll be grateful for anything you'd give us." Cassie had told her. So, that's what she'd done. After working at the Bakery for a little while now, she'd asked Laney to show her how to make a few things, just in case she'd have to look after the shop on her own someday. Laney's skills and teachings had paid off as after she'd made her very first Thanksgiving pumpkin pie, it looked somewhat half decent.

Success!

There was still more than enough time until she had to make her way over to the ranch, as she'd baked the pie in plenty of time for it to cook but still be somewhat warm when it arrived with her later on. Ralph had insisted on stopping by to pick her up but she'd politely declined, telling him that she planned to bring a surprise with her so he wasn't to get a glimpse at it. Knowing Ralph, he'd at least try to peak even if never actually did.

Seeing as everything looked okay from the food perspective, she headed on upstairs to fix herself a bath.

As her bath was filling up with her favourite bubble bath scent, spiced berries, she dug her laptop out her laptop back from a room she'd since made into her makeshift office/editing room/library expansion. She was mostly way through her first draft of the book she'd decided to continue writing. At one stage, she almost gave up. She'd fallen sick earlier this year around March and it zapped her energy that much, she almost lost all of the will to write.

The only thing in which had changed that was reading Robinne Lee's book, *The Idea of You*. A story about a 40-something woman crushing on and harbouring feelings for a man half of her age. Believe it or not, she found the story beyond gripping and by the time she got to the end, she was demanding as many people were, a second book to add to the characters' stories. Robinne Lee was the reason she began writing again, and write she would until she got her story out there.

Shortly, her bath was ready thanks to the top of the range bath of her choice had been installed during the re-build. She'd went nuts when she saw the price of some of the items she'd been asked to personally pick out over email. Never would she make someone pay that much for something which she'd be happy to have basic of. Yet, here she was, sliding into a bath the interior designer had convinced her was more than affordable to buy and fit.

Shed of any clothes, she slid down into the bath and immediately closed her eyes, relaxing in the soothing smells and feel of the bath and all its glorious contents.

Who said heaven didn't exist? They were wrong.
Very wrong.

A little over an hour later she was clean, dressed and ready to go. She'd just finished wrapping up the pie to take, double checking one last time that it was still decent to take over. It was, thankfully. The last thing she had to do was pick up Ralph's gift on her way out and she was all set.

"Keys, check. Purse, don't need it. Phone, check." She mumbled to herself, picking up the pie as she walked out of the kitchen, through the front room and into the hallway. Picking up the gift for Ralph as she left the house, locking up behind her.

On her way over to the Jenkins ranch, she couldn't help but sing (rather badly) along to her favourite Irish songs which she'd put to disc, Yes, she still did that. Where custom cd playlists were still considered a bit of a 90s thing to do, it was the only way she'd get all her favourite Irish songs in one place, as her truck wasn't a new one so she couldn't link up her phone to it.

She'd picked up a love of Irish music thanks to her grandma. When she was alive, they'd often spend the days she'd visit listening to them, with her grandma telling her stories she'd often remember when listening. Often would she be treated to the sight of her grandma trying to 'dance' along to the tunes while negotiating her tricky knees, tricky hip and minding her pacemaker. Still, those were the memories she now harboured and cherished deeply. She didn't know what her grandma would make of her now, here, but she hoped that wherever she was, she'd be looking down at her and smiling for her granddaughter still loved her Irish tunes.

A short while later she parked up at the Jenkins' main ranch house, with the very moment she'd parked up, the front door came open and her heart kicked up a gear at the person who'd come out.

Ralph.

He'd always wait where he could watch her arrive, coming out when she'd just parked up so she didn't have to come all the way to the door on her own. Bless him.

He came to her just as her door was opening, giving her a hand as she hopped out of her truck. "Glad you could make it." he said, pressing a kiss to her cheek before a follow-up kiss on her neck, making her giggle.

"Mmm, it helped that you were texting me every fifteen minutes, counting down the time until I had to be here." She smirked.

She wasn't lying, he did. It was rather sweet. Ralph was a very protective man of what was finally now his and to be fair, she was just as looking forward to seeing him as he was to seeing her. The little message attached to the countdown were really sweet too, they just added to his cuteness. Yes, men can be cute as well as beautiful.

"C'mon, let's get you and your goodies inside so they don't get cold." She arched a brow. "My 'goodies'?"

He chuckled. Clearly he hadn't thought about how it would come out before he said it. Surprisingly, he wasn't a dirty-minded man by nature, but he did have his moments.

"Your food. Though, I wouldn't mind your other goodies coming in too, since they're attached to a rather fetching woman." He winked.

She gently smacked his arm. "You're terrible."

Ralph winked at her again, "Don't you forget it."

Between them, they carried her things inside and made their way straight out to the back porch and garden where the thanksgiving festivities were taking place. She'd only ever seen Thanksgiving being held inside in movies but, this was Texas. They didn't do anything small so all of the major events of the year happened out in the open, for as long as the weather would allow for anyway.

"Look who's here!" Ralph called out to his family, taking her light coat off her shoulders as they came out onto the back porch.

Everyone who'd gathered outside turned to call out a greeting to her, before turning back to whatever they were doing when she and Ralph emerged. He joined her once he'd gone to hang up her coat, only to be called over by Cassie who was attempting to carry more than what she could over to the table.

"Go." She smiled, nodding to him when he gave her an apologetic look. "It's okay go help her."

Watching Ralph dash off to go over and help his mother, she felt a hand on her left shoulder. Turning around, she was met by the smiling face of her male best friend.

"Ryder, good to see you!" she beamed, giving him a brief hug before pulling away again. "How have you been?"

Though she saw him last week, he'd been busy working so they'd not had the chance to meet up or chat at any time. She knew ranchers were pretty beat by the end of the day, so she'd learned not to be too put out if he or anyone else didn't get back to her when they were finished for the day.

He shrugged, "Tired but, I'm good. How's things going between the two of you now?"

Guessing he means Ralph.

"We're great, thanks. I don't think I could say a bad word about him right now. Quite a change from not too long ago huh?"

Ryder chuckled, nodding. "You can say that again. I had all faith you'd get together eventually, but things looked a bit sketchy there for a bit. Looked as if it wasn't going to happen."

Admittedly, she thought so too at one stage. Never before had she ever been glad to be proved wrong before.

"I couldn't be more glad that they did." She replied, feeling her cheeks warm at the mere thought of her man.

My man!

"Me too." The object of her thought said, walking up to them with the biggest, silliest, proudest grin adorning his glorious face, wrapping an arm around Robinne's waist and bringing her to his side. "Trying to take away my woman, Ry?"

Ryder chuckled, shaking his head. "Not at all. For once, I'm happy to let you have something or rather, someone, all to yourself. Lord knows you deserve her. You deserve to be happy." He said, clapping Ralph on the shoulder.

Having not had any siblings to grow up and into adults with, Robinne missed out on moments like this where she would show her pride and happiness for something one of her brothers, or sisters, would've had or achieved. Though, Ryder and the other Jenkins brothers had become less and less friend-like over the time she'd known and worked with them, and more like pseudo brothers, having them take her under their wings and into their family fold. She fit right in with them, somewhere she never would've expected when she first landed here.

"Boys! Robinne! Dinner's ready, come and get it!" Cassie's voice called out, halting their conversation.

Ralph and Ryder turned to look in the direction where their mother called from, before sharing a familial smile between them.

"Guess that's the cue. C'mon, let's go eat!" Ryder said enthusiastically, never one to turn down a meal. Even if it was one of his own. He left their side and swiftly sat down in a chair, ready to dig in.

Robinne was guided over to the table out the back, which has since been fitted with an added chair for her, since she was now considered an official part of the family with her now being Ralph's girlfriend.

When it became official news to Ralph's family, especially his parents, they'd all been beyond over the moon. His mother had embraced her and said how she couldn't have been more perfect for her 'baby boy', saying that she should consider Cassie as her 'mother' if she felt comfortable doing so. Which she did. Finally that day at twenty-three years old, she officially had a mother. His father had done similarly with both embracing her and praising her for being the one to complete his son. His brothers? Well they'd each enveloped her in a bear hug, welcoming her to the family as their 'little sister', each making a different vow to protect, love, care, support and stand by her for as long as they lived and breathed.

You would've thought we were getting married, not announcing the end of Ralph's bachelorhood.

From then on out, they carried out their promises when having needed to. Not that there were a lot of times she needed it multiple times in a short space of time. It was still nice to have three older brothers and one younger, as Roland was eighteen to her twenty-three.

Naturally as she took her seat, she now sat beside Ralph. Ryder sat to her left with Ralph on her right. Sandwiched between two scrumptious samples of sapiens wasn't a bad place to be, what with being best friends with one and girlfriend to the other. Life was good, at last.

The food currently at their table was soon blessed, as was the custom she'd come to follow upon moving here after her first time eating with the Jenkins'. Soon after the blessing ended, food began to pile onto plates and an assortments of dishes passed through her hand, being passed around the table to who had requested a particular item.

"So, what are we all thankful for this year?" Joe piped up, being the first to speak after the food blessing.

Robinne looked up from the food she'd started to eat, casting her eyes over the family, wondering who'd be the first to say what they were thankful for this year. Shortly, her question was answered.

"If I may?" Ralph piped up. She should've predicted he would be the first to speak, but she didn't. Robinne wasn't much for making speeches to a big or small audience, so she was glad he'd at least spoken up first so she'd know the sort of thing to say. Though she'd say what she was thankful for, not what he was about to say.

Joe nodded at him, silently giving him permission to continue.

Ralph cleared his throat.

"I think you all know what I'm about to say, though I'm going to say it anyway." He said smiling. Chuckles echoed around the table before he continued. "A year ago, I couldn't have predicted this wonderful woman sitting here right beside me. Heck even two months ago I would've laughed anyone off if they said I'd find someone to love who'd be way outside of my league yet, she loves me anyway." He turned to her, giving her hand a squeeze under the table. "I'm thankful for whoever the powers to be up there are, for sending her my way and becoming one of the new pieces added to our family. I'll be thankful for her not just today, but for every day for the rest of my life. That's a promise." He lifted her hand and kissed the back of it, his eyes doing their best no to spill the tears brimming his beautiful eyes.

Robinne was fighting back her own tears at this point, finding it hard to keep them and more at bay after his touching speech. Reaching up, she touched her hand to his cheek and smiled softly at him. Their moment was swiftly interrupted by a collective coughing coming from the table, the two of them turning their heads to see all of Ralph's other brothers smiling at them.

"Need more time alone?" Rowan smirked, throwing a wink in for good measure.

"They'd need more than that, look at them." Reed pitched in, chuckling as he ate another mouthful of food.

Cassie watched her and Ralph with soft eyes for a moment longer, before stepping in to chastise her two sons who'd spoken up. "Now boys, behave. That'll be you someday soon enough, so don't be too quick to tease."

Reed, Rowan, Ryder and Roland all gave each other eyebrow-raising looks, as if they didn't quite believe their mother. Of course, they did. It just seemed that the fact their minds escaped this fact for a moment. Where there was no guarantee that any of them would actually find someone, it was obvious that they'd had this talk with their mother at some stage, hence the alarmed expression.

Joe clapped his hands, bringing everyone's attention back to the present moment. "Okay, so who wants to go next?"

Much to her relief, the rest of the meal passed without incident or fun being made in either hers or Ralph's direction. Each of the remaining table members upon their turn said what they were thankful for that year, with Robinne's turn coming up last. Purposely done so she'd hear what was usually said.

All eyes turned to her when her turn came. She took a breath and calmed herself before speaking, keeping Ralph's hand tight in her own where it'd remained for the entirety of the meal.

"First I'd like to thank you all for inviting me here tonight for my first Thanksgiving. I'm very honoured you all want to include me in American traditions and someday, I'd like to share mine from my country with you all. For now, I've finally decided what I'm thankful for and I want to share it with you all. When I first moved here, I was thankful for the chance I was able to take it upon myself to start over. I came to find myself, try new things. Or not." She smirked, looking at Ralph. "Now that I'm here, I've found brand new things to be thankful for in the short time I've known you all. I'm thankful that I don't have to go through the hard things alone anymore. I'm thankful for the physical and emotional support you've all been giving me. I'm thankful for having friends who'll actually stand by my side, treat me as an equal and include me in things. I'm thankful for finally being given the family I've dreamed of having since I was a child. Especially two people who are just like the parents I've always wanted." She swallowed, trying to hold back her own tears as she looked at Joe and Cassie in turn. Each of them beaming with pride and love. "Most of all though…" she said, turning once more to the man who'd become her everything. "I'm thankful for being given the chance to be loved by someone. Something I never thought would happen to me. I'm thankful for everything I've dreamed of and more being sent to me in the form of this man here. I'm thankful for someone I'm proud to have had my first kiss with, someone who'll finally hold me when I need him, someone who'll see me through this journey we call life before we head on into the next one. I'm thankful that he chose me. Thank you, Ralph."

This time, there wasn't a dry eye at the table when she'd finished saying what she was thankful for. She even thought she saw tough nut Roland wipe away a tear.

"Happy Thanksgiving, everyone!" Ralph said, never taking his eyes off Robinne as he lifted his glass in the air, offering up a toast.

"Happy Thanksgiving!"

Ralph leaned down and gave her a not so quick kiss on the lips. Leaving them to linger over hers to thank her in a way in which words could never do, for what she'd just said, she assumed.

This time when they kissed though, no one complained. They were too enthralled in Cassie's cooking to care what the two of them were doing, immersed once more in their own world, happily talking through the art of kissing as they'd discovered once, it was a more effective way to get across just what was in their hears. Without having to say one thousand and one words each time they had something to say.

"Don't ever change Robinne James." Ralph purred, his voice low and husky.

"I won't if you won't." she countered.

He chuckled. "Deal."

* * *

Robinne felt her eyes drooping just as the sun set behind the vastness of the horizon stretching out as far as the eye can see from the back of Ryder's property. Thinking about the events of that Thanksgiving day not too long ago made her tired, as the games and activities that followed the meal and drinks more than wore her out, being more activity than she was used to. Even now.

Unable to hold it back, a yawn broke through.

"Sorry darlin', am I keeping you up?" Ralph's voice rumbled above her head, his chin resting gently on the top of it.

Manoeuvring herself from under his face she stretched her arms out wide, shaking her head. "Mmm, no. Not at all. I'm just tired. I've been on that thing all day." She nodded to the laptop, "I've also got to be up early tomorrow, I'm cooking with Laney in the morning and Ryder and I are checking fence lines in the afternoon before it's my turn to clean and tidy the barn in the evening."

Ralph sighed, "My family's got you running about like a slave."

She hit him playfully, knowing he was secretly proud of her that she was mucking in and keeping busy. His sighs didn't fool her.

"Well in that case, I think I should get you into bed."

Before she knew what was happening, she was lifted from her place on the porch seat and up into Ralph's arms. An amazing feat considering she was no lightweight. Though he never complained or moaned about it one bit as in fact, he relished her being in his arms every time he carried her to bed. Even if his voice did suggest he had ulterior motives, he did simply mean get her to bed and that being the only thing that happened. Sleep that is. They weren't at a place to go all the way just yet.

"Oh, if you must." She smiled.

Ralph scoffed, "Believe me, it would be my pleasure if I must."

I don't doubt that for a second.

Not a second.

CHAPTER TWENTY-TWO
~ Ralph ~

Ralph always hated having to get up first thing in the morning, as it now meant that he had to leave the warm bed and the even warmer body inside the bed beside him. He'd come to love and be thankful for Robinne being there, but it made it twice as hard to fight the urge to stay in bed. Mostly, his sheer determination won out and he usually got out of bed. Today? He wasn't going to fight. He was going to happily give in and spend a few more minutes snuggling with his lady.

Only, he would. If she was in bed with him in the first place.

Reaching out to the other side of the bed, his hand came up empty. Coming across nothing but the same bedsheets and cover that adorned his own body.

Huh…where'd she go?

Sitting up, he stretched his arms and scratched at his chest. It took him a minute to come too from sleep to remember where Robinne said she'd be that day.

Oh yeah, she's at the bakery with Laney…

I hope they have leftovers, I could go for something sugary today.

He had his own full agenda today. What with winter knocking on their backdoor, there were things that needed to be done before it was too late. Though they were blessed in Texas not to have it as rough as other states during the winter, you never knew what could happen. You had to be prepared for any possibility.

After a quick shower and a shave, Ralph sat down on his side of the bed wrapped only in a towel secured around his waist. He picked up his phone from the nightstand and fired off a quick message to Robinne. As he probably wouldn't get to see her until late in the day, this would have to do for now.

Ralph: Hey Darlin'. Good morning. Don't push yourself too hard today, you'll need your strength for when I return the favour on sneakin' out on me this morning. See you tonight. Love you darlin', R x

Yes, he signs off his messages. Only to Robinne though, no one else. It just felt…special, giving it to only her in some way.

I've turned into such a sap.

A happy sap.

Robinne's sap.

Shortly after he'd sent his message, his phone buzzed in his hand. Robinne never went anywhere without her phone in case someone needed her, so it never took her long to reply unless she was busy.

Robinne: Morning Handsome! I won't push myself, I promise. You looked so peaceful sleeping, I couldn't bear to wake you. YOU work too hard. Saved you a muffin…or two ;) You're welcome. Can't wait to see you tonight, I love you too! <3 x

What more could a man ask for to start his way right, than the person he loves thinking about him and professing their love? Some might argue that there was a lot more. Ralph wasn't one of those men. The simple things far satisfied him more than overly kinky, dirty or sexual things ever would. Because if you ever took away those things or if they fizzled out someday, he'd still be blessed with the same worth of relationship he had with those things. Unlike how some people parted when the 'spark' fizzled out. He wouldn't be one of them.

Putting his phone back on the nightstand, he stood from the bed and finished getting himself ready for the rest of the day and whatever it brought him. Keen to work hard to pass the day until the time he could have the very air he breathed back in his arms.

Time simply couldn't move fast enough.

The day passed a lot slower than Ralph cared for, with constant hold-ups and being made to wait, it made the day crawl by at a much smaller rate. By the time the early afternoon crawled around, he felt as if he'd been working all day instead of until now.

Ralph arrived back at his own place for a quick break before heading back out there, instead of stopping by the main ranch house for lunch which he usually would do. His mother would be at the B&B today as she was most days, but sometimes she'd be at the house or Ryder would to make lunch, and today wasn't a day he could afford to wait any more.

Everyone he'd been waiting on to come see him today or that he'd had to meet had either been held up, late, cancelled last-minute or didn't show up. He understood that things sometimes happened, but today was one of those rare days where no one or anything went as planned or as close to planned as possible.

It can only get better from here. Right?

Of course the question even in his own head went unanswered, the voice up there refusing to answer or wake up until it'd been fed at least a drop or two of coffee. He wasn't a massive coffee drinker, but times like this on days like this often called for a cup.

Sitting down at the table, he pulled his phone out of his pocket and fired off another message to Robinne. He wasn't one to bombard a woman with messages but, he'd never felt this way about anyone and ever since he was given a second chance with her, no way was he missing a chance to show or tell her that he loved her. Or to just speak to her.

Ralph: Hey Darlin'! Hope you've kept to your promise, don't push yourself too hard. Missing you like mad. Tonight is too far away, can't wait to see you. Still love you darlin'. R x

He got through his cup of coffee before Robinne replied to him, a good ten to fifteen minutes.

Robinne: Sorry! I was driving! Didn't want to text and drive. Just got to Ryder's to go check the fences soon. My arse is going to be sore from being in the saddle all afternoon, splendid! Not... Can't wait to see you either. Seeing you later is what's keeping me going. Love you too handsome! X

Nothing could strip the stupid grin that had formed on his face while reading Robinne's message, she turned him from a bear of a man into a pile of happy mush in next to no time. A pile of mush he'd happily be if it meant he wasn't going to go back to who he was before he met Robinne. That was a man he never wished to be again. Ever.

He trusted Robinne with his brother. If there was one other person in this world he trusted with the light of his life, it was him. They'd formed a close friendship in which he had no cause to worry. She needed a best friend and he couldn't be happier that his brother had stepped into that role. He never was one to judge against women having male best friends, as he had a female 'best friend' in kindergarten and into elementary school. The friendship didn't last though. It wasn't a big loss but still, he saw no wrong in opposite genders being friends without it having to go further.

Ryder would watch over her like a big brother and that was enough to sate him until he would have her back in his arms again.

Putting away his phone, he rose up from the table and washed up his mug. The less washing up to do at night the better, even if it was just a mug. A mug could take away seconds better spent with a certain someone.

Get your head in the game Ralph. It's time to work now.

Often he found himself thinking about Robinne while he worked. Not that thinking about her was a bad thing. In fact, he relished in thinking about her. It was just that sometimes he often found himself stopping to think about her when he needed to hustle. Which is what he should be doing right about now.

Giving his head a mental shake, he strode out of his house and headed towards his truck. Hoping to whoever was up there, that no more interruptions, hold-ups or strokes of bad luck would spoil his day.

God willing.

Hours later after thankfully a less stressful afternoon, Ralph was finally done with all of his work for the day. Closing the tailgate of his truck he took off his Stetson, wiping his brow with the back of his hand. Sweat felt like it was pouring down his face when really, the back of his hand only had a few beads on it.

Finally, all done.

He'd worked hard over the hours since he'd last stopped for a drink, thankfully only being interrupted once by his Ma, asking if he and Robinne were planning to stop by the main house for their dinner tonight. He'd replied saying that he'd let her know as soon as he'd picked Robinne up, as no doubt she'd be tired after such a long day, she might not want to stay out for much longer.

Hopping back up into his truck, he was about to start his engine when his phone started buzzing in his pocket. He'd planned to ignore any and all calls until he'd collected Robinne, but a feeling in his stomach told him that he should be taking this call.

It was his mother.

"Ma, is everything alright?"

The fear that was blooming in the bottom of his belly, came out in full force when his Ma finally found the words to speak.

"Ralph…" she sobbed. "Come quick…the barn…it's on fire…" her voice wobbled, unable to complete her sentence. He didn't need to hear anymore.

Hanging up, he wasted no time in starting his engine and flooring it, heading in the direction of the main ranch house and its outer buildings. If there was one thing he was taught from an early age, it was to never ignore a gut feeling. Good or bad, pay attention to it.

As he drove faster than possibly Steve McQueen himself, he tried to place in his mind as to where everyone was. His gut was still ringing out loud and clear that something wasn't quite right. No way was he going to ignore it now.

Ma's fine, as she phoned. Roland won't be there, he's in town tonight. Reed and Rowan are probably helping with whatever's caused this fire. Ryder…where would Ryder be.

He knew once Ryder was done for the day, he could go pretty much wherever the hell he wanted. Having no other commitments for the night, he'd be free to go home or wherever he wanted to.

As he drove, his phone buzzed on the dashboard of his truck. Still not picking it up, he glanced over at the name. Ryder.

Oh thank God. Everyone's okay, thank God.

He was able to relax just the slightest as he drove frantically towards home, the roaring glow of what he assumed was the barn fire growing bigger and brighter as he got closer, a beacon of distressing light surrounded by the pitch black of the Texas night.

Screeching to a halt once he'd reached the main ranch house, he wasted no time in booking it through the home and out into the back garden area. The barn was just starting to catch on a second wall, with thin tendrils of flames slowly snaking their way up towards the roof.

How on Earth could this happen…how?

Before he could ponder another thought, men came rushing from all directions to help put out the flames. Drayton, Luca, Mike, Grant, Drake, Brant, Reed, Rowan and surprisingly, Roland, all rallying with what they had to had to try to contain the flames until the town fire service would get here.

Where the hell were they?

"Ralph!" Ryder's voice called to him. He turned to see his bother all black and covered in dirt running up to him, panting and wearing an expression he could only describe as pure fear, written and plastered all over his face. "Thank God you're here…I'm so sorry…I…" he coughed, a real hacking sort of cough.

"Later. Tell me later. Where are Ma and Pa? Are they okay?" he said, fear coating his every word.

Ryder nodded, "Y-yes, they're fine. They got the animals and the hands away from the barn. But they didn't know…they…they…"

He took a hold of his brother's shoulders, giving them a stiff shake. "They didn't know what? Spit it out! What didn't they know?"

It was then at that moment, that all the colour that had remained on his brother's face, completely vanished before his eyes. As for his own stomach? Well if the feeling there went any lower, he'd have to start looking on the floor for his own innards.

"Ro…Rob…Robinne. S-she was in…she was in the barn! I-I left her to do the evening chores on her own. She said…she said it was her turn and she'd be alright. Oh God Ralph…I'm so sorry!"

Robinne…Robinne! No! Oh God no!

Don't take her from me!

Not now! Please!

If it wasn't for the fact that he was still holding onto Ryder's shoulders, Ralph was pretty sure he'd be on the ground on his knees. His gut was right. Someone *was* in danger. Someone who had become his soul reason for existing. His everything and here he stood, trying to process it all instead of getting in there and getting her out.

He heard his name being called from what sounded like far away, as his mind was wandering to places it never ever should go. Ryder was now the one shaking *his* shoulders, bringing him back to the overly important and critical matter at hand. "I'm so sorry, it's all my fault! I should've never left her alone…I'm so sorry…"

In no way was his brother to blame for this. For any of this. No one knew what the cause of the fire was yet and that wasn't the main priority. Getting Robinne out was the main priority, and the now reason he knew why so many men had gathered around the barn, instead of letting the barn burn down in a controlled manor.

I'm coming Robinne, I won't let you die! Just hold on! I'm coming!

Leaving Ryder's side in a split second, he ignored all voices around him calling for him to stop. No way in hell was he going to stop now. Robinne needed saving and that was enough driving force, along with imaging living without her again, to spur him into action at last. Grabbing at the flame-licked barn door, he gave it three sharp and powerful tugs, feeling it finally break open upon the third try.

A barrage of smoke and dirt blasted out of the now partially open door, with the other barn door remaining stuck fast. Half a door open was better than no door open at all, even if the contents within caused him to temporarily step back, shielding his eyes.

"ROBINNE!" he yelled into the barn, hoping to hear even the smallest noise coming from within to answer his call. Nothing. No sound. No voice. No nothing. His fear levels went up into overdrive as he tried not to imagine the worst before he could at least get in there to try and save her.

No. I WILL save her!

Ignoring the voices and the hands now pulling at him, he wrestled them off and with no second thought as to his safety, ducked inside the building. It didn't matter to him if he was hurt during this process or not, finding and getting Robinne was his one and only priority. Everything else would simply wait until the situation was well under control.

Using one hand to cover his mouth and the other to move some of the smoke from his eyes he squinted into the bleakness, doing his best to locate Robinne. He looked for a few more moments before a sound came from the back of the barn that he wasn't expecting to hear, but a sound he would forever be grateful for hearing.

Chance.

He knew the sound of his horse when he heard it. Wasting no more time, he headed in the direction where he heard Chance whinnying from, careful to keep his mouth as covered as much as possible through the thickening smoke. He spotted Chance down at the back corner of one of the stalls in the barn they used to comb down and tend to the horses before putting them in the stables. Chance must've been in here with Robinne when the fire started.

But where is she?!

At the sight of him, Chance stood up and started scraping his front right hoof on the ground, indicating to Ralph that something was wrong. They'd trained him to do that if ever an animal or anyone was in danger, time well spent as now he could save both his horse and his love in turn.

Removing his hand from his mouth, he grabbed the reins that were still adorning Chance's mouth, moving him forward and out of the way. "Woah…good boy." He coughed. "Good boy. Now go on, get out of here!" he gave Chance a gentle slap on his hind quarters, sending him on his way towards the half a door which thankfully, he made it out of.

Turning back around, he spotted the familiar figure in the corner of the stall in which Chance had been literally guarding with his very life. Robinne.

Oh thank God!

The flames that were beginning to lick the second wall had more than spread to other areas of the barn, raising both the danger factor and heat factor in turn. He had to get her and get out quick or they were both going to be in a worse spot of bother than where things currently stood.

Taking one last breath, his last before he made it out with Robinne, he quickly shucked off his coat and put it over Robinne's lifeless-like body, picking her up the next second. He was worried that he was too late, not knowing how long she'd remained conscious before passing out, inhaling far too much smoke than what he'd been exposed to. Trying his best not to cough his brains out, he tucked Robinne as close to his chest as he could without hurting her, making a mad dash in the same direction as Chance did moments before.

He could hear the barn creaking and groaning around him, the sound of the flames growing louder and louder with each item caught in its path. As he blindly made his way across the barn floor, he felt his eyes start to sting in protest against the amount of smoke they were fighting to see again. What he *was* able to see through it all though, was that the half a barn door he'd come in through was now semi-on fire. Leaving only an even smaller opening for him and Robinne to get through.

Lord, keep her safe. Let me take the hit.

One…two…three…

On the count of three in his head, he ran like the quarterback he was back in his high school days, making it to the outside just in time to avoid the barn roof collapsing in on the rest of the building. If they were in there for even a second later, both their numbers would've been up and for that he was sadly almost certain.

He released the breath he'd been holding in since picking Robinne up, a hacking cough he directed away from Robinne's face. He'd been lucky in comparison to her. Though she herself had been luckier than he'd imagined going in. Chance had saved her life by shielding her body with his much bigger one, providing her with a small pocket of air for her to breathe even while unconscious.

His knees gave way beneath him, the adrenaline wearing off from his brave yet stupid decision to go into that barn. Where he knew going in was a risk to his own life, he'd come to the realisation that he'd do literally anything to make sure the woman now in his arms would remain safe, healthy and alive. His life's mission was now to be her on Earth guardian angel, even if she wasn't aware of it. He was careful not to hurt her as he laid her down on the ground in front of him, removing his coat as people surrounded them.

There was a bombardment of voices all around him, none of which he was remotely listening to. His entire focus was assessing Robinne's condition. Putting two fingers to her neck, he was relieved to feel the very faintest of pulses. She'd need to get to hospital as quickly as possible. Checking over the rest of her, he could see that from the trickle of blood down her face, she'd hit her head at some stage. Probably falling to the ground or something along those lines. Bruises were starting to form on the parts of her skin that were exposed, namely her arms, chest bone area and neck. His poor angel had taken a fair bit of damage, the likes of which he wished he had inflicted upon himself instead of him. This never should've happened to her.

I should've volunteered to do the chores today.

This should've been me.

I wish this was me…oh god…how I wish it was me instead of her.

Sirens of all kinds came out of nowhere, their noise and flashing lights bringing him out of his self-inflicted guilt and back to the moment. In a matter of moments, Robinne was removed from in front of him and whisked straight into an ambulance. He waved off someone's offer to check him over, as he knew there was nothing wrong with him. He'd only inhaled a small amount of smoke, nothing that would damage his health. The main cause of his concern was now inside an ambulance, once more being whisked away from him but to a place he knew would look after her, care for her until he'd be at her side once again.

Stay safe my love, I'm not done living with you yet.

What felt like days later but was in fact only a matter of an hour or two, Ralph and his family all sat in the waiting room of the local hospital, waiting for news on Robinne's condition. Of course, he was paying to even God himself that it would be good news, as his soul would split in two at the thought of his beloved having to go through anything traumatic. Even more so than what she'd already been through.

Ryder sat slumped in his waiting room chair, looking like he'd been dealt the worst news of his life. He'd not said a word on the way over, still probably feeling like this whole thing was his fault for not insisting he should do the chores instead of Robinne. Ralph knew the truth however, which he'll speak to Ryder about when all of this is over and when he was reassured that Robinne would be alright.

Reed, Rowan, Roland and his Pa all sat in other chairs around the waiting room, all sporting various states of weariness and worry. They'd all been at action stations ever since he'd arrived at the ranch and were bound to be tired. Mentally and physically. The barn wasn't a big loss to their overall day to day running of the place, it was just a complete mystery as to how the hell it happened in the first place.

The fire crew had managed to dampen down the fire enough for them to leave to come to the hospital, assuring them they'd get it fully under control by the time they got back. He knew the head of the station well, Gage Danvers. Former SEAL now working for the local fire department after an honourable discharge. He knew Gage would keep his word until he or one of his other family members returned home.

"Here you go sweetie." His mother's voice called out to him. Looking up, she stood in front of him holding a to-go cup from one of the hospital's coffee vending machines. "It's not as good as mine, but it'll do the job for now." Bless her heart for trying to cheer him up, even just a little. Mothers were truly wonderful people.

He accepted the cup, mumbling a word of thanks to his Ma as she took a seat beside him. "She's going to be alright baby boy, she's a fighter. I promise you she'll make it."

How can you be so sure?

"I'm sure because I am listening to my gut, just like I've taught you all of your life." She said, laying a hand on his forearm.

I'm convinced she can read minds.

He exhaled.

"I've finally found someone I never thought I'd ever be blessed to have in my life, let alone possibly and hopefully spend the rest of it with. I'm just…scared. Scared that she'll be taken away from me, and me from her. I can't even bare to think of a life without her again, it's too darn painful." He gripped the coffee cup a bit tighter, feeling its cardboard flex under his grip.

"You'll get your chance to spend today and every day for the rest of your life with her Ralph. Don't you see? She gave you a second chance, and the good Lord has *literally* given her a second *Chance*. That horse saved her and has given you another chance with her. I'm a big believer in signs my dear boy, and that was a doozie if ever there was one." she chuckled lightly, patting his arm.

Deep down, he knew his Ma was right. If Robinne was meant to perish in that fire, she would've. Chance was there for a reason and he liked to think that his prior thoughts of his protection of his girl, along with what his Ma had just told him, were both pointing towards a better and positive outcome. For him and for Robinne.

He drained the contents of the coffee cup just in time to hear a pair of feet walking in their direction. Everyone in the waiting room looked up from where they sat, including himself. A doctor in scrubs came to stand before them, removing a mask from his face before he spoke. "Family of Robinne James?" he looked around at them all. "Relative?"

Ralph immediately stood up, walking to stand with the doctor. He held out his hand. "I'm her boyfriend, Ralph Jenkins. How is she? Is she okay?" he said, his voice laced with worry and urgency.

The doctor looked like a kindly older-ish gentleman, late forties if Ralph had to guess, with hair only beginning to show the faintest signs of greying. He shook Ralph's hand in a firm grip as he addressed him. "We had to operate on her, Mr Jenkins. She had too much smoke in her lungs to clear it using a machine." He paused, assessing the faces around him before continuing. "Don't worry, she'll make a full recovery. Things will be a little slow on recovery for a short while but, no permanent damage was done and with a little TLC, she'll be right in time for Christmas."

All the stress and worry lifted right off of Ralph's shoulders with every word the doctor said.

She's alive.

She's alive.

She's…she's alive!

Thank you God! Thank you so much! Thank you for saving her…my everything.

Ralph pumped the doctor's hand hard as soon as his hand finally caught up with his brain, "When can I see her?"

"She should be getting settled into her room so…" the doctor looked at his watch. "I'd say you can see her in about half an hour. It'll allow for the nurses to hook her up with all the necessaries. One at a time to visit her, two at a push. Once she's awake, we'll see about adding another if she's up to it. Looks like she's got a lot of admirers." The doctor smiled, flicking his gaze above and behind Ralph's shoulders.

He turned around to see what the doctor meant for himself. In the time that they'd been talking, more people had shown up that had been touched by Robinne, and those who cared deeply about her. All of his friends from the ranch were here, his buddies, Niall, Hannah and Laney were all here too. Word must've spread about what had happened, not that he didn't expect it to in such a small town.

All of these people were here for a woman who once thought that no one cared about her, that no one could want her for anything other than to use her, lie to her and deceive her. He was never happier that she was wrong, for her being wrong this time filled his heart with immense pride. None of these wonderful people before were here because they *had* to be. They were here because they *wanted* to be.

Thank you all. Thank you all so much…

After greeting all of his guests…Robinne's guests, personally, it was around half an hour later. The time given to him by the doctor that they'd all be able to see Robinne, even if she wasn't awake from her surgery yet.

He hung back when they were given the green light, just to give anyone a chance to see her before he went in there and claimed his seat beside her bed. A seat he had no intention of leaving until she was ready to leave the hospital with him. However long that would be.

A hand came to rest on his shoulder. He turned to see that it belonged to his Pa, who looked upon him with the most fatherly of looks. A warm smile and a twinkle in his aging eye. "Go on son. She needs you."

And I need her.

He looked around everyone in the room one more time, seeing nothing but smiles and nods of agreement at his father's words. Seeing that there wasn't any more time or reason to waste, he left the company of his friends and family, striding towards the room in which held his present, his future, his everything.

I'm coming my love. When you open your eyes again, I'll be there.
I'll always be there.
I promise.

CHAPTER TWENTY-THREE
~ Robinne ~

"Ralph, I said I'm fine. You don't have to hover over me anymore." Robinne pleaded with him for what felt to her like the millionth time. Ever since her being caught up in the barn a week ago, he'd been hovering over her like a mother hen. Even when she'd been given the okay to go around, albeit carefully, like she normally would do.

The fire itself had happened a few days after thanksgiving. Today was December 1st, the day they would be decorating all of their houses for Christmas. Or as her American family counterparts would say, 'for the holidays'. It still was odd to her that they called it that as a holiday to her, was physically going somewhere for a break. They called that a 'vacation', though. It was fun teaching them her terminologies, with her picking up on some of theirs which she'd managed to skip by somehow.

She'd been cleared to move around normally that very morning but Ralph being Ralph, still insisted on hovering around her like she was a fragile newborn baby.

"Darlin', I almost lost you. You can bet your beautiful behind that I'm not going to relax up just yet. It's only been a week." Ralph argued back, his voice still reeking of worry and concern.

I can't exactly blame him though. I'd be hovering if this were the other way around.

Much to her surprise, she'd been released from the hospital only a couple of days after her admittance. Considering she'd had surgery, she thought she'd be in there a whole lot longer than two days. Though her surgery was classed as 'minor', as it wasn't a case of it saving her life as the doctors had no doubt even from before operating on her, that she would make it. How they could be *that* confident, she'll never know. She'd just always be grateful for them working on her and doing what they could to assist her diagnosis and recovery.

Of course, the events leading up to her admittance were still confusing. Not just to her, but to everyone else too. She'd been in the barn beginning to sort out Chance when she'd heard the barn doors close rather loudly. It didn't strike her to think of it as unusual, as the wind could've easily blown them too. It was only when she started getting hotter and hotter that things didn't seem entirely right.

Soon after this realisation, the barn had been engulfed in flames and the contents within started to burn. Rather too quickly. She vaguely remembers smelling a very pungent, chemically sort of smell. However, she never got the time to figure out what the source of it was before she'd passed out right there in the stall area her and Chance stood in. Ever since her illness when she'd gotten very ill, she couldn't be in spaces which had no air or felt like they had no air. She wasn't a diagnosed claustrophobic, it just happened that way. Anyone in a stuffy room would struggle to breathe.

She woke up to the surprise of being in a hospital bed in a hospital room, having no idea that what had happened to her had been worse than she could've imagined. To her anyway. Having never being admitted into hospital for anything in her life other than the virus, this was a massive deal for her to wake up to. Other than the beautiful eyes of her boyfriend, that is. Ralph had been the very first thing or rather, person, she'd seen when opening her tired eyes that day.

Robinne encountered another surprise when opening her eyes that morning. Ralph with tears rolling down his cheeks. In all the time she'd seen and spent with him, not once had she seen him cry. They were tears of relief and happiness. Relief for the fact that she'd made it through all the ordeals, surgery included. Happiness because someone up above had listened to his silent prayers. Both of which she'd learned when they'd had the moment alone to talk.

And talk they did.

For at least an hour, he'd recalled all the events up until the point in which she'd blacked out, filling in the blanks for her. After which, she'd had a constant flow of visitors and well-wishers, all praying for a safe and speedy recovery for her. Including a few for a lesser action-packed future free from life-threatening situations.

Where that last point wasn't an absolute guarantee, she promised that she'd do her best not to get into too many scrapes.

I can't guarantee a clumsy-free life though. That'll always be one of my flaws.

Which brought her to where she sat now, on Ralph's back porch with him worrying like a mother hen and her newborn chick.

"And I told you, I'm fine." She smiled, patting the spot beside her.

Ralph came and sat beside her, taking her hand in his.

"You still need to rest and take it easy. I can't leave you just yet."

She rolled her eyes, "Yes you can. You know Ryder's coming by to take his turn keeping an eye on me, you're safe to leave while he's here. Nothing will happen and I'll listen to his every word, just like I've done with all of you. I never go back on my word."

Ever since her release from hospital, Ralph and his family had been taking turns in looking after her. Keeping watch on her. It wasn't that they didn't trust her to be alone, it was to aid her recovery to make sure she was doing everything right. A stipulation for being released earlier than normal for such an injury/situation as hers.

Ralph had stayed with her for the first twenty-four hours after her release, then came his mother and father, who'd stayed with her the longest.

Ryder visited shortly after, where then both Reed, Rowan and Roland kept her company until Ralph took another day off to care for her.

Where she will always be thankful and grateful for all of them taking time out of their days to stay with and care for her, her conscience couldn't bear to take liberty of any of them for much longer. One way or another, she'd get this amazing man at her side to relax a little and get on with whatever has been holding him back from taking care of her.

Ralph leaned in and gave her a gentle kiss on the corner of her mouth, his eyes looking down on her with that ever present puppy dog look of love in them. A look she'd never get tired of seeing. "I didn't say that you wouldn't, it's just…"

"Fretting again dear brother?" a familiar voice interrupted Ralph. Ryder walked out onto the back porch, a cheeky grin plastered on his face as he came to sand before them.

She chuckled while Ralph rolled his eyes, standing up to embrace his brother in a 'bro hug', southern style.

"Yes, yes he was." She laughed, extending her arms when Ryder came over and hugged her. "Now you can kindly tell him that I'm perfectly fine here with you while he goes out for a while. Won't you?"

Ryder chuckled at the same time Ralph let out a groan of defeat.

"I won't win, will I?"

"No" she and Ryder said in unison.

Seeing that there was no going against herself and Ryder, she watched with a smirk on her face as Ralph held up both of his hands in mock surrender. "Alright, alright. I don't like leaving but…I will admit, I would like to get a few things done while there's still daylight left."

"Thank God, he's seen sense!"

"I see you've lost none of that sarcasm I just love so much." Ralph said, coming over to her and pressing a kiss against her lips. "Then again, I can't not like anything you say with that thrilling accent of yours darlin'. I have a feeling that even if you were mad as hell at me, I'd simply be standing there grinning like a fool on Tuesday."

Oh I can say the same to you darling man, I can so say the same.

"Alright we get it, you two are irresistible to one another. Ralph, get your butt outta here and Robinne." Ryder turned to her, "You just stay where you are and I'll fix us up something nice to eat."

"Don't I get anything?" Ralph asked, his brows raising in interest.

"Nope, you can get something while you're out. Now get!"

Robinne couldn't help but watch as Ryder manoeuvred Ralph off the back porch and through the house, no doubt guiding him towards his truck and finally getting him to stop hovering around. Ralph had blown her a kiss on his way out, which she'd caught and held close to her heart.

Lord, thank you for keeping me safe and bringing me back to him.

He's my everything.

A short while later, Ryder returned to her side with a platter of sandwiches, sides and a few pieces of fruit thrown in there, placing them down on the table in front of them.

"How does this look? Up for giving this a go?"

She nodded, "Oh yes! It all looks great, I could eat about anything. There's nothing wrong with my appetite that's for sure."

Ryder chuckled.

"No doubting that. Though I'm glad you don't pack as much away as any of my brothers, you'd run out of space to find it all."

She gently smacked his arm, laughing at his attempt to make her feel like she was smaller than she knew she was. "You're awful."

Robinne tucked into one of the sandwiches on the plate just as she heard the familiar rumble of Ralph's truck start up and fade into the distance. As she ate, she noticed that Ryder was now rather silent. Not a normal thing for her best friend to be, as when they were together, they often enjoyed a chat about many things.

Not wanting to pry into whatever was on his mind, she kept quiet. A few moments later, Ryder broke the silence between them by a heavy sigh. A sigh that sounded as if he had the whole weight of the world on his shoulders.

"Robinne, I have something to say. Will you…will you hear me out? Please?"

She set her sandwich down, turning to face him. "Of course I will. What's troubling you?"

Ryder let out another worried sigh before he continued.

"I know we've spent a few moments together since you got out of hospital, but I've been stuck as to what to say to you which would accurately try to convey what I've been trying to say. You know, in the right words." He swallowed. "It's no great secret that I feel as if what happened to you was my fault. I still do feel that way. Any one of us could've volunteered to take your place, namely me. I was with you that day after we mended the fences, I could've stepped in but I didn't. I let you carry on and look what happened. You got hurt. That could've been me. No. That *should've* been me. Ralph has tried his best to convince me that it wasn't my fault, but it's no use. Night after night as I've gone to bed I've thought about it and how all of it was my fault." He turned to face Robinne, removing his Stetson and setting it aside. "You've come to mean as close as to what I assume a best friend would feel like. See, I've never had one before. I was too into my own world to think about having a best friend. Some best friend I've come to be to you. I'm supposed to be there for you as you have been for me and look what happens. You get hurt on my watch."

She went to interrupt him, to tell him how wrong he was but he held his hand up politely, indicating that he wasn't quite done speaking.

"I've come to terms with what happened, as awful as it was. It was going to happen no matter who was inside, weather that was me or you it was meant to happen. What I can't come to terms with is what you went through afterwards. I would never wish surgery on you and it's been hell watching you suffer as you recover, for both Ralph and I. To see him torn up cut me deep, real deep. See, we're close him and I. Yes I know we're brothers, but not always are brothers as close as we are. I look up to him and he's everything I wished I could ever be. And I hurt him by hurting you." He reached and put his hand on her shoulder. A friendly gesture. "I promise from here on out, that I will look after you as your best friend better than I have been doing so far. You won't ever be put in a position of danger like that again. I promise you."

Oh this poor man, he had to have been hurting all this time.

There was no way that any of this was his fault. As he'd so rightly said, anyone could've been in that barn instead of her and the same thing would've happened. Therefore, the blame could not rest on him one bit. He had to know that and it was more than time to set the record straight once and for all.

"Ryder James Jenkins, listen to me and listen to me good. Okay?"

At her tone, Ryder sat up straight where he sat. "Y-yes ma'am!"

"This is the only time I'll say this to you. You are *NOT* to blame for what happened to me. If this was the other way around and you were in there instead of me, would you even let me feel one bit of guilt? No. Of course you wouldn't. You'd say everything and anything possible to make me feel better, wouldn't you? Yes you would. So you putting the blame on yourself here is pointless. Whoever was with me that day if it wasn't you would also blame themselves. The only people who are to blame here is me, for going inside when I could've gone elsewhere, and whoever or whatever made the barn catch fire. No one else. When we find out what the hell happened, the blame can lie there and on nothing and no one else? Understand? I forgive you for leaving me alone and please, let you mind be at ease now. I'm alive, I'm healing and I'm going to be fine. So, don't worry anymore. For me? Please?"

If there was anything else that she should've said, she couldn't think of it. She'd said all that she had to say and she was praying that poor Ryder would finally be at ease.

By the look on Ryder's face, her words seem to have done the trick. Finally. Seeing him going around looking so forlorn was slowly chipping away at her heart.

After a moment's pause, Ryder huffed a laugh of defeat. Shaking his head while fighting back a grin pulling at the corners of his mouth.

"I don't know how you did it, but you convinced me." He held his hands up again, "You've won me over."

"Good. Perhaps we can move on now? I'm really hungry and I was enjoying your sandwiches."

Ryder chuckled, nodding in agreement. "That sounds perfect."

Much to Robinne's relief, Ryder never mentioned the barn or his guilt for the rest of lunch or thereafter.

They spent the rest of their lunch instead talking about much lighter topics. Like what Ryder planned to do next for the ranch, his questions about how she was getting on with her book and what her and Ralph had been up to when they'd had moments alone together. Finally, they unanimously agreed that she'd been cooped up for too long in Ralph's place. The doctor said she was alright to begin normal movements and activities, if taken slowly and carefully. So, Ryder suggested a drive to get her out. A chance for her to sit and rest while getting some well-needed air.

With everything cleared away after they were done eating, Ryder carefully helped Robinne into his truck and off they went. He'd chosen to drive around the lesser seen parts of the town, places she'd yet to have explored or visited with anyone else. The drive was pleasant as was the weather, not too cold or too anything else for her at this point in time for Texas weather.

They'd been driving around and talking for about an hour when Ryder's phone began to ring. He pulled over and cut the engine so he could take the call. "Hello? Yes this is Ryder…She's with me…you do?…We'll be right there!" he hung up the quick call.

"Who was it?"

Ryder turned to look at her as he started the truck engine again. "That was the police station. They think they've got the man who set the barn ablaze. They want to talk to you to get your account of things. Are you up for it?"

"As up for it as I'll ever be."

Turning the truck around, they now headed towards the centre of town where the police station was located. Hopefully and finally finding out who the hell did this to Ralph's family and why.

Please, let justice be done. Don't make them suffer for any longer.

An hour or so later, Robinne excited the police station with Ryder supporting her at her elbow, guiding her back into his truck which he'd been lucky to be able to park right outside, so it wasn't far for her to walk at all.

What they'd gone into do was for Robinne to give her case of events, and leave. That's it. Ryder was told that they *might* have a lead on who set the barn on fire, but that was only speculation. That was, until they'd actually gone into the police station and were told the full story upon arrival.

When they'd arrived, they were ushered into a private room where Robinne did in fact give her account of the events in question. Only, when they were almost done, they were interrupted by another officer saying that the man they'd brought in had owned up to everything. Considering it had happened to her and she was there, she was privy to this information and was told by the officer they were talking to, once he'd seen to the man, what exactly he had said.

It turns out that one of the ranch hands who helped out occasionally at the Jenkins' ranch, began to get extremely jealous of how Ralph was the one who was with Robinne and he wasn't. The man actually thought that he stood a chance of getting to know and being with Robinne, despite never having even approached her in his life. She'd seen the man around the place a few times when she'd been helping out, but she'd never got the chance to stop and say hello because he was always so busy.

Thank God that I didn't...

"We need to tell everyone what happened, they have a right to know." She told Ryder as he pulled out of the parking space.

He nodded.

"Let's head back to the main house now. Everyone should be there right about now if we're lucky. How're you holding up?"

"Do you know what? I think I'm alright." She smiled. Genuinely smiled. She genuinely felt lighter for the first time since she'd woken up in the hospital room a week ago. "You?"

Ryder beamed, "Never better."

They headed back in the direction as fast as the speed limit would allow for. The last thing they needed was to be given a ticket. Almost at the road leading to the house, they spotted two vehicles on the side of the road. One appeared to be broken down and the other, the other was very familiar. It was Ralph's truck.

Why is he on the side of the road?

I hope he's okay.

Ryder pulled in behind Ralph's truck, giving Robinne a clear view of both the driver's sides of Ryder's truck and the car in front. As the truck came to a stop, they were both able to get a clearer view of what was going on. Ralph was leaning inside the truck and appeared to be....talking? Just as Ryder was about to get out and see if he could help in any way, Ralph began to emerge from the person's car. His lips attached directly to a woman's lips.

What the...

The person in question who Ralph's lips were attached to, shortly followed him out of the car. Letting his lips go.

Delilah.

She was kissing Ralph. *Kissing him!*

The bottom of Robinne's stomach fell completely through. She couldn't believe what she was seeing. Ralph was kissing Delilah and she was kissing him back, there was no doubt about it. She was seeing it with her own two eyes with another set sitting right beside her.

Both of them were stunned to silence watching the scene unfold between them. Only when Ralph looked up and in their direction did either of them have anything to say. He looked completely surprised and caught off-guard seeing Ryder's truck behind his own with her sitting inside of it. His eyes widened and his skin paled, that much she could tell even sitting as far back as she was.

"Drive." She said to Ryder, her tone flat and emotionless.

Ryder didn't need to be told twice. He quickly backed the truck up and peeled out of the space they'd pulled in to, just in time to avoid Ralph who'd begun to advance on them and the truck.

Robinne had nothing more to say as Ryder booked the truck as far away from the scene as he could. Her mind once clear from the confession of the ranch hand setting the barn alight, was jumbled beyond comprehension again. Everything had been going to well between her and Ralph, better than they had ever gone between them since they'd first met. So how and why was he kissing that harlot on the side of the road?

It doesn't matter now. Nothing matters.

I should've known things were too good to be true. They always are.

You've blown it Ralph. Blown it big time.

A single tear trickled down her cheek as they continued to drive, the only outward sign that she'd been affected by what they'd just seen.

My heart, it hurts too much. What was left of it.

Good job Ralph, you've destroyed what was left of my heart.

Never again. Never again will I trust anyone, all thanks to you.

It hurts, so much.

CHAPTER TWENTY-FOUR
~ Robinne ~

Robinne groaned a sigh of relief as she finally clicked the 'publish' button on Kindle Direct Publishing, KDP for short. She'd spent the last eight days nailing down last checks and going over her third draft manuscript for any errors, inconsistencies or parts she wanted to change/add before hitting the 'publish' button at last.

It had been taxing to get her book finished and uploaded to the site before her deadline, but she'd done it. It was a tremendous help that she had plenty of time on her hands to get it all done in, working around the clock and every opportunity in between. Though as to the reason why she had all of this time on her hands, it brought her great pain every time she found her mind wandering back to it.

Just over a week ago as she and Ryder were driving back from the station to tell everyone the good news of catching the barn fire culprit, they'd caught Ralph kissing a woman in her car, which had turned out to be his old friend and flame Delilah. Since then, she's avoided talking or seeing him at all costs. No matter what he could possibly say to her would change what she saw or what he did. Neither has she spoken to any of his family, as any reminder of him like before, would be far too painful than what she's feeling right now. That pain was bad enough without adding to it.

She'd thrown herself into her writing and anything else that would take away from any and all thoughts of Ralph. For the most part, her distractions worked. It was only when she had a spare moment to think that her mind would wander back to thoughts of him, where she would quickly do something in which would distract her all over again.

Now that there was nothing more to do on her book, other than to post on her Instagram and other social media accounts about its release today and on the days that would follow, she found herself in need of something else to do. Most of the day had been spent on finishing this, so when she looked at the clock and saw it read almost four in the afternoon, there were very few options. Especially on a Sunday.

Setting her laptop aside, she made her way up the stairs, planning on rewarding her efforts with the longest bubble bath known to man. At least, that was the plan if not for her doorbell ringing, halting her in her steps.

Great, who could it possibly be?

Hoping against all hope that it was the one person she definitely didn't want to see right now, she made her way back down the stairs and reluctantly opened the door. Thankfully upon opening the door, it was someone she would always be welcome to see. Laney stood on her doorstep, a smile upon her beautiful face.

"Hello there you!"

"H-hi?"

She scratched the back of her neck, not quite sure as to why Laney would show up without sending at least a text before doing so. Ever since she'd started recovering from her surgery, Laney had insisted that Robinne rest up and wait at least until after Christmas to come back to work. Insisting that she could cope with spending a little more time with help from Luca to see her through the Christmas rush. With a little insisting on Laney's part, she reluctantly agreed to take the time off. Secretly being thankful for the opportunity.

"I really don't want to sound rude but, why um…what's brought you here?"

Taking it all in her stride, Laney merely shrugged and kept the smile on her face. "I'm here to take you into town for an early dinner of course! Girl you've been cooped up for over a week and I know if this was me, I'd be going stir-crazy right about now."

That's…true

'Since you're refusing to come and be a part of the outside world, I'm going to take you there. Just you and me. Dinner, music and a good drink. Well, for you anyway. I'm driving again."

Laney was right. About everything. Her friend rarely didn't see straight through her, what she was thinking or what her mind was doing. Thanks to the two of them becoming fast friends, they'd gotten to know one another on an equal level.

"You're not going to take no for an answer, are you?"

"Nope." Laney winked, "Now get your stuff together and be back out here in ten."

Without another word, Laney spun on her heals and headed back to her car with a spring in her step. It was clear to Robinne that Laney was clearly up to something, it was just *what* specifically she was up to that escaped her.

Seeing no reason to argue against not going, she made short work of picking up her phone, purse and keys, meeting Laney back outside exactly ten minutes later. Laney made short work of pulling away from the pavement, keen to be getting to wherever she was taking her for dinner.

"So, got anywhere in mind that you're kidnapping me to?"

Laney rolled her eyes, "It's hardly kidnapping if you're coming willingly. But no. I just thought we'd hit up wherever took our fancy."

I know what I fancy. And what I fancy is an ass of the highest order.

She didn't say another word on their drive into the town, happily contented at watching the scenery that rolled by her window, enclosed in the beauty that was the night. As they approached the town, the beauty of the night faded away with each new light they came across.

On the day that she'd found out about Ralph's kiss with Delilah, the town and surrounding streets had switched on their Christmas lights and adorned the place with decorations galore both traditional and modern. A meeting of two worlds coming together, she liked that very much. Though she hadn't been at the light up ceremony itself, she had seen pictures of the night on the town hall's website. It looked like a very beautiful night and she'd pleased to see the turnout of the local community.

As it was a small town, they didn't go all out as major cities like London or Birmingham would've done back home. No, their decorations seemed to add just the right about of festive feeling and cheer to the place. Going overboard was never her forte, so she appreciated what everyone had spent time doing to make everyone happier this season.

Well, almost everyone.

Laney parked her car down a small side street just off of the main street in town, one which was lesser decorated and had plenty of parking spaces for the local people to park. This would never happen back home. No one would keep a street or two free for people to park in, as people sadly were more focused on capitalising on making people pay, rather than giving them actual places to park in.

They both got out of the car, stretching their limbs before heading towards the main street.

"Got any ideas where you want to eat yet?" she called out to Laney, following behind her as they walked.

"I'll know it when I see it." Laney cheerfully replied. She was still acting a little strangely as she did back at her place, though Robinne wasn't any more the wiser as to why.

Shortly, they made their way out of the back street and onto the main street. That is, as close to actually getting *on* to main street as possible, if not for all the people crowding around them. She'd never seen so many people in one place before, not even at a one day Christmas market back home. It was if the whole town had come out tonight, but why?

"Is there anything going on tonight?" she whispered into Laney's ear, not wanting to draw attention to herself.

It was then that Laney turned to her, with the smile already on her face turning up tenfold. "Oh yes."

What is she up to?

Before she got a chance to ask her friend what she was planning, the people who were standing around in front of them parted like the Red Sea. They now stood with a gap between them, resembling knights of old that would hold their swords up when a newlywed couple would come out of the church having been declared as man and wife. Except, these people didn't have swords, they carried candles in their hands and smiles on their faces as they now looked upon her.

"Come on." Laney encouraged, sliding her arm through Robinne's and guiding her through the throng of people and to the beginning of…a red carpet?

"Laney, what on Earth is going on?"

The nervousness in her stomach kicked right up to one hundred from its blindly contented zero from when they'd arrived, thinking that she was going to catch something to eat with her friend. Had she been lied to? Deceived? No. Something in her stomach told her that it was going to be so much more than that.

"Good luck." Laney whispered to her, leaving her side and vanishing into the crowd.

Good luck? Why on Earth would I need luck?
What's going on?!

The gap that had once opened up to her and Laney was now closed again, the people back in their places. A new gap had opened up to her right, heading directly along the main street in town and revealing the rest of the red carpet, lined with people once more holding candles. Now that she had a chance to look as her feet froze her to the spot she stood, everyone appeared to be holding candles. As if lighting her way. To what though?

Her questions were soon answered, as a very familiar voice called out to her.

"Darlin'? Could you come here a minute? I have something I'd like to say to you."

Ralph.

Finding the will in her body to get her feet to move from their frozen position, Robinne slowly walked down the red carpet lined either side with people holding the candles, getting closer and closer to what she now could see was a makeshift wooden stage at the end. Sitting in the middle of the stage was the very person her body knew the voice belonged to. Ralph. He had a guitar across his lap and a mic in front of him.

He looked the most nervous she'd ever seen since she'd known him. She knew the expression well, as no doubt she was sporting a similar one right this very moment. Without waiting for her to speak, he continued now that she was standing as close as she could bear to be.

"There's something I want to say to you darlin'. So please, hear me out."

Background music started to play from speakers that she couldn't see, with Ralph picking up his guitar and starting to pluck at its strings.

Is he...going to sing?

Her question was soon answered, as her handsome cowboy clad in his best Stetson, plaid shirt, trousers and boots started to sing.

"One word, that's all was said,
Something in your voice called me, caused me to turn my head.
Your smile just captured me, you were in my future as far as I could see.
And I don't know how it happened, but it happens still.
You ask me if I love you, if I always will

Well, you had me from "Hello"
I felt love start to grow the moment I looked into your eyes,
You won me, it was over from the start.
You completely stole my heart, and now you won't let go.
I never even had a chance you know?
You had me from "Hello"

Inside I built a wall so high around my heart, I thought I'd never fall.
One touch, you brought it down
Bricks of my defences scattered on the ground
And I swore to me that I wasn't going to love again
The last time was the last time I'd let someone in

Well, you had me from "Hello"
I felt love start to grow the moment I looked into your eyes,
You won me, it was over from the start.
You completely stole my heart, and now you won't let go.
I never even had a chance you know?
You had me from "Hello"

That's all you said
Something in your voice calls me, caused me to turn my head
You had me from "Hello"
You had me from "Hello"
Girl, I've loved you from "Hello"."

She recognised the song from the moment he sung the first line. It was Kenny Chesney's 'You Had Me From Hello'. As a fan of country music, she knew the song well. Though she never imagined in her wildest dreams that she would be standing here, listening to Ralph sing it to her. She never even had any idea that he could sing.

When he finished, he laid the guitar in the stand next to his seat and stood, raising the mic as he did so. The crowd remained as silent as she, waiting to see what the two of them would do next.

One thing for sure she know she was doing, was battling to let the tears fall from her eyes. If anyone else here had a dry eye, they would truly have to be heartless. Regardless of what he'd done to her, she couldn't deny that both his voice and choice of song were far more beautiful than words could say. The man could sing and boy, did his words strike her heart true.

"I have something else I'd like to say to you darlin'. So, would you come up here? Please?"

How could she say no when she was literally the centre of attention in front of all of these people? She would look like the biggest fool ever if she said no and left. Holding her nose slightly aloft, she squared off her shoulders and approached the steps on the side leading up to the stage.

As she came to stand on the stage, Ralph removed the mic from the stand and gently pulled her into the middle of the makeshift stage, never letting go of the hand in which he'd gently pulled her with.

"I've almost lost you twice now darlin', I really don't want to make it a third. You see, what you saw isn't what you thought. I'm willing to tell you the truth in front of everyone here today, to prove that I'm not lying to you. If you'll let me, that is."

She nodded after a moment's pause. Ralph used her nod as a cue to continue.

"I was on my way back from running an errand, I saw a car on the side of the road and I had to stop and help. I had no idea that the person inside would be Delilah."

There was a collective 'boo' from the crowd. Clearly they were as much of a fan of hers as Robinne was.

"She told me that her engine had cut out and she couldn't get her car running again. She also told me that there was something wrong with the steering wheel. I saw no reason not to believe her, as car faults aren't a new thing around these parts. So I leaned in to take a look when she got a hold of me and kissed me. That was when you and my brother pulled up, seeing me 'kissing her'. Not once during that whole moment did I ever return the kiss, I swear it. It was all her. If it was me even remotely, I wouldn't be up here to purposely make a fool out of myself. I can do that all on my own."

She smiled at that, just a little bit. Only because she knew it to be true.

"I've spent this time we've been apart doing a lot of thinking, and somehow I've not managed to hurt my head during the process." He laughed. "I knew I hadn't done anything wrong that would upset you, but I knew I had to do something that would put your mind at ease and prove to you that there are people out there who you can trust. I know you've been put through the mill more than anyone I know, therefore I knew just exactly what to do. I had to give you the best birthday present you deserve and need in kind."

Birthday present? It's not…oh.

Oops.

Today's my 24th birthday…

Ralph nodded behind her, gesturing her to take a look. "They've all come for you my darlin'" She turned around to see Ralph's family standing off to the side watching them both, smiles and looks of adoration adorning all of their faces. Even Roland's. She hadn't seen any of them since she'd hid away over a week ago, yet here they all stood. Nothing but love on their faces for a girl they considered one of their own.

She turned back around to listen to the rest of what Ralph had to say. Only, he wasn't in her line of sight when she turned back around. She knew he was still there as she felt his hand slide from hers when she'd turned around to look at his family. He was in fact, still there. Just on one knee before her instead of standing.

One knee? One knee!

Ralph was indeed on one knee before her, an open blue velvet box on his palm. The most beautiful ring she'd ever seen was staring back at her. A stunning platinum ring too. Modern yet with a traditional twist to it.

"Robinne James, I knew from the moment you fled from the side of the road, that I needed to do something that would truly convey how much you are the *only* woman for me. The only person that I will ever love for the rest of my life. The person that can bring you solace in times of need, day or night for as long as you need me. The person that can hold your hand and hold you in their arms no matter how much they get tired. The person that will never ever force you to live another day on your own emotionally or physically, regardless of how much or little sleep they've had. Most of all, I want to be the person you can rely on to never use you, to never lie or deceive you or toss you out when I'm done with you. Which will never happen because my darlin' love, hell will have to freeze over before that even happens. I'll be there for you through the good times and bad, I'll help guide you through your dreams and support your every decision regardless of it being a good or bad one, I'll stand there and cheer you on. I'll wake you up every day for the rest of our lives with a kiss that will feel like it'll be our first, promising that each day I will love you even more than the last. I finally understand now why hearts are made the way they are, because from the moment you came into my life, you slid right up inside of mine and planted yourself there without any chance of leaving. Now I couldn't even imagine living a single day without you, at my side or not. For as long as I know you're mine no matter where you are on this Earth, I'll know true content and happiness in my heart and soul. Forever isn't forever without you, and I intend to spend forever with you in this life and the next. So my one and only darlin' love, will you marry me? Become my wife? Share sunsets with me and let me love you until the very last breath has left my body?"

If she wasn't trembling before, she was now. Noises and faces of the crowed beside them faded away with each word he said, until the only two people there that she was aware of, were Ralph and herself.

She'd expected to come out here tonight to go to dinner with Laney, albeit it wasn't going to be what she had planned to do, the dinner was what she was expecting. Now she was here, with the sweetest, loveliest and most genuine man she's ever known, who was kneeling before her and asking her to be his wife.

Robinne knew when to admit that she was wrong, and when other people were telling the truth because when they spoke the truth, the words they spoke came straight from the heart. Ralph was doing just that. She knew just exactly what Delilah was capable of. Though it was unplanned that she would stop at the roadside at that moment, she knew Delilah would make the most of it just to make her suffer because she knew who Ralph's heart truly lay with. And it wasn't her.

She'd been foolish to ignore him and avoid his family without giving him a chance to explain how things were not as they seemed. But boy was her singing heart glad that she didn't for if she did, she wouldn't be experiencing the most romantic moment of her life both physically and verbally. She most certainly didn't plan to keep this darling man in suspense for longer than she had to, as she already had her answer.

Kneeling down in front of him with Ralph remaining down on one knee, she wiped the falling tears from her eyes as she placed one hand over his heart, and the other on his cheek.

"You Ralph Joseph Jenkins, are probably the most important person to me on this whole entire planet. No one else has ever come close to how much you mean to me, stupid actions or not. You rescued me during my darkest days and were literally the answer to my prayers when I asked God to send me an angel. You make me laugh, cry, fill my days with nothing but the stuff I've only ever dreamed of. You've given me so many firsts I've missed out for so many years, I couldn't ever imagine experiencing a lifetime of firsts with anyone else but who's before me right now." She sniffled, smiling as she took a breath between her happy, relieved tears. "So my answer is yes. Yes I will become your wife. Yes I will be your everything and more in this life as you will be mine. Yes to absolutely everything. I love you, so much. Yes I will marry you."

The moment she'd uttered her last word, her feet literally came away from the ground as Ralph enveloped her close to his body and spun her around, letting out the most wondrous sound her ears had ever heard. Setting her down on her feet at the sound of the roaring, cheering crowd, he removed the ring from its box and onto her finger. Setting into place on her ring finger with ease.

"A perfect fit my love." Ralph beamed, his eyes shining with tears of his own that promised to fall.

"Yes." She said, her voice cracking as she fought to contain the mountain of emotions building up inside of her.

They shared a smile between them that held the promise of only a brighter future ahead of them. Ralph's head descended towards her own and soon her lips were finally enclosed with his, their rightful place today, tomorrow and forever more. His hands held her back steady as he moved her in the most movie cliché of dip-kisses, pouring the love that was once in his words directly from his lips and onto hers, spreading throughout the every fibre of her being.

No longer did she care about avoiding clichés, no longer did she care about avoiding things in life that were 'only for book characters', as for those very things brought her the man that in her heart know that she was put on this very Earth to meet. They'd been designed for each other from the very beginning, and this indeed was the very start of their brand new beginning.

Together.

She was always alone, no more.

Epilogue
~ Robinne ~
* 3 Weeks later - Christmas Eve, 5pm *

Robinne stood looking at her own reflection in the mirror of Ralph's bedroom at the Jenkins' ranch, seeing with her own eyes a reflection that she never imagined she would ever see. On a day that she never thought she'd ever be privileged to be a part of.

Her wedding day.

Ever since Ralph had asked her to marry him on that makeshift stage on her twenty-fourth birthday, they'd knew exactly the day they wanted to get married. Christmas Eve. There was no doubt in their minds that they wanted to marry as soon as was feasible, both of them had spent enough time on their own to have any doubts about marrying on this day.

After receiving congratulations from his family and all the well-wishers that Ralph had somehow managed to wrangle into being there that night, he'd whisked her away for the most romantic night of her life. A night which she'd never seen coming. He'd made the most special night of any girl's life, somehow ever more special. His touch was so soft and tender, his movements were thoughtful and gentle. Making a woman of her and finally connecting them together in the beautiful art of making love had been everything she'd dreamed of and more. Neither of them wanted to wait for their wedding day for him to take her virginity, as they'd agreed that twenty-four years was more than enough time to wait.

Since then, things had only got better and kicked well into gear as wedding talks began.

The barn had been levelled and was soon scheduled to start re-building. Of course, Ralph and his brothers were going to see to that. A blessing in disguise with them all being so used to constructing houses, it would be like second nature to them. For now, it would be the site that held a dark wood wedding gazebo which they'd both picked out to say their vows to one another. At the place where so much hurt and destruction had taken place, they couldn't think of a better one to write it in with something as monumentally right as their wedding vows. Once a place of division would now be remembered as a place filled with only happy memories and love, especially when the new barn would be placed upon the self-same ground.

Wedding preparations had spun into overdrive from there, with Cassie thankfully at the helm for most of it. This wasn't the first speedy wedding in Dripping Springs, so thankfully all who were involved had things under control in no time at all with as minimal input from her and Ralph as possible. They'd told everyone what they wanted and from there, things were taken care of.

The only thing that truly required all of Robinne's attention was her wedding dress. She'd managed to get a custom dress made and fitted in under a month which in itself, was a feat worthy of a Guinness World Record. As Cassie's wedding dress didn't fit her remotely, the only decisions left were to either buy one from the local wedding dress store. Or get one custom made. She'd gone with the latter.

Considering she never thought she'd get married, Robinne was grateful she already had an idea of what she'd love her dress to look like. She'd seen the most beautiful dress worn by Anastasia Steele in one of her favourite movies ever, *Fifty Shades Freed,* knowing that someday if she was fortunate to get married, she'd want her dress to somewhat resemble that one in some way. As a carbon copy isn't what she wasn't about being.

The only alteration to the ideal design of the dress, bearing in mind what the dress in the movie looked like, was that instead of having it form-fitted from the bodice area, she'd gone with a flowing dress with a billowing skirt down to the floor that hid her feet. A typical bell-like shape which hid her curves and flattered the natural shape she was born with. It settled her mind to know that what she wanted hidden was hidden, boosting her sense of self-confidence to wear such a dress as this. The shoulder-less, lace-sleeved gown topped off with white-heeled shoes, was one typically worn by a princess, not someone like herself. Though today, that didn't matter. She *was* a princess and she was about to go marry the cowboy prince of her dreams. Her overall 'princess' look was topped off by a head to floor veil, with Cassie's wedding tiara sitting proudly underneath, and a necklace given to her by her stand in 'father' Joe, who was doing the honour of giving her away.

A knock on the door interrupted her thoughts.

Turning around, she saw the man in question in the doorway. A smile of pride on his face upon seeing her. "Don't you look like a pretty picture? Boy is my son a lucky man."

She laughed, "He sure is. I'm luckier because I get to marry him."

"That you do sweetheart, that you do. Now, what's say we get this show on the road so I can proudly show you off as my official daughter-in-law." He said, offering her his elbow.

Taking a deep breath, she picked up her rose wedding bouquet, sliding her hand in to rest on the crook of Joe's arm. "Let's do this."

After three weeks of waiting, it was time to go marry her man.

Outside as they left the back doors of the main house, Robinne could see just how much effort had gone into transforming the back garden into their wedding and reception venue. Every rail was twined with white lace and lights, making the whole back of the house turn into something beyond beautiful. A white carpet had been laid from the back porch steps, which atop it were scattered rose petals leading to the gazebo in which a few short moments, she'd be exchanging her vows.

The guests were seated on handmade wooden chairs, which had been decorated with an azure blue fabric across the backs to match the colour theme of their wedding. These chairs would also serve as the chairs used at the wedding reception. Each chair was full with friends and family for both Ralph and herself, with her abandoning the 'bride's side', with her saying it was pointless to have one when everyone invited would be a friend of both of theirs. So everyone sat where they wanted to, with the front row on both sides reserved for the Jenkins', Hannah, Niall and a few of Ralph's friends.

Laney came out behind them and picked up the train of Robinne's dress, a job she proudly held as the matron of honour. Gripping Joe's arm, she took a deep breath as the bride's wedding march started up, courtesy of the local town band.

Making her feet work against the frozen feeling that had started to creep into them, she and Joe made their way down the aisle and towards the man who'd shortly become her husband. With each step that she took, she could see just how handsome Ralph looked, Ryder standing at his side as his best man. Ralph had chosen to go with the traditional country-style inspired cowboy wedding look. He wore a fitted blue suit and white dress shirt with black cowboy boots peeking out from underneath the ends of his suit trousers, a black Stetson on his head topped off with a bolo tie at his neck with the Jenkins' ranch crest shining proudly.

Oh my, that's one handsome cowboy groom.

And he's all mine.

The moment their eyes met, it seemed like they were back on the makeshift stage where it felt like it was just the two of them. His eyes shone with the prospect of tears spilling, a sure sign that he liked what he saw when his eyes travelled up and down her, checking her out in her wedding dress and all that came with it. At the sight of his eyes, she fought back shedding her own tears. If she allowed them to spill though, she'd feel the wrath from Laney, as she'd worked her magic doing her hair and makeup for today.

A few steps later, she was standing side by side with the man of her dreams, Joe perfectly handing her over to his son with the declaration that he was the man who was giving her to the man beside her.

Handing her flowers off to Laney who now stood at her side, she joined her hands with Ralph, facing him for the first time.

"My darlin' British beauty bride, restart my heart because my God, you're beyond beautiful" he whispered only for her to hear, sending her a wink which made her blush right down to her toes.

She dipped her eyes before raising them again, the priest taking his place beside them, beginning the proceedings.

"Dearly beloved, we are gathered here on this lovely evening in the sight of God to join this man and this woman, together in holy matrimony. Please both repeat after me. Ralph. I Ralph Joseph Jenkins, take you, Robinne James to be my lawfully wedded wife. To have and to hold from this day forward, for better or for worse, for richer or poorer, in sickness and in health for today and forever."

Ralph took a deep breath before saying his vows, his voice whiskey-dipped and filled with emotion, "I Ralph Joseph Jenkins, take you, Robinne James to be my lawfully wedded wife. To have and to hold from this day forward, for better or for worse, for richer or poorer, in sickness and in health for today and forever."

Amen.

The priest turned to Robinne, as it was now time for her to say her vows. "Robinne."

She nodded, smiling under her veil as she said her vows to her dearest love. "I Robinne James, take you, Ralph Joseph Jenkins to be my lawfully wedded husband. To have and to hold from this day forward, for better or for worse, for richer or poorer, in sickness and in health for today and forever."

They'd chosen to go with the traditional vows, as each had prepared a speech each for their wedding reception, where they'd have more time to say all that they wanted to say.

With both of their vows spoken, the priest turned to Ryder and asked for the rings which without hesitation, he placed the respective rings into both her hand and Ralph's. Ralph moved first, sliding her wedding ring onto her finger to join her engagement ring. She then acted in kind and slid his much larger wedding ring onto his wedding finger, joining both of their hands together once he'd placed a kiss on hers.

"Now that they have each spoken their vows, I ask that if any man or woman know why these two wonderful people should not be joined together, let them speak now or forever hold their peace." The priest announced, waiting to hear if any of the guests would speak up.

Robinne's heart sped up, fearing for just a moment that anyone would dare to speak up. Thankfully after a moment's pause, no one spoke. Ralph and Robinne exhaled a sigh of relief, sharing a smile between them.

"Then with the holy power vested in my by the state of Texas, I now pronounce you man and wife. Ralph, you may *finally* kiss your bride."

I'm married! Holy cow I'm married!

The priest's words drew a round of laughter from the guests, before Ralph released her hands to lift her veil, cupping her cheeks gently with his hands as her own came to rest on his. "At last, my love. At last." Those were his last words to her before their lips joined, sharing their first kiss as man and wife.

Cheers and claps burst forth from their friends, family and honoured guests. Though the only sound that the two of them could hear was the collective beating of their hearts finally beating as one.

"Ladies and gentlemen, I now pronounce to you, Mr and Mrs Ralph Jenkins."

Their kiss ended only when the two of them needed to come up for air, resting their foreheads together as the priest announced their new title to the adoring crowd before them.

"I love you, Mrs Jenkins. You're not alone anymore."

"I love you too, Mr Jenkins. Forever and always."

They kissed briefly one more time before turning towards their guests, with Robinne accepting her flowers from Laney just in time for her to head back down the aisle with Ralph. Her husband, as the skies opened up and showered them with a light snowfall, perfectly completing their exit into a bright and prosperous future. Together.

Love always finds a way, and my way is Ralph Jenkins.
Well, Ralph and his mini me to-be. I can't wait to tell him.
Never again will I be always alone.
Thank you God. Thank you.

THE END

THANK YOU/
ACKNOWLEDGMENTS

I have quite a few people I want to thank for supporting me and being so amazing in following my journey to this book's completion, so strap yourselves in. Here we go!

To my non-biological sister, Gabrielle Marie Dickens. Thank you for being a constant person in my life where many have come and often left again. I've never known what it was truly like to have a sister until I met you. You're everything and more that I could've asked for in a sister, proving truly that family isn't always blood. It's who you meet that makes you feel like family. I wish you only the best, and may we know each other for many years to come. I'll love you for a thousand years!

To my American family, Pete & Melanie Dickens. Thank you both for taking me under your wings and dubbing me your 'London daughter', and making me part of your family. There's not many places where I feel that I belong, so I'm very honoured and thankful that I feel there with you both. I can't wait to see you both again very soon.

To my former work colleagues Lis, Megan, Grace, Emma, Laura, Clive & Jonathan. You all brought out the person within me that I should've always been, you all brought me out of my shell in your own way in the year I worked with you all. Your advice, support, company and faith in me hasn't gone unnoticed one bit. I am the person I am today thanks to you amazing people. Thank you for what truly was an unforgettable year together, I won't ever forget you all.

To my many Twitter and Instagram supporters: Lyn Hewitson, Amber Miller, Natasha Rumana, Jasmine & Tiffany Stells, Emma B, Zoya, Vanessa Viner, Barbie Straub, Silvia, Rorato Silvia, Paula Gomez, Lorna McCorkell, Nikki G, Rebecca Andrýsková, Wendy Powell, Laura, Shirley Jones, Diane Abboud, Amber Procter, Victoria Riddell, Ben Sansom, Christiana, Karen Bourne, Kerry Murphy, Millie Woodburne, Marjorie Madden, Denise Harbison & her daughter Jinifer, Rosie Matthew, Jennifer, Helen (Jamie-Dornan.Net), Lindsey Lenfesty-Zegeling, Pachy and so, so many more. These last five years knowing some of you and bonding over Fifty Shades/Jamie Dornan has been something I never will ever trade anything for in the world. Thank you to every single one of you that has supported me and continues to be a valued person in my life, both during my darkest hours and my best of times. You all should be superheroes because you all are uniquely amazing and I'm proud to know all of you.

To Kellie Sheridan, for letting me be one of her amazing remote editorial interns for way longer than I ever thought I would be. I've had the pleasure of editing manuscripts for her and other authors, while also picking up other editorial and publishing knowledge including proof-reading, copy-editing and learning how to design book covers, I wouldn't be writing this book today without having gained more experience and learning through your wonderful guidance.

To my parents, my grandma and my three grandparents (the last three sadly not on this earth anymore) who are watching me from heaven, I hope that I have made every single one of you proud. I wouldn't be alive today if none of you had ever met and I hope I didn't disappoint you all on my journey that is life.

Lastly, to two amazing ladies who this book is dedicated to. E.L.James & Robinne Lee. These two sensational ladies have inspired me in more ways than I care to list, leading me to name my main character, Robinne James, after parts of their names respectively. I've had the absolute pleasure of being recognised by the two of you on many occasions over the years I've been a fan of both of yours. Reading both of your books is what has truly inspired me into sitting down and writing this one, plucking up the courage to finally put a big part of me out there for the world to see. I hope I have the pleasure of meeting you both in person someday, even to just hug you both and say thank you for being truly incredible and inspirations that both men and women can look up to and aspire to be like. May you both only know success from here on out along with love, good health and happiness. You two deserve it. Thank you both so much!

SONG PLAYLIST

Note – The songs below are not specific to every scene in the book, just the odd one here and there that stuck out most to me.

I'm On My Way – The Proclaimers – *Robinne leaves her home in England and journeys to her new home in America.*

3 Things – Jason Mraz – *Robinne rides the bus to her new home in Dripping Springs, Texas*

Start Of Something Good – Daughtry – *Robinne walks into Cassie's B&B and stays the night.*

Outlaw In 'Em - Waylon – *Ralph walks into and meets two of his brothers at the local bar after finishing checking on their latest house build, Robinne's house.*

Beautiful Day – Michael Bublé – *Robinne walks into town to get her groceries, walking to the main street in the town centre.*

Eyes On You - Chase Rice – *Ralph catches Robinne naked in the bathroom of his parents' main ranch house.*

Night Shift – Jon Pardi – *Robinne eats at the Jenkins' weekly BBQ*

I Don't Know About You – Chris Lane – *Ralph shows Robinne around the ranch when it starts to rain, ushering her inside the barn.*

You Are The Reason – Callum Scott & Leona Lewis – *Ralph gives Robinne her first kiss inside the barn at the BBQ night.*

Cowboys & Angels – Dustin Lynch -– *Robinne flees the ranch after finding out about Ralph's lies and deception.*

You Make It Easy – Jason Aldean – *Ryder finds Robinne and takes her back to his place to safely spend the night so she won't be alone.*

Brand New Day – David Nail – *Robinne starts work for her new friend Laney at the bakery, after deciding not to drown her sorrows pining over Ralph.*

Back To Us – Rascal Flatts – *Ralph watches Robinne as she works at Laney's bakery, unbeknown to her that he was there watching her unintentionally.*

When It Rains It Pours – Luke Combs -–- *Ralph heads on over to his friend Luca's place to try and put Robinne out of his mind for a little bit.*

I Miss My Friend – Darryl Worley *Ralph thinks about Robinne as he goes about his day on the ranch, after promising her he'll give her distance.*

Caught Up In The Country – Rodney Atkins -– *Laney drives her and Robinne out to the English-style pub just outside of Dripping Springs*

Best Shot – Jimmie Allen – *Ralph drives a drunk Robinne back to her place after the night out with Laney at the pub.*

So Close – Jon McLaughlin – *Ralph and Robinne dance at the annual charity ball.*

Give Into Me – Garrett Hedlund – *Robinne and Ralph drive out to and swim in the cavern just outside of Dripping Springs, rekindling their relationship.*

St Elmo's Fire – John Parr – *Ralph saves Robinne from the burning barn fire on the Jenkins' ranch.*

The Long Way – Brett Eldridge – *Robinne and Ralph sit on his back porch and think about how far they've come since giving themselves a second chance.*

Tonight I Wanna Cry – Keith Urban – *Robinne spots Ralph kissing Delilah on the side of the road and tells Ryder to get her away from there as fast as possible.*

You Had Me From Hello – Kenny Chesney – *Ralph sings to Robinne in the middle of the town centre on the main street, after orchestrating the whole town to be there for his apology speech and proposal.*

Up Where We Belong – Jon Cocker & Jennifer Warnes – *Ralph and Robinne walk down the aisle of their ranch wedding after saying their vows, becoming husband and wife.*

Printed in Poland
by Amazon Fulfillment
Poland Sp. z o.o., Wrocław

58418166R00154